商務印書館編輯部　編

方平　譯

THE ARABIAN NIGHTS

一千零一夜

商務印書館

本書譯文由上海譯文出版社有限公司授權使用

責任編輯	陳朝暉
裝幀設計	郭梓琪
排　版	周　榮
責任校對	趙會明
印　務	龍寶祺

一千零一夜 *The Arabian Nights*

選　輯	商務印書館編輯部
譯　者	方　平
出　版	商務印書館 (香港) 有限公司
	香港筲箕灣耀興道 3 號東滙廣場 8 樓
	http://www.commercialpress.com.hk
發　行	香港聯合書刊物流有限公司
	香港新界荃灣德士古道 220-248 號荃灣工業中心 16 樓
印　刷	永經堂印刷有限公司
	香港新界荃灣德士古道 188-202 號立泰工業中心第 1 座 3 樓
版　次	2024 年 7 月第 1 版第 1 次印刷
	© 2024 商務印書館 (香港) 有限公司
	ISBN 978 962 07 0441 3
	Printed in China

Publisher's Note 出版説明

《一千零一夜》是一部豐富多彩的阿拉伯民間故事集。本書精選了六個膾炙人口的故事，讓廣大讀者能夠領略這部古老而神奇的文學經典的魅力。

意外發現藏寶洞祕密的阿里巴巴憑藉智慧和勇氣，與強盜們巧妙周旋；偶獲神燈的阿拉丁實現心願，戰勝邪惡巫師；仙巴歷經重重阻難，險象迭生；三妹飽受算計，終於沉冤昭雪，重獲幸福；能力超凡的神馬為波斯王子帶來真愛和好運；漁夫面對強大的妖怪毫不畏縮，以智取勝⋯⋯

《一千零一夜》以其獨特的想象力、奇幻的故事情節、鮮明的人物形象和深刻的主題思想，成為享譽世界的文學巨著。讀者不僅能從中感受到閱讀的樂趣，更能領悟生活的真諦。

初、中級英語程度讀者使用本書時，先閱讀英文原文，如遇到理解障礙，則參考中譯作為輔助。在英文原文後附加註解，標註古英語、非現代詞彙拼寫形式及語法；在譯文後附加註釋，以幫助讀者理解原文背景。讀者如有餘力，可在閱讀原文部分段落後，查閱相應中譯，揣摩同樣詞句在雙語中的不同表達。

商務印書館 (香港) 有限公司

編輯出版部

Contents 目錄

Preface to the Chinese Translation 中文譯本序　261

1　Ali Baba and the Forty Thieves /
阿里巴巴與四十大盜　1 / 266

2　Aladdin and the Magic Lamp / 阿拉丁與神燈　34 / 288

3　The Seven Voyages of Sindbad / 仙巴歷險記　93 / 361

4　The Story of Two Sisters Who Were Jealous of
Their Younger Sister / 三姐妹的故事　144 / 403

5　The Enchanted Horse / 神馬　178 / 427

6　The Story of the Fisherman / 漁夫的故事　209 / 439

The Arabian Nights

Ali Baba and the Forty Thieves

There once lived in a town of Persia two brothers, one named Cassim and the other Ali Baba. Their father divided a small inheritance equally between them. Cassim married a very rich wife, and became a wealthy merchant. Ali Baba married a woman as poor as himself, and lived by cutting wood, and bringing it upon three asses into the town to sell.

One day, when Ali Baba was in the forest and had just cut wood enough to load his asses, he saw at a distance a great cloud of dust, which seemed to approach him. He observed it with attention, and distinguished soon after a body of horsemen, whom he suspected might be robbers. He determined to leave his asses to save himself. He climbed up a large tree, planted on a high rock, whose branches were thick enough to conceal him, and yet enabled him to see all that passed without being discovered.

The troop, who were to the number of forty, all well mounted and armed, came to the foot of the rock on which the tree stood, and there dismounted. Every man unbridled his horse, tied him to some shrub, and hung about his neck a bag of corn which they had brought behind them. Then each of them took off his saddlebag, which seemed to Ali Baba from its weight to be full of gold and silver. One, whom he took to be their captain, came under the tree in which Ali Baba was concealed; and making his way through some shrubs, pronounced these words: 'Open,

Sesame!' As soon as the captain of the robbers had thus spoken, a door opened in the rock; and after he had made all his troop enter before him, he followed them, when the door shut again of itself.

The robbers stayed some time within the rock, during which Ali Baba, fearful of being caught, remained in the tree.

At last the door opened again, and as the captain went in last, so he came out first, and stood to see them all pass by him; when Ali Baba heard him make the door close by pronouncing these words, 'Shut, Sesame!' Every man at once went and bridled his horse, fastened his wallet, and mounted again. When the captain saw them all ready, he put himself at their head, and they returned the way they had come.

Ali Baba followed them with his eyes as far as he could see them; and afterward stayed a considerable time before he descended. Remembering the words the captain of the robbers used to cause the door to open and shut, he had the curiosity to try if his pronouncing them would have the same effect. Accordingly, he went among the shrubs, and perceiving the door concealed behind them, stood before it, and said, 'Open, Sesame!' The door instantly flew wide open.

Ali Baba, who expected a dark, dismal cavern, was surprised to see a well-lighted and spacious chamber, which received the light from an opening at the top of the rock, and in which were all sorts of provisions, rich bales of silk, stuff, brocade, and valuable carpeting, piled upon one another, gold and silver ingots in great heaps, and money in bags. The sight of all these riches made him suppose that this cave must have been occupied for ages by robbers, who had succeeded one another.

Ali Baba went boldly into the cave, and collected as much of the gold coin, which was in bags, as he thought his three asses could carry. When he had loaded them with the bags, he laid wood over them in such a manner that they could not be seen. When he had passed in and out as often as he wished, he stood before the door, and pronouncing the words, 'Shut, Sesame!' the door closed of itself. He then made the best of his way to town.

When Ali Baba got home he drove his asses into a little yard, shut the gates very carefully, threw off the wood that covered the panniers, carried the bags into his house, and ranged them in order before his wife. He then emptied the bags, which raised such a great heap of gold as dazzled his wife's eyes, and then he told her the whole adventure from beginning to end, and, above all, recommended her to keep it secret.

The wife rejoiced greatly at their good fortune, and would count all the gold piece by piece.

'Wife,' replied Ali Baba, 'you do not know what you undertake, when you pretend to count the money; you will never have done. I will dig a hole, and bury it. There is no time to be lost.'

'You are in the right, husband,' replied she, 'but let us know, as nigh as possible, how much we have. I will borrow a small measure, and measure it, while you dig the hole.'

Away the wife ran to her brother-in-law Cassim, who lived just by, and addressing herself to his wife, desired that she lend her a measure for a little while. Her sister-in-law asked her whether she would have a great or a small one. The other asked for a small one. She bade her stay a little, and she would readily fetch one.

The sister-in-law did so, but as she knew Ali Baba's poverty, she was curious to know what sort of grain his wife wanted to measure, and artfully putting some suet at the bottom of the measure, brought it to her, with an excuse that she was sorry that she had made her stay so long, but that she could not find it sooner.

Ali Baba's wife went home, set the measure upon the heap of gold, filled it, and emptied it often upon the sofa, till she had done, when she was very well satisfied to find the number of measures amounted to so many as they did, and went to tell her husband, who had almost finished digging the hole. When Ali Baba was burying the gold, his wife, to show her exactness and diligence to her sister-in-law, carried the measure back again, but without taking notice that a piece of gold had stuck to the bottom.

'Sister,' said she, giving it to her again, 'you see that I have not kept your measure long. I am obliged to you for it, and return it with thanks.'

As soon as Ali Baba's wife was gone, Cassim's looked at the bottom of the measure, and was in inexpressible surprise to find a piece of gold sticking to it. Envy immediately possessed her breast.

'What!' said she, 'has Ali Baba gold so plentiful as to measure it? Whence[1] has he all this wealth?'

Cassim, her husband, was at his counting house. When he came home his wife said to him, 'Cassim, I know you think yourself rich, but Ali Baba is infinitely richer than you. He does not count his money, but measures it.'

Cassim desired her to explain the riddle, which she did, by telling him the stratagem she had used to make the discovery, and showed him the piece of money, which was so old that they could not tell in what prince's reign it was coined.

Cassim, after he had married the rich widow, had never treated Ali Baba as a brother, but neglected him; and now, instead of being pleased, he conceived a base envy at his brother's prosperity. He could not sleep all that night, and went to him in the morning before sunrise.

'Ali Baba,' said he, 'I am surprised at you. You pretend to be miserably poor, and yet you measure gold. My wife found this at the bottom of the measure you borrowed yesterday.'

By this discourse, Ali Baba perceived that Cassim and his wife, through his own wife's folly, knew what they had so much reason to conceal; but what was done could not be undone. Therefore, without showing the least surprise or trouble, he confessed all, and offered his brother part of his treasure to keep the secret.

'I expect as much,' replied Cassim haughtily; 'but I must know exactly where this treasure is, and how I may visit it myself when I choose. Otherwise I will go and inform against you, and then you will not only get no more, but will lose all you have, and I shall have a share for my information.'

Ali Baba told him all he desired, even to the very words he was to use to gain admission into the cave.

Cassim rose the next morning long before the sun, and set out for the forest with ten mules bearing great chests, which he designed to fill, and followed the road which Ali Baba had pointed out to him. He was not long before he reached the rock, and found out the place, by the tree and other marks which his brother had given him. When he reached the entrance of the cavern, he pronounced the words, 'Open, Sesame!' The door immediately opened, and, when he was in, closed upon him. In examining the cave, he was in great admiration to find much more riches than he had expected from Ali Baba's relation. He quickly laid as many bags of gold as he could carry at the door of the cavern; but his thoughts were so full of the great riches he should possess that he could not think of the necessary word to make it open, but instead of 'Sesame,' said, 'Open, Barley!' and was much amazed to find that the door remained fast shut. He named several sorts of grain, but still the door would not open.

Cassim had never expected such an incident, and was so alarmed at the danger he was in, that the more he endeavoured to remember the word 'Sesame,' the more his memory was confounded, and he had as much forgotten it as if he had never heard it mentioned. He threw down the bags he had loaded himself with, and walked distractedly up and down the cave, without having the least regard to the riches that were around him.

About noon the robbers visited their cave. At some distance they saw Cassim's mules straggling about the rock, with great chests on their backs. Alarmed at this, they galloped full speed to the cave. They drove away the mules, who strayed through the forest so far that they were soon out of sight, and went directly, with their naked sabres in their hands, to the door, which, on their captain pronouncing the proper words, immediately opened.

Cassim, who heard the noise of the horses' feet, at once guessed the arrival of the robbers, and resolved to make one effort for his life. He rushed to the door, and no sooner saw the door open, than he ran out and threw the leader down, but could not escape the other robbers, who with their scimitars soon deprived him of life.

The first care of the robbers after this was to examine the cave. They found all the bags which Cassim had brought to the door, to be ready to load his mules, and carried them again to their places, but they did not miss what Ali Baba had taken away before. Then holding a council, and deliberating upon this occurrence, they guessed that Cassim, when he was in, could not get out again, but could not imagine how he had learned the secret words by which alone he could enter. They could not deny the fact of his being there; and to terrify any person or accomplice who should attempt the same thing, they agreed to cut Cassim's body into four quarters—to hang two on one side, and two on the other, within the door of the cave. They had no sooner taken this resolution than they put it in execution; and when they had nothing more to detain them, left the place of their hoards well closed. They mounted their horses, went to beat the roads again, and to attack the caravans they might meet.

In the meantime, Cassim's wife was very uneasy when night came, and her husband was not returned. She ran to Ali Baba in great alarm, and said, 'I believe, brother-in-law, that you know Cassim is gone to the forest, and upon what account. It is now night, and he has not returned. I am afraid some misfortune has happened to him.'

Ali Baba told her that she need not frighten herself, for that certainly Cassim would not think it proper to come into the town till the night should be pretty far advanced.

Cassim's wife, considering how much it concerned her husband to keep the business secret, was the more easily persuaded to believe her brother-in-law. She went home again, and waited patiently till midnight. Then her fear redoubled, and her grief was the more sensible because she was forced to keep it to herself. She repented of her foolish curiosity, and cursed her desire of prying into the affairs of her brother and sister-in-law. She spent all the night in weeping; and as soon as it was day went to them, telling them, by her tears, the cause of her coming.

Ali Baba did not wait for his sister-in-law to desire him to go to see what was become of Cassim, but departed immediately with his three asses, begging of her first to moderate her grief.

He went to the forest, and when he came near the rock, having seen neither his brother nor his mules on his way, was seriously alarmed at finding some blood spilt near the door, which he took for an ill omen; but when he had pronounced the word, and the door had opened, he was struck with horror at the dismal sight of his brother's body. He was not long in determining how he should pay the last dues to his brother; but without adverting to the little fraternal affection he had shown for him, went into the cave, to find something to enshroud his remains. Having loaded one of his asses with them, he covered them over with wood. The other two asses he loaded with bags of gold, covering them with wood also as before; and then, bidding the door shut, he came away; but was so cautious as to stop some time at the end of the forest, that he might not go into the town before night. When he came home he drove the two asses loaded with gold into his little yard, and left the care of unloading them to his wife, while he led the other to his sister-in-law's house.

Ali Baba knocked at the door, which was opened by Morgiana, a clever, intelligent slave, who was fruitful in inventions to meet the most difficult circumstances. When he came into the court he unloaded the ass, and taking Morgiana aside, said to her, 'You must observe an inviolable secrecy. Your master's body is contained in these two panniers. We must bury him as if he had died a natural death. Go now and tell your mistress. I leave the matter to your wit and skilful devices.'

Ali Baba helped to place the body in Cassim's house, again recommended to Morgiana to act her part well, and then returned with his ass.

Morgiana went out early the next morning to a druggist and asked for a sort of lozenge which was considered efficacious in the most dangerous disorders. The apothecary inquired who was ill. She replied, with a sigh, her good master Cassim himself; and that he could neither eat nor speak.

In the evening Morgiana went to the same druggist again, and with tears in her eyes, asked for an essence which they used to give to sick people only when in the last extremity.

'Alas!' said she, taking it from the apothecary, 'I am afraid that this remedy will have no better effect than the lozenges; and that I shall lose my good master.'

On the other hand, as Ali Baba and his wife were often seen to go between Cassim's and their own house all that day, and to seem melancholy, nobody was surprised in the evening to hear the lamentable shrieks and cries of Cassim's wife and Morgiana, who gave out everywhere that her master was dead. The next morning at daybreak, Morgiana went to an old cobbler whom she knew to be always ready at his stall, and bidding him good morrow, put a piece of gold into his hand, saying, 'Baba Mustapha, you must bring with you your sewing tackle, and come with me; but I must tell you, I shall blindfold you when you come to such a place.'

Baba Mustapha seemed to hesitate a little at these words. 'Oh! Oh!' replied he, 'you would have me do something against my conscience, or against my honour?'

'God forbid,' said Morgiana, putting another piece of gold into his hand, 'that I should ask anything that is contrary to your honour! Only come along with me, and fear nothing.'

Baba Mustapha went with Morgiana, who, after she had bound his eyes with a handkerchief at the place she had mentioned, conveyed him to her deceased master's house, and never unloosed his eyes till he had entered the room where she had put the corpse together. 'Baba Mustapha,' said she, 'you must make haste and sew the parts of this body together; and when you have done, I will give you another piece of gold.'

After Baba Mustapha had finished his task, she blindfolded him again, gave him the third piece of gold as she had promised, and recommending secrecy to him, carried him back to the place where she first bound his eyes, pulled off the bandage, and let him go home, but watched him that he returned toward his stall, till he was quite out of sight, for fear he should have the curiosity to return and dodge her; she then went home.

Morgiana, on her return, warmed some water to wash the body, and at the same time Ali Baba perfumed it with incense, and wrapped it in the burying clothes with the accustomed ceremonies. Not long after the proper officer brought the bier, and when the attendants of the mosque, whose business it was to wash the dead, offered to perform their duty, she told them it was done already. Shortly after this the imam and the other ministers of the mosque arrived. Four neighbours carried the corpse to the burying ground, following the imam, who recited some prayers. Ali Baba came after with some neighbours, who often relieved the others in carrying the bier to the burying ground. Morgiana, a slave to the deceased, followed in the procession, weeping, beating her breast, and tearing her hair. Cassim's wife stayed at home mourning, uttering lamentable cries with the women of the neighbourhood, who came, according to custom, during the funeral, and joining their lamentations with hers filled the quarter far and near with sounds of sorrow.

In this manner Cassim's melancholy death was concealed and hushed up between Ali Baba, his widow, and Morgiana his slave, with so much contrivance that nobody in the city had the least knowledge or suspicion of the cause of it. Three or four days after the funeral, Ali Baba removed his few goods openly to his sister's house, in which it was agreed that he should in future live; but the money he had taken from the robbers he conveyed thither[2] by night. As for Cassim's warehouse, he entrusted it entirely to the management of his eldest son.

While these things were being done, the forty robbers again visited their retreat in the forest. Great, then, was their surprise to find Cassim's body taken away, with some of their bags of gold. 'We are certainly discovered,' said the captain. 'The removal of the body and the loss of some of our money, plainly shows that the man whom we killed had an accomplice: and for our own lives' sake we must try to find him. What say you, my lads?'

All the robbers unanimously approved of the captain's proposal.

'Well,' said the captain, 'one of you, the boldest and most skilful among you, must go into the town, disguised as a traveller and a stranger, to try if he can hear any talk of the man whom we have killed, and endeavour to find out who he was, and where he lived. This is a matter of the first importance, and for fear of any treachery I propose that whoever undertakes this business without success, even though the failure arises only from an error of judgment, shall suffer death.'

Without waiting for the sentiments of his companions, one of the robbers started up, and said, 'I submit to this condition, and think it an honour to expose my life to serve the troop.'

After this robber had received great commendations from the captain and his comrades, he disguised himself so that nobody would take him for what he was; and taking his leave of the troop that night, he went into the town just at daybreak. He walked up and down, till accidentally he came to Baba Mustapha's stall, which was always open before any of the shops.

Baba Mustapha was seated with an awl in his hand, just going to work. The robber saluted him, bidding him good morrow; and perceiving that he was old, said, 'Honest man, you begin to work very early; is it possible that one of your age can see so well? I question, even if it were somewhat lighter, whether you could see to stitch.'

'You do not know me,' replied Baba Mustapha; 'for old as I am, I have extraordinary good eyes; and you will not doubt it when I tell you that I sewed the body of a dead man together in a place where I had not so much light as I have now.'

'A dead body!' exclaimed the robber, with affected amazement.

'Yes, yes,' answered Baba Mustapha. 'I see you want me to speak out, but you shall know no more.'

The robber felt sure that he had discovered what he sought. He pulled out a piece of gold, and putting it into Baba Mustapha's hand, said to him, 'I do not want to learn your secret, though I can assure you you might safely trust me with it. The only thing I desire of you is to show me the house where you stitched up the dead body.'

'If I were disposed to do you that favour,' replied Baba Mustapha, 'I assure you I cannot. I was taken to a certain place, whence I was led blindfold to the house, and afterward brought back in the same manner. You see, therefore, the impossibility of my doing what you desire.'

'Well,' replied the robber, 'you may, however, remember a little of the way that you were led blindfold. Come, let me blind your eyes at the same place. We will walk together; perhaps you may recognise some part, and as everyone should be paid for his trouble here is another piece of gold for you; gratify me in what I ask you.' So saying, he put another piece of gold into his hand.

The two pieces of gold were great temptations to Baba Mustapha. He looked at them a long time in his hand, without saying a word, but at last he pulled out his purse and put them in.

'I cannot promise,' said he to the robber, 'that I can remember the way exactly; but since you desire, I will try what I can do.'

At these words Baba Mustapha rose up, to the great joy of the robber, and led him to the place where Morgiana had bound his eyes.

'It was here,' said Baba Mustapha, 'I was blindfolded; and I turned this way.'

The robber tied his handkerchief over his eyes, and walked by him till he stopped directly at Cassim's house, where Ali Baba then lived. The thief, before he pulled off the band, marked the door with a piece of chalk, which he had ready in his hand, and then asked him if he knew whose house that was; to which Baba Mustapha replied that as he did not live in that neighbourhood, he could not tell.

The robber, finding that he could discover no more from Baba Mustapha, thanked him for the trouble he had taken, and left him to go back to his stall, while he returned to the forest, persuaded that he should be very well received.

A little after the robber and Baba Mustapha had parted, Morgiana went out of Ali Baba's house upon some errand, and upon her return, seeing the mark the robber had made, stopped to observe it.

'What can be the meaning of this mark?' said she to herself. 'Somebody intends my master no good. However, with whatever intention it was done, it is advisable to guard against the worst.'

Accordingly, she fetched a piece of chalk, and marked two or three doors on each side in the same manner, without saying a word to her master or mistress.

In the meantime the robber rejoined his troop in the forest, and recounted to them his success, expatiating upon his good fortune in meeting so soon with the only person who could inform him of what he wanted to know. All the robbers listened to him with the utmost satisfaction. Then the captain, after commending his diligence, addressing himself to them all, said, 'Comrades, we have no time to lose. Let us set off well armed, without its appearing who we are; but that we may not excite any suspicion, let only one or two go into the town together, and join at our rendezvous, which shall be the great square. In the meantime, our comrade who brought us the good news and I will go and find out the house, that we may consult what had best be done.'

This speech and plan was approved of by all, and they were soon ready. They filed off in parties of two each, after some interval of time, and got into the town without being in the least suspected. The captain, and he who had visited the town in the morning as spy, came in the last. He led the captain into the street where he had marked Ali Baba's residence; and when they came to the first of the houses which Morgiana had marked, he pointed it out. But the captain observed that the next door was chalked in the same manner, and in the same place; and showing it to his guide, asked him which house it was, that, or the first. The guide was so confounded, that he knew not what answer to make; but he was still more puzzled when he and the captain saw five or six houses similarly marked. He assured the captain, with an oath, that he had marked but one, and could not tell who had chalked the rest, so that he could not distinguish the house which the cobbler had stopped at.

The captain, finding that their design had proved abortive, went directly to their place of rendezvous, and told his troop that they had lost their labour, and must return to their cave. He himself set them the example, and they all returned as they had come.

When the troop was all got together, the captain told them the reason of their returning; and presently the conductor was declared by all worthy of death. He condemned himself, acknowledging that he ought to have taken better precaution, and prepared to receive the stroke from him who was appointed to cut off his head.

But as the safety of the troop required the discovery of the second intruder into the cave, another of the gang, who promised himself that he should succeed better, presented himself, and his offer being accepted he went and corrupted Baba Mustapha as the other had done; and being shown the house, marked it in a place more remote from sight, with red chalk.

Not long after, Morgiana, whose eyes nothing could escape, went out, and seeing the red chalk, and arguing with herself as she had done before, marked the other neighbours' houses in the same place and manner.

The robber, on his return to his company, valued himself much on the precaution he had taken, which he looked upon as an infallible way of distinguishing Ali Baba's house from the others; and the captain and all of them thought it must succeed. They conveyed themselves into the town with the same precaution as before; but when the robber and his captain came to the street, they found the same difficulty; at which the captain was enraged, and the robber in as great confusion as his predecessor.

Thus the captain and his troop were forced to retire a second time, and much more dissatisfied; while the robber who had been the author of the mistake underwent the same punishment, which he willingly submitted to.

The captain, having lost two brave fellows of his troop, was afraid of diminishing it too much by pursuing this plan to get information of the residence of their plunderer. He found by their example that their heads were not so good as their hands on such occasions; and therefore resolved to take upon himself the important commission.

Accordingly, he went and addressed himself to Baba Mustapha, who did him the same service he had done to the other robbers. He did not set any particular mark on the house, but examined and observed it so carefully, by passing often by it, that it was impossible for him to mistake it.

The captain, well satisfied with his attempt, and informed of what he wanted to know, returned to the forest: and when he came into the cave, where the troop waited for him, said, 'Now, comrades, nothing can prevent our full revenge, as I am certain of the house; and on my way hither[3] I have thought how to put it into execution, but if anyone can form a better expedient, let him communicate it.'

He then told them his contrivance; and as they approved of it, ordered them to go into the villages about, and buy nineteen mules, with thirty-eight large leather jars, one full of oil, and the others empty.

In two or three days' time the robbers had purchased the mules and jars, and as the mouths of the jars were rather too narrow for his purpose, the captain caused them to be widened, and after having put one of his men into each, with the weapons which he thought fit, leaving open the seam which had been undone to leave them room to breathe, he rubbed the jars on the outside with oil from the full vessel.

Things being thus prepared, when the nineteen mules were loaded with thirty-seven robbers in jars, and the jar of oil, the captain, as their driver, set out with them, and reached the town by the dusk of the evening, as he had intended. He led them through the streets, till he came to Ali Baba's, at whose door he designed to have knocked; but was prevented by his sitting there after supper to take a little fresh air. He stopped his mules, addressed himself to him, and said, 'I have brought some oil a great way, to sell at to-morrow's market; and it is now so late that I do not know where to lodge. If I should not be troublesome to you, do me the favour to let me pass the night with you, and I shall be very much obliged by your hospitality.'

Though Ali Baba had seen the captain of the robbers in the forest, and had heard him speak, it was impossible to know him in the disguise of an oil merchant. He told him he should be welcome, and immediately opened his gates for the mules to go into the yard. At the same time he called to a slave, and ordered him, when the mules were unloaded, to put them into the stable, and to feed them; and then went to Morgiana, to bid her get a good supper for his guest.

After they had finished supper, Ali Baba, charging Morgiana afresh to take care of his guest, said to her, 'To-morrow morning I design to go to the bath before day; take care my bathing linen be ready, give them to Abdalla (which was the slave's name), and make me some good broth against I return.' After this he went to bed.

In the meantime the captain of the robbers went into the yard, and took off the lid of each jar, and gave his people orders what to do. Beginning at the first jar, and so on to the last, he said to each man: 'As soon as I throw some stones out of the chamber window where I lie, do not fail to come out, and I will immediately join you.'

After this he returned into the house, when Morgiana, taking up a light, conducted him to his chamber, where she left him; and he, to avoid any suspicion, put the light out soon after, and laid himself down in his clothes, that he might be the more ready to rise.

Morgiana, remembering Ali Baba's orders, got his bathing linen ready, and ordered Abdalla to set on the pot for the broth; but while she was preparing it the lamp went out, and there was no more oil in the house, nor any candles. What to do she did not know, for the broth must be made. Abdalla, seeing her very uneasy, said, 'do not fret and tease yourself, but go into the yard, and take some oil out of one of the jars.'

Morgiana thanked Abdalla for his advice, took the oil pot, and went into the yard; when, as she came nigh the first jar, the robber within said softly, 'Is it time?'

Though naturally much surprised at finding a man in the jar instead of the oil she wanted, she immediately felt the importance of keeping silence, as Ali Baba, his family, and herself were in great danger; and collecting herself, without showing the least emotion, she answered, 'Not yet, but presently.' She went quietly in this manner to all the jars, giving the same answer, till she came to the jar of oil.

By this means Morgiana found that her master Ali Baba had admitted thirty-eight robbers into his house, and that this pretended oil merchant was their captain. She made what haste she could to fill her oil pot, and returned into the kitchen, where, as soon as she had lighted her lamp, she took a great kettle, went again to the oil jar, filled the kettle, set it on a large wood fire, and as soon as it boiled, went and poured enough into every jar to stifle and destroy the robber within.

When this action, worthy of the courage of Morgiana, was executed without any noise, as she had projected, she returned into the kitchen with the empty kettle; and having put out the great fire she had made to boil the oil, and leaving just enough to make the broth, put out the lamp also, and remained silent, resolving not to go to rest till, through a window of the kitchen, which opened into the yard, she had seen what might follow.

She had not waited long before the captain of the robbers got up, opened the window, and, finding no light and hearing no noise or any one stirring in the house, gave the appointed signal, by throwing little stones, several of which hit the jars, as he doubted not by the sound they gave. He then listened, but not hearing or perceiving anything whereby he could judge that his companions stirred, he began to grow very uneasy, threw stones again a second and also a third time, and could not comprehend the reason that none of them should answer his signal. Much alarmed, he went softly down into the yard, and going to the first jar, while asking the robber, whom he thought alive, if he was in readiness, smelt the hot boiled oil, which sent forth a steam out of the jar. Hence he knew that his plot to murder Ali Baba and plunder his house was discovered. Examining all the jars, one after another, he found that all his gang were dead; and, enraged to despair at having failed in his design, he forced the lock of a door that led from the yard to the garden, and climbing over the walls made his escape.

When Morgiana saw him depart, she went to bed, satisfied and pleased to have succeeded so well in saving her master and family.

Ali Baba rose before day, and, followed by his slave, went to the baths, entirely ignorant of the important event which had happened at home.

When he returned from the baths he was very much surprised to see the oil jars, and to learn that the merchant was not gone with the mules. He asked Morgiana, who opened the door, the reason of it.

'My good master,' answered she, 'God preserve you and all your family. You will be better informed of what you wish to know when you have seen what I have to show you, if you will follow me.'

As soon as Morgiana had shut the door, Ali Baba followed her, when she requested him to look into the first jar, and see if there was any oil. Ali Baba did so, and seeing a man, started back in alarm, and cried out.

'Do not be afraid,' said Morgiana; 'the man you see there can neither do you nor anybody else any harm. He is dead.'

'Ah, Morgiana,' said Ali Baba, 'what is it you show me? Explain yourself.'

'I will,' replied Morgiana. 'Moderate your astonishment, and do not excite the curiosity of your neighbours; for it is of great importance to keep this affair secret. Look into all the other jars.'

Ali Baba examined all the other jars, one after another; and when he came to that which had the oil in it, found it prodigiously sunk, and stood for some time motionless, sometimes looking at the jars and sometimes at Morgiana, without saying a word, so great was his surprise.

At last, when he had recovered himself, he said, 'And what is become of the merchant?'

'Merchant!' answered she; 'he is as much one as I am. I will tell you who he is, and what is become of him; but you had better hear the story in your own chamber; for it is time for your health that you had your broth after your bathing.'

Morgiana then told him all she had done, from the first observing the mark upon the house, to the destruction of the robbers, and the flight of their captain.

On hearing of these brave deeds from the lips of Morgiana, Ali Baba said to her—'God, by your means, has delivered me from the snares of these robbers laid for my destruction. I owe, therefore, my life to you; and, for the first token of my acknowledgment, I give you your liberty from this moment, till I can complete your recompense as I intend.'

Ali Baba's garden was very long, and shaded at the farther end by a great number of large trees. Near these he and the slave

Abdalla dug a trench, long and wide enough to hold the bodies of the robbers; and as the earth was light, they were not long in doing it. When this was done, Ali Baba hid the jars and weapons; and as he had no occasion for the mules, he sent them at different times to be sold in the market by his slave.

While Ali Baba was taking these measures the captain of the forty robbers returned to the forest with inconceivable mortification. He did not stay long; the loneliness of the gloomy cavern became frightful to him. He determined, however, to avenge the death of his companions, and to accomplish the death of Ali Baba. For this purpose he returned to the town, and took a lodging in a khan, disguising himself as a merchant in silks. Under this assumed character he gradually conveyed a great many sorts of rich stuffs and fine linen to his lodging from the cavern, but with all the necessary precautions to conceal the place whence he brought them. In order to dispose of the merchandise, when he had thus amassed them together, he took a warehouse, which happened to be opposite to Cassim's, which Ali Baba's son had occupied since the death of his uncle.

He took the name of Cogia Houssain, and, as a newcomer, was, according to custom, extremely civil and complaisant to all the merchants his neighbours. Ali Baba's son was, from his vicinity, one of the first to converse with Cogia Houssain, who strove to cultivate his friendship more particularly. Two or three days after he was settled, Ali Baba came to see his son, and the captain of the robbers recognised him at once, and soon learned from his son who he was. After this he increased his assiduities, caressed him in the most engaging manner, made him some small presents, and often asked him to dine and sup with him, when he treated him very handsomely.

Ali Baba's son did not choose to lie under such obligation to Cogia Houssain; but was so much straitened for want of room in his house that he could not entertain him. He therefore acquainted his father, Ali Baba, with his wish to invite him in return.

Ali Baba with great pleasure took the treat upon himself. 'Son,' said he, 'to-morrow being Friday, which is a day that the shops of such great merchants as Cogia Houssain and yourself are shut, get him to accompany you, and as you pass by my door, call in. I will go and order Morgiana to provide a supper.'

The next day Ali Baba's son and Cogia Houssain met by appointment, took their walk, and as they returned, Ali Baba's son led Cogia Houssain through the street where his father lived, and when they came to the house, stopped and knocked at the door.

'This, sir,' said he, 'is my father's house, who, from the account I have given him of your friendship, charged me to procure him the honour of your acquaintance; and I desire you to add this pleasure to those for which I am already indebted to you.'

Though it was the sole aim of Cogia Houssain to introduce himself into Ali Baba's house, that he might kill him without hazarding his own life or making any noise, yet he excused himself, and offered to take his leave; but a slave having opened the door, Ali Baba's son took him obligingly by the hand, and, in a manner, forced him in.

Ali Baba received Cogia Houssain with a smiling countenance, and in the most obliging manner he could wish. He thanked him for all the favours he had done his son; adding, withal, the obligation was the greater as he was a young man, not much acquainted with the world, and that he might contribute to his information.

Cogia Houssain returned the compliment by assuring Ali Baba that though his son might not have acquired the experience of older men, he had good sense equal to the experience of many others. After a little more conversation on different subjects, he offered again to take his leave, when Ali Baba, stopping him, said, 'Where are you going, sir, in so much haste? I beg you will do me the honour to sup with me, though my entertainment may not be worthy your acceptance. Such as it is, I heartily offer it.'

'Sir,' replied Cogia Houssain, 'I am thoroughly persuaded of your good will; but the truth is, I can eat no victuals that have any salt in them; therefore judge how I should feel at your table.'

'If that is the only reason,' said Ali Baba, 'it ought not to deprive me of the honour of your company; for, in the first place, there is no salt ever put into my bread, and as to the meat we shall have to-night, I promise you there shall be none in that. Therefore you must do me the favour to stay. I will return immediately.'

Ali Baba went into the kitchen, and ordered Morgiana to put no salt to the meat that was to be dressed that night; and to make quickly two or three ragouts besides what he had ordered, but be sure to put no salt in them.

Morgiana, who was always ready to obey her master, could not help being surprised at his strange order.

'Who is this strange man,' said she, 'who eats no salt with his meat? Your supper will be spoiled, if I keep it back so long.'

'Do not be angry, Morgiana,' replied Ali Baba. 'He is an honest man, therefore do as I bid you.'

Morgiana obeyed, though with no little reluctance, and had a curiosity to see this man who ate no salt. To this end, when she had finished what she had to do in the kitchen, she helped Abdalla to carry up the dishes; and looking at Cogia Houssain, she knew him at first sight, notwithstanding his disguise, to be the captain of the robbers, and examining him very carefully, perceived that he had a dagger under his garment.

'I am not in the least amazed,' said she to herself, 'that this wicked man, who is my master's greatest enemy, would eat no salt with him, since he intends to assassinate him; but I will prevent him.'

Morgiana, while they were at supper, determined in her own mind to execute one of the boldest acts ever meditated. When Abdalla came for the dessert of fruit, and had put it with the wine and glasses before Ali Baba, Morgiana retired, dressed herself neatly with a suitable headdress like a dancer, girded her waist with a silver-gilt girdle, to which there hung a poniard with a hilt and guard of the same metal, and put a handsome mask on her face. When she had thus disguised herself, she said to Abdalla, 'Take your tabor, and let us go and divert our master and his son's friend, as we do sometimes when he is alone.'

Abdalla took his tabor, and played all the way into the hall before Morgiana, who, when she came to the door, made a low obeisance by way of asking leave to exhibit her skill, while Abdalla left off playing.

'Come in, Morgiana,' said Ali Baba, 'and let Cogia Houssain see what you can do, that he may tell us what he thinks of your performance.'

Cogia Houssain, who did not expect this diversion after supper, began to fear he should not be able to take advantage of the opportunity he thought he had found; but hoped, if he now missed his aim, to secure it another time, by keeping up a friendly correspondence with the father and son; therefore, though he could have wished Ali Baba would have declined the dance, he pretended to be obliged to him for it, and had the complaisance to express his satisfaction at what he saw, which pleased his host.

As soon as Abdalla saw that Ali Baba and Cogia Houssain had done talking, he began to play on the tabor, and accompanied it with an air, to which Morgiana, who was an excellent performer, danced in such a manner as would have created admiration in any company.

After she had danced several dances with much grace, she drew the poniard, and holding it in her hand, began a dance in which she outdid herself by the many different figures, light movements, and the surprising leaps and wonderful exertions with which she accompanied it. Sometimes she presented the poniard to one breast, sometimes to another, and oftentimes seemed to strike her own. At last, she snatched the tabor from Abdalla with her left hand, and holding the dagger in her right presented the other side of the tabor, after the manner of those who get a livelihood by dancing, and solicit the liberality of the spectators.

Ali Baba put a piece of gold into the tabor, as did also his son; and Cogia Houssain, seeing that she was coming to him, had pulled his purse out of his bosom to make her a present; but while he was putting his hand into it, Morgiana, with a courage and resolution worthy of herself, plunged the poniard into his heart.

Ali Baba and his son, shocked at this action, cried out aloud.

'Unhappy woman!' exclaimed Ali Baba, 'what have you done, to ruin me and my family?'

'It was to preserve, not to ruin you,' answered Morgiana; 'for see here,' continued she, opening the pretended Cogia Houssain's garment, and showing the dagger, 'what an enemy you had entertained! Look well at him, and you will find him to be both the fictitious oil merchant, and the captain of the gang of forty robbers. Remember, too, that he would eat no salt with you; and what would you have more to persuade you of his wicked design? Before I saw him, I suspected him as soon as you told me you had such a guest. I knew him, and you now find that my suspicion was not groundless.'

Ali Baba, who immediately felt the new obligation he had to Morgiana for saving his life a second time, embraced her: 'Morgiana,' said he, 'I gave you your liberty, and then promised you that my gratitude should not stop there, but that I would soon give you higher proofs of its sincerity, which I now do by making you my daughter-in-law.'

Then addressing himself to his son, he said, 'I believe you, son, to be so dutiful a child, that you will not refuse Morgiana for your wife. You see that Cogia Houssain sought your friendship with a treacherous design to take away my life; and if he had succeeded, there is no doubt but he would have sacrificed you also to his revenge. Consider, that by marrying Morgiana you marry the preserver of my family and your own.'

The son, far from showing any dislike, readily consented to the marriage; not only because he would not disobey his father, but also because it was agreeable to his inclination. A few days afterward, Ali Baba celebrated the nuptials of his son and Morgiana with great solemnity, a sumptuous feast, and the usual dancing and spectacles; and had the satisfaction to see that his friends and neighbours, whom he invited, had no knowledge of the true motives of the marriage; but that those who were not unacquainted with Morgiana's good qualities commended his generosity and goodness of heart. Ali Baba did not visit the robber's cave for a whole year, as he supposed the other two, whom he could get no account of, might be alive.

At the year's end, when he found they had not made any attempt to disturb him, he had the curiosity to make another journey. He mounted his horse, and when he came to the cave he alighted, tied his horse to a tree, and approaching the entrance, pronounced the words, 'Open, Sesame!' and the door opened. He entered the cavern, and by the condition he found things in, judged that nobody had been there since the captain had fetched the goods for his shop. From this time he believed he was the only person in the world who had the secret of opening the cave, and that all the treasure was at his sole disposal. He put as much gold into his saddlebag as his horse would carry, and returned to town. Some years later he carried his son to the cave, and taught him the secret, which he handed down to his posterity, who, using their good fortune with moderation, lived in great honour and splendour.

2
Aladdin and the Magic Lamp

In one of the large and rich cities of China there once lived a tailor named Mustapha. He was very poor. He could hardly, by his daily labour, maintain himself and his family, which consisted only of his wife and a son.

His son, who was called Aladdin, was a very careless and idle fellow. He was disobedient to his father and mother, and would go out early in the morning and stay out all day, playing in the streets and public places with idle children of his own age.

When he was old enough to learn a trade his father took him into his own shop, and taught him how to use his needle; but all his father's endeavours to keep him to his work were vain, for no sooner was his back turned than the boy was gone for that day. Mustapha chastised him, but Aladdin was incorrigible, and his father, to his great grief, was forced to abandon him to his idleness. He was so much troubled about him, that he fell sick and died in a few months.

Aladdin, who was now no longer restrained by the fear of a father, gave himself over entirely to his idle habits, and was never out of the streets from his companions. This course he followed till he was fifteen years old, without giving his mind to any useful pursuit, or the least reflection on what would become of him. As he was one day playing in the street with his evil associates, according to custom, a stranger passing by stood to observe him.

This stranger was a sorcerer, known as the African magician, as he had been but two days arrived from Africa, his native country.

The African magician, observing in Aladdin's countenance something which assured him that he was a fit boy for his purpose, inquired his name and history of his companions. When he had learned all he desired to know, he went up to him, and taking him aside from his comrades, said, 'Child, was not your father called Mustapha the tailor?'

'Yes, sir,' answered the boy, 'but he has been dead a long time.'

At these words the African magician threw his arms about Aladdin's neck, and kissed him several times, with tears in his eyes, saying, 'I am your uncle. Your worthy father was my own brother. I knew you at first sight, you are so like him.'

Then he gave Aladdin a handful of small money, saying, 'Go, my son, to your mother. Give my love to her, and tell her that I will visit her to-morrow, that I may see where my good brother lived so long, and ended his days.'

Aladdin ran to his mother, overjoyed at the money his uncle had given him.

'Mother,' said he, 'have I[4] an uncle?'

'No, child,' replied his mother, 'you have no uncle by your father's side or mine.'

'I am[5] just now come,' said Aladdin, 'from a man who says he is my uncle, and my father's brother. He cried, and kissed me, when I told him my father was dead, and gave me money, sending his love to you, and promising to come and pay you a visit, that he may see the house my father lived and died in.'

'Indeed, child,' replied the mother, 'your father had no brother, nor have you an uncle.'

The next day the magician found Aladdin playing in another part of the town, and embracing him as before, put two pieces of gold into his hand, and said to him, 'Carry this, child, to your mother. Tell her that I will come and see her to-night, and bid her get us something for supper. But first show me the house where you live.'

Aladdin showed the African magician the house, and carried the two pieces of gold to his mother, who went out and bought provisions; and considering she wanted various utensils, borrowed them of her neighbours. She spent the whole day in preparing the supper; and at night, when it was ready, said to her son, 'Perhaps the stranger knows not how to find our house; go and bring him, if you meet with him.'

Aladdin was just ready to go, when the magician knocked at the door, and came in loaded with wine and all sorts of fruits, which he brought for a dessert. After he had given what he brought into Aladdin's hands, he saluted his mother, and desired her to show him the place where his brother Mustapha used to sit on the sofa; and when she had so done, he fell down, and kissed it several times, crying out, with tears in his eyes, 'My poor brother! how unhappy am I, not to have come soon enough to give you one last embrace!'

Aladdin's mother desired him to sit down in the same place, but he declined.

'No,' said he, 'I shall not do that; but give me leave to sit opposite to it, that although I see not the master of a family so dear to me, I may at least behold the place where he used to sit.'

When the magician had made choice of a place, and sat down, he began to enter into discourse with Aladdin's mother.

'My good sister,' said he, 'do not be surprised at your never having seen me all the time you have been married to my brother Mustapha of happy memory. I have been forty years absent from this country, which is my native place as well as my late brother's. During that time I have travelled into the Indies, Persia, Arabia, and Syria, and afterward crossed over into Africa, where I took up my abode in Egypt. At last, as it is natural for a man, I was desirous to see my native country again, and to embrace my dear brother; and finding I had strength enough to undertake so long a journey, I made the necessary preparations, and set out. Nothing ever afflicted me so much as hearing of my brother's death. But God be praised for all things! It is a comfort for me to find, as it were, my brother in a son, who has his most remarkable features.'

The African magician, perceiving that the widow wept at the remembrance of her husband, changed the conversation, and turning toward her son, asked him, 'What business do you follow? Are you of any trade?'

At this question the youth hung down his head, and was not a little abashed when his mother answered, 'Aladdin is an idle fellow. His father, when alive, strove all he could to teach him his trade, but could not succeed; and since his death, notwithstanding all I can say to him, he does nothing but idle away his time in the streets, as you saw him, without considering he is no longer a child; and if you do not make him ashamed of it, I despair of his ever coming to any good. For my part, I am resolved, one of these days, to turn him out of doors, and let him provide for himself.'

After these words, Aladdin's mother burst into tears; and the magician said, 'This is not well, nephew; you must think of helping yourself, and getting your livelihood. There are many sorts of trades; perhaps you do not like your father's, and would prefer another; I will endeavour to help you. If you have no mind to learn any handicraft, I will take a shop for you, furnish it with all sorts of fine stuffs and linens; and then with the money you make of them you can lay in fresh goods, and live in an honourable way. Tell me freely what you think of my proposal; you shall always find me ready to keep my word.'

This plan just suited Aladdin, who hated work. He told the magician he had a greater inclination to that business than to any other, and that he should be much obliged to him for his kindness. 'Well, then,' said the African magician, 'I will carry you with me to-morrow, clothe you as handsomely as the best merchants in the city, and afterward we will open a shop as I mentioned.'

The widow, after his promise of kindness to her son, no longer doubted that the magician was her husband's brother. She thanked him for his good intentions; and after having exhorted Aladdin to render himself worthy of his uncle's favour, she served up supper, at which they talked of several indifferent matters; and then the magician took his leave and retired.

He came again the next day, as he had promised, and took Aladdin with him to a merchant, who sold all sorts of clothes for different ages and ranks, ready made, and a variety of fine stuffs, and bade Aladdin choose those he preferred, which he paid for.

When Aladdin found himself so handsomely equipped, he returned his uncle thanks, who thus addressed him: 'As you are soon to be a merchant, it is proper you should frequent these shops, and become acquainted with them.'

He then showed him the largest and finest mosques, carried him to the khans or inns where the merchants and travellers lodged, and afterward to the sultan's palace, where he had free access; and at last brought him to his own khan, where, meeting with some merchants he had become acquainted with since his arrival, he gave them a treat, to bring them and his pretended nephew acquainted.

This entertainment lasted till night, when Aladdin would have taken leave of his uncle to go home. The magician would not let him go by himself, but conducted him to his mother, who, as soon as she saw him so well dressed, was transported with joy, and bestowed a thousand blessings upon the magician.

Early the next morning the magician called again for Aladdin, and said he would take him to spend that day in the country, and on the next he would purchase the shop. He then led him out at one of the gates of the city, to some magnificent palaces, to each of which belonged beautiful gardens, into which anybody might enter. At every building he came to he asked Aladdin if he did not think it fine; and the youth was ready to answer, when any one presented itself, crying out, 'Here is a finer house, uncle, than any we have yet seen.'

By this artifice the cunning magician led Aladdin some way into the country; and as he meant to carry him farther, to execute his design, pretending to be tired, he took an opportunity to sit down in one of the gardens, on the brink of a fountain of clear water which discharged itself by a lion's mouth of bronze into a basin.

'Come, nephew,' said he, 'you must be weary as well as I. Let us rest ourselves, and we shall be better able to pursue our walk.'

The magician next pulled from his girdle a handkerchief with cakes and fruit, and during this short repast he exhorted his nephew to leave off bad company, and to seek that of wise and prudent men, to improve by their conversation. 'For,' said he, 'you will soon be at man's estate, and you cannot too early begin to imitate their example.'

When they had eaten as much as they liked, they got up, and pursued their walk through gardens separated from one another only by small ditches, which marked out the limits without interrupting the communication; so great was the confidence the inhabitants reposed in each other.

By this means the African magician drew Aladdin insensibly beyond the gardens, and crossed the country, till they nearly reached the mountains.

At last they arrived between two mountains of moderate height and equal size, divided by a narrow valley, where the magician intended to execute the design that had brought him from Africa to China.

'We will go no farther now,' said he to Aladdin. 'I will show you here some extraordinary things, which, when you have seen, you will thank me for; but while I strike a light, gather up all the loose dry sticks you can see, to kindle a fire with.'

Aladdin found so many dried sticks that he soon collected a great heap. The magician presently set them on fire; and when they were in a blaze he threw in some incense, pronouncing several magical words, which Aladdin did not understand.

He had scarcely done so when the earth opened just before the magician, and disclosed a stone with a brass ring fixed in it.

Aladdin was so frightened that he would have run away, but the magician caught hold of him, and gave him such a box on the ear that he knocked him down. Aladdin got up trembling, and, with tears in his eyes, said to the magician, 'What have I done, uncle, to be treated in this severe manner?'

'I am your uncle,' answered the magician; 'I supply the place of your father, and you ought to make no reply. But, child,' added he, softening, 'do not be afraid; for I shall not ask anything of you, but that, if you obey me punctually, you will reap the advantages which I intend you. Know, then, that under this stone there is hidden a treasure, destined to be yours, and which will make you richer than the greatest monarch in the world. No person but yourself is permitted to lift this stone, or enter the cave; so you must punctually execute what I may command, for it is a matter of great consequence both to you and to me.'

Aladdin, amazed at all he saw and heard, forgot what was past, and rising said, 'Well, uncle, what is to be done? Command me. I am ready to obey.'

'I am overjoyed, child,' said the African magician, embracing him. 'Take hold of the ring, and lift up that stone.'

'Indeed, uncle,' replied Aladdin, 'I am not strong enough; you must help me.'

'You have no occasion for my assistance,' answered the magician; 'if I help you, we shall be able to do nothing. Take hold of the ring, and lift it up; you will find it will come easily.' Aladdin did as the magician bade him, raised the stone with ease, and laid it on one side.

When the stone was pulled up there appeared a staircase about three or four feet deep, leading to a door.

'Descend those steps, my son,' said the African magician, 'and open that door. It will lead you into a palace, divided into three great halls. In each of these you will see four large brass cisterns placed on each side, full of gold and silver; but take care you do not meddle with them. Before you enter the first hall, be sure to tuck up your robe, wrap it about you, and then pass through the second into the third without stopping. Above all things, have a care that you do not touch the walls so much as with your clothes; for if you do, you will die instantly. At the end of the third hall you will find a door which opens into a garden planted with fine trees loaded with fruit. Walk directly across the garden to a terrace, where you will see a niche before you, and in that niche a lighted lamp. Take the lamp down and put it out. When you have thrown away the wick and poured out the liquor, put it in your waistband and bring it to me. Do not be afraid that the liquor will spoil your clothes, for it is not oil, and the lamp will be dry as soon as it is thrown out.'

After these words the magician drew a ring off his finger, and put it on one of Aladdin's, saying, 'It is a talisman against all evil, so long as you obey me. Go, therefore, boldly, and we shall both be rich all our lives.'

Aladdin descended the steps, and, opening the door, found the three halls just as the African magician had described. He went through them with all the precaution the fear of death could inspire, crossed the garden without stopping, took down the lamp from the niche, threw out the wick and the liquor, and, as the magician had desired, put it in his waistband. But as he came down from the terrace, seeing it was perfectly dry, he stopped in the garden to observe the trees, which were loaded with extraordinary fruit of different colours on each tree. Some bore fruit entirely white, and some clear and transparent as crystal; some pale red, and others deeper; some green, blue, and purple, and others yellow; in short, there was fruit of all colours. The white were pearls; the clear and transparent, diamonds; the deep red, rubies; the paler, ballas rubies; the green, emeralds; the blue, turquoises; the purple, amethysts; and the yellow, sapphires. Aladdin, ignorant of their value, would have preferred figs, or grapes, or pomegranates; but as he had his uncle's permission, he resolved to gather some of every sort. Having filled the two new purses his uncle had bought for him with his clothes, he wrapped some up in the skirts of his vest, and crammed his bosom as full as it could hold.

Aladdin, having thus loaded himself with riches of which he knew not the value, returned through the three halls with the utmost precaution, and soon arrived at the mouth of the cave, where the African magician awaited him with the utmost impatience.

As soon as Aladdin saw him, he cried out, 'Pray, uncle, lend me your hand, to help me out.'

'Give me the lamp first,' replied the magician; 'it will be troublesome to you.'

'Indeed, uncle,' answered Aladdin, 'I cannot now; but I will as soon as I am up.'

The African magician was determined that he would have the lamp before he would help him up; and Aladdin, who had encumbered himself so much with his fruit that he could not well get at it, refused to give it to him till he was out of the cave. The African magician, provoked at this obstinate refusal, flew into a passion, threw a little of his incense into the fire, and pronounced two magical words, when the stone which had closed the mouth of the staircase moved into its place, with the earth over it in the same manner as it lay at the arrival of the magician and Aladdin.

This action of the magician plainly revealed to Aladdin that he was no uncle of his, but one who designed him evil. The truth was that he had learned from his magic books the secret and the value of this wonderful lamp, the owner of which would be made richer than any earthly ruler, and hence his journey to China. His art had also told him that he was not permitted to take it himself, but must receive it as a voluntary gift from the hands of another person. Hence he employed young Aladdin, and hoped by a mixture of kindness and authority to make him obedient to his word and will.

When he found that his attempt had failed, he set out to return to Africa, but avoided the town, lest any person who had seen him leave in company with Aladdin should make inquiries after the youth.

Aladdin, being suddenly enveloped in darkness, cried, and called out to his uncle to tell him he was ready to give him the lamp. But in vain, since his cries could not be heard.

He descended to the bottom of the steps, with a design to get into the palace, but the door, which was opened before by enchantment, was now shut by the same means. He then redoubled his cries and tears, sat down on the steps without any hopes of ever seeing light again, and in an expectation of passing from the present darkness to a speedy death.

In this great emergency he said, 'There is no strength or power but in the great and high God'; and in joining his hands to pray he rubbed the ring which the magician had put on his finger. Immediately a genie of frightful aspect appeared, and said, 'What wouldst[6] thou[7] have? I am ready to obey thee[8]. I serve him who possesses the ring on thy[9] finger; I, and the other slaves of that ring.'

At another time Aladdin would have been frightened at the sight of so extraordinary a figure, but the danger he was in made him answer without hesitation, 'Whoever thou art[10], deliver me from this place.' He had no sooner spoken these words than he found himself on the very spot where the magician had last left him, and no sign of cave or opening, nor disturbance of the earth. Returning thanks to God for being once more in the world, he made the best of his way home. When he got within his mother's door, joy at seeing her and weakness for want of sustenance made him so faint that he remained for a long time as dead. As soon as he recovered, he related to his mother all that had happened to him, and they were both very vehement in their complaints of the cruel magician.

Aladdin slept very soundly till late the next morning, when the first thing he said to his mother was, that he wanted something to eat, and wished she would give him his breakfast.

'Alas! child,' said she, 'I have not a bit of bread to give you; you ate up all the provisions I had in the house yesterday; but I have a little cotton which I have spun; I will go and sell it, and buy bread and something for our dinner.'

'Mother,' replied Aladdin, 'keep your cotton for another time, and give me the lamp I brought home with me yesterday. I will go and sell it, and the money I shall get for it will serve both for breakfast and dinner, and perhaps supper too.'

Aladdin's mother took the lamp and said to her son, 'Here it is, but it is very dirty. If it were a little cleaner I believe it would bring something more.'

She took some fine sand and water to clean it. But she had no sooner begun to rub it, than in an instant a hideous genie of gigantic size appeared before her, and said to her in a voice of thunder, 'What wouldst thou have? I am ready to obey thee as thy slave, and the slave of all those who have that lamp in their hands; I, and the other slaves of the lamp.'

Aladdin's mother, terrified at the sight of the genie, fainted; when Aladdin, who had seen such a phantom in the cavern, snatched the lamp out of his mother's hand, and said to the genie boldly, 'I am hungry. Bring me something to eat.'

The genie disappeared immediately, and in an instant returned with a large silver tray, holding twelve covered dishes of the same metal, which contained the most delicious viands; six large white bread cakes on two plates, two flagons of wine, and two silver cups. All these he placed upon a carpet and disappeared; this was done before Aladdin's mother recovered from her swoon.

Aladdin had fetched some water, and sprinkled it in her face to recover her. Whether that or the smell of the meat effected her cure, it was not long before she came to herself.

'Mother,' said Aladdin, 'be not afraid. Get up and eat. Here is what will put you in heart, and at the same time satisfy my extreme hunger.'

His mother was much surprised to see the great tray, twelve dishes, six loaves, the two flagons and cups, and to smell the savoury odour which exhaled from the dishes.

'Child,' said she, 'to whom are we obliged for this great plenty and liberality? Has the sultan been made acquainted with our poverty, and had compassion on us?'

'It is no matter, mother,' said Aladdin. 'Let us sit down and eat; for you have almost as much need of a good breakfast as I myself. When we have done, I will tell you.'

Accordingly, both mother and son sat down and ate with the better relish as the table was so well furnished. But all the time Aladdin's mother could not forbear looking at and admiring the tray and dishes, though she could not judge whether they were silver or any other metal, and the novelty more than the value attracted her attention.

The mother and son sat at breakfast till it was dinner time, and then they thought it would be best to put the two meals together. Yet, after this they found they should have enough left for supper, and two meals for the next day.

When Aladdin's mother had taken away and set by what was left, she went and sat down by her son on the sofa, saying, 'I expect now that you will satisfy my impatience, and tell me exactly what passed between the genie and you while I was in a swoon.'

He readily complied with her request.

She was in as great amazement at what her son told her as at the appearance of the genie, and said to him, 'But, son, what have we to do with genies? I never heard that any of my acquaintance had ever seen one. How came that vile genie to address himself to me, and not to you, to whom he had appeared before in the cave?'

'Mother,' answered Aladdin, 'the genie you saw is not the one who appeared to me. If you remember, he that I first saw called himself the slave of the ring on my finger; and this you saw, called himself the slave of the lamp you had in your hand; but I believe you did not hear him, for I think you fainted as soon as he began to speak.'

'What!' cried the mother, 'was your lamp then the occasion of that cursed genie's addressing himself to me rather than to you? Ah! my son, take it out of my sight, and put it where you please. I had rather you would sell it than run the hazard of being frightened to death again by touching it; and if you would take my advice, you would part also with the ring, and not have anything to do with genies, who, as our prophet has told us, are only devils.'

'With your leave, mother,' replied Aladdin, 'I shall now take care how I sell a lamp which may be so serviceable both to you and me. That false and wicked magician would not have undertaken so long a journey to secure this wonderful lamp if he had not known its value to exceed that of gold and silver. And since we have honestly come by it, let us make a profitable use of it, without making any great show and exciting the envy and jealousy of our neighbours. However, since the genies frighten you so much, I will take it out of your sight, and put it where I may find it when I want it. The ring I cannot resolve to part with; for without that you had never seen me again; and though I am alive now, perhaps, if it were gone, I might not be so some moments hence. Therefore I hope you will give me leave to keep it, and to wear it always on my finger.'

Aladdin's mother replied that he might do what he pleased; for her part, she would have nothing to do with genies, and never say anything more about them.

By the next night they had eaten all the provisions the genie had brought; and the next day Aladdin, who could not bear the thought of hunger, putting one of the silver dishes under his vest, went out early to sell it. Addressing himself to a Jew whom he met in the streets, he took him aside, and pulling out the plate, asked him if he would buy it.

The cunning Jew took the dish, examined it, and as soon as he found that it was good silver, asked Aladdin at how much he valued it.

Aladdin, who had never been used to such traffic, told him he would trust to his judgment and honour. The Jew was somewhat confounded at this plain dealing; and doubting whether Aladdin understood the material or the full value of what he offered to sell, took a piece of gold out of his purse and gave it him, though it was but the sixtieth part of the worth of the plate. Aladdin, taking the money very eagerly, retired with so much haste that the Jew, not content with the exorbitancy of his profit, was vexed he had not penetrated into his ignorance, and was going to run after him, to endeavour to get some change out of the piece of gold. But the boy ran so fast, and had got so far, that it would have been impossible to overtake him.

Before Aladdin went home he called at a baker's, bought some cakes of bread, changed his money, and on his return gave the rest to his mother, who went and purchased provisions enough to last them some time. After this manner they lived, until Aladdin had sold the twelve dishes singly, as necessity pressed, to the Jew, for the same money; who, after the first time, durst not offer him less, for fear of losing so good a bargain. When he had sold the last dish, he had recourse to the tray, which weighed ten times as much as the dishes, and would have carried it to his old purchaser, but that it was too large and cumbersome; therefore he was obliged to bring him home with him to his mother's, where, after the Jew had examined the weight of the tray, he laid down ten pieces of gold, with which Aladdin was very well satisfied.

When all the money was spent, Aladdin had recourse again to the lamp. He took it in his hands, looked for the part where his mother had rubbed it with the sand, and rubbed it also. The genie immediately appeared, and said, 'What wouldst thou have? I am ready to obey thee as thy slave, and the slave of all those who have that lamp in their hands; I, and the other slaves of the lamp.'

'I am hungry,' said Aladdin. 'Bring me something to eat.'

The genie disappeared, and presently returned with a tray holding the same number of covered dishes as before, set it down, and vanished.

As soon as Aladdin found that their provisions were again expended, he took one of the dishes, and went to look for his

Jew chapman. But as he was passing by a goldsmith's shop, the goldsmith perceiving him, called to him, and said, 'My lad, I imagine that you have something to sell to the Jew, whom I often see you visit. Perhaps you do not know that he is the greatest rogue even among the Jews. I will give you the full worth of what you have to sell, or I will direct you to other merchants who will not cheat you.'

This offer induced Aladdin to pull his plate from under his vest and show it to the goldsmith. At first sight he perceived that it was made of the finest silver, and asked if he had sold such as that to the Jew. When Aladdin told him he had sold him twelve such, for a piece of gold each, 'What a villain!' cried the goldsmith. 'But,' added he, 'my son, what is past cannot be recalled. By showing you the value of this plate, which is of the finest silver we use in our shops, I will let you see how much the Jew has cheated you.'

The goldsmith took a pair of scales, weighed the dish, and assured him that his plate would fetch by weight sixty pieces of gold, which he offered to pay down immediately.

Aladdin thanked him for his fair dealing, and never after went to any other person.

Though Aladdin and his mother had an inexhaustible treasure in their lamp, and might have had whatever they wished for, yet they lived with the same frugality as before, and it may easily be supposed that the money for which Aladdin had sold the dishes and tray was sufficient to maintain them some time.

During this interval, Aladdin frequented the shops of the principal merchants, where they sold cloth of gold and silver, linens, silk stuffs, and jewellery, and, oftentimes joining in their conversation, acquired a knowledge of the world, and a desire to improve himself. By his acquaintance among the jewellers, he came to know that the fruits which he had gathered when he took the lamp were, instead of coloured glass, stones of inestimable value; but he had the prudence not to mention this to any one, not even to his mother.

One day as Aladdin was walking about the town he heard an order proclaimed, commanding the people to shut up their shops and houses, and keep within doors while the Princess Buddir al Buddoor, the sultan's daughter, went to the bath and returned.

This proclamation inspired Aladdin with eager desire to see the princess's face, which he determined to gratify by placing himself behind the door of the bath, so that he could not fail to see her face.

Aladdin had not long concealed himself before the princess came. She was attended by a great crowd of ladies, slaves, and mutes, who walked on each side and behind her. When she came within three or four paces of the door of the bath, she took off her veil, and gave Aladdin an opportunity of a full view of her face.

The princess was a noted beauty; her eyes were large, lively, and sparkling; her smile bewitching; her nose faultless; her mouth small; her lips vermilion. It is not therefore surprising that Aladdin, who had never before seen such a blaze of charms, was dazzled and enchanted.

After the princess had passed by, and entered the bath, Aladdin quitted his hiding place, and went home. His mother perceived him to be more thoughtful and melancholy than usual, and asked what had happened to make him so, or if he were ill. He then told his mother all his adventure, and concluded by declaring, 'I love the princess more than I can express, and am resolved that I will ask her in marriage of the sultan.'

Aladdin's mother listened with surprise to what her son told her. When he talked of asking the princess in marriage, she laughed aloud.

'Alas! child,' said she, 'what are you thinking of? You must be mad to talk thus.'

'I assure you, mother,' replied Aladdin, 'that I am not mad, but in my right senses. I foresaw that you would reproach me with folly and extravagance; but I must tell you once more that I am resolved to demand the princess of the sultan in marriage; nor do I despair of success. I have the slaves of the lamp and of the ring to help me, and you know how powerful their aid is. And I have another secret to tell you; those pieces of glass, which I got from the trees in the garden of the subterranean palace, are jewels of inestimable value, and fit for the greatest monarchs. All the precious stones the jewellers have in Bagdad are not to be compared to mine for size or beauty; and I am sure that the offer of them will secure the favour of the sultan. You have a large porcelain dish fit to hold them; fetch it, and let us see how they will look, when we have arranged them according to their different colours.'

Aladdin's mother brought the china dish. Then he took the jewels out of the two purses in which he had kept them, and placed them in order, according to his fancy. But the brightness and lustre they emitted in the daytime, and the variety of the colours, so dazzled the eyes both of mother and son that they were astonished beyond measure. Aladdin's mother, emboldened by the sight of these rich jewels, and fearful lest her son should be guilty of greater extravagance, complied with his request, and promised to go early the next morning to the palace of the sultan. Aladdin rose before daybreak, awakened his mother, pressing her to go to the sultan's palace and to get admittance, if possible, before the grand vizier, the other viziers, and the great officers of state went in to take their seats in the divan, where the sultan always attended in person.

Aladdin's mother took the china dish, in which they had put the jewels the day before, wrapped it in two fine napkins, and set forward for the sultan's palace. When she came to the gates the grand vizier, the other viziers, and most distinguished lords of the court were just gone in; but notwithstanding the crowd of people was great, she got into the divan, a spacious hall, the entrance into which was very magnificent. She placed herself just before the sultan, and the grand vizier and the great lords, who sat in council on his right and left hand. Several causes were called, according to their order, pleaded and adjudged, until the time the divan generally broke up, when the sultan, rising, returned to his apartment, attended by the grand vizier; the other viziers and ministers of state then retired, as also did all those whose business had called them thither.

Aladdin's mother, seeing the sultan retire, and all the people depart, judged rightly that he would not sit again that day, and resolved to go home. On her arrival she said, with much simplicity, 'Son, I have seen the sultan, and am very well persuaded he has seen me, too, for I placed myself just before him; but he was so much taken up with those who attended on all sides of him that I pitied him, and wondered at his patience. At last I believe he was heartily tired, for he rose up suddenly, and would not hear a great many who were ready prepared to speak to him, but went away, at which I was well pleased, for indeed I began to lose all patience, and was extremely fatigued with staying so long. But there is no harm done; I will go again to-morrow. Perhaps the sultan may not be so busy.'

The next morning she repaired to the sultan's palace with the present as early as the day before; but when she came there, she found the gates of the divan shut. She went six times afterward on the days appointed, placed herself always directly before the sultan, but with as little success as the first morning.

On the sixth day, however, after the divan was broken up, when the sultan returned to his own apartment he said to his grand vizier: 'I have for some time observed a certain woman, who attends constantly every day that I give audience, with something wrapped up in a napkin; she always stands up from the beginning to the breaking up of the audience, and effects to place herself just before me. If this woman comes to our next audience, do not fail to call her, that I may hear what she has to say.'

The grand vizier made answer by lowering his hand, and then lifting it up above his head, signifying his willingness to lose it if he failed.

On the next audience day, when Aladdin's mother went to the divan, and placed herself in front of the sultan as usual, the grand vizier immediately called the chief of the mace-bearers, and pointing to her bade him bring her before the sultan. The old woman at once followed the mace-bearer, and when she reached the sultan, bowed her head down to the carpet which covered the platform of the throne, and remained in that posture until he bade her rise.

She had no sooner done so, than he said to her, 'Good woman, I have observed you to stand many days from the beginning to the rising of the divan. What business brings you here?'

At these words, Aladdin's mother prostrated herself a second time, and when she arose, said, 'Monarch of monarchs, I beg of you to pardon the boldness of my petition, and to assure me of your pardon and forgiveness.'

'Well,' replied the sultan, 'I will forgive you, be it what it may, and no hurt shall come to you. Speak boldly.'

When Aladdin's mother had taken all these precautions, for fear of the sultan's anger, she told him faithfully the errand on which her son had sent her, and the event which led to his making so bold a request in spite of all her remonstrances.

The sultan hearkened to this discourse without showing the least anger. But before he gave her any answer, he asked her what she had brought tied up in the napkin. She took the china dish which she had set down at the foot of the throne, untied it, and presented it to the sultan.

The sultan's amazement and surprise were inexpressible, when he saw so many large, beautiful, and valuable jewels collected in the dish. He remained for some time lost in admiration. At last, when he had recovered himself, he received the present from Aladdin's mother's hand, saying, 'How rich, how beautiful!'

After he had admired and handled all the jewels one after another, he turned to his grand vizier, and showing him the dish, said, 'Behold, admire, wonder! And confess that your eyes never beheld jewels so rich and beautiful before.'

The vizier was charmed.

'Well,' continued the sultan, 'what sayest thou to such a present? Is it not worthy of the princess my daughter? And ought I not to bestow her on one who values her at so great a price?'

'I cannot but own,' replied the grand vizier, 'that the present is worthy of the princess; but I beg of your majesty to grant me three months before you come to a final resolution. I hope, before that time, my son, whom you have regarded with your favour, will be able to make a nobler present than this Aladdin, who is an entire stranger to your majesty.'

The sultan granted his request, and he said to the old woman, 'Good woman, go home, and tell your son that I agree to the proposal you have made me; but I cannot marry the princess my daughter for three months. At the expiration of that time, come again.'

Aladdin's mother returned home much more gratified than she had expected, and told her son with much joy the condescending answer she had received from the sultan's own mouth; and that she was to come to the divan again that day three months.

At hearing this news, Aladdin thought himself the most happy of all men, and thanked his mother for the pains she had taken in the affair, the good success of which was of so great importance to his peace that he counted every day, week, and even hour as it passed. When two of the three months were passed, his mother one evening, having no oil in the house, went out to buy some, and found a general rejoicing—the houses dressed with foliage, silks, and carpeting, and every one striving to show his joy according to his ability. The streets were crowded with officers in habits of ceremony, mounted on horses richly caparisoned, each attended by a great many footmen. Aladdin's mother asked the oil merchant what was the meaning of all this preparation of public festivity.

'Whence came you, good woman,' said he, 'that you don't know that the grand vizier's son is to marry the Princess Buddir al

Buddoor, the sultan's daughter, to-night? She will presently return from the bath; and these officers whom you see are to assist at the cavalcade to the palace, where the ceremony is to be solemnised.'

Aladdin's mother, on hearing this news, ran home very quickly.

'Child,' cried she, 'you are undone! The sultan's fine promises will come to naught. This night the grand vizier's son is to marry the Princess Buddir al Buddoor.'

At this account Aladdin was thunderstruck. He bethought himself of the lamp, and of the genie who had promised to obey him; and without indulging in idle words against the sultan, the vizier, or his son, he determined, if possible, to prevent the marriage.

When Aladdin had got into his chamber he took the lamp, and rubbing it in the same place as before, immediately the genie appeared, and said to him, 'What wouldst thou have? I am ready to obey thee as thy slave; I, and the other slaves of the lamp.'

'Hear me,' said Aladdin. 'Thou hast hitherto[11] obeyed me, but now I am about to impose on thee a harder task. The sultan's daughter, who was promised me as my bride, is this night married to the son of the grand vizier. Bring them both hither to me immediately they retire to their bedchamber.'

'Master,' replied the genie, 'I obey you.'

Aladdin supped with his mother as was their wont, and then went to his own apartment, and sat up to await the return of the genie, according to his commands.

In the meantime the festivities in honour of the princess's marriage were conducted in the sultan's palace with great magnificence. The ceremonies were at last brought to a conclusion, and the princess and the son of the vizier retired to the bedchamber prepared for them. No sooner had they entered it, and dismissed their attendants, than the genie, the faithful slave of the lamp, to the great amazement and alarm of the bride and bridegroom took up the bed, and by an agency invisible to them, transported it in an instant into Aladdin's chamber, where he set it down.

'Remove the bridegroom,' said Aladdin to the genie, 'and keep him a prisoner till to-morrow dawn, and then return with him here.' On Aladdin being left alone with the princess, he endeavoured to assuage her fears, and explained to her the treachery practiced upon him by the sultan her father. He then laid himself down beside her, putting a drawn scimitar between them, to show that he was determined to secure her safety, and to treat her with the utmost possible respect. At break of day, the genie appeared at the appointed hour, bringing back the bridegroom, whom by breathing upon he had left motionless and entranced at the door of Aladdin's chamber during the night, and at Aladdin's command transported the couch, with the bride and bridegroom on it, by the same invisible agency, into the palace of the sultan.

At the instant that the genie had set down the couch with the bride and bridegroom in their own chamber, the sultan came to the door to offer his good wishes to his daughter. The grand vizier's son, who was almost perished with cold, by standing in his thin under-garment all night, no sooner heard the knocking at the door than he got out of bed, and ran into the robing-chamber, where he had undressed himself the night before.

The sultan, having opened the door, went to the bed-side, and kissed the princess on the forehead, but was extremely surprised to see her look so melancholy. She only cast at him a sorrowful look, expressive of great affliction. He suspected there was something extraordinary in this silence, and thereupon went immediately to the sultaness's apartment, told her in what a state he found the princess, and how she had received him.

'Sire,' said the sultaness, 'I will go and see her. She will not receive me in the same manner.'

The princess received her mother with sighs and tears, and signs of deep dejection. At last, upon her pressing on her the duty of telling her all her thoughts, she gave to the sultaness a precise description of all that happened to her during the night; on which the sultaness enjoined on her the necessity of silence and discretion, as no one would give credence to so strange a tale. The grand vizier's son, elated with the honour of being the sultan's son-in-law, kept silence on his part, and the events of the night were not allowed to cast the least gloom on the festivities on the following day, in continued celebration of the royal marriage.

When night came, the bride and bridegroom were again attended to their chamber with the same ceremonies as on the preceding evening. Aladdin, knowing that this would be so, had already given his commands to the genie of the lamp; and no sooner were they alone than their bed was removed in the same mysterious manner as on the preceding evening; and having passed the night in the same unpleasant way, they were in the morning conveyed to the palace of the sultan. Scarcely had they been replaced in their apartment, when the sultan came to make his compliments to his daughter. The princess could no longer conceal from him the unhappy treatment she had been subjected to, and told him all that had happened, as she had already related it to her mother.

The sultan, on hearing these strange tidings, consulted with the grand vizier; and finding from him that his son had been subjected by an invisible agency to even worse treatment, he determined to declare the marriage cancelled, and all the festivities, which were yet to last for several days, countermanded and terminated.

This sudden change in the mind of the sultan gave rise to various speculations and reports. Nobody but Aladdin knew the secret, and he kept it with the most scrupulous silence. Neither the sultan nor the grand vizier, who had forgotten Aladdin and his request, had the least thought that he had any hand in the strange adventures that befell the bride and bridegroom.

On the very day that the three months contained in the sultan's promise expired, the mother of Aladdin again went to the palace, and stood in the same place in the divan. The sultan knew her again, and directed his vizier to have her brought before him.

After having prostrated herself, she made answer, in reply to the sultan: 'Sire, I come at the end of three months to ask of you the fulfilment of the promise you made to my son.'

The sultan little thought the request of Aladdin's mother was made to him in earnest, or that he would hear any more of the matter. He therefore took counsel with his vizier, who suggested that the sultan should attach such conditions to the marriage that no one of the humble condition of Aladdin could possibly fulfil. In accordance with this suggestion of the vizier, the sultan replied to the mother of Aladdin: 'Good woman, it is true sultans ought to abide by their word, and I am ready to keep mine, by making your son happy in marriage with the princess my daughter. But as I cannot marry her without some further proof of your son being able to support her in royal state, you may tell him I will fulfil my promise as soon as he shall send me forty trays of massy gold, full of the same sort of jewels you have already made me a present of, and carried by the like number of black slaves, who shall be led by as many young and handsome white slaves, all dressed magnificently. On these conditions I am ready to bestow the princess my daughter upon him; therefore, good woman, go and tell him so, and I will wait till you bring me his answer.'

Aladdin's mother prostrated herself a second time before the sultan's throne, and retired. On her way home, she laughed within herself at her son's foolish imagination. 'Where,' said she, 'can he get so many large gold trays, and such precious stones to fill them? It is altogether out of his power, and I believe he will not be much pleased with my embassy this time.'

When she came home, full of these thoughts, she told Aladdin all the circumstances of her interview with the sultan, and the conditions on which he consented to the marriage. 'The sultan expects your answer immediately,' said she; and then added, laughing, 'I believe he may wait long enough!'

'Not so long, mother, as you imagine,' replied Aladdin. 'This demand is a mere trifle, and will prove no bar to my marriage with the princess. I will prepare at once to satisfy his request.'

Aladdin retired to his own apartment and summoned the genie of the lamp, and required him to immediately prepare and present the gift, before the sultan closed his morning audience, according to the terms in which it had been prescribed. The genie professed his obedience to the owner of the lamp, and disappeared. Within a very short time, a train of forty black slaves, led by the same number of white slaves, appeared opposite the house in which Aladdin lived. Each black slave carried on his head a basin of massy gold, full of pearls, diamonds, rubies, and emeralds.

Aladdin then addressed his mother: 'Madam, pray lose no time; before the sultan and the divan rise, I would have you return to the palace with this present as the dowry demanded for the princess, that he may judge by my diligence and exactness of the ardent and sincere desire I have to procure myself the honour of this alliance.'

As soon as this magnificent procession, with Aladdin's mother at its head, had begun to march from Aladdin's house, the whole city was filled with the crowds of people desirous to see so grand a sight. The graceful bearing, elegant form, and wonderful likeness of each slave; their grave walk at an equal distance from each other, the lustre of their jewelled girdles, and the brilliancy of the aigrettes of precious stones in their turbans, excited the greatest admiration in the spectators. As they had to pass through several streets to the palace, the whole length of the way was lined with files of spectators. Nothing, indeed, was ever seen so beautiful and brilliant in the sultan's palace, and the richest robes of the emirs of his court were not to be compared to the costly dresses of these slaves, whom they supposed to be kings.

As the sultan, who had been informed of their approach, had given orders for them to be admitted, they met with no obstacle, but went into the divan in regular order, one part turning to the right and the other to the left. After they were all entered, and had formed a semi-circle before the sultan's throne, the black slaves laid the golden trays on the carpet, prostrated themselves, touching the carpet with their foreheads, and at the same time the white slaves did the same. When they rose, the black slaves uncovered the trays, and then all stood with their arms crossed over their breasts.

In the meantime, Aladdin's mother advanced to the foot of the throne, and having prostrated herself, said to the sultan, 'Sire, my son knows this present is much below the notice of Princess Buddir al Buddoor; but hopes, nevertheless, that your majesty will accept of it, and make it agreeable to the princess, and with the greater confidence since he has endeavoured to conform to the conditions you were pleased to impose.'

The sultan, overpowered by the sight of such more than royal magnificence, replied without hesitation to the words of Aladdin's mother: 'Go and tell your son that I wait with open arms to embrace him; and the more haste he makes to come and receive the princess my daughter from my hands, the greater pleasure he will do me.'

As soon as Aladdin's mother had retired, the sultan put an end to the audience. Rising from his throne, he ordered that the princess's attendants should come and carry the trays into their mistress's apartment, whither[12] he went himself to examine them with her at his leisure. The fourscore slaves were conducted into the palace; and the sultan, telling the princess of their magnificent apparel, ordered them to be brought before her apartment, that she might see through the lattices he had not exaggerated in his account of them.

In the meantime Aladdin's mother reached home, and showed in her air and countenance the good news she brought to her son. 'My son,' said she, 'you may rejoice you are arrived at the height of your desires. The sultan has declared that you shall marry the Princess Buddir al Buddoor. He waits for you with impatience.'

Aladdin, enraptured with this news, made his mother very little reply, but retired to his chamber. There he rubbed his lamp, and the obedient genie appeared.

'Genie,' said Aladdin, 'convey me at once to a bath, and supply me with the richest and most magnificent robe ever worn by a monarch.'

No sooner were the words out of his mouth than the genie rendered him, as well as himself, invisible, and transported him into a hummum of the finest marble of all sorts of colours; where he was undressed, without seeing by whom, in a magnificent and spacious hall. He was then well rubbed and washed with various scented waters. After he had passed through several degrees of heat, he came out quite a different man from what he was before. His skin was clear as that of a child, his body lightsome and free; and when he returned into the hall, he found, instead of his own poor raiment, a robe, the magnificence of which astonished him. The genie helped him to dress, and when he had done, transported him back to his own chamber, where he asked him if he had any other commands.

'Yes,' answered Aladdin, 'bring me a charger that surpasses in beauty and goodness the best in the sultan's stables; with a saddle, bridle, and other caparisons to correspond with his value. Furnish also twenty slaves, as richly clothed as those who carried the present to the sultan, to walk by my side and follow me, and twenty more to go before me in two ranks. Besides these, bring my mother six women slaves to attend her, as richly dressed at least as any of the Princess Buddir al Buddoor's, each carrying a complete dress fit for any sultaness. I want also ten thousand pieces of gold in ten purses; go, and make haste.'

As soon as Aladdin had given these orders, the genie disappeared, but presently returned with the horse, the forty slaves, ten of whom carried each a purse containing ten thousand pieces of gold, and six women slaves, each carrying on her head a different dress for Aladdin's mother, wrapped up in a piece of silver tissue, and presented them all to Aladdin.

He presented the six women slaves to his mother, telling her they were her slaves, and that the dresses they had brought were for her use. Of the ten purses Aladdin took four, which he gave to his mother, telling her those were to supply her with necessaries; the other six he left in the hands of the slaves who brought them, with an order to throw them by handfuls among the people as they went to the sultan's palace. The six slaves who carried the purses he ordered likewise to march before him, three on the right hand and three on the left.

When Aladdin had thus prepared himself for his first

interview with the sultan, he dismissed the genie, and immediately mounting his charger, began his march, and though he never was on horseback before, appeared with a grace the most experienced horseman might envy. The innumerable concourse of people through whom he passed made the air echo with their acclamations, especially every time the six slaves who carried the purses threw handfuls of gold among the populace.

On Aladdin's arrival at the palace, the sultan was surprised to find him more richly and magnificently robed than he had ever been himself, and was impressed with his good looks and dignity of manner, which were so different from what he expected in the son of one so humble as Aladdin's mother. He embraced him with all the demonstrations of joy, and when he would have fallen at his feet, held him by the hand, and made him sit near his throne. He shortly after led him, amidst the sounds of trumpets, hautboys, and all kinds of music, to a magnificent entertainment, at which the sultan and Aladdin ate by themselves, and the great lords of the court, according to their rank and dignity, sat at different tables.

After the feast, the sultan sent for the chief cadi, and commanded him to draw up a contract of marriage between the Princess Buddir al Buddoor and Aladdin. When the contract had been drawn, the sultan asked Aladdin if he would stay in the palace and complete the ceremonies of the marriage that day.

'Sire,' said Aladdin, 'though great is my impatience to enter on the honour granted me by your majesty, yet I beg you to permit me first to build a palace worthy to receive the princess your daughter. I pray you to grant me sufficient ground near your palace, and I will have it completed with the utmost expedition.'

The sultan granted Aladdin his request, and again embraced him. After which he took his leave with as much politeness as if he had been bred up and had always lived at court.

Aladdin returned home in the order he had come, amidst the acclamations of the people, who wished him all happiness and prosperity. As soon as he dismounted, he retired to his own chamber, took the lamp, and summoned the genie as usual, who professed his allegiance.

'Genie,' said Aladdin, 'build me a palace fit to receive the Princess Buddir al Buddoor. Let its materials be made of nothing less than porphyry, jasper, agate, lapis lazuli, and the finest marble. Let its walls be massive gold and silver bricks and laid alternately. Let each front contain six windows, and let the lattices of these (except one, which must be left unfinished) be enriched with diamonds, rubies, and emeralds, so that they shall exceed everything of the kind ever seen in the world. Let there be an inner and outer court in front of the palace, and a spacious garden; but above all things, provide a safe treasure house, and fill it with gold and silver. Let there be also kitchens and storehouses, stables full of the finest horses, with their equerries and grooms, and hunting equipage, officers, attendants, and slaves, both men and women, to form a retinue for the princess and myself. Go and execute my wishes.'

When Aladdin gave these commands to the genie, the sun was set. The next morning at daybreak the genie presented himself, and, having obtained Aladdin's consent, transported him in a moment to the palace he had made. The genie led him through all the apartments, where he found officers and slaves, habited according to their rank and the services to which they were appointed. The genie then showed him the treasury, which was opened by a treasurer, where Aladdin saw large vases of different sizes, piled up to the top with money, ranged all around the chamber. The genie thence[13] led him to the stables, where were some of the finest horses in the world, and the grooms busy in dressing them; from thence they went to the storehouses, which were filled with all things necessary, both for food and ornament.

When Aladdin had examined every portion of the palace, and particularly the hall with the four-and-twenty windows, and found it far to exceed his fondest expectations, he said, 'Genie, there is one thing wanting, a fine carpet for the princess to walk upon from the sultan's palace to mine. Lay one down immediately.' The genie disappeared, and Aladdin saw what he desired executed in an instant. The genie then returned, and carried him to his own home.

When the sultan's porters came to open the gates, they were amazed to find what had been an unoccupied garden filled up with a magnificent palace, and a splendid carpet extending to it all the way from the sultan's palace. They told the strange tidings to the grand vizier, who informed the sultan.

'It must be Aladdin's palace,' the sultan exclaimed, 'which I gave him leave to build for my daughter. He has wished to surprise us, and let us see what wonders can be done in only one night.'

Aladdin, on his being conveyed by the genie to his own home, requested his mother to go to the Princess Buddir al Buddoor, and tell her that the palace would be ready for her reception in the evening. She went, attended by her women slaves, in the same order as on the preceding day. Shortly after her arrival at the princess's apartment the sultan himself came in, and was surprised to find her, whom he knew only as his suppliant at his divan in humble guise, more richly and sumptuously attired than his own daughter. This gave him a higher opinion of Aladdin, who took such care of his mother, and made her share his wealth and honours.

Shortly after her departure, Aladdin, mounting his horse and attended by his retinue of magnificent attendants, left his paternal home forever, and went to the palace in the same pomp as on the day before. Nor did he forget to take with him the wonderful lamp, to which he owed all his good fortune, nor to wear the ring which was given him as a talisman.

The sultan entertained Aladdin with the utmost magnificence, and at night, on the conclusion of the marriage ceremonies, the princess took leave of the sultan her father. Bands of music led the procession, followed by a hundred state ushers, and the like number of black mutes, in two files, with their officers at their head. Four hundred of the sultan's young pages carried flambeaux on each side, which, together with the illuminations of the sultan's and Aladdin's palaces, made it as light as day. In this order the princess, conveyed in her litter, and accompanied also by Aladdin's mother, carried in a superb litter and attended by her women slaves, proceeded on the carpet which was spread from the sultan's palace to that of Aladdin.

On her arrival Aladdin was ready to receive her at the entrance, and led her into a large hall, illuminated with an infinite number of wax candles, where a noble feast was served up. The dishes were of massy gold, and contained the most delicate viands. The vases, basins, and goblets were gold also, and of exquisite workmanship, and all the other ornaments and embellishments of the hall were answerable to this display. The princess, dazzled to see so much riches collected in one place, said to Aladdin, 'I thought, prince, that nothing in the world was so beautiful as the sultan my father's palace, but the sight of this hall alone is sufficient to show I was mistaken.'

When the supper was ended, there entered a company of female dancers, who performed, according to the custom of the country, singing at the same time verses in praise of the bride and bridegroom. About midnight Aladdin's mother conducted the bride to the nuptial apartment, and he soon after retired.

The next morning the attendants of Aladdin presented themselves to dress him, and brought him another habit, as rich and magnificent as that worn the day before. He then ordered one of the horses to be got ready, mounted him, and went in the midst of a large troop of slaves to the sultan's palace to entreat him to take a repast in the princess's palace, attended by his grand vizier and all the lords of his court. The sultan consented with pleasure, rose up immediately, and, preceded by the principal officers of his palace, and followed by all the great lords of his court, accompanied Aladdin.

The nearer the sultan approached Aladdin's palace, the more he was struck with its beauty; but when he entered it, when he came into the hall and saw the windows, enriched with diamonds, rubies, emeralds, all large perfect stones, he was completely surprised, and said to his son-in-law, 'This palace is one of the wonders of the world; for where in all the world besides shall we find walls built of massy gold and silver, and diamonds, rubies, and emeralds composing the windows? But what most surprises me is that a hall of this magnificence should be left with one of its windows incomplete and unfinished.'

'Sire,' answered Aladdin, 'the omission was by design, since I wished that you should have the glory of finishing this hall.'

'I take your intention kindly,' said the sultan, 'and will give orders about it immediately.'

After the sultan had finished this magnificent entertainment, provided for him and for his court by Aladdin, he was informed that the jewellers and goldsmiths attended; upon which he returned to the hall, and showed them the window which was unfinished.

'I sent for you,' said he, 'to fit up this window in as great perfection as the rest. Examine them well, and make all the dispatch you can.'

The jewellers and goldsmiths examined the three-and-twenty windows with great attention, and after they had consulted together, to know what each could furnish, they returned, and presented themselves before the sultan, whose principal jeweller, undertaking to speak for the rest, said, 'Sire, we are all willing to exert our utmost care and industry to obey you; but among us all we cannot furnish jewels enough for so great a work.'

'I have more than are necessary,' said the sultan. 'Come to my palace, and you shall choose what may answer your purpose.'

When the sultan returned to his palace he ordered his jewels to be brought out, and the jewellers took a great quantity, particularly those Aladdin had made him a present of, which they soon used, without making any great advance in their work. They came again several times for more, and in a month's time had not finished half their work. In short, they used all the jewels the sultan had, and borrowed of the vizier, but yet the work was not half done.

Aladdin, who knew that all the sultan's endeavours to make this window like the rest were in vain, sent for the jewellers and goldsmiths, and not only commanded them to desist from their work, but ordered them to undo what they had begun, and to carry all their jewels back to the sultan and to the vizier. They undid in a few hours what they had been six weeks about, and retired, leaving Aladdin alone in the hall. He took the lamp, which he carried about him, rubbed it, and presently the genie appeared.

'Genie,' said Aladdin, 'I ordered thee to leave one of the four-and-twenty windows of this hall imperfect, and thou hast executed my commands exactly; now I would have thee make it like the rest.'

The genie immediately disappeared. Aladdin went out of the hall, and returning soon after, found the window, as he wished it to be, like the others.

In the meantime the jewellers and goldsmiths repaired to the palace, and were introduced into the sultan's presence, where the chief jeweller presented the precious stones which he had brought back. The sultan asked them if Aladdin had given them any reason for so doing, and they answering that he had given them none, he ordered a horse to be brought, which he mounted, and rode to his son-in-law's palace, with some few attendants on foot, to inquire why he had ordered the completion of the window to be stopped.

Aladdin met him at the gate, and without giving any reply to his inquiries conducted him to the grand saloon, where the sultan, to his great surprise, found that the window, which was left imperfect, corresponded exactly with the others. He fancied at first that he was mistaken, and examined the two windows on each side, and afterward all the four-and-twenty; but when he was convinced that the window which several workmen had been so long about was finished in so short a time, he embraced Aladdin and kissed him between his eyes.

'My son,' said he, 'what a man you are to do such surprising things always in the twinkling of an eye! There is not your fellow in the world; the more I know, the more I admire you.'

The sultan returned to the palace, and after this went frequently to the window to contemplate and admire the wonderful palace of his son-in-law.

Aladdin did not confine himself in his palace, but went with much state, sometimes to one mosque, and sometimes to another, to prayers, or to visit the grand vizier or the principal lords of the court. Every time he went out he caused two slaves, who walked by the side of his horse, to throw handfuls of money among the people as he passed through the streets and squares. This generosity gained him the love and blessings of the people, and it was common for them to swear by his head. Thus Aladdin, while he paid all respect to the sultan, won by his affable behaviour and liberality the affection of the people.

Aladdin had conducted himself in this manner several years, when the African magician, who had for some years dismissed him from his recollection, determined to inform himself with certainty whether he perished, as he supposed, in the subterranean cave or not. After he had resorted to a long course of magic ceremonies, and had formed a horoscope by which to ascertain Aladdin's fate, what was his surprise to find the appearances to declare that Aladdin, instead of dying in the cave, had made his escape, and was living in royal splendour by the aid of the genie of the wonderful lamp!

On the very next day the magician set out, and travelled with the utmost haste to the capital of China, where, on his arrival, he took up his lodgings in a khan.

He then quickly learned about the wealth, charities, happiness, and splendid palace of Prince Aladdin. Directly he saw the wonderful fabric, he knew that none but the genies, the slaves of the lamp, could have performed such wonders, and, piqued to the quick at Aladdin's high estate, he returned to the khan.

On his return he had recourse to an operation of geomancy to find out where the lamp was—whether Aladdin carried it about with him, or where he left it. The result of his consultation informed him, to his great joy, that the lamp was in the palace.

'Well,' said he, rubbing his hands in glee, 'I shall have the lamp, and I shall make Aladdin return to his original mean condition.'

The next day the magician learned from the chief superintendent of the khan where he lodged that Aladdin had gone on a hunting expedition which was to last for eight days, of which only three had expired. The magician wanted to know no more. He resolved at once on his plans. He went to a coppersmith, and asked for a dozen copper lamps; the master of the shop told him he had not so many by him, but if he would have patience till the next day he would have them ready. The magician appointed his time, and desired him to take care that they should be handsome and well polished.

The next day the magician called for the twelve lamps, paid the man his full price, put them into a basket hanging on his arm, and went directly to Aladdin's palace. As he approached, he began crying, 'Who will exchange old lamps for new?' And as he went along, a crowd of children collected, who hooted, and thought him, as did all who chanced to be passing by, a madman or a fool to offer to exchange new lamps for old.

The African magician regarded not their scoffs, hootings, or all they could say to him, but still continued crying, 'Who will exchange old lamps for new?' He repeated this so often, walking backward and forward in front of the palace, that the princess, who was then in the hall of the four-and-twenty windows, hearing a man cry something, and seeing a great mob crowding about him, sent one of her women slaves to know what he cried.

The slave returned, laughing so heartily that the princess rebuked her.

'Madam,' answered the slave, laughing still, 'who can forbear laughing, to see an old man with a basket on his arm, full of fine new lamps, asking to exchange them for old ones? The children and mob, crowding about him so that he can hardly stir, make all the noise they can in derision of him.'

Another female slave, hearing this, said, 'Now you speak of lamps, I know not whether the princess may have observed it, but there is an old one upon a shelf of the Prince Aladdin's robing room, and whoever owns it will not be sorry to find a new one in its stead. If the princess chooses, she may have the pleasure of trying if this old man is so silly as to give a new lamp for an old one, without taking anything for the exchange.'

The princess, who knew not the value of the lamp and the interest that Aladdin had to keep it safe, entered into the pleasantry and commanded a slave to take it and make the exchange. The slave obeyed, went out of the hall, and no sooner got to the palace gates than he saw the African magician, called to him, and showing him the old lamp, said, 'Give me a new lamp for this.'

The magician never doubted but this was the lamp he wanted. There could be no other such in this palace, where every utensil was gold or silver. He snatched it eagerly out of the slave's hand, and thrusting it as far as he could into his breast, offered him his basket, and bade him choose which he liked best. The slave picked out one and carried it to the princess; but the change was no sooner made than the place rang with the shouts of the children, deriding the magician's folly.

The African magician stayed no longer near the palace, nor cried any more, 'New lamps for old,' but made the best of his way to his khan. His end was answered, and by his silence he got rid of the children and the mob.

As soon as he was out of sight of the two palaces he hastened down the least-frequented streets. Having no more occasion for his lamps or basket, he set all down in a spot where nobody saw him; then going down another street or two, he walked till he came to one of the city gates, and pursuing his way through the suburbs, which were very extensive, at length he reached a lonely spot, where he stopped till the darkness of the night, as the most suitable time for the design he had in contemplation.

When it became quite dark, he pulled the lamp out of his breast and rubbed it. At that summons the genie appeared, and said, 'What wouldst thou have? I am ready to obey thee as thy slave, and the slave of all those who have that lamp in their hands; both I and the other slaves of the lamp.'

'I command thee,' replied the magician, 'to transport me immediately, and the palace which thou and the other slaves of the lamp have built in this city, with all the people in it, to Africa.'

The genie made no reply, but with the assistance of the other genies, the slaves of the lamp, immediately transported him and the palace, entire, to the spot whither he had been desired to convey it.

Early the next morning when the sultan, according to custom, went to contemplate and admire Aladdin's palace, his amazement was unbounded to find that it could nowhere be seen. He could not comprehend how so large a palace, which he had seen plainly every day for some years, should vanish so soon and not leave the least remains behind. In his perplexity he ordered the grand vizier to be sent for with expedition.

The grand vizier, who, in secret, bore no good will to Aladdin, intimated his suspicion that the palace was built by magic, and that Aladdin had made his hunting excursion an excuse for the removal of his palace with the same suddenness with which it had been erected. He induced the sultan to send a detachment of his guard, and to have Aladdin seized as a prisoner of state.

On his son-in-law being brought before him, the sultan would not hear a word from him, but ordered him to be put to death. But the decree caused so much discontent among the people, whose affection Aladdin had secured by his largesses and charities, that the sultan, fearful of an insurrection, was obliged to grant him his life.

When Aladdin found himself at liberty, he again addressed the sultan: 'Sire, I pray you to let me know the crime by which I have thus lost the favour of thy countenance.'

'Your crime!' answered the sultan. 'Wretched man, do you not know it? Follow me, and I will show you.'

The sultan then took Aladdin into the apartment from whence he was wont to look at and admire his palace, and said, 'You ought to know where your palace stood; look, mind, and tell me what has become of it.'

Aladdin did so, and being utterly amazed at the loss of his palace, was speechless. At last recovering himself, he said, 'It is true, I do not see the palace. It is vanished; but I had no concern in its removal. I beg you to give me forty days, and if in that time I cannot restore it, I will offer my head to be disposed of at your pleasure.'

'I give you the time you ask, but at the end of the forty days forget not to present yourself before me.'

Aladdin went out of the sultan's palace in a condition of exceeding humiliation. The lords who had courted him in the days of his splendour now declined to have any communication with him. For three days he wandered about the city, exciting the wonder and compassion of the multitude by asking everybody he met if they had seen his palace, or could tell him anything of it. On the third day he wandered into the country, and as he was approaching a river he fell down the bank with so much violence that he rubbed the ring which the magician had given him so hard, by holding on to the rock to save himself, that immediately the same genie appeared whom he had seen in the cave where the magician had left him.

'What wouldst thou have?' said the genie. 'I am ready to obey thee as thy slave, and the slave of all those that have that ring on their finger; both I and the other slaves of the ring.'

Aladdin, agreeably surprised at an offer of help so little expected, replied, 'Genie, show me where the palace I caused to be built now stands, or transport it back where it first stood.'

'Your command,' answered the genie, 'is not wholly in my power; I am only the slave of the ring, and not of the lamp.'

'I command thee, then,' replied Aladdin, 'by the power of the ring, to transport me to the spot where my palace stands, in what part of the world soever it may be.'

These words were no sooner out of his mouth than the genie transported him into Africa, to the midst of a large plain, where his palace stood at no great distance from a city, and, placing him exactly under the window of the princess's apartment, left him.

Now it so happened that shortly after Aladdin had been transported by the slave of the ring to the neighbourhood of his palace, that one of the attendants of the Princess Buddir al Buddoor, looking through the window, perceived him and instantly told her mistress. The princess, who could not believe the joyful tidings, hastened herself to the window, and seeing Aladdin, immediately opened it. The noise of opening the window made Aladdin turn his head that way, and perceiving the princess, he saluted her with an air that expressed his joy.

'To lose no time,' said she to him, 'I have sent to have the private door opened for you; enter, and come up.'

The private door, which was just under the princess's apartment, was soon opened, and Aladdin was conducted up into the chamber. It is impossible to express the joy of both at seeing each other, after so cruel a separation. After embracing and shedding tears of joy, they sat down, and Aladdin said, 'I beg of you, princess, to tell me what is become of an old lamp which stood upon a shelf in my robing chamber.'

'Alas!' answered the princess, 'I was afraid our misfortune might be owing to that lamp; and what grieves me most is that I have been the cause of it. I was foolish enough to exchange the old lamp for a new one, and the next morning I found myself in this unknown country, which I am told is Africa.'

'Princess,' said Aladdin, interrupting her, 'you have explained all by telling me we are in Africa. I desire you only to tell me if you know where the old lamp now is.'

'The African magician carries it carefully wrapped up in his bosom,' said the princess; 'and this I can assure you, because he pulled it out before me, and showed it to me in triumph.'

'Princess,' said Aladdin, 'I think I have found the means to deliver you and to regain possession of the lamp, on which all my prosperity depends. To execute this design, it is necessary for me to go to the town. I shall return by noon, and will then tell you what must be done by you to insure success. In the meantime, I shall disguise myself, and I beg that the private door may be opened at the first knock.'

When Aladdin was out of the palace, he looked round him on all sides, and perceiving a peasant going into the country, hastened after him. When he had overtaken him, he made a proposal to him to change clothes, which the man agreed to. When they had made the exchange, the countryman went about his business, and Aladdin entered the neighbouring city. After traversing several streets, he came to that part of the town where the merchants and artisans had their particular streets according to their trades. He went into that of the druggists; and entering one of the largest and best furnished shops, asked the druggist if he had a certain powder, which he named.

The druggist, judging Aladdin by his habit to be very poor, told him he had it, but that it was very dear; upon which Aladdin, penetrating his thoughts, pulled out his purse, and showing him some gold, asked for half a dram of the powder, which the druggist weighed and gave him, telling him the price was a piece of gold. Aladdin put the money into his hand, and hastened to the palace, which he entered at once by the private door.

When he came into the princess's apartment he said to her, 'Princess, you must take your part in the scheme which I propose for our deliverance. You must overcome your aversion for the magician, and assume a most friendly manner toward him, and ask him to oblige you by partaking of an entertainment in your apartments. Before he leaves, ask him to exchange cups with you, which he, gratified at the honour you do him, will gladly do, when you must give him the cup containing this powder. On drinking it he will instantly fall asleep, and we will obtain the lamp, whose slaves will do all our bidding, and restore us and the palace to the capital of China.'

The princess obeyed to the utmost her husband's instructions. She assumed a look of pleasure on the next visit of the magician, and asked him to an entertainment, which he most willingly accepted. At the close of the evening, during which the princess had tried all she could to please him, she asked him to exchange cups with her, and giving the signal, had the drugged cup brought to her, which she gave to the magician. Out of compliment to the princess he drank it to the very last drop, when he fell back lifeless on the sofa.

The princess, in anticipation of the success of her scheme, had so placed her women from the great hall to the foot of the staircase that the word was no sooner given that the African magician was fallen backward, than the door was opened, and Aladdin admitted to the hall. The princess rose from her seat, and ran, overjoyed, to embrace him; but he stopped her, and said, 'Princess, retire to your apartment; and let me be left alone, while I endeavour to transport you back to China as speedily as you were brought from thence.'

When the princess, her women, and slaves were gone out of the hall, Aladdin shut the door, and going directly to the dead body of the magician, opened his vest, took out the lamp, which was carefully wrapped up, and rubbing it, the genie immediately appeared.

'Genie,' said Aladdin, 'I command thee to transport this palace instantly to the place from whence it was brought hither.'

The genie bowed his head in token of obedience, and disappeared. Immediately the palace was transported into China, and its removal was felt only by two little shocks, the one when it was lifted up, the other when it was set down, and both in a very short interval of time.

On the morning after the restoration of Aladdin's palace the sultan was looking out of his window, mourning over the fate of his daughter, when he thought that he saw the vacancy created by the disappearance of the palace to be again filled up.

On looking more attentively, he was convinced beyond the power of doubt that it was his son-in-law's palace. Joy and gladness succeeded to sorrow and grief. He at once ordered a horse to be saddled, which he mounted that instant, thinking he could not make haste enough to the place.

Aladdin rose that morning by daybreak, put on one of the most magnificent habits his wardrobe afforded, and went up into the hall of the twenty-four windows, from whence he perceived the sultan approaching, and received him at the foot of the great staircase, helping him to dismount.

He led the sultan into the princess's apartment. The happy father embraced her with tears of joy; and the princess, on her side, afforded similar testimonies of her extreme pleasure. After a short interval, devoted to mutual explanations of all that had happened, the sultan restored Aladdin to his favour, and expressed his regret for the apparent harshness with which he had treated him.

'My son,' said he, 'be not displeased at my proceedings against you; they arose from my paternal love, and therefore you ought to forgive the excesses to which it hurried me.'

'Sire,' replied Aladdin, 'I have not the least reason to complain of your conduct, since you did nothing but what your duty required. This infamous magician, the basest of men, was the sole cause of my misfortune.'

The African magician, who was thus twice foiled in his endeavour to rain Aladdin, had a younger brother, who was as skilful a magician as himself and exceeded him in wickedness and hatred of mankind. By mutual agreement they communicated with each other once a year, however widely separate might be their place of residence from each other. The younger brother, not having received as usual his annual communication, prepared to take a horoscope and ascertain his brother's proceedings. He, as well as his brother, always carried a geomantic square instrument about him; he prepared the sand, cast the points, and drew the figures. On examining the planetary crystal, he found that his brother was no longer living, but had been poisoned; and by another observation, that he was in the capital of the kingdom of China; also, that the person who had poisoned him was of mean birth, though married to a princess, a sultan's daughter.

When the magician had informed himself of his brother's fate he resolved immediately to avenge his death, and at once departed for China; where, after crossing plains, rivers, mountains, deserts, and a long tract of country without delay, he arrived after incredible fatigues. When he came to the capital of China he took a lodging at a khan. His magic art soon revealed to him that Aladdin was the person who had been the cause of the death of his brother. He had heard, too, all the persons of repute in the city talking of a woman called Fatima, who was retired from the world, and of the miracles she wrought. As he fancied that this woman might be serviceable to him in the project he had conceived, he made more minute inquiries, and requested to be informed more particularly who that holy woman was, and what sort of miracles she performed.

'What!' said the person whom he addressed, 'have you never seen or heard of her? She is the admiration of the whole town, for her fasting, her austerities, and her exemplary life. Except Mondays and Fridays, she never stirs out of her little cell; and on those days on which she comes into the town she does an infinite deal of good; for there is not a person who is diseased but she puts her hand on him and cures him.'

Having ascertained the place where the hermitage of this holy woman was, the magician went at night, and plunged a poniard into her heart—killed this good woman. In the morning he dyed his face of the same hue as hers, and arraying himself in her garb, taking her veil, the large necklace she wore round her waist, and her stick, went straight to the palace of Aladdin.

As soon as the people saw the holy woman, as they imagined him to be, they presently gathered about him in a great crowd. Some begged his blessing, others kissed his hand, and others, more reserved, kissed only the hem of his garment; while others, suffering from disease, stooped for him to lay his hands upon them; which he did, muttering some words in form of prayer, and, in short, counterfeiting so well that everybody took him for the holy woman. He came at last to the square before Aladdin's palace. The crowd and the noise were so great that the princess, who was in the hall of the four-and-twenty windows, heard it, and asked what was the matter. One of her women told her it was a great crowd of people collected about the holy woman to be cured of diseases by the imposition of her hands.

The princess, who had long heard of this holy woman, but had never seen her, was very desirous to have some conversation with her. The chief officer perceiving this, told her it was an easy matter to bring the woman to her if she desired and commanded it; and the princess expressing her wishes, he immediately sent four slaves for the pretended holy woman.

As soon as the crowd saw the attendants from the palace, they made way; and the magician, perceiving also that they were coming for him, advanced to meet them, overjoyed to find his plot succeed so well.

'Holy woman,' said one of the slaves, 'the princess wishes to see you, and has sent us for you.'

'The princess does me too great an honour,' replied the false Fatima; 'I am ready to obey her command.' And at the same time he followed the slaves to the palace.

When the pretended Fatima had made his obeisance, the princess said, 'My good mother, I have one thing to request, which you must not refuse me; it is, to stay with me, that you may edify me with your way of living, and that I may learn from your good example.'

'Princess,' said the counterfeit Fatima, 'I beg of you not to ask what I cannot consent to without neglecting my prayers and devotion.'

'That shall be no hindrance to you,' answered the princess; 'I have a great many apartments unoccupied; you shall choose which you like best, and have as much liberty to perform your devotions as if you were in your own cell.'

The magician, who really desired nothing more than to introduce himself into the palace, where it would be a much easier matter for him to execute his designs, did not long excuse himself from accepting the obliging offer which the princess made him.

'Princess,' said he, 'whatever resolution a poor wretched woman as I am may have made to renounce the pomp and grandeur of this world, I dare not presume to oppose the will and commands of so pious and charitable a princess.'

Upon this the princess, rising up, said, 'Come with me. I will show you what vacant apartments I have, that you may make choice of that you like best.'

The magician followed the princess, and of all the apartments she showed him, made choice of that which was the worst, saying that was too good for him, and that he only accepted it to please her.

Afterward the princess would have brought him back again into the great hall to make him dine with her; but he, considering that he should then be obliged to show his face, which he had always taken care to conceal with Fatima's veil, and fearing that the princess would find out that he was not Fatima, begged of her earnestly to excuse him, telling her that he never ate anything but bread and dried fruits, and desiring to eat that slight repast in his own apartment.

The princess granted his request, saying, 'You may be as free here, good mother, as if you were in your own cell: I will order you a dinner, but remember, I expect you as soon as you have finished your repast.'

After the princess had dined, and the false Fatima had been sent for by one of the attendants, he again waited upon her. 'My good mother,' said the princess, 'I am overjoyed to see so holy a woman as yourself, who will confer a blessing upon this palace. But now I am speaking of the palace, pray how do you like it? And before I show it all to you, tell me first what you think of this hall.'

Upon this question, the counterfeit Fatima surveyed the hall from one end to the other. When he had examined it well, he said to the princess, 'As far as such a solitary being as I am, who am unacquainted with what the world calls beautiful, can judge, this hall is truly admirable; there wants but one thing.'

'What is that, good mother?' demanded the princess; 'tell me, I conjure you. For my part, I always believed, and have heard say, it wanted nothing; but if it does, it shall be supplied.'

'Princess,' said the false Fatima, with great dis-simulation, 'forgive me the liberty I have taken; but my opinion is, if it can be of any importance, that if a roc's egg were hung up in the middle of the dome, this hall would have no parallel in the four quarters of the world, and your palace would be the wonder of the universe.'

'My good mother,' said the princess, 'what is a roc, and where may one get an egg?'

'Princess,' replied the pretended Fatima, 'it is a bird of prodigious size, which inhabits the summit of Mount Caucasus; the architect who built your palace can get you one.'

After the princess had thanked the false Fatima for what she believed her good advice, she conversed with her upon other matters; but she could not forget the roc's egg, which she resolved to request of Aladdin when next he should visit his apartments. He did so in the course of that evening, and shortly after he entered, the princess thus addressed him: 'I always believed that our palace was the most superb, magnificent, and complete in the world: but I will tell you now what it wants, and that is a roc's egg hung up in the midst of the dome.'

'Princess,' replied Aladdin, 'it is enough that you think it wants such an ornament; you shall see by the diligence which I use in obtaining it, that there is nothing which I would not do for your sake.'

Aladdin left the Princess Buddir al Buddoor that moment, and went up into the hall of four-and-twenty windows, where, pulling out of his bosom the lamp, which after the danger he had been exposed to he always carried about him, he rubbed it; upon which the genie immediately appeared.

'Genie,' said Aladdin, 'I command thee, in the name of this lamp, bring a roc's egg to be hung up in the middle of the dome of the hall of the palace.'

Aladdin had no sooner pronounced these words than the hall shook as if ready to fall; and the genie said, in a loud and terrible voice, 'Is it not enough that I and the other slaves of the lamp have done everything for you, but you, by an unheard-of ingratitude, must command me to bring my master, and hang him up in the midst of this dome? This attempt deserves that you, the princess, and the palace should be immediately reduced to ashes; but you are spared because this request does not come from yourself. Its true author is the brother of the African magician, your enemy whom you have destroyed. He is now in your palace, disguised in the habit of the holy woman Fatima, whom he has murdered; at his suggestion your wife makes this pernicious demand. His design is to kill you; therefore take care of yourself.' After these words the genie disappeared.

Aladdin resolved at once what to do. He returned to the princess's apartment, and without mentioning a word of what had happened, sat down, and complained of a great pain which had suddenly seized his head. On hearing this, the princess told him how she had invited the holy Fatima to stay with her, and that she was now in the palace; and at the request of the prince, ordered her to be summoned to her at once.

When the pretended Fatima came, Aladdin said, 'Come hither, good mother; I am glad to see you here at so fortunate a time. I am tormented with a violent pain in my head, and request your assistance, and hope you will not refuse me that cure which you impart to afflicted persons.'

So saying, he arose, but held down his head. The counterfeit Fatima advanced toward him, with his hand all the time on a dagger concealed in his girdle under his gown. Observing this, Aladdin snatched the weapon from his hand, pierced him to the heart with his own dagger, and then pushed him down on the floor.

'My dear prince, what have you done?' cried the princess, in surprise. 'You have killed the holy woman!

'No, my princess,' answered Aladdin, with emotion, 'I have not killed Fatima, but a villain who would have assassinated me, if I had not prevented him. This wicked man,' added he, uncovering his face, 'is the brother of the magician who attempted our ruin.

He has strangled the true Fatima, and disguised himself in her clothes with intent to murder me.'

Aladdin then informed her how the genie had told him these facts, and how narrowly she and the palace had escaped destruction though his treacherous suggestion which had led to her request.

Thus was Aladdin delivered from the persecution of the two brothers, who were magicians. Within a few years the sultan died in a good old age, and as he left no male children, the Princess Buddir al Buddoor succeeded him, and she and Aladdin reigned together many years, and left a numerous and illustrious posterity.

3

The Seven Voyages of Sindbad

First Voyage

I had inherited considerable wealth from my parents, and being young and foolish I at first squandered it recklessly upon every kind of pleasure, but presently, finding that riches speedily take to themselves wings if managed as badly as I was managing mine, and remembering also that to be old and poor is misery indeed, I began to bethink me of how I could make the best of what still remained to me. I sold all my household goods by public auction, and joined a company of merchants who traded by sea, embarking with them at Balsora in a ship which we had fitted out between us.

We set sail and took our course towards the East Indies by the Persian Gulf, having the coast of Persia upon our left hand and upon our right the shores of Arabia Felix. I was at first much troubled by the uneasy motion of the vessel, but speedily recovered my health, and since that hour have been no more plagued by sea-sickness.

From time to time we landed at various islands, where we sold or exchanged our merchandise, and one day, when the wind dropped suddenly, we found ourselves becalmed close to a small island like a green meadow, which only rose slightly above the surface of the water. Our sails were furled, and the captain gave permission to all who wished to land for a while and amuse themselves. I was among the number, but when after strolling about for some time we lighted a fire and sat down to enjoy the repast which we had brought with us, we were startled by a sudden and violent trembling of the island, while at the same moment those left upon the ship set up an outcry bidding us come on board for our lives, since what we had taken for an island was nothing but the back of a sleeping whale. Those who were nearest to the boat threw themselves into it, others sprang into the sea, but before I could save myself the whale plunged suddenly into the depths of the ocean, leaving me clinging to a piece of the wood which we had brought to make our fire. Meanwhile a breeze had sprung up, and in the confusion that ensued on board our vessel in hoisting the sails and taking up those who were in the boat and clinging to its sides, no one missed me and I was left at the mercy of the waves. All that day I floated up and down, now beaten this way, now that, and when night fell I despaired for my life; but, weary and spent as I was, I clung to my frail support, and great was my joy when the morning light showed me that I had drifted against an island.

The cliffs were high and steep, but luckily for me some tree-roots protruded in places, and by their aid I climbed up at last, and stretched myself upon the turf at the top, where I lay, more dead than alive, till the sun was high in the heavens. By that time I was very hungry, but after some searching I came upon some eatable herbs, and a spring of clear water, and much refreshed I set out to explore the island. Presently I reached a great plain where a grazing horse was tethered, and as I stood looking at it I heard voices talking apparently underground, and in a moment a man appeared who asked me how I came upon the island. I told him my adventures, and heard in return that he was one of the grooms of Mihrage, the King of the island, and that each year they came to feed their master's horses in this plain. He took me to a cave where his companions were assembled, and when I had eaten of the food they set before me, they bade me think myself fortunate to have come upon them when I did, since they were going back to their master on the morrow, and without their aid I could certainly never have found my way to the inhabited part of the island.

Early the next morning we accordingly set out, and when we reached the capital I was graciously received by the King, to whom I related my adventures, upon which he ordered that I should be well cared for and provided with such things as I needed. Being a merchant I sought out men of my own profession, and particularly those who came from foreign countries, as I hoped in this way to hear news from Bagdad, and find out some means of returning thither, for the capital was situated upon the sea-shore, and visited by vessels from all parts of the world. In the meantime I heard many curious things, and answered many questions concerning my own country, for I talked willingly with all who came to me. Also to while away the time of waiting I explored a little island named Cassel, which belonged to King Mihrage, and which was supposed to be inhabited by a spirit named Deggial. Indeed, the sailors assured me that often at night the playing of timbals could be heard upon it. However, I saw nothing strange upon my voyage, saving some fish that were full two hundred cubits long, but were fortunately more in dread of us than even we were of them, and fled from us if we did but strike upon a board to frighten them. Other fishes there were only a cubit long which had heads like owls.

One day after my return, as I went down to the quay, I saw a ship which had just cast anchor, and was discharging her cargo, while the merchants to whom it belonged were busily directing the removal of it to their warehouses. Drawing nearer I presently noticed that my own name was marked upon some of the packages, and after having carefully examined them, I felt sure that they were indeed those which I had put on board our ship at Balsora. I then recognised the captain of the vessel, but as I was certain that he believed me to be dead, I went up to him and asked who owned the packages that I was looking at.

'There was on board my ship,' he replied, 'a merchant of Bagdad named Sindbad. One day he and several of my other passengers landed upon what we supposed to be an island, but which was really an enormous whale floating asleep upon the waves. No sooner did it feel upon its back the heat of the fire which had been kindled, than it plunged into the depths of the sea. Several of the people who were upon it perished in the waters, and among others this unlucky Sindbad. This merchandise is his, but I have resolved to dispose of it for the benefit of his family if I should ever chance to meet with them.'

'Captain,' said I, 'I am that Sindbad whom you believe to be dead, and these are my possessions!'

When the captain heard these words he cried out in amazement, 'Lackaday! and what is the world coming to? In these days there is not an honest man to be met with. Did I not with my own eyes see Sindbad drown, and now you have the audacity to tell me that you are he! I should have taken you to be a just man, and yet for the sake of obtaining that which does not belong to you, you are ready to invent this horrible falsehood.'

'Have patience, and do me the favour to hear my story,' said I.

'Speak then,' replied the captain, 'I am all attention.'

So I told him of my escape and of my fortunate meeting with

the king's grooms, and how kindly I had been received at the palace. Very soon I began to see that I had made some impression upon him, and after the arrival of some of the other merchants, who showed great joy at once more seeing me alive, he declared that he also recognised me.

Throwing himself upon my neck he exclaimed, 'Heaven be praised that you have escaped from so great a danger. As to your goods, I pray you take them, and dispose of them as you please.' I thanked him, and praised his honesty, begging him to accept several bales of merchandise in token of my gratitude, but he would take nothing. Of the choicest of my goods I prepared a present for King Mihrage, who was at first amazed, having known that I had lost my all. However, when I had explained to him how my bales had been miraculously restored to me, he graciously accepted my gifts, and in return gave me many valuable things. I then took leave of him, and exchanging my merchandise for sandal and aloes-wood, camphor, nutmegs, cloves, pepper, and ginger, I embarked upon the same vessel and traded so successfully upon our homeward voyage that I arrived in Balsora with about one hundred thousand sequins. My family received me with as much joy as I felt upon seeing them once more. I bought land and slaves, and built a great house in which I resolved to live happily, and in the enjoyment of all the pleasures of life to forget my past sufferings.

Here Sindbad paused, and commanded the musicians to play again, while the feasting continued until evening. When the time came for the porter to depart, Sindbad gave him a purse containing one hundred sequins, saying, 'Take this, Hindbad, and go home, but to-morrow come again and you shall hear more of my adventures.'

The porter retired quite overcome by so much generosity, and you may imagine that he was well received at home, where his wife and children thanked their lucky stars that he had found such a benefactor.

The next day Hindbad, dressed in his best, returned to the voyager's house, and was received with open arms. As soon as all the guests had arrived the banquet began as before, and when they had feasted long and merrily, Sindbad addressed them thus:

'My friends, I beg that you will give me your attention while I relate the adventures of my second voyage, which you will find even more astonishing than the first.'

Second Voyage

I had resolved, as you know, on my return from my first voyage, to spend the rest of my days quietly in Bagdad, but very soon I grew tired of such an idle life and longed once more to find myself upon the sea.

I procured, therefore, such goods as were suitable for the places I intended to visit, and embarked for the second time in a good ship with other merchants whom I knew to be honourable men. We went from island to island, often making excellent bargains, until one day we landed at a spot which, though covered with fruit trees and abounding in springs of excellent water, appeared to possess neither houses nor people. While my companions wandered here and there gathering flowers and fruit I sat down in a shady place, and, having heartily enjoyed the provisions and the wine I had brought with me, I fell asleep, lulled by the murmur of a clear brook which flowed close by.

How long I slept I know not, but when I opened my eyes and started to my feet I perceived with horror that I was alone and that the ship was gone. I rushed to and fro like one distracted, uttering cries of despair, and when from the shore I saw the vessel under full sail just disappearing upon the horizon, I wished bitterly enough that I had been content to stay at home in safety. But since wishes could do me no good, I presently took courage and looked about me for a means of escape. When I had climbed a tall tree I first of all directed my anxious glances towards the sea; but, finding nothing hopeful there, I turned landward, and my curiosity was excited by a huge dazzling white object, so far off that I could not make out what it might be.

Descending from the tree I hastily collected what remained of my provisions and set off as fast as I could go towards it. As I drew near it seemed to me to be a white ball of immense size and height, and when I could touch it, I found it marvellously smooth and soft. As it was impossible to climb it--for it presented no foot-hold-- I walked round about it seeking some opening, but there was none. I counted, however, that it was at least fifty paces round. By this time the sun was near setting, but quite suddenly it fell dark, something like a huge black cloud came swiftly over me, and I saw with amazement that it was a bird of extraordinary size which was hovering near. Then I remembered that I had often heard the sailors speak of a wonderful bird called a roc, and it occurred to me that the white object which had so puzzled me must be its egg.

Sure enough the bird settled slowly down upon it, covering it with its wings to keep it warm, and I cowered close beside the egg in such a position that one of the bird's feet, which was as large as the trunk of a tree, was just in front of me. Taking off my turban I bound myself securely to it with the linen in the hope that the roc, when it took flight next morning, would bear me away with it from the desolate island. And this was precisely what did happen. As soon as the dawn appeared the bird rose into the air carrying me up and up till I could no longer see the earth, and then suddenly it descended so swiftly that I almost lost consciousness. When I became aware that the roc had settled and that I was once again upon solid ground, I hastily unbound my turban from its foot and freed myself, and that not a moment too soon; for the bird, pouncing upon a huge snake, killed it with a few blows from its powerful beak, and seizing it up rose into the air once more and soon disappeared from my view. When I had looked about me I began to doubt if I had gained anything by quitting the desolate island.

The valley in which I found myself was deep and narrow, and surrounded by mountains which towered into the clouds, and were so steep and rocky that there was no way of climbing up their sides. As I wandered about, seeking anxiously for some means of escaping from this trap, I observed that the ground was strewed with diamonds, some of them of an astonishing size. This sight gave me great pleasure, but my delight was speedily damped when I saw also numbers of horrible snakes so long and so large that the smallest of them could have swallowed an elephant with ease. Fortunately for me they seemed to hide in caverns of the rocks by day, and only came out by night, probably because of their enemy the roc.

All day long I wandered up and down the valley, and when it grew dusk I crept into a little cave, and having blocked up the entrance to it with a stone, I ate part of my little store of food and lay down to sleep, but all through the night the serpents crawled to and fro, hissing horribly, so that I could scarcely close my eyes for terror. I was thankful when the morning light appeared, and when I judged by the silence that the serpents had retreated to their dens I came tremblingly out of my cave and wandered up and down the valley once more, kicking the diamonds contemptuously out of my path, for I felt that they were indeed vain things to a man in my situation. At last, overcome with weariness, I sat down upon a rock, but I had hardly closed my eyes when I was startled by something which fell to the ground with a thud close beside me.

It was a huge piece of fresh meat, and as I stared at it several more pieces rolled over the cliffs in different places. I had always thought that the stories the sailors told of the famous valley of diamonds, and of the cunning way which some merchants had devised for getting at the precious stones, were mere travellers' tales invented to give pleasure to the hearers, but now I perceived that they were surely true. These merchants came to the valley at the time when the eagles, which keep their eyries in the rocks, had hatched their young. The merchants then threw great lumps of meat into the valley. These, falling with so much force upon the diamonds, were sure to take up some of the precious stones with them, when the eagles pounced upon the meat and carried it off to their nests to feed their hungry broods. Then the merchants, scaring away the parent birds with shouts and outcries, would secure their treasures. Until this moment I had looked upon the valley as my grave, for I had seen no possibility of getting out of it alive, but now I took courage and began to devise a means of escape. I began by picking up all the largest diamonds I could find and storing them carefully in the leathern wallet which had held my provisions; this I tied securely to my belt. I then chose the piece of meat which seemed most suited to my purpose, and with the aid of my turban bound it firmly to my back; this done I laid down upon my face and awaited the coming of the eagles. I soon heard the flapping of their mighty wings above me, and had the satisfaction of feeling one of them seize upon my piece of meat, and me with it, and rise slowly towards his nest, into which he presently dropped me. Luckily for me the merchants were on the watch, and setting up their usual outcries they rushed to the nest scaring away the eagle. Their amazement was great when they discovered me, and also their disappointment, and with one accord they fell to abusing me for having robbed them of their usual profit. Addressing myself to the one who seemed most aggrieved, I said:

'I am sure, if you knew all that I have suffered, you would show more kindness towards me, and as for diamonds, I have enough here of the very best for you and me and all your company.' So saying I showed them to him. The others all crowded round me, wondering at my adventures and admiring the device by which I had escaped from the valley, and when they had led me to their camp and examined my diamonds, they assured me that in all the years that they had carried on their trade they had seen no stones to be compared with them for size and beauty.

I found that each merchant chose a particular nest, and took his chance of what he might find in it. So I begged the one who owned the nest to which I had been carried to take as much as he would of my treasure, but he contented himself with one stone, and that by no means the largest, assuring me that with such a gem his fortune was made, and he need toil no more. I stayed with the merchants several days, and then as they were journeying homewards I gladly accompanied them. Our way lay across high mountains infested with frightful serpents, but we had the good luck to escape them and came at last to the seashore. Thence we sailed to the isle of Rohat where the camphor trees grow to such a size that a hundred men could shelter under one of them with ease. The sap flows from an incision made high up in the tree into a vessel hung there to receive it, and soon hardens into the substance called camphor, but the tree itself withers up and dies when it has been so treated.

In this same island we saw the rhinoceros, an animal which is smaller than the elephant and larger than the buffalo. It has one horn about a cubit long which is solid, but has a furrow from the base to the tip. Upon it is traced in white lines the figure of a man. The rhinoceros fights with the elephant, and transfixing him with his horn carries him off upon his head, but becoming blinded with the blood of his enemy, he falls helpless to the ground, and then comes the roc, and clutches them both up in his talons and takes them to feed his young. This doubtless astonishes you, but if you do not believe my tale go to Roha and see for yourself. For fear of wearying you I pass over in silence many other wonderful things which we saw in this island. Before we left I exchanged one of my diamonds for much goodly merchandise by which I profited greatly on our homeward way. At last we reached Balsora, whence I hastened to Bagdad, where my first action was to bestow large sums of money upon the poor, after which I settled down to enjoy tranquilly the riches I had gained with so much toil and pain.

Having thus related the adventures of his second voyage, Sindbad again bestowed a hundred sequins upon Hindbad, inviting him to come again on the following day and hear how he fared upon his third voyage. The other guests also departed to their homes, but all returned at the same hour next day, including the porter, whose former life of hard work and poverty had already begun to seem to him like a bad dream. Again after the feast was over did Sindbad claim the attention of his guests and began the account of his third voyage.

Third Voyage

After a very short time the pleasant easy life I led made me quite forget the perils of my two voyages. Moreover, as I was still in the prime of life, it pleased me better to be up and doing. So once more providing myself with the rarest and choicest merchandise of Bagdad, I conveyed it to Balsora, and set sail with other merchants of my acquaintance for distant lands. We had touched at many ports and made much profit, when one day upon the open sea we were caught by a terrible wind which blew us completely out of our reckoning, and lasting for several days finally drove us into harbour on a strange island.

'I would rather have come to anchor anywhere than here,' quoth our captain. 'This island and all adjoining it are inhabited by hairy savages, who are certain to attack us, and whatever these dwarfs may do we dare not resist, since they swarm like locusts, and if one of them is killed the rest will fall upon us, and speedily make an end of us.'

These words caused great consternation among all the ship's company, and only too soon we were to find out that the captain spoke truly. There appeared a vast multitude of hideous savages, not more than two feet high and covered with reddish fur. Throwing themselves into the waves they surrounded our vessel. Chattering meanwhile in a language we could not understand, and clutching at ropes and gangways, they swarmed up the ship's side with such speed and agility that they almost seemed to fly.

You may imagine the rage and terror that seized us as we watched them, neither daring to hinder them nor able to speak a word to deter them from their purpose, whatever it might be. Of this we were not left long in doubt. Hoisting the sails, and cutting the cable of the anchor, they sailed our vessel to an island which lay a little further off, where they drove us ashore; then taking possession of her, they made off to the place from which they had come, leaving us helpless upon a shore avoided with horror by all mariners for a reason which you will soon learn.

Turning away from the sea we wandered miserably inland, finding as we went various herbs and fruits which we ate, feeling that we might as well live as long as possible though we had no hope of escape. Presently we saw in the far distance what seemed to us to be a splendid palace, towards which we turned our weary steps, but when we reached it we saw that it was a castle, lofty, and strongly built. Pushing back the heavy ebony doors we entered the courtyard, but upon the threshold of the great hall beyond it we paused, frozen with horror, at the sight which greeted us. On one side lay a huge pile of bones--human bones, and on the other numberless spits for roasting! Overcome with despair we sank trembling to the ground, and lay there without speech or motion. The sun was setting when a loud noise aroused us, the door of the hall was violently burst open and a horrible giant entered. He was as tall as a palm tree, and perfectly black, and had one eye, which flamed like a burning coal in the middle of his forehead. His teeth were long and sharp and grinned horribly, while his lower lip hung down upon his chest, and he had ears like elephant's ears, which covered his shoulders, and nails like the claws of some fierce bird.

At this terrible sight our senses left us and we lay like dead men. When at last we came to ourselves the giant sat examining us attentively with his fearful eye. Presently when he had looked at us enough he came towards us, and stretching out his hand took me by the back of the neck, turning me this way and that, but feeling that I was mere skin and bone he set me down again and went on to the next, whom he treated in the same fashion; at last he came to the captain, and finding him the fattest of us all, he took him up in one hand and stuck him upon a spit and proceeded to kindle a huge fire at which he presently roasted him. After the giant had supped he lay down to sleep, snoring like the loudest thunder, while we lay shivering with horror the whole night through, and when day broke he awoke and went out, leaving us in the castle.

When we believed him to be really gone we started up bemoaning our horrible fate, until the hall echoed with our despairing cries. Though we were many and our enemy was alone it did not occur to us to kill him, and indeed we should have found that a hard task, even if we had thought of it, and no plan could we devise to deliver ourselves. So at last, submitting to our sad fate, we spent the day in wandering up and down the island eating such fruits as we could find, and when night came we returned to the castle, having sought in vain for any other place of shelter. At sunset the giant returned, supped upon one of our unhappy comrades, slept and snored till dawn, and then left us as before. Our condition seemed to us so frightful that several of my companions thought it would be better to leap from the cliffs and perish in the waves at once, rather than await so miserable an end; but I had a plan of escape which I now unfolded to them, and which they at once agreed to attempt.

'Listen, my brothers,' I added. 'You know that plenty of driftwood lies along the shore. Let us make several rafts, and carry them to a suitable place. If our plot succeeds, we can wait patiently for the chance of some passing ship which would rescue us from this fatal island. If it fails, we must quickly take to our rafts; frail as they are, we have more chance of saving our lives with them than we have if we remain here.'

All agreed with me, and we spent the day in building rafts, each capable of carrying three persons. At nightfall we returned to the castle, and very soon in came the giant, and one more of our number was sacrificed. But the time of our vengeance was at hand! As soon as he had finished his horrible repast he lay down to sleep as before, and when we heard him begin to snore I, and nine of the boldest of my comrades, rose softly, and took each a spit, which we made red-hot in the fire, and then at a given signal we plunged it with one accord into the giant's eye, completely blinding him. Uttering a terrible cry, he sprang to his feet clutching in all directions to try to seize one of us, but we had all fled different ways as soon as the deed was done, and thrown ourselves flat upon the ground in corners where he was not likely to touch us with his feet.

After a vain search he fumbled about till he found the door, and fled out of it howling frightfully. As for us, when he was gone we made haste to leave the fatal castle, and, stationing ourselves beside our rafts, we waited to see what would happen. Our idea was that if, when the sun rose, we saw nothing of the giant, and no longer heard his howls, which still came faintly through the darkness, growing more and more distant, we should conclude that he was dead, and that we might safely stay upon the island and need not risk our lives upon the frail rafts. But alas! morning light showed us our enemy approaching us, supported on either hand by two giants nearly as large and fearful as himself, while a crowd of others followed close upon their heels. Hesitating no longer we clambered upon our rafts and rowed with all our might out to sea. The giants, seeing their prey escaping them, seized up huge pieces of rock, and wading into the water hurled them after us with such good aim that all the rafts except the one I was upon were swamped, and their luckless crews drowned, without our being able to do anything to help them. Indeed I and my two companions had all we could do to keep our own raft beyond the reach of the giants, but by dint of hard rowing we at last gained the open sea. Here we were at the mercy of the winds and waves, which tossed us to and fro all that day and night, but the next morning we found ourselves near an island, upon which we gladly landed.

There we found delicious fruits, and having satisfied our hunger we presently lay down to rest upon the shore. Suddenly we were aroused by a loud rustling noise, and starting up, saw that it was caused by an immense snake which was gliding towards us over the sand. So swiftly it came that it had seized one of my comrades before he had time to fly, and in spite of his cries and struggles speedily crushed the life out of him in its mighty coils and proceeded to swallow him. By this time my other companion and

I were running for our lives to some place where we might hope to be safe from this new horror, and seeing a tall tree we climbed up into it, having first provided ourselves with a store of fruit off the surrounding bushes. When night came I fell asleep, but only to be awakened once more by the terrible snake, which after hissing horribly round the tree at last reared itself up against it, and finding my sleeping comrade who was perched just below me, it swallowed him also, and crawled away leaving me half dead with terror.

When the sun rose I crept down from the tree with hardly a hope of escaping the dreadful fate which had over-taken my comrades; but life is sweet, and I determined to do all I could to save myself. All day long I toiled with frantic haste and collected quantities of dry brushwood, reeds and thorns, which I bound with faggots, and making a circle of them under my tree I piled them firmly one upon another until I had a kind of tent in which I crouched like a mouse in a hole when she sees the cat coming. You may imagine what a fearful night I passed, for the snake returned eager to devour me, and glided round and round my frail shelter seeking an entrance. Every moment I feared that it would succeed in pushing aside some of the faggots, but happily for me they held together, and when it grew light my enemy retired, baffled and hungry, to his den. As for me I was more dead than alive! Shaking with fright and half suffocated by the poisonous breath of the monster, I came out of my tent and crawled down to the sea, feeling that it would be better to plunge from the cliffs and end my life at once than pass such another night of horror. But to my joy and relief I saw a ship sailing by, and by shouting wildly and waving my turban I managed to attract the attention of her crew.

A boat was sent to rescue me, and very soon I found myself

on board surrounded by a wondering crowd of sailors and merchants eager to know by what chance I found myself in that desolate island. After I had told my story they regaled me with the choicest food the ship afforded, and the captain, seeing that I was in rags, generously bestowed upon me one of his own coats. After sailing about for some time and touching at many ports we came at last to the island of Salahat, where sandal wood grows in great abundance. Here we anchored, and as I stood watching the merchants disembarking their goods and preparing to sell or exchange them, the captain came up to me and said,

'I have here, brother, some merchandise belonging to a passenger of mine who is dead. Will you do me the favour to trade with it, and when I meet with his heirs I shall be able to give them the money, though it will be only just that you shall have a portion for your trouble.'

I consented gladly, for I did not like standing by idle. Whereupon he pointed the bales out to me, and sent for the person whose duty it was to keep a list of the goods that were upon the ship. When this man came he asked in what name the merchandise was to be registered.

'In the name of Sindbad the Sailor,' replied the captain.

At this I was greatly surprised, but looking carefully at him I recognised him to be the captain of the ship upon which I had made my second voyage, though he had altered much since that time. As for him, believing me to be dead it was no wonder that he had not recognised me.

'So, captain,' said I, 'the merchant who owned those bales was called Sindbad?'

'Yes,' he replied. 'He was so named. He belonged to Bagdad,

and joined my ship at Balsora, but by mischance he was left behind upon a desert island where we had landed to fill up our water-casks, and it was not until four hours later that he was missed. By that time the wind had freshened, and it was impossible to put back for him.'

'You suppose him to have perished then?' said I.

'Alas! yes,' he answered.

'Why, captain!' I cried, 'look well at me. I am that Sindbad who fell asleep upon the island and awoke to find himself abandoned!'

The captain stared at me in amazement, but was presently convinced that I was indeed speaking the truth, and rejoiced greatly at my escape.

'I am glad to have that piece of carelessness off my conscience at any rate,' said he. 'Now take your goods, and the profit I have made for you upon them, and may you prosper in future.'

I took them gratefully, and as we went from one island to another I laid in stores of cloves, cinnamon, and other spices. In one place I saw a tortoise which was twenty cubits long and as many broad, also a fish that was like a cow and had skin so thick that it was used to make shields. Another I saw that was like a camel in shape and colour. So by degrees we came back to Balsora, and I returned to Bagdad with so much money that I could not myself count it, besides treasures without end. I gave largely to the poor, and bought much land to add to what I already possessed, and thus ended my third voyage.

When Sindbad had finished his story he gave another hundred sequins to Hindbad, who then departed with the other guests, but next day when they had all reassembled, and the banquet was ended, their host continued his adventures.

Fourth Voyage

Rich and happy as I was after my third voyage, I could not make up my mind to stay at home altogether. My love of trading, and the pleasure I took in anything that was new and strange, made me set my affairs in order, and begin my journey through some of the Persian provinces, having first sent off stores of goods to await my coming in the different places I intended to visit. I took ship at a distant seaport, and for some time all went well, but at last, being caught in a violent hurricane, our vessel became a total wreck in spite of all our worthy captain could do to save her, and many of our company perished in the waves. I, with a few others, had the good fortune to be washed ashore clinging to pieces of the wreck, for the storm had driven us near an island, and scrambling up beyond the reach of the waves we threw ourselves down quite exhausted, to wait for morning.

At daylight we wandered inland, and soon saw some huts, to which we directed our steps. As we drew near their black inhabitants swarmed out in great numbers and surrounded us, and we were led to their houses, and as it were divided among our captors. I with five others was taken into a hut, where we were made to sit upon the ground, and certain herbs were given to us, which the blacks made signs to us to eat. Observing that they themselves did not touch them, I was careful only to pretend to taste my portion; but my companions, being very hungry, rashly ate up all that was set before them, and very soon I had the horror of seeing them become perfectly mad. Though they chattered incessantly I could not understand a word they said, nor did they heed when I spoke to them. The savages now produced large bowls full of rice prepared with cocoanut oil, of which my crazy comrades ate eagerly, but I only tasted a few grains, understanding clearly that the object of our captors was to fatten us speedily for their own eating, and this was exactly what happened. My unlucky companions having lost their reason, felt neither anxiety nor fear, and ate greedily all that was offered them. So they were soon fat and there was an end of them, but I grew leaner day by day, for I ate but little, and even that little did me no good by reason of my fear of what lay before me. However, as I was so far from being a tempting morsel, I was allowed to wander about freely, and one day, when all the blacks had gone off upon some expedition leaving only an old man to guard me, I managed to escape from him and plunged into the forest, running faster the more he cried to me to come back, until I had completely distanced him.

For seven days I hurried on, resting only when the darkness stopped me, and living chiefly upon cocoanuts, which afforded me both meat and drink, and on the eighth day I reached the seashore and saw a party of white men gathering pepper, which grew abundantly all about. Reassured by the nature of their occupation, I advanced towards them and they greeted me in Arabic, asking who I was and whence I came. My delight was great on hearing this familiar speech, and I willingly satisfied their curiosity, telling them how I had been shipwrecked, and captured by the blacks. 'But these savages devour men!' said they. 'How did you escape?' I repeated to them what I have just told you, at which they were mightily astonished. I stayed with them until they had collected as much pepper as they wished, and then they took me back to their own country and presented me to their king, by whom I was hospitably received. To him also I had to relate my adventures, which surprised him much, and when I had finished he ordered that I should be supplied with food and raiment and treated with consideration.

The island on which I found myself was full of people, and abounded in all sorts of desirable things, and a great deal of traffic went on in the capital, where I soon began to feel at home and contented. Moreover, the king treated me with special favour, and in consequence of this everyone, whether at the court or in the town, sought to make life pleasant to me. One thing I remarked which I thought very strange; this was that, from the greatest to the least, all men rode their horses without bridle or stirrups. I one day presumed to ask his majesty why he did not use them, to which he replied, 'You speak to me of things of which I have never before heard!' This gave me an idea. I found a clever workman, and made him cut out under my direction the foundation of a saddle, which I wadded and covered with choice leather, adorning it with rich gold embroidery. I then got a lock-smith to make me a bit and a pair of spurs after a pattern that I drew for him, and when all these things were completed I presented them to the king and showed him how to use them. When I had saddled one of his horses he mounted it and rode about quite delighted with the novelty, and to show his gratitude he rewarded me with large gifts. After this I had to make saddles for all the principal officers of the king's household, and as they all gave me rich presents I soon became very wealthy and quite an important person in the city.

One day the king sent for me and said, 'Sindbad, I am going to ask a favour of you. Both I and my subjects esteem you, and wish you to end your days amongst us. Therefore I desire that you will marry a rich and beautiful lady whom I will find for you, and think no more of your own country.'

As the king's will was law I accepted the charming bride he presented to me, and lived happily with her. Nevertheless I had every intention of escaping at the first opportunity, and going back to Bagdad. Things were thus going prosperously with me when it happened that the wife of one of my neighbours, with whom I had struck up quite a friendship, fell ill, and presently died. I went to his house to offer my consolations, and found him in the depths of woe.

'Heaven preserve you,' said I, 'and send you a long life!'

'Alas!' he replied, 'what is the good of saying that when I have but an hour left to live!'

'Come, come!' said I, 'surely it is not so bad as all that. I trust that you may be spared to me for many years.'

'I hope,' answered he, 'that your life may be long, but as for me, all is finished. I have set my house in order, and to-day I shall be buried with my wife. This has been the law upon our island from the earliest ages--the living husband goes to the grave with his dead wife, the living wife with her dead husband. So did our fathers, and so must we do. The law changes not, and all must submit to it!'

As he spoke the friends and relations of the unhappy pair began to assemble. The body, decked in rich robes and sparkling with jewels, was laid upon an open bier, and the procession started, taking its way to a high mountain at some distance from the city, the wretched husband, clothed from head to foot in a black mantle, following mournfully.

When the place of interment was reached the corpse was lowered, just as it was, into a deep pit. Then the husband, bidding farewell to all his friends, stretched himself upon another bier,

upon which were laid seven little loaves of bread and a pitcher of
water, and he also was let down-down-down to the depths of the
horrible cavern, and then a stone was laid over the opening, and
the melancholy company wended its way back to the city.

You may imagine that I was no unmoved spectator of these
proceedings; to all the others it was a thing to which they had been
accustomed from their youth up; but I was so horrified that I could
not help telling the king how it struck me.

'Sire,' I said, 'I am more astonished than I can express to you at
the strange custom which exists in your dominions of burying the
living with the dead. In all my travels I have never before met with
so cruel and horrible a law.'

'What would you have, Sindbad?' he replied. 'It is the law for everybody. I myself should be buried with the Queen if she were the first to die.'

'But, your Majesty,' said I, 'dare I ask if this law applies to foreigners also?'

'Why, yes,' replied the king smiling, in what I could but consider a very heartless manner, 'they are no exception to the rule if they have married in the country.'

When I heard this I went home much cast down, and from that time forward my mind was never easy. If only my wife's little finger ached I fancied she was going to die, and sure enough before very long she fell really ill and in a few days breathed her last. My dismay was great, for it seemed to me that to be buried alive was even a worse fate than to be devoured by cannibals, nevertheless there was no escape. The body of my wife, arrayed in her richest robes and decked with all her jewels, was laid upon the bier. I followed it, and after me came a great procession, headed by the king and all his nobles, and in this order we reached the fatal mountain, which was one of a lofty chain bordering the sea.

Here I made one more frantic effort to excite the pity of the king and those who stood by, hoping to save myself even at this last moment, but it was of no avail. No one spoke to me, they even appeared to hasten over their dreadful task, and I speedily found myself descending into the gloomy pit, with my seven loaves and pitcher of water beside me. Almost before I reached the bottom the stone was rolled into its place above my head, and I was left to my fate. A feeble ray of light shone into the cavern through some chink, and when I had the courage to look about me I could see that I was in a vast vault, bestrewn with bones and bodies of the dead. I even fancied that I heard the expiring sighs of those who, like myself, had come into this dismal place alive. All in vain did I shriek aloud with rage and despair, reproaching myself for the love of gain and adventure which had brought me to such a pass, but at length, growing calmer, I took up my bread and water, and wrapping my face in my mantle I groped my way towards the end of the cavern, where the air was fresher.

Here I lived in darkness and misery until my provisions were exhausted, but just as I was nearly dead from starvation the rock was rolled away overhead and I saw that a bier was being lowered into the cavern, and that the corpse upon it was a man. In a moment my mind was made up, the woman who followed had nothing to expect but a lingering death; I should be doing her a service if I shortened her misery. Therefore when she descended, already insensible from terror, I was ready armed with a huge bone, one blow from which left her dead, and I secured the bread and water which gave me a hope of life. Several times did I have recourse to this desperate expedient, and I know not how long I had been a prisoner when one day I fancied that I heard something near me, which breathed loudly. Turning to the place from which the sound came I dimly saw a shadowy form which fled at my movement, squeezing itself through a cranny in the wall. I pursued it as fast as I could, and found myself in a narrow crack among the rocks, along which I was just able to force my way. I followed it for what seemed to me many miles, and at last saw before me a glimmer of light which grew clearer every moment until I emerged upon the sea shore with a joy which I cannot describe. When I was sure that I was not dreaming, I realised that it was doubtless some little animal which had found its way into the cavern from the sea, and when disturbed had fled, showing me a means of escape which I could never have discovered for myself. I hastily surveyed my surroundings, and saw that I was safe from all pursuit from the town.

The mountains sloped sheer down to the sea, and there was no road across them. Being assured of this I returned to the cavern, and amassed a rich treasure of diamonds, rubies, emeralds, and jewels of all kinds which strewed the ground. These I made up into bales, and stored them into a safe place upon the beach, and then waited hopefully for the passing of a ship. I had looked out for two days, however, before a single sail appeared, so it was with much delight that I at last saw a vessel not very far from the shore, and by waving my arms and uttering loud cries succeeded in attracting the attention of her crew. A boat was sent off to me, and in answer to the questions of the sailors as to how I came to be in such a plight, I replied that I had been shipwrecked two days before, but had managed to scramble ashore with the bales which I pointed out to them. Luckily for me they believed my story, and without even looking at the place where they found me, took up my bundles, and rowed me back to the ship. Once on board, I soon saw that the captain was too much occupied with the difficulties of navigation to pay much heed to me, though he generously made me welcome, and would not even accept the jewels with which I offered to pay my passage. Our voyage was prosperous, and after visiting many lands, and collecting in each place great store of goodly merchandise, I found myself at last in Bagdad once more with unheard of riches of every description. Again I gave large sums of money to the poor, and enriched all the mosques in the city, after which I gave myself up to my friends and relations, with whom I passed my time in feasting and merriment.

Here Sindbad paused, and all his hearers declared that the adventures of his fourth voyage had pleased them better than anything they had heard before. They then took their leave, followed by Hindbad, who had once more received a hundred sequins, and with the rest had been bidden to return next day for the story of the fifth voyage.

When the time came all were in their places, and when they had eaten and drunk of all that was set before them Sindbad began his tale.

Fifth Voyage

Not even all that I had gone through could make me contented with a quiet life. I soon wearied of its pleasures, and longed for change and adventure. Therefore I set out once more, but this time in a ship of my own, which I built and fitted out at the nearest seaport. I wished to be able to call at whatever port I chose, taking my own time; but as I did not intend carrying enough goods for a full cargo, I invited several merchants of different nations to join me. We set sail with the first favourable wind, and after a long voyage upon the open seas we landed upon an unknown island which proved to be uninhabited. We determined, however, to explore it, but had not gone far when we found a roc's egg, as large as the one I had seen before and evidently very nearly hatched, for the beak of the young bird had already pierced the shell. In spite of all I could say to deter them, the merchants who were with me fell upon it with their hatchets, breaking the shell, and killing the young roc. Then lighting a fire upon the ground they hacked morsels from the bird, and proceeded to roast them while I stood by aghast.

Scarcely had they finished their ill-omened repast, when the air above us was darkened by two mighty shadows. The captain of my ship, knowing by experience what this meant, cried out to us that the parent birds were coming, and urged us to get on board with all speed. This we did, and the sails were hoisted, but before we had made any way the rocs reached their despoiled nest and hovered about it, uttering frightful cries when they discovered the mangled remains of their young one. For a moment we lost sight of them, and were flattering ourselves that we had escaped, when they reappeared and soared into the air directly over our vessel, and we saw that each held in its claws an immense rock ready to crush us. There was a moment of breathless suspense, then one bird loosed its hold and the huge block of stone hurtled through the air, but thanks to the presence of mind of the helmsman, who turned our ship violently in another direction, it fell into the sea close beside us, cleaving it asunder till we could nearly see the bottom. We had hardly time to draw a breath of relief before the other rock fell with a mighty crash right in the midst of our luckless vessel, smashing it into a thousand fragments, and crushing, or hurling into the sea, passengers and crew. I myself went down with the rest, but had the good fortune to rise unhurt, and by holding on to a piece of driftwood with one hand and swimming with the other I kept myself afloat and was presently washed up by the tide on to an island. Its shores were steep and rocky, but I scrambled up safely and threw myself down to rest upon the green turf.

When I had somewhat recovered I began to examine the spot in which I found myself, and truly it seemed to me that I had reached a garden of delights. There were trees everywhere, and they were laden with flowers and fruit, while a crystal stream wandered in and out under their shadow. When night came I slept sweetly in a cosy nook, though the remembrance that I was alone in a strange land made me sometimes start up and look around me in alarm, and then I wished heartily that I had stayed at home at ease. However, the morning sunlight restored my courage, and I once more wandered among the trees, but always with some anxiety as to what I might see next. I had penetrated some distance into the island when I saw an old man bent and feeble sitting upon the river bank, and at first I took him to be some ship-wrecked mariner like myself. Going up to him I greeted him in a friendly way, but he only nodded his head at me in reply. I then asked what he did there, and he made signs to me that he wished to get across the river to gather some fruit, and seemed to beg me to carry him on my back. Pitying his age and feebleness, I took him up, and wading across the stream I bent down that he might more easily reach the bank, and bade him get down. But instead of allowing himself to be set upon his feet (even now it makes me laugh to think of it!), this creature who had seemed to me so decrepit leaped nimbly upon my shoulders, and hooking his legs round my neck gripped me so tightly that I was well-nigh choked, and so overcome with terror that I fell insensible to the ground. When I recovered my enemy was still in his place, though he had released his hold enough to allow me breathing space, and seeing me revive he prodded me adroitly first with one foot and then with the other, until I was forced to get up and stagger about with him under the trees while he gathered and ate the choicest fruits. This went on all day, and even at night, when I threw myself down half dead with weariness, the terrible old man held on tight to my neck, nor did he fail to greet the first glimmer of morning light by drumming upon me with his heels, until I perforce awoke and resumed my dreary march with rage and bitterness in my heart.

It happened one day that I passed a tree under which lay several dry gourds, and catching one up I amused myself with scooping out its contents and pressing into it the juice of several bunches of grapes which hung from every bush. When it was full I left it propped in the fork of a tree, and a few days later, carrying the hateful old man that way, I snatched at my gourd as I passed it and had the satisfaction of a draught of excellent wine so good and refreshing that I even forgot my detestable burden, and began to sing and caper.

The old monster was not slow to perceive the effect which my draught had produced and that I carried him more lightly than usual, so he stretched out his skinny hand and seizing the gourd first tasted its contents cautiously, then drained them to the very last drop. The wine was strong and the gourd capacious, so he also began to sing after a fashion, and soon I had the delight of feeling the iron grip of his goblin legs unclasp, and with one vigorous effort I threw him to the ground, from which he never moved again. I was so rejoiced to have at last got rid of this uncanny old man that I ran leaping and bounding down to the sea shore, where, by the greatest good luck, I met with some mariners who had anchored off the island to enjoy the delicious fruits, and to renew their supply of water.

They heard the story of my escape with amazement, saying, 'You fell into the hands of the Old Man of the Sea, and it is a mercy that he did not strangle you as he has everyone else upon whose shoulders he has managed to perch himself. This island is well known as the scene of his evil deeds, and no merchant or sailor who lands upon it cares to stray far away from his comrades.' After we had talked for a while they took me back with them on board their ship, where the captain received me kindly, and we soon set sail, and after several days reached a large and prosperous-looking town where all the houses were built of stone. Here we anchored, and one of the merchants, who had been very friendly to me on the way, took me ashore with him and showed me a lodging set apart for strange merchants. He then provided me with a large sack, and pointed out to me a party of others equipped in like manner.

'Go with them,' said he, 'and do as they do, but beware of losing sight of them, for if you strayed your life would be in danger.'

With that he supplied me with provisions, and bade me farewell, and I set out with my new companions. I soon learnt that the object of our expedition was to fill our sacks with cocoanuts, but when at length I saw the trees and noted their immense height and the slippery smoothness of their slender trunks, I did not at all understand how we were to do it. The crowns of the cocoa-palms were all alive with monkeys, big and little, which skipped from one to the other with surprising agility, seeming to be curious about us and disturbed at our appearance, and I was at first surprised when my companions after collecting stones began to throw them at the lively creatures, which seemed to me quite harmless. But very soon I saw the reason of it and joined them heartily, for the monkeys, annoyed and wishing to pay us back in our own coin, began to tear the nuts from the trees and cast them at us with angry and spiteful gestures, so that after very little labour our sacks were filled with the fruit which we could not otherwise have obtained.

As soon as we had as many as we could carry we went back to the town, where my friend bought my share and advised me to continue the same occupation until I had earned money enough to carry me to my own country. This I did, and before long had amassed a considerable sum. Just then I heard that there was a trading ship ready to sail, and taking leave of my friend I went on board, carrying with me a goodly store of cocoanuts; and we sailed first to the islands where pepper grows, then to Comari where the best aloes wood is found, and where men drink no wine by an unalterable law. Here I exchanged my nuts for pepper and good aloes wood, and went a-fishing for pearls with some of the other merchants, and my divers were so lucky that very soon I had an immense number, and those very large and perfect. With all these treasures I came joyfully back to Bagdad, where I disposed of them for large sums of money, of which I did not fail as before to give the tenth part to the poor, and after that I rested from my labours and comforted myself with all the pleasures that my riches could give me.

Having thus ended his story, Sindbad ordered that one hundred sequins should be given to Hindbad, and the guests then withdrew; but after the next day's feast he began the account of his sixth voyage as follows.

Sixth Voyage

It must be a marvel to you how, after having five times met with shipwreck and unheard of perils, I could again tempt fortune and risk fresh trouble. I am even surprised myself when I look back, but evidently it was my fate to rove, and after a year of repose I prepared to make a sixth voyage, regardless of the entreaties of my friends and relations, who did all they could to keep me at home. Instead of going by the Persian Gulf, I travelled a considerable way overland, and finally embarked from a distant Indian port with a captain who meant to make a long voyage. And truly he did so, for we fell in with stormy weather which drove us completely out of our course, so that for many days neither captain nor pilot knew where we were, nor where we were going. When they did at last discover our position we had small ground for rejoicing, for the captain, casting his turban upon the deck and tearing his beard, declared that we were in the most dangerous spot upon the whole wide sea, and had been caught by a current which was at that minute sweeping us to destruction. It was too true! In spite of all the sailors could do we were driven with frightful rapidity towards the foot of a mountain, which rose sheer out of the sea, and our vessel was dashed to pieces upon the rocks at its base, not, however, until we had managed to scramble on shore, carrying with us the most precious of our possessions. When we had done this the captain said to us:

'Now we are here we may as well begin to dig our graves at once, since from this fatal spot no shipwrecked mariner has ever returned.'

This speech discouraged us much, and we began to lament over our sad fate.

The mountain formed the seaward boundary of a large island, and the narrow strip of rocky shore upon which we stood was strewn with the wreckage of a thousand gallant ships, while the bones of the luckless mariners shone white in the sunshine, and we shuddered to think how soon our own would be added to the heap. All around, too, lay vast quantities of the costliest merchandise, and treasures were heaped in every cranny of the rocks, but all these things only added to the desolation of the scene. It struck me as a very strange thing that a river of clear fresh water, which gushed out from the mountain not far from where we stood, instead of flowing into the sea as rivers generally do, turned off sharply, and flowed out of sight under a natural archway of rock, and when I went to examine it more closely I found that inside the cave the walls were thick with diamonds, and rubies, and masses of crystal, and the floor was strewn with ambergris. Here, then, upon this desolate shore we abandoned ourselves to our fate, for there was no possibility of scaling the mountain, and if a ship had appeared it could only have shared our doom. The first thing our captain did was to divide equally amongst us all the food we possessed, and then the length of each man's life depended on the time he could make his portion last. I myself could live upon very little.

Nevertheless, by the time I had buried the last of my companions my stock of provisions was so small that I hardly thought I should live long enough to dig my own grave, which I set about doing, while I regretted bitterly the roving disposition which was always bringing me into such straits, and thought longingly of all the comfort and luxury that I had left. But luckily for me the fancy took me to stand once more beside the river where it plunged out of sight in the depths of the cavern, and as I did so an idea struck me. This river which hid itself underground doubtless emerged again at some distant spot. Why should I not build a raft and trust myself to its swiftly flowing waters? If I perished before I could reach the light of day once more I should be no worse off than I was now, for death stared me in the face, while there was always the possibility that, as I was born under a lucky star, I might find myself safe and sound in some desirable land. I decided at any rate to risk it, and speedily built myself a stout raft of drift-wood with strong cords, of which enough and to spare lay strewn upon the beach. I then made up many packages of rubies, emeralds, rock crystal, ambergris, and precious stuffs, and bound them upon my raft, being careful to preserve the balance, and then I seated myself upon it, having two small oars that I had fashioned laid ready to my hand, and loosed the cord which held it to the bank. Once out in the current my raft flew swiftly under the gloomy archway, and I found myself in total darkness, carried smoothly forward by the rapid river. On I went as it seemed to me for many nights and days. Once the channel became so small that I had a narrow escape of being crushed against the rocky roof, and after that I took the precaution of lying flat upon my precious bales. Though I only ate what was absolutely necessary to keep myself alive, the inevitable moment came when, after swallowing my last morsel of food, I began to wonder if I must after all die of hunger. Then, worn out with anxiety and fatigue, I fell into a deep sleep, and when I again opened my eyes I was once more in the light of day; a beautiful country lay before me, and my raft, which was tied to the river bank, was surrounded by friendly looking black men. I rose and saluted them, and they spoke to me in return, but I could not understand a word of their language. Feeling perfectly bewildered by my sudden return to life and light, I murmured to myself in Arabic, 'Close thine[14] eyes, and while thou sleepest Heaven will change thy fortune from evil to good.'

One of the natives, who understood this tongue, then came forward saying:

'My brother, be not surprised to see us; this is our land, and as we came to get water from the river we noticed your raft floating down it, and one of us swam out and brought you to the shore. We have waited for your awakening; tell us now whence you come and where you were going by that dangerous way?'

I replied that nothing would please me better than to tell them, but that I was starving, and would fain eat something first. I was soon supplied with all I needed, and having satisfied my hunger I told them faithfully all that had befallen me. They were lost in wonder at my tale when it was interpreted to them, and said that adventures so surprising must be related to their king only by the man to whom they had happened. So, procuring a horse, they mounted me upon it, and we set out, followed by several strong men carrying my raft just as it was upon their shoulders. In this order we marched into the city of Serendib, where the natives presented me to their king, whom I saluted in the Indian fashion, prostrating myself at his feet and kissing the ground; but the monarch bade me rise and sit beside him, asking first what was my name.

'I am Sindbad,' I replied, 'whom men call "the Sailor," for I have voyaged much upon many seas.'

'And how come you here?' asked the king.

I told my story, concealing nothing, and his surprise and delight were so great that he ordered my adventures to be written in letters of gold and laid up in the archives of his kingdom.

Presently my raft was brought in and the bales opened in his presence, and the king declared that in all his treasury there were no such rubies and emeralds as those which lay in great heaps before him. Seeing that he looked at them with interest, I ventured to say that I myself and all that I had were at his disposal, but he answered me smiling:

'Nay,[15] Sindbad. Heaven forbid that I should covet your riches; I will rather add to them, for I desire that you shall not leave my kingdom without some tokens of my good will.' He then commanded his officers to provide me with a suitable lodging at his expense, and sent slaves to wait upon me and carry my raft and my bales to my new dwelling place. You may imagine that I praised his generosity and gave him grateful thanks, nor did I fail to present myself daily in his audience chamber, and for the rest of my time I amused myself in seeing all that was most worthy of attention in the city. The island of Serendib being situated on the equinoctial line, the days and nights there are of equal length. The chief city is placed at the end of a beautiful valley, formed by the highest mountain in the world, which is in the middle of the island. I had the curiosity to ascend to its very summit, for this was the place to which Adam was banished out of Paradise. Here are found rubies and many precious things, and rare plants grow abundantly, with cedar trees and cocoa palms. On the seashore and at the mouths of the rivers the divers seek for pearls, and in some valleys diamonds are plentiful. After many days I petitioned the king that I might return to my own country, to which he graciously consented. Moreover, he loaded me with rich gifts, and when I went to take leave of him he entrusted me with a royal present and a letter to the Commander of the Faithful, our sovereign lord, saying, 'I pray you give these to the Caliph Haroun al Raschid, and assure him of my friendship.'

I accepted the charge respectfully, and soon embarked upon the vessel which the king himself had chosen for me. The king's letter was written in blue characters upon a rare and precious skin of yellowish colour, and these were the words of it: 'The King of the Indies, before whom walk a thousand elephants, who lives in a palace, of which the roof blazes with a hundred thousand rubies, and whose treasure house contains twenty thousand diamond crowns, to the Caliph Haroun al Raschid sends greeting. Though the offering we present to you is unworthy of your notice, we pray you to accept it as a mark of the esteem and friendship which we cherish for you, and of which we gladly send you this token, and we ask of you a like regard if you deem us worthy of it. Adieu, brother.'

The present consisted of a vase carved from a single ruby, six inches high and as thick as my finger; this was filled with the choicest pearls, large, and of perfect shape and lustre; secondly, a huge snake skin, with scales as large as a sequin, which would preserve from sickness those who slept upon it. Then quantities of aloes wood, camphor, and pistachio-nuts; and lastly, a beautiful slave girl, whose robes glittered with precious stones.

After a long and prosperous voyage we landed at Balsora, and I made haste to reach Bagdad, and taking the king's letter I presented myself at the palace gate, followed by the beautiful slave, and various members of my own family, bearing the treasure.

As soon as I had declared my errand I was conducted into the presence of the Caliph, to whom, after I had made my obeisance, I gave the letter and the king's gift, and when he had examined them he demanded of me whether the Prince of Serendib was really as rich and powerful as he claimed to be.

'Commander of the Faithful,' I replied, again bowing humbly before him, 'I can assure your Majesty that he has in no way exaggerated his wealth and grandeur. Nothing can equal the magnificence of his palace. When he goes abroad his throne is prepared upon the back of an elephant, and on either side of him ride his ministers, his favourites, and courtiers. On his elephant's neck sits an officer, his golden lance in his hand, and behind him stands another bearing a pillar of gold, at the top of which is an emerald as long as my hand. A thousand men in cloth of gold, mounted upon richly caparisoned elephants, go before him, and as the procession moves onward the officer who guides his elephant cries aloud, "Behold the mighty monarch, the powerful and valiant Sultan of the Indies, whose palace is covered with a hundred thousand rubies, who possesses twenty thousand diamond crowns. Behold a monarch greater than Solomon and Mihrage in all their glory!"'

'Then the one who stands behind the throne answers: "This king, so great and powerful, must die, must die, must die!"'

'And the first takes up the chant again, "All praise to Him who lives for evermore."'

'Further, my lord, in Serendib no judge is needed, for to the king himself his people come for justice.'

The Caliph was well satisfied with my report.

'From the king's letter,' said he, 'I judged that he was a wise man. It seems that he is worthy of his people, and his people of him.'

So saying he dismissed me with rich presents, and I returned in peace to my own house.

When Sindbad had done speaking his guests withdrew, Hindbad having first received a hundred sequins, but all returned next day to hear the story of the seventh voyage, Sindbad thus began.

Seventh and Last Voyage

After my sixth voyage I was quite determined that I would go to sea no more. I was now of an age to appreciate a quiet life, and I had run risks enough. I only wished to end my days in peace. One day, however, when I was entertaining a number of my friends, I was told that an officer of the Caliph wished to speak to me, and when he was admitted he bade me follow him into the presence of Haroun al Raschid, which I accordingly did. After I had saluted him, the Caliph said:

'I have sent for you, Sindbad, because I need your services. I have chosen you to bear a letter and a gift to the King of Serendib in return for his message of friendship.'

The Caliph's commandment fell upon me like a thunderbolt.

'Commander of the Faithful,' I answered, 'I am ready to do all that your Majesty commands, but I humbly pray you to remember that I am utterly disheartened by the unheard of sufferings I have undergone. Indeed, I have made a vow never again to leave Bagdad.'

With this I gave him a long account of some of my strangest adventures, to which he listened patiently.

'I admit,' said he, 'that you have indeed had some extraordinary experiences, but I do not see why they should hinder you from doing as I wish. You have only to go straight to Serendib and give my message, then you are free to come back and do as you will. But go you must; my honour and dignity demand it.'

Seeing that there was no help for it, I declared myself willing to obey; and the Caliph, delighted at having got his own way, gave me a thousand sequins for the expenses of the voyage. I was soon ready to start, and taking the letter and the present I embarked at Balsora, and sailed quickly and safely to Serendib. Here, when I had disclosed my errand, I was well received, and brought into the presence of the king, who greeted me with joy.

'Welcome, Sindbad,' he cried. 'I have thought of you often, and rejoice to see you once more.'

After thanking him for the honour that he did me, I displayed the Caliph's gifts. First a bed with complete hangings all cloth of gold, which cost a thousand sequins, and another like to it of crimson stuff. Fifty robes of rich embroidery, a hundred of the finest white linen from Cairo, Suez, Cufa, and Alexandria. Then more beds of different fashion, and an agate vase carved with the figure of a man aiming an arrow at a lion, and finally a costly table, which had once belonged to King Solomon. The King of Serendib received with satisfaction the assurance of the Caliph's friendliness toward him, and now my task being accomplished I was anxious to depart, but it was some time before the king would think of letting me go. At last, however, he dismissed me with many presents, and I lost no time in going on board a ship, which sailed at once, and for four days all went well. On the fifth day we had the misfortune to fall in with pirates, who seized our vessel, killing all who resisted, and making prisoners of those who were prudent enough to submit at once, of whom I was one. When they had despoiled us of all we possessed, they forced us to put on vile raiment, and sailing to a distant island there sold us for slaves. I fell into the hands of a rich merchant, who took me home with him, and clothed and fed me well, and after some days sent for me and questioned me as to what I could do.

I answered that I was a rich merchant who had been captured by pirates, and therefore I knew no trade.

'Tell me,' said he, 'can you shoot with a bow?'

I replied that this had been one of the pastimes of my youth, and that doubtless with practice my skill would come back to me.

Upon this he provided me with a bow and arrows, and mounting me with him upon his own elephant took the way to a vast forest which lay far from the town. When we had reached the wildest part of it we stopped, and my master said to me: 'This forest swarms with elephants. Hide yourself in this great tree, and shoot at all that pass you. When you have succeeded in killing one come and tell me.'

So saying he gave me a supply of food, and returned to the town, and I perched myself high up in the tree and kept watch. That night I saw nothing, but just after sunrise the next morning a large herd of elephants came crashing and trampling by. I lost no time in letting fly several arrows, and at last one of the great animals fell to the ground dead, and the others retreated, leaving me free to come down from my hiding place and run back to tell my master of my success, for which I was praised and regaled with good things. Then we went back to the forest together and dug a mighty trench in which we buried the elephant I had killed, in order that when it became a skeleton my master might return and secure its tusks.

For two months I hunted thus, and no day passed without my securing, an elephant. Of course I did not always station myself in the same tree, but sometimes in one place, sometimes in another. One morning as I watched the coming of the elephants I was surprised to see that, instead of passing the tree I was in, as they usually did, they paused, and completely surrounded it, trumpeting horribly, and shaking the very ground with their heavy tread, and when I saw that their eyes were fixed upon me I was terrified, and my arrows dropped from my trembling hand. I had indeed good reason for my terror when, an instant later, the largest of the animals wound his trunk round the stem of my tree, and with one mighty effort tore it up by the roots, bringing me to the ground entangled in its branches. I thought now that my last hour was surely come; but the huge creature, picking me up gently enough, set me upon its back, where I clung more dead than alive, and followed by the whole herd turned and crashed off into the dense forest. It seemed to me a long time before I was once more set upon my feet by the elephant, and I stood as if in a dream watching the herd, which turned and trampled off in another direction, and were soon hidden in the dense underwood. Then, recovering myself, I looked about me, and found that I was standing upon the side of a great hill, strewn as far as I could see on either hand with bones and tusks of elephants. 'This then must be the elephants' burying place,' I said to myself, 'and they must have brought me here that I might cease to persecute them, seeing that I want nothing but their tusks, and here lie more than I could carry away in a lifetime.'

Whereupon I turned and made for the city as fast as I could go, not seeing a single elephant by the way, which convinced me that they had retired deeper into the forest to leave the way open to the Ivory Hill, and I did not know how sufficiently to admire their sagacity. After a day and a night I reached my master's house, and was received by him with joyful surprise.

'Ah! poor Sindbad,' he cried, 'I was wondering what could have become of you. When I went to the forest I found the tree newly uprooted, and the arrows lying beside it, and I feared I should never see you again. Pray tell me how you escaped death.'

I soon satisfied his curiosity, and the next day we went together to the Ivory Hill, and he was overjoyed to find that I had told him nothing but the truth. When we had loaded our elephant with as many tusks as it could carry and were on our way back to the city, he said:

'My brother--since I can no longer treat as a slave one who has enriched me thus--take your liberty and may Heaven prosper you. I will no longer conceal from you that these wild elephants have killed numbers of our slaves every year. No matter what good advice we gave them, they were caught sooner or later. You alone have escaped the wiles of these animals, therefore you must be under the special protection of Heaven. Now through you the whole town will be enriched without further loss of life, therefore you shall not only receive your liberty, but I will also bestow a fortune upon you.'

To which I replied, 'Master, I thank you, and wish you all prosperity. For myself I only ask liberty to return to my own country.'

'It is well,' he answered, 'the monsoon will soon bring the ivory ships hither, then I will send you on your way with somewhat to pay your passage.'

So I stayed with him till the time of the monsoon, and every day we added to our store of ivory till all his ware-houses were overflowing with it. By this time the other merchants knew the secret, but there was enough and to spare for all. When the ships at last arrived my master himself chose the one in which I was to sail, and put on board for me a great store of choice provisions, also ivory in abundance, and all the costliest curiosities of the country, for which I could not thank him enough, and so we parted. I left the ship at the first port we came to, not feeling at ease upon the sea after all that had happened to me by reason of it, and having disposed of my ivory for much gold, and bought many rare and costly presents, I loaded my pack animals, and joined a caravan of merchants. Our journey was long and tedious, but I bore it patiently, reflecting that at least I had not to fear tempests, nor pirates, nor serpents, nor any of the other perils from which I had suffered before, and at length we reached Bagdad. My first care was to present myself before the Caliph, and give him an account of my embassy. He assured me that my long absence had disquieted him much, but he had nevertheless hoped for the best. As to my adventure among the elephants he heard it with amazement, declaring that he could not have believed it had not my truthfulness been well known to him.

By his orders this story and the others I had told him were written by his scribes in letters of gold, and laid up among his treasures. I took my leave of him, well satisfied with the honours and rewards he bestowed upon me; and since that time I have rested from my labours, and given myself up wholly to my family and my friends.

Thus Sindbad ended the story of his seventh and last voyage, and turning to Hindbad he added:

'Well, my friend, and what do you think now? Have you ever heard of anyone who has suffered more, or had more narrow escapes than I have? Is it not just that I should now enjoy a life of ease and tranquillity?'

Hindbad drew near, and kissing his hand respectfully, replied, 'Sir, you have indeed known fearful perils; my troubles have been nothing compared to yours. Moreover, the generous use you make of your wealth proves that you deserve it. May you live long and happily in the enjoyment in it.'

Sindbad then gave him a hundred sequins, and henceforward counted him among his friends; also he caused him to give up his profession as a porter, and to eat daily at his table that he might all his life remember Sindbad the Sailor.

4

The Story of Two Sisters Who Were Jealous of Their Younger Sister

Once upon a time there reigned over Persia a Sultan named Kosrouschah, who from his boyhood had been fond of putting on a disguise and seeking adventures in all parts of the city, accompanied by one of his officers, disguised like himself. And no sooner was his father buried and the ceremonies over that marked his accession to the throne, than the young man hastened to throw off his robes of state, and calling to his vizier to make ready likewise, stole out in the simple dress of a private citizen into the less known streets of the capital.

Passing down a lonely street, the Sultan heard women's voices in loud discussion; and peeping through a crack in the door, he saw three sisters, sitting on a sofa in a large hall, talking in a very lively and earnest manner. Judging from the few words that reached his ear, they were each explaining what sort of men they wished to marry.

'I ask nothing better,' cried the eldest, 'than to have the Sultan's baker for a husband. Think of being able to eat as much as one wanted, of that delicious bread that is baked for his Highness alone! Let us see if your wish is as good as mine.'

'I,' replied the second sister, 'should be quite content with the Sultan's head cook. What delicate stews I should feast upon! And, as I am persuaded that the Sultan's bread is used all through the palace, I should have that into the bargain. You see, my dear sister, my taste is as good as yours.'

It was now the turn of the youngest sister, who was by far the most beautiful of the three, and had, besides, more sense than the other two. 'As for me,' she said, 'I should take a higher flight; and if we are to wish for husbands, nothing less than the Sultan himself will do for me.'

The Sultan was so much amused by the conversation he had overheard, that he made up his mind to gratify their wishes, and turning to the grand-vizier, he bade him note the house, and on the following morning to bring the ladies into his presence.

The grand-vizier fulfilled his commission, and hardly giving them time to change their dresses, desired the three sisters to follow him to the palace. Here they were presented one by one, and when they had bowed before the Sultan, the sovereign abruptly put the question to them:

'Tell me, do you remember what you wished for last night, when you were making merry? Fear nothing, but answer me the truth.'

These words, which were so unexpected, threw the sisters into great confusion, their eyes fell, and the blushes of the youngest did not fail to make an impression on the heart of the Sultan. All three remained silent, and he hastened to continue: 'Do not be afraid, I have not the slightest intention of giving you pain, and let me tell you at once, that I know the wishes formed by each one. You,' he said, turning to the youngest, 'who desired to have me for an husband, shall be satisfied this very day. And you,' he added, addressing himself to the other two, 'shall be married at the same moment to my baker and to my chief cook.'

When the Sultan had finished speaking the three sisters flung themselves at his feet, and the youngest faltered out, 'Oh, sire, since you know my foolish words, believe, I pray you, that they were only said in joke. I am unworthy of the honour you propose to do me, and I can only ask pardon for my boldness.'

The other sisters also tried to excuse themselves, but the Sultan would hear nothing.

'No, no,' he said, 'my mind is made up. Your wishes shall be accomplished.'

So the three weddings were celebrated that same day, but with a great difference. That of the youngest was marked by all the magnificence that was customary at the marriage of the Shah of Persia, while the festivities attending the nuptials of the Sultan's baker and his chief cook were only such as were suitable to their conditions.

This, though quite natural, was highly displeasing to the elder sisters, who fell into a passion of jealousy, which in the end caused a great deal of trouble and pain to several people. And the first time that they had the opportunity of speaking to each other, which was not till several days later at a public bath, they did not attempt to disguise their feelings.

'Can you possibly understand what the Sultan saw in that little cat,' said one to the other, 'for him to be so fascinated by her?'

'He must be quite blind,' returned the wife of the chief cook. 'As for her looking a little younger than we do, what does that matter? You would have made a far better Sultana than she.'

'Oh, I say nothing of myself,' replied the elder, 'and if the Sultan had chosen you it would have been all very well; but it really grieves me that he should have selected a wretched little creature like that. However, I will be revenged on her somehow, and I beg you will give me your help in the matter, and to tell me anything that you can think of that is likely to mortify her.'

In order to carry out their wicked scheme the two sisters met constantly to talk over their ideas, though all the while they pretended to be as friendly as ever towards the Sultana, who, on her part, invariably treated them with kindness. For a long time no plan occurred to the two plotters that seemed in the least likely to meet with success, but at length the expected birth of an heir gave them the chance for which they had been hoping.

They obtained permission of the Sultan to take up their abode in the palace for some weeks, and never left their sister night or day. When at last a little boy, beautiful as the sun, was born, they laid him in his cradle and carried it down to a canal which passed through the grounds of the palace. Then, leaving it to its fate, they informed the Sultan that instead of the son he had so fondly desired the Sultana had given birth to a puppy. At this dreadful news the Sultan was so overcome with rage and grief that it was with great difficulty that the grand-vizier managed to save the Sultana from his wrath.

Meanwhile the cradle continued to float peacefully along the canal till, on the outskirts of the royal gardens, it was suddenly perceived by the intendant, one of the highest and most respected officials in the kingdom.

'Go,' he said to a gardener who was working near, 'and get that cradle out for me.'

The gardener did as he was bid, and soon placed the cradle in the hands of the intendant.

The official was much astonished to see that the cradle, which he had supposed to be empty, contained a baby, which, young though it was, already gave promise of great beauty. Having no children himself, although he had been married some years, it at once occurred to him that here was a child which he could take and bring up as his own. And, bidding the man pick up the cradle and follow him, he turned towards home.

'My wife,' he exclaimed as he entered the room, 'heaven has denied us any children, but here is one that has been sent in their place. Send for a nurse, and I will do what is needful publicly to recognise it as my son.'

The wife accepted the baby with joy, and though the intendant saw quite well that it must have come from the royal palace, he did not think it was his business to inquire further into the mystery.

The following year another prince was born and sent adrift, but happily for the baby, the intendant of the gardens again was walking by the canal, and carried it home as before.

The Sultan, naturally enough, was still more furious the second time than the first, but when the same curious accident was repeated in the third year he could control himself no longer, and, to the great joy of the jealous sisters, commanded that the Sultana should be executed. But the poor lady was so much beloved at Court that not even the dread of sharing her fate could prevent the grand-vizier and the courtiers from throwing themselves at the Sultan's feet and imploring him not to inflict so cruel a punishment for what, after all, was not her fault.

'Let her live,' entreated the grand-vizier, 'and banish her from your presence for the rest of her days. That in itself will be punishment enough.'

His first passion spent, the Sultan had regained his self-command. 'Let her live then,' he said, 'since you have it so much at heart. But if I grant her life it shall only be on one condition, which shall make her daily pray for death. Let a box be built for her at the door of the principal mosque, and let the window of the box be always open. There she shall sit, in the coarsest clothes, and every Mussulman who enters the mosque shall spit in her face in passing. Anyone that refuses to obey shall be exposed to the same punishment himself. You, vizier, will see that my orders are carried out.'

The grand-vizier saw that it was useless to say more, and, full of triumph, the sisters watched the building of the box, and then listened to the jeers of the people at the helpless Sultana sitting inside. But the poor lady bore herself with so much dignity and meekness that it was not long before she had won the sympathy of those that were best among the crowd.

But it is now time to return to the fate of the third baby, this time a princess. Like its brothers, it was found by the intendant of the gardens, and adopted by him and his wife, and all three were brought up with the greatest care and tenderness.

As the children grew older their beauty and air of distinction became more and more marked, and their manners had all the grace and ease that is proper to people of high birth. The princes had been named by their foster-father Bahman and Perviz, after two of the ancient kings of Persia, while the princess was called Parizade, or the child of the genii.

The intendant was careful to bring them up as befitted their real rank, and soon appointed a tutor to teach the young princes how to read and write. And the princess, determined not to be left behind, showed herself so anxious to learn with her brothers, that the intendant consented to her joining in their lessons, and it was not long before she knew as much as they did.

From that time all their studies were done in common. They had the best masters for the fine arts, geography, poetry, history and science, and even for sciences which are learned by few, and every branch seemed so easy to them, that their teachers were astonished at the progress they made. The princess had a passion for music, and could sing and play upon all sorts of instruments she could also ride and drive as well as her brothers, shoot with a bow and arrow, and throw a javelin with the same skill as they, and sometimes even better.

In order to set off these accomplishments, the intendant resolved that his foster children should not be pent up any longer in the narrow borders of the palace gardens, where he had always lived, so he bought a splendid country house a few miles from the capital, surrounded by an immense park. This park he filled with wild beasts of various sorts, so that the princes and princess might hunt as much as they pleased.

When everything was ready, the intendant threw himself

at the Sultan's feet, and after referring to his age and his long services, begged his Highness's permission to resign his post. This was granted by the Sultan in a few gracious words, and he then inquired what reward he could give to his faithful servant. But the intendant declared that he wished for nothing except the continuance of his Highness's favour, and prostrating himself once more, he retired from the Sultan's presence.

Five or six months passed away in the pleasures of the country, when death attacked the intendant so suddenly that he had no time to reveal the secret of their birth to his adopted children, and as his wife had long been dead also, it seemed as if the princes and the princess would never know that they had been born to a higher station than the one they filled. Their sorrow for their father was very deep, and they lived quietly on in their new home, without feeling any desire to leave it for court gaieties or intrigues.

One day the princes as usual went out to hunt, but their sister remained alone in her apartments. While they were gone an old Mussulman devotee appeared at the door, and asked leave to enter, as it was the hour of prayer. The princess sent orders at once that the old woman was to be taken to the private oratory in the grounds, and when she had finished her prayers was to be shown the house and gardens, and then to be brought before her.

Although the old woman was very pious, she was not at all indifferent to the magnificence of all around her, which she seemed to understand as well as to admire, and when she had seen it all she was led by the servants before the princess, who was seated in a room which surpassed in splendour all the rest.

'My good woman,' said the princess pointing to a sofa, 'come and sit beside me. I am delighted at the opportunity of speaking for a few moments with so holy a person.' The old woman made some objections to so much honour being done her, but the princess refused to listen, and insisted that her guest should take the best seat, and as she thought she must be tired ordered refreshments.

While the old woman was eating, the princess put several questions to her as to her mode of life, and the pious exercises she practiced, and then inquired what she thought of the house now that she had seen it.

'Madam,' replied the pilgrim, 'one must be hard indeed to please to find any fault. It is beautiful, comfortable and well ordered, and it is impossible to imagine anything more lovely than the garden. But since you ask me, I must confess that it lacks three things to make it absolutely perfect.'

'And what can they be?' cried the princess. 'Only tell me, and I will lose no time in getting them.'

'The three things, madam,' replied the old woman, 'are, first, the Talking Bird, whose voice draws all other singing birds to it, to join in chorus. And second, the Singing Tree, where every leaf is a song that is never silent. And lastly the Golden Water, of which it is only needful to pour a single drop into a basin for it to shoot up into a fountain, which will never be exhausted, nor will the basin ever overflow.'

'Oh, how can I thank you,' cried the princess, 'for telling me of such treasures! But add, I pray you, to your goodness by further informing me where I can find them.'

'Madam,' replied the pilgrim, 'I should ill repay the hospitality you have shown me if I refused to answer your question. The three things of which I have spoken are all to be found in one place, on the borders of this kingdom, towards India. Your messenger has only to follow the road that passes by your house, for twenty days, and at the end of that time, he is to ask the first person he meets for the Talking Bird, the Singing Tree, and the Golden Water.' She then rose, and bidding farewell to the princess, went her way.

The old woman had taken her departure so abruptly that the Princess Parizade did not perceive till she was really gone that the directions were hardly clear enough to enable the search to be successful. And she was still thinking of the subject, and how delightful it would be to possess such rarities, when the princes, her brothers, returned from the chase.

'What is the matter, my sister?' asked Prince Bahman; 'why are you so grave? Are you ill? Or has anything happened?'

Princess Parizade did not answer directly, but at length she raised her eyes, and replied that there was nothing wrong.

'But there must be something,' persisted Prince Bahman, 'for you to have changed so much during the short time we have been absent. Hide nothing from us, I beseech you, unless you wish us to believe that the confidence we have always had in one another is now to cease.'

'When I said that it was nothing,' said the princess, moved by his words, 'I meant that it was nothing that affected you, although I admit that it is certainly of some importance to me. Like myself, you have always thought this house that our father built for us was perfect in every respect, but only to-day I have learned that three things are still lacking to complete it. These are the Talking Bird, the Singing Tree, and the Golden Water.' After explaining the peculiar qualities of each, the princess continued: 'It was a

Mussulman devotee who told me all this, and where they might all be found. Perhaps you will think that the house is beautiful enough as it is, and that we can do quite well without them; but in this I cannot agree with you, and I shall never be content until I have got them. So counsel me, I pray, whom to send on the undertaking.'

'My dear sister,' replied Prince Bahman, 'that you should care about the matter is quite enough, even if we took no interest in it ourselves. But we both feel with you, and I claim, as the elder, the right to make the first attempt, if you will tell me where I am to go, and what steps I am to take.'

Prince Perviz at first objected that, being the head of the family, his brother ought not to be allowed to expose himself to danger; but Prince Bahman would hear nothing, and retired to make the needful preparations for his journey.

The next morning Prince Bahman got up very early, and after bidding farewell to his brother and sister, mounted his horse. But just as he was about to touch it with his whip, he was stopped by a cry from the princess.

'Oh, perhaps after all you may never come back; one never can tell what accidents may happen. Give it up, I implore you, for I would a thousand times rather lose the Talking Bird, and the Singing Tree and the Golden Water, than that you should run into danger.'

'My dear sister,' answered the prince, 'accidents only happen to unlucky people, and I hope that I am not one of them. But as everything is uncertain, I promise you to be very careful. Take this knife,' he continued, handing her one that hung sheathed from his belt, 'and every now and then draw it out and look at it. As long as it keeps bright and clean as it is to-day, you will know that I am living; but if the blade is spotted with blood, it will be a sign that I am dead, and you shall weep for me.'

So saying, Prince Bahman bade them farewell once more, and started on the high road, well mounted and fully armed. For twenty days he rode straight on, turning neither to the right hand nor to the left, till he found himself drawing near the frontiers of Persia. Seated under a tree by the wayside he noticed a hideous old man, with a long white moustache, and beard that almost fell to his feet. His nails had grown to an enormous length, and on his head he wore a huge hat, which served him for an umbrella.

Prince Bahman, who, remembering the directions of the old woman, had been since sunrise on the look-out for some one, recognised the old man at once to be a dervish. He dismounted from his horse, and bowed low before the holy man, saying by way of greeting, 'My father, may your days be long in the land, and may all your wishes be fulfilled!'

The dervish did his best to reply, but his moustache was so thick that his words were hardly intelligible, and the prince, perceiving what was the matter, took a pair of scissors from his saddle pockets, and requested permission to cut off some of the moustache, as he had a question of great importance to ask the dervish. The dervish made a sign that he might do as he liked, and when a few inches of his hair and beard had been pruned all round the prince assured the holy man that he would hardly believe how much younger he looked. The dervish smiled at his compliments, and thanked him for what he had done.

'Let me,' he said, 'show you my gratitude for making me more comfortable by telling me what I can do for you.'

'Gentle dervish,' replied Prince Bahman, 'I come from far, and I seek the Talking Bird, the Singing Tree, and the Golden Water. I know that they are to be found somewhere in these parts, but I am ignorant of the exact spot. Tell me, I pray you, if you can, so that I may not have travelled on a useless quest.' While he was speaking, the prince observed a change in the countenance of the dervish, who waited for some time before he made reply.

'My lord,' he said at last, 'I do know the road for which you ask, but your kindness and the friendship I have conceived for you make me loth to point it out.'

'But why not?' inquired the prince. 'What danger can there be?'

'The very greatest danger,' answered the dervish. 'Other men, as brave as you, have ridden down this road, and have put me that question. I did my best to turn them also from their purpose, but it was of no use. Not one of them would listen to my words, and not one of them came back. Be warned in time, and seek to go no further.'

'I am grateful to you for your interest in me,' said Prince Bahman, 'and for the advice you have given, though I cannot follow it. But what dangers can there be in the adventure which courage and a good sword cannot meet?'

'And suppose,' answered the dervish, 'that your enemies are invisible, how then?'

'Nothing will make me give it up,' replied the prince, 'and for the last time I ask you to tell me where I am to go.'

When the dervish saw that the prince's mind was made up, he drew a ball from a bag that lay near him, and held it out. 'If it must be so,' he said, with a sigh, 'take this, and when you have mounted your horse throw the ball in front of you. It will roll on till it reaches the foot of a mountain, and when it stops you will stop also. You will then throw the bridle on your horse's neck without any fear of his straying, and will dismount. On each side you will see vast heaps of big black stones, and will hear a multitude of insulting voices, but pay no heed to them, and, above all, beware of ever turning your head. If you do, you will instantly become a black stone like the rest. For those stones are in reality men like yourself, who have been on the same quest, and have failed, as I fear that you may fail also. If you manage to avoid this pitfall, and to reach the top of the mountain, you will find there the Talking Bird in a splendid cage, and you can ask of him where you are to seek the Singing Tree and the Golden Water. That is all I have to say. You know what you have to do, and what to avoid, but if you are wise you will think of it no more, but return whence you have come.'

The prince smilingly shook his head, and thanking the dervish once more, he sprang on his horse and threw the ball before him.

The ball rolled along the road so fast that Prince Bahman had much difficulty in keeping up with it, and it never relaxed its speed till the foot of the mountain was reached. Then it came to a sudden halt, and the prince at once got down and flung the bridle on his horse's neck. He paused for a moment and looked round him at the masses of black stones with which the sides of the mountain were covered, and then began resolutely to ascend. He had hardly gone four steps when he heard the sound of voices around him, although not another creature was in sight.

'Who is this imbecile?' cried some, 'stop him at once.' 'Kill him,' shrieked others, 'Help! robbers! murderers! help! help!' 'Oh, let him alone,' sneered another, and this was the most trying of all, 'he is such a beautiful young man; I am sure the bird and the cage must have been kept for him.'

At first the prince took no heed to all this clamour, but continued to press forward on his way. Unfortunately this conduct, instead of silencing the voices, only seemed to irritate them the more, and they arose with redoubled fury, in front as well as behind. After some time he grew bewildered, his knees began to tremble, and finding himself in the act of falling, he forgot altogether the advice of the dervish. He turned to fly down the mountain, and in one moment became a black stone.

As may be imagined, Prince Perviz and his sister were all this time in the greatest anxiety, and consulted the magic knife, not once but many times a day. Hitherto the blade had remained bright and spotless, but on the fatal hour on which Prince Bahman and his horse were changed into black stones, large drops of blood appeared on the surface. 'Ah! my beloved brother,' cried the princess in horror, throwing the knife from her, 'I shall never see you again, and it is I who have killed you. Fool that I was to listen to the voice of that temptress, who probably was not speaking the truth. What are the Talking Bird and the Singing Tree to me in comparison with you, passionately though I long for them!'

Prince Perviz's grief at his brother's loss was not less than that of Princess Parizade, but he did not waste his time on useless lamentations.

'My sister,' he said, 'why should you think the old woman was deceiving you about these treasures, and what would have been her object in doing so! No, no, our brother must have met his death by some accident, or want of precaution, and to-morrow I will start on the same quest.'

Terrified at the thought that she might lose her only remaining brother, the princess entreated him to give up his project, but he remained firm. Before setting out, however, he gave her a chaplet of a hundred pearls, and said, 'When I am absent, tell this over daily for me. But if you should find that the beads stick, so that they will not slip one after the other, you will know that my brother's fate has befallen me. Still, we must hope for better luck.'

Then he departed, and on the twentieth day of his journey fell in with the dervish on the same spot as Prince Bahman had met him, and began to question him as to the place where the Talking Bird, the Singing Tree and the Golden Water were to be found. As in the case of his brother, the dervish tried to make him give up his project, and even told him that only a few weeks since a young man, bearing a strong resemblance to himself, had passed that way, but had never come back again.

'That, holy dervish,' replied Prince Perviz, 'was my elder brother, who is now dead, though how he died I cannot say.'

'He is changed into a black stone,' answered the dervish, 'like all the rest who have gone on the same errand, and you will become one likewise if you are not more careful in following my directions.' Then he charged the prince, as he valued his life, to take no heed of the clamour of voices that would pursue him up the mountain, and handing him a ball from the bag, which still seemed to be half full, he sent him on his way.

When Prince Perviz reached the foot of the mountain he jumped from his horse, and paused for a moment to recall the instructions the dervish had given him. Then he strode boldly on, but had scarcely gone five or six paces when he was startled by a man's voice that seemed close to his ear, exclaiming: 'Stop, rash fellow, and let me punish your audacity.' This outrage entirely put the dervish's advice out of the prince's head. He drew his sword, and turned to avenge himself, but almost before he had realised that there was nobody there, he and his horse were two black stones.

Not a morning had passed since Prince Perviz had ridden away without Princess Parizade telling her beads, and at night she even hung them round her neck, so that if she woke she could assure herself at once of her brother's safety. She was in the very act of moving them through her fingers at the moment that the prince fell a victim to his impatience, and her heart sank when the first pearl remained fixed in its place. However she had long made up her mind what she would do in such a case, and the following morning the princess, disguised as a man, set out for the mountain.

As she had been accustomed to riding from her childhood, she managed to travel as many miles daily as her brothers had done, and it was, as before, on the twentieth day that she arrived at the place where the dervish was sitting. 'Good dervish,' she said politely, 'will you allow me to rest by you for a few moments, and perhaps you will be so kind as to tell me if you have ever heard of a Talking Bird, a Singing Tree, and some Golden Water that are to be found somewhere near this?'

'Madam,' replied the dervish, 'for in spite of your manly dress your voice betrays you, I shall be proud to serve you in any way I can. But may I ask the purpose of your question?'

'Good dervish,' answered the princess, 'I have heard such glowing descriptions of these three things, that I cannot rest till I possess them.'

'Madam,' said the dervish, 'they are far more beautiful than any description, but you seem ignorant of all the difficulties that stand in your way, or you would hardly have undertaken such an adventure. Give it up, I pray you, and return home, and do not ask me to help you to a cruel death.'

'Holy father,' answered the princess, 'I come from far, and I should be in despair if I turned back without having attained my object. You have spoken of difficulties; tell me, I entreat you, what they are, so that I may know if I can overcome them, or see if they are beyond my strength.'

So the dervish repeated his tale, and dwelt more firmly than before on the clamour of the voices, the horrors of the black stones, which were once living men, and the difficulties of climbing the mountain; and pointed out that the chief means of success was never to look behind till you had the cage in your grasp.

'As far as I can see,' said the princess, 'the first thing is not to mind the tumult of the voices that follow you till you reach the cage, and then never to look behind. As to this, I think I have enough self-control to look straight before me; but as it is quite possible that I might be frightened by the voices, as even the boldest men have been, I will stop up my ears with cotton, so that, let them make as much noise as they like, I shall hear nothing.'

'Madam,' cried the dervish, 'out of all the number who have asked me the way to the mountain, you are the first who has ever suggested such a means of escaping the danger! It is possible that you may succeed, but all the same, the risk is great.'

'Good dervish,' answered the princess, 'I feel in my heart that I shall succeed, and it only remains for me to ask you the way I am to go.'

Then the dervish said that it was useless to say more, and he gave her the ball, which she flung before her.

The first thing the princess did on arriving at the mountain was to stop her ears with cotton, and then, making up her mind which was the best way to go, she began her ascent. In spite of the cotton, some echoes of the voices reached her ears, but not so as to trouble her. Indeed, though they grew louder and more insulting the higher she climbed, the princess only laughed, and said to herself that she certainly would not let a few rough words stand between her and the goal. At last she perceived in the distance the cage and the bird, whose voice joined itself in tones of thunder to those of the rest: 'Return, return! never dare to come near me.'

At the sight of the bird, the princess hastened her steps, and without vexing herself at the noise which by this time had grown deafening, she walked straight up to the cage, and seizing it, she said: 'Now, my bird, I have got you, and I shall take good care that you do not escape.' As she spoke she took the cotton from her ears, for it was needed no longer.

'Brave lady,' answered the bird, 'do not blame me for having joined my voice to those who did their best to preserve my freedom. Although confined in a cage, I was content with my lot, but if I must become a slave, I could not wish for a nobler mistress than one who has shown so much constancy, and from this moment I swear to serve you faithfully. Some day you will put me to the proof, for I know who you are better than you do yourself. Meanwhile, tell me what I can do, and I will obey you.'

'Bird,' replied the princess, who was filled with a joy that seemed strange to herself when she thought that the bird had cost her the lives of both her brothers. 'bird, let me first thank you for your good will, and then let me ask you where the Golden Water is to be found.'

The bird described the place, which was not far distant, and the princess filled a small silver flask that she had brought with her for the purpose. She then returned to the cage, and said: 'Bird, there is still something else, where shall I find the Singing Tree?'

'Behind you, in that wood,' replied the bird, and the princess wandered through the wood, till a sound of the sweetest voices told her she had found what she sought. But the tree was tall and strong, and it was hopeless to think of uprooting it.

'You need not do that,' said the bird, when she had returned to ask counsel. 'Break off a twig, and plant it in your garden, and it will take root, and grow into a magnificent tree.'

When the Princess Parizade held in her hands the three wonders promised her by the old woman, she said to the bird, 'All that is not enough. It was owing to you that my brothers became black stones. I cannot tell them from the mass of others, but you must know, and point them out to me, I beg you, for I wish to carry them away.'

For some reason that the princess could not guess these words seemed to displease the bird, and he did not answer. The princess waited a moment, and then continued in severe tones, 'Have you forgotten that you yourself said that you are my slave to do my bidding, and also that your life is in my power?'

'No, I have not forgotten,' replied the bird, 'but what you ask is very difficult. However, I will do my best. If you look round,' he went on, 'you will see a pitcher standing near. Take it, and, as you go down the mountain, scatter a little of the water it contains over every black stone and you will soon find your two brothers.'

Princess Parizade took the pitcher, and, carrying with her besides the cage the twig and the flask, returned down the mountain side. At every black stone she stopped and sprinkled it with water, and as the water touched it the stone instantly became a man. When she suddenly saw her brothers before her, her delight was mixed with astonishment.

'Why, what are you doing here?' she cried.

'We have been asleep,' they said.

'Yes,' returned the princess, 'but without me your sleep would probably have lasted till the day of judgment. Have you forgotten that you came here in search of the Talking Bird, the Singing Tree, and the Golden Water, and the black stones that were heaped up along the road? Look round and see if there is one left. These gentlemen, and yourselves, and all your horses were changed into these stones, and I have delivered you by sprinkling you with the water from this pitcher. As I could not return home without you, even though I had gained the prizes on which I had set my heart, I forced the Talking Bird to tell me how to break the spell.'

On hearing these words Prince Bahman and Prince Perviz understood all they owed their sister, and the knights who stood by declared themselves her slaves and ready to carry out her wishes. But the princess, while thanking them for their politeness, explained that she wished for no company but that of her brothers, and that the rest were free to go where they would.

So saying the princess mounted her horse, and, declining to allow even Prince Bahman to carry the cage with the Talking Bird, she entrusted him with the branch of the Singing Tree, while Prince Perviz took care of the flask containing the Golden Water.

Then they rode away, followed by the knights and gentlemen, who begged to be permitted to escort them.

It had been the intention of the party to stop and tell their adventures to the dervish, but they found to their sorrow that he was dead, whether from old age, or whether from the feeling that his task was done, they never knew.

As they continued their road their numbers grew daily smaller, for the knights turned off one by one to their own homes, and only the brothers and sister finally drew up at the gate of the palace.

The princess carried the cage straight into the garden, and, as soon as the bird began to sing, nightingales, larks, thrushes, finches, and all sorts of other birds mingled their voices in chorus. The branch she planted in a corner near the house, and in a few days it had grown into a great tree. As for the Golden Water it was poured into a great marble basin specially prepared for it, and it swelled and bubbled and then shot up into the air in a fountain twenty feet high.

The fame of these wonders soon spread abroad, and people came from far and near to see and admire.

After a few days Prince Bahman and Prince Perviz fell back into their ordinary way of life, and passed most of their time hunting. One day it happened that the Sultan of Persia was also hunting in the same direction, and, not wishing to interfere with his sport, the young men, on hearing the noise of the hunt approaching, prepared to retire, but, as luck would have it, they turned into the very path down which the Sultan was coming. They threw themselves from their horses and prostrated themselves to the earth, but the Sultan was curious to see their faces, and commanded them to rise.

The princes stood up respectfully, but quite at their ease, and the Sultan looked at them for a few moments without speaking, then he asked who they were and where they lived.

'Sire,' replied Prince Bahman, 'we are sons of your Highness's late intendant of the gardens, and we live in a house that he built a short time before his death, waiting till an occasion should offer itself to serve your Highness.'

'You seem fond of hunting,' answered the Sultan.

'Sire,' replied Prince Bahman, 'it is our usual exercise, and one that should be neglected by no man who expects to comply with the ancient customs of the kingdom and bear arms.'

The Sultan was delighted with this remark, and said at once, 'In that case I shall take great pleasure in watching you. Come, choose what sort of beasts you would like to hunt.'

The princes jumped on their horses and followed the Sultan at a little distance. They had not gone very far before they saw a number of wild animals appear at once, and Prince Bahman started to give chase to a lion and Prince Perviz to a bear. Both used their javelins with such skill that, directly they arrived within striking range, the lion and the bear fell, pierced through and through. Then Prince Perviz pursued a lion and Prince Bahman a bear, and in a very few minutes they, too, lay dead. As they were making ready for a third assault the Sultan interfered, and, sending one of his officials to summon them, he said smiling, 'If I let you go on, there will soon be no beasts left to hunt. Besides, your courage and manners have so won my heart that I will not have you expose yourselves to further danger. I am convinced that some day or other I shall find you useful as well as agreeable.'

He then gave them a warm invitation to stay with him altogether, but with many thanks for the honour done them, they begged to be excused, and to be suffered to remain at home.

The Sultan who was not accustomed to see his offers rejected inquired their reasons, and Prince Bahman explained that they did not wish to leave their sister, and were accustomed to do nothing without consulting all three together.

'Ask her advice, then,' replied the Sultan, 'and to-morrow come and hunt with me, and give me your answer.'

The two princes returned home, but their adventure made so little impression on them that they quite forgot to speak to their sister on the subject. The next morning when they went to hunt they met the Sultan in the same place, and he inquired what advice their sister had given. The young men looked at each other and blushed. At last Prince Bahman said, 'Sire, we must throw ourselves on your Highness's mercy. Neither my brother nor myself remembered anything about it.'

'Then be sure you do not forget to-day,' answered the Sultan, 'and bring me back your reply to-morrow.'

When, however, the same thing happened a second time, they feared that the Sultan might be angry with them for their carelessness. But he took it in good part, and, drawing three little golden balls from his purse, he held them out to Prince Bahman, saying, 'Put these in your bosom and you will not forget a third time, for when you remove your girdle to-night the noise they will make in falling will remind you of my wishes.'

It all happened as the Sultan had foreseen, and the two brothers appeared in their sister's apartments just as she was in the act of stepping into bed, and told their tale.

The Princess Parizade was much disturbed at the news, and did not conceal her feelings. 'Your meeting with the Sultan is very honourable to you,' she said, 'and will, I dare say, be of service to you, but it places me in a very awkward position. It is on my account, I know, that you have resisted the Sultan's wishes, and I am very grateful to you for it. But kings do not like to have their offers refused, and in time he would bear a grudge against you, which would render me very unhappy. Consult the Talking Bird, who is wise and far-seeing, and let me hear what he says.'

So the bird was sent for and the case laid before him.

'The princes must on no account refuse the Sultan's proposal,' said he, 'and they must even invite him to come and see your house.'

'But, bird,' objected the princess, 'you know how dearly we love each other; will not all this spoil our friendship?'

'Not at all,' replied the bird, 'it will make it all the closer.'

'Then the Sultan will have to see me,' said the princess.

The bird answered that it was necessary that he should see her, and everything would turn out for the best.

The following morning, when the Sultan inquired if they had spoken to their sister and what advice she had given them, Prince Bahman replied that they were ready to agree to his Highness's wishes, and that their sister had reproved them for their hesitation about the matter. The Sultan received their excuses with great kindness, and told them that he was sure they would be equally faithful to him, and kept them by his side for the rest of the day, to the vexation of the grand-vizier and the rest of the court.

When the procession entered in this order the gates of the capital, the eyes of the people who crowded the streets were fixed on the two young men, strangers to every one.

'Oh, if only the Sultan had had sons like that!' they murmured, 'they look so distinguished and are about the same age that his sons would have been!'

The Sultan commanded that splendid apartments should be prepared for the two brothers, and even insisted that they should sit at table with him. During dinner he led the conversation to various scientific subjects, and also to history, of which he was especially fond, but whatever topic they might be discussing he found that the views of the young men were always worth listening to. 'If they were my own sons,' he said to himself, 'they could not be better educated!' and aloud he complimented them on their learning and taste for knowledge.

At the end of the evening the princes once more prostrated themselves before the throne and asked leave to return home; and then, encouraged by the gracious words of farewell uttered by the Sultan, Prince Bahman said: 'Sire, may we dare to take the liberty of asking whether you would do us and our sister the honour of resting for a few minutes at our house the first time the hunt passes that way?'

'With the utmost pleasure,' replied the Sultan; 'and as I am all impatience to see the sister of such accomplished young men you may expect me the day after to-morrow.'

The princess was of course most anxious to entertain the Sultan in a fitting way, but as she had no experience in court customs she ran to the Talking Bird, and begged he would advise her as to what dishes should be served.

'My dear mistress,' replied the bird, 'your cooks are very good and you can safely leave all to them, except that you must be careful to have a dish of cucumbers, stuffed with pearl sauce, served with the first course.'

'Cucumbers stuffed with pearls!' exclaimed the princess. 'Why, bird, who ever heard of such a dish? The Sultan will expect a dinner he can eat, and not one he can only admire! Besides, if I were to use all the pearls I possess, they would not be half enough.'

'Mistress,' replied the bird, 'do what I tell you and nothing but good will come of it. And as to the pearls, if you go at dawn to-morrow and dig at the foot of the first tree in the park, on the right hand, you will find as many as you want.'

The princess had faith in the bird, who generally proved to be right, and taking the gardener with her early next morning followed out his directions carefully. After digging for some time they came upon a golden box fastened with little clasps.

These were easily undone, and the box was found to be full of pearls, not very large ones, but well-shaped and of a good colour. So leaving the gardener to fill up the hole he had made under the tree, the princess took up the box and returned to the house.

The two princes had seen her go out, and had wondered what could have made her rise so early. Full of curiosity they got up and dressed, and met their sister as she was returning with the box under her arm.

'What have you been doing?' they asked, 'and did the gardener come to tell you he had found a treasure?'

'On the contrary,' replied the princess, 'it is I who have found one,' and opening the box she showed her astonished brothers the pearls inside. Then, on the way back to the palace, she told them of her consultation with the bird, and the advice it had given her. All three tried to guess the meaning of the singular counsel, but they were forced at last to admit the explanation was beyond them, and they must be content blindly to obey.

The first thing the princess did on entering the palace was to send for the head cook and to order the repast for the Sultan When she had finished she suddenly added, 'Besides the dishes I have mentioned there is one that you must prepare expressly for the Sultan, and that no one must touch but yourself. It consists of a stuffed cucumber, and the stuffing is to be made of these pearls.'

The head cook, who had never in all his experience heard of such a dish, stepped back in amazement.

'You think I am mad,' answered the princess, who perceived what was in his mind. 'But I know quite well what I am doing. Go, and do your best, and take the pearls with you.'

The next morning the princes started for the forest, and were soon joined by the Sultan. The hunt began and continued till midday, when the heat became so great that they were obliged to leave off. Then, as arranged, they turned their horses' heads towards the palace, and while Prince Bahman remained by the side of the Sultan, Prince Perviz rode on to warn his sister of their approach.

The moment his Highness entered the courtyard, the princess flung herself at his feet, but he bent and raised her, and gazed at her for some time, struck with her grace and beauty, and also with the indefinable air of courts that seemed to hang round this country girl. 'They are all worthy one of the other,' he said to himself, 'and I am not surprised that they think so much of her opinions. I must know more of them.'

By this time the princess had recovered from the first embarrassment of meeting, and proceeded to make her speech of welcome.

'This is only a simple country house, sire,' she said, 'suitable to people like ourselves, who live a quiet life. It cannot compare with the great city mansions, much less, of course, with the smallest of the Sultan's palaces.'

'I cannot quite agree with you,' he replied; 'even the little that

I have seen I admire greatly, and I will reserve my judgment until you have shown me the whole.'

The princess then led the way from room to room, and the Sultan examined everything carefully. 'Do you call this a simple country house?' he said at last. 'Why, if every country house was like this, the towns would soon be deserted. I am no longer astonished that you do not wish to leave it. Let us go into the gardens, which I am sure are no less beautiful than the rooms.'

A small door opened straight into the garden, and the first object that met the Sultan's eyes was the Golden Water.

'What lovely coloured water!' he exclaimed; 'where is the spring, and how do you make the fountain rise so high? I do not believe there is anything like it in the world.' He went forward to examine it, and when he had satisfied his curiosity, the princess conducted him towards the Singing Tree.

As they drew near, the Sultan was startled by the sound of strange voices, but could see nothing. 'Where have you hidden your musicians?' he asked the princess; 'are they up in the air, or under the earth? Surely the owners of such charming voices ought not to conceal themselves!'

'Sire,' answered the princess, 'the voices all come from the tree which is straight in front of us; and if you will deign to advance a few steps, you will see that they become clearer.'

The Sultan did as he was told, and was so wrapt in delight at what he heard that he stood some time in silence.

'Tell me, madam, I pray you,' he said at last, 'how this marvellous tree came into your garden? It must have been brought from a great distance, or else, fond as I am of all curiosities, I could not have missed hearing of it! What is its name?'

'The only name it has, sire,' replied she, 'is the Singing Tree, and it is not a native of this country. Its history is mixed up with those of the Golden Water and the Talking Bird, which you have not yet seen. If your Highness wishes I will tell you the whole story, when you have recovered from your fatigue.'

'Indeed, madam,' returned he, 'you show me so many wonders that it is impossible to feel any fatigue. Let us go once more and look at the Golden Water; and I am dying to see the Talking Bird.'

The Sultan could hardly tear himself away from the Golden Water, which puzzled him more and more. 'You say,' he observed to the princess, 'that this water does not come from any spring, neither is brought by pipes. All I understand is, that neither it nor the Singing Tree is a native of this country.'

'It is as you say, sire,' answered the princess, 'and if you examine the basin, you will see that it is all in one piece, and therefore the water could not have been brought through it. What is more astonishing is, that I only emptied a small flaskful into the basin, and it increased to the quantity you now see.'

'Well, I will look at it no more to-day,' said the Sultan. 'Take me to the Talking Bird.'

On approaching the house, the Sultan noticed a vast quantity of birds, whose voices filled the air, and he inquired why they were so much more numerous here than in any other part of the garden.

'Sire,' answered the princess, 'do you see that cage hanging in one of the windows of the saloon? that is the Talking Bird, whose voice you can hear above them all, even above that of the nightingale. And the birds crowd to this spot, to add their songs to his.'

The Sultan stepped through the window, but the bird took no notice, continuing his song as before.

'My slave,' said the princess, 'this is the Sultan; make him a pretty speech.'

The bird stopped singing at once, and all the other birds stopped too.

'The Sultan is welcome,' he said. 'I wish him long life and all prosperity.'

'I thank you, good bird,' answered the Sultan, seating himself before the repast, which was spread at a table near the window, 'and I am enchanted to see in you the Sultan and King of the Birds.'

The Sultan, noticing that his favourite dish of cucumber was placed before him, proceeded to help himself to it, and was amazed to and that the stuffing was of pearls. 'A novelty, indeed!' cried he, 'but I do not understand the reason of it; one cannot eat pearls!'

'Sire,' replied the bird, before either the princes or the princess could speak, 'surely your Highness cannot be so surprised at beholding a cucumber stuffed with pearls, when you believed without any difficulty that the Sultana had presented you, instead of children, with a dog, a cat, and a log of wood.'

'I believed it,' answered the Sultan, 'because the women attending on her told me so.'

'The women, sire,' said the bird, 'were the sisters of the Sultana, who were devoured with jealousy at the honour you had done her, and in order to revenge themselves invented this story. Have them examined, and they will confess their crime. These are your children, who were saved from death by the intendant of your gardens, and brought up by him as if they were his own.'

Like a flash the truth came to the mind of the Sultan. 'Bird,' he cried, 'my heart tells me that what you say is true. My children,' he added, 'let me embrace you, and embrace each other, not only as brothers and sister, but as having in you the blood royal of Persia which could flow in no nobler veins.'

When the first moments of emotion were over, the Sultan hastened to finish his repast, and then turning to his children he exclaimed: 'To-day you have made acquaintance with your father. To-morrow I will bring you the Sultana your mother. Be ready to receive her.'

The Sultan then mounted his horse and rode quickly back to the capital. Without an instant's delay he sent for the grand-vizier, and ordered him to seize and question the Sultana's sisters that very day. This was done. They were confronted with each other and proved guilty, and were executed in less than an hour.

But the Sultan did not wait to hear that his orders had been carried out before going on foot, followed by his whole court to the door of the great mosque, and drawing the Sultana with his own hand out of the narrow prison where she had spent so many years, 'Madam,' he cried, embracing her with tears in his eyes, 'I have come to ask your pardon for the injustice I have done you, and to repair it as far as I may. I have already begun by punishing the authors of this abominable crime, and I hope you will forgive me when I introduce you to our children, who are the most charming and accomplished creatures in the whole world. Come with me, and take back your position and all the honour that is due to you.'

This speech was delivered in the presence of a vast multitude of people, who had gathered from all parts on the first hint of what was happening, and the news was passed from mouth to mouth in a few seconds.

Early next day the Sultan and Sultana, dressed in robes of state and followed by all the court, set out for the country house of their children. Here the Sultan presented them to the Sultana one by one, and for some time there was nothing but embraces and tears and tender words. Then they ate of the magnificent dinner which had been prepared for them, and after they were all refreshed they went into the garden, where the Sultan pointed out to his wife the Golden Water and the Singing Tree. As to the Talking Bird, she had already made acquaintance with him.

In the evening they rode together back to the capital, the princes on each side of their father, and the princess with her mother. Long before they reached the gates the way was lined with people, and the air filled with shouts of welcome, with which were mingled the songs of the Talking Bird, sitting in its cage on the lap of the princess, and of the birds who followed it.

And in this manner they came back to their father's palace.

5

The Enchanted Horse

It was the Feast of the New Year, the oldest and most splendid of all the feasts in the Kingdom of Persia, and the day had been spent by the king in the city of Schiraz, taking part in the magnificent spectacles prepared by his subjects to do honour to the festival. The sun was setting, and the monarch was about to give his court the signal to retire, when suddenly an Indian appeared before his throne, leading a horse richly harnessed, and looking in every respect exactly like a real one.

'Sire,' said he, prostrating himself as he spoke, 'although I make my appearance so late before your Highness, I can confidently assure you that none of the wonders you have seen during the day can be compared to this horse, if you will deign to cast your eyes upon him.'

'I see nothing in it,' replied the king, 'except a clever imitation of a real one; and any skilled workman might do as much.'

'Sire,' returned the Indian, 'it is not of his outward form that I would speak, but of the use that I can make of him. I have only to mount him, and to wish myself in some special place, and no matter how distant it may be, in a very few moments I shall find myself there. It is this, Sire, that makes the horse so marvellous, and if your Highness will allow me, you can prove it for yourself.'

The King of Persia, who was interested in every thing out

of the common, and had never before come across a horse with such qualities, bade the Indian mount the animal, and show what he could do. In an instant the man had vaulted on his back, and inquired where the monarch wished to send him.

'Do you see that mountain?' asked the king, pointing to a huge mass that towered into the sky about three leagues from Schiraz; 'go and bring me the leaf of a palm that grows at the foot.'

The words were hardly out of the king's mouth when the Indian turned a screw placed in the horse's neck, close to the saddle, and the animal bounded like lightning up into the air, and was soon beyond the sight even of the sharpest eyes. In a quarter of an hour the Indian was seen returning, bearing in his hand the palm, and, guiding his horse to the foot of the throne, he dismounted, and laid the leaf before the king.

Now the monarch had no sooner proved the astonishing speed of which the horse was capable than he longed to possess it himself, and indeed, so sure was he that the Indian would be quite ready to sell it, that he looked upon it as his own already.

'I never guessed from his mere outside how valuable an animal he was,' he remarked to the Indian, 'and I am grateful to you for having shown me my error,' said he. 'If you will sell it, name your own price.'

'Sire,' replied the Indian, 'I never doubted that a sovereign so wise and accomplished as your Highness would do justice to my horse, when he once knew its power; and I even went so far as to think it probable that you might wish to possess it. Greatly as I prize it, I will yield it up to your Highness on one condition. The horse was not constructed by me, but it was given me by the inventor, in exchange for my only daughter, who made me take a solemn oath that I would never part with it, except for some object of equal value.'

'Name anything you like,' cried the monarch, interrupting him. 'My kingdom is large, and filled with fair cities. You have only to choose which you would prefer, to become its ruler to the end of your life.'

'Sire,' answered the Indian, to whom the proposal did not seem nearly so generous as it appeared to the king, 'I am most grateful to your Highness for your princely offer, and beseech you not to be offended with me if I say that I can only deliver up my horse in exchange for the hand of the princess your daughter.'

A shout of laughter burst from the courtiers as they heard these words, and Prince Firouz Schah, the heir apparent, was filled with anger at the Indian's presumption. The king, however, thought that it would not cost him much to part from the princess in order to gain such a delightful toy, and while he was hesitating as to his answer the prince broke in.

'Sire,' he said, 'it is not possible that you can doubt for an instant what reply you should give to such an insolent bargain. Consider what you owe to yourself, and to the blood of your ancestors.'

'My son,' replied the king, 'you speak nobly, but you do not realise either the value of the horse, or the fact that if I reject the proposal of the Indian, he will only make the same to some other monarch, and I should be filled with despair at the thought that anyone but myself should own this Seventh Wonder of the World. Of course I do not say that I shall accept his conditions, and perhaps he may be brought to reason, but meanwhile I should like you to examine the horse, and, with the owner's permission, to make trial of its powers.'

The Indian, who had overheard the king's speech, thought that he saw in it signs of yielding to his proposal, so he joyfully agreed to the monarch's wishes, and came forward to help the prince to mount the horse, and show him how to guide it: but, before he had finished, the young man turned the screw, and was soon out of sight.

They waited some time, expecting that every moment he might be seen returning in the distance, but at length the Indian grew frightened, and prostrating himself before the throne, he said to the king, 'Sire, your Highness must have noticed that the prince, in his impatience, did not allow me to tell him what it was necessary to do in order to return to the place from which he started. I implore you not to punish me for what was not my fault, and not to visit on me any misfortune that may occur.'

'But why,' cried the king in a burst of fear and anger, 'why did you not call him back when you saw him disappearing?'

'Sire,' replied the Indian, 'the rapidity of his movements took me so by surprise that he was out of hearing before I recovered my speech. But we must hope that he will perceive and turn a second screw, which will have the effect of bringing the horse back to earth.'

'But supposing he does!' answered the king, 'what is to hinder the horse from descending straight into the sea, or dashing him to pieces on the rocks?'

'Have no fears, your Highness,' said the Indian; 'the horse has the gift of passing over seas, and of carrying his rider wherever he wishes to go.'

'Well, your head shall answer for it,' returned the monarch, 'and if in three months he is not safe back with me, or at any rate does not send me news of his safety, your life shall pay the penalty.' So saying, he ordered his guards to seize the Indian and throw him into prison.

Meanwhile, Prince Firouz Schah had gone gaily up into the air, and for the space of an hour continued to ascend higher and higher, till the very mountains were not distinguishable from the plains. Then he began to think it was time to come down, and took for granted that, in order to do this, it was only needful to turn the screw the reverse way; but, to his surprise and horror, he found that, turn as he might, he did not make the smallest impression. He then remembered that he had never waited to ask how he was to get back to earth again, and understood the danger in which he stood. Luckily, he did not lose his head, and set about examining the horse's neck with great care, till at last, to his intense joy, he discovered a tiny little peg, much smaller than the other, close to the right ear. This he turned, and found him-self dropping to the earth, though more slowly than he had left it.

It was now dark, and as the prince could see nothing, he was obliged, not without some feeling of disquiet, to allow the horse to direct his own course, and midnight was already passed before Prince Firouz Schah again touched the ground, faint and weary from his long ride, and from the fact that he had eaten nothing since early morning.

The first thing he did on dismounting was to try to find out where he was, and, as far as he could discover in the thick darkness, he found himself on the terraced roof of a huge palace, with a balustrade of marble running round. In one corner of the terrace stood a small door, opening on to a staircase which led down into the palace.

Some people might have hesitated before exploring further, but not so the prince. 'I am doing no harm,' he said, 'and whoever the owner may be, he will not touch me when he sees I am unarmed,' and in dread of making a false step, he went cautiously down the staircase. On a landing, he noticed an open door, beyond which was a faintly lighted hall.

Before entering, the prince paused and listened, but he heard nothing except the sound of men snoring. By the light of a lantern suspended from the roof, he perceived a row of black guards sleeping, each with a naked sword lying by him, and he understood that the hall must form the ante-room to the chamber of some queen or princess.

Standing quite still, Prince Firouz Schah looked about him, till his eyes grew accustomed to the gloom, and he noticed a bright light shining through a curtain in one corner. He then made his way softly towards it, and, drawing aside its folds, passed into a magnificent chamber full of sleeping women, all lying on low couches, except one, who was on a sofa; and this one, he knew, must be the princess.

Gently stealing up to the side of her bed he looked at her, and saw that she was more beautiful than any woman he had ever beheld. But, fascinated though he was, he was well aware of the danger of his position, as one cry of surprise would awake the guards, and cause his certain death.

So sinking quietly on his knees, he took hold of the sleeve of the princess and drew her arm lightly towards him. The princess opened her eyes, and seeing before her a handsome well-dressed man, she remained speechless with astonishment.

This favourable moment was seized by the prince, who bowing low while he knelt, thus addressed her:

'You behold, madam, a prince in distress, son to the King of Persia, who, owing to an adventure so strange that you will scarcely believe it, finds himself here, a suppliant for your protection. But yesterday, I was in my father's court, engaged in the celebration of our most solemn festival; to-day, I am in an unknown land, in danger of my life.'

Now the princess whose mercy Prince Firouz Schah implored was the eldest daughter of the King of Bengal, who was enjoying rest and change in the palace her father had built her, at a little distance from the capital. She listened kindly to what he had to say, and then answered:

'Prince, be not uneasy; hospitality and humanity are practised as widely in Bengal as they are in Persia. The protection you ask will be given you by all. You have my word for it.' And as the prince was about to thank her for her goodness, she added quickly, 'However great may be my curiosity to learn by what means you have travelled here so speedily, I know that you must be faint for want of food, so I shall give orders to my women to take you to one of my chambers, where you will be provided with supper, and left to repose.'

By this time the princess's attendants were all awake, and listening to the conversation. At a sign from their mistress they rose, dressed themselves hastily, and snatching up some of the tapers which lighted the room, conducted the prince to a large and lofty room, where two of the number prepared his bed, and the rest went down to the kitchen, from which they soon returned with all sorts of dishes. Then, showing him cupboards filled with dresses and linen, they quitted the room.

During their absence the Princess of Bengal, who had been greatly struck by the beauty of the prince, tried in vain to go to sleep again. It was of no use: she felt broad awake, and when her women entered the room, she inquired eagerly if the prince had all he wanted, and what they thought of him.

'Madam,' they replied, 'it is of course impossible for us to tell what impression this young man has made on you. For ourselves, we think you would be fortunate if the king your father should allow you to marry anyone so amiable. Certainly there is no one in the Court of Bengal who can be compared with him.'

These flattering observations were by no means displeasing to the princess, but as she did not wish to betray her own feelings she merely said, 'You are all a set of chatterboxes; go back to bed, and let me sleep.'

When she dressed the following morning, her maids noticed that, contrary to her usual habit, the princess was very particular about her toilette, and insisted on her hair being dressed two or three times over. 'For,' she said to herself, 'if my appearance was not displeasing to the prince when he saw me in the condition I was, how much more will he be struck with me when he beholds me with all my charms.'

Then she placed in her hair the largest and most brilliant

diamonds she could find, with a necklace, bracelets and girdle, all of precious stones. And over her shoulders her ladies put a robe of the richest stuff in all the Indies, that no one was allowed to wear except members of the royal family. When she was fully dressed according to her wishes, she sent to know if the Prince of Persia was awake and ready to receive her, as she desired to present herself before him.

When the princess's messenger entered his room, Prince Firouz Schah was in the act of leaving it, to inquire if he might be allowed to pay his homage to her mistress: but on hearing the princess's wishes, he at once gave way. 'Her will is my law,' he said, 'I am only here to obey her orders.'

In a few moments the princess herself appeared, and after the usual compliments had passed between them, the princess sat down on a sofa, and began to explain to the prince her reasons for not giving him an audience in her own apartments. 'Had I done so,' she said, 'we might have been interrupted at any hour by the chief of the eunuchs, who has the right to enter whenever it pleases him, whereas this is forbidden ground. I am all impatience to learn the wonderful accident which has procured the pleasure of your arrival, and that is why I have come to you here, where no one can intrude upon us. Begin then, I entreat you, without delay.'

So the prince began at the beginning, and told all the story of the festival of Nedrouz held yearly in Persia, and of the splendid spectacles celebrated in its honour. But when he came to the enchanted horse, the princess declared that she could never have imagined anything half so surprising. 'Well then,' continued the prince, 'you can easily understand how the King my father, who has a passion for all curious things, was seized with a violent desire to possess this horse, and asked the Indian what sum he would take for it.

'The man's answer was absolutely absurd, as you will agree, when I tell you that it was nothing less than the hand of the princess my sister; but though all the bystanders laughed and mocked, and I was beside myself with rage, I saw to my despair that my father could not make up his mind to treat the insolent proposal as it deserved. I tried to argue with him, but in vain. He only begged me to examine the horse with a view (as I quite understood) of making me more sensible of its value.'

'To please my father, I mounted the horse, and, without waiting for any instructions from the Indian, turned the peg as I had seen him do. In an instant I was soaring upwards, much quicker than an arrow could fly, and I felt as if I must be getting so near the sky that I should soon hit my head against it! I could see nothing beneath me, and for some time was so confused that I did not even know in what direction I was travelling. At last, when it was growing dark, I found another screw, and on turning it, the horse began slowly to sink towards the earth. I was forced to trust to chance, and to see what fate had in store, and it was already past midnight when I found myself on the roof of this palace. I crept down the little staircase, and made directly for a light which I perceived through an open door--I peeped cautiously in, and saw, as you will guess, the eunuchs lying asleep on the floor. I knew the risks I ran, but my need was so great that I paid no attention to them, and stole safely past your guards, to the curtain which concealed your doorway.

'The rest, Princess, you know; and it only remains for me to thank you for the kindness you have shown me, and to assure you of my gratitude. By the law of nations, I am already your slave, and I have only my heart, that is my own, to offer you. But what am I saying? My own? Alas, madam, it was yours from the first moment I beheld you!'

The air with which he said these words could have left no doubt on the mind of the princess as to the effect of her charms, and the blush which mounted to her face only increased her beauty.

'Prince,' returned she as soon as her confusion permitted her to speak, 'you have given me the greatest pleasure, and I have followed you closely in all your adventures, and though you are positively sitting before me, I even trembled at your danger in the upper regions of the air! Let me say what a debt I owe to the chance that has led you to my house; you could have entered none which would have given you a warmer welcome. As to your being a slave, of course that is merely a joke, and my reception must itself have assured you that you are as free here as at your father's court. As to your heart,' continued she in tones of encouragement, 'I am quite sure that must have been disposed of long ago, to some princess who is well worthy of it, and I could not think of being the cause of your unfaithfulness to her.'

Prince Firouz Schah was about to protest that there was no lady with any prior claims, but he was stopped by the entrance of one of the princess's attendants, who announced that dinner was served, and, after all, neither was sorry for the interruption.

Dinner was laid in a magnificent apartment, and the table was covered with delicious fruits; while during the repast richly dressed girls sang softly and sweetly to stringed instruments. After the prince and princess had finished, they passed into a small room hung with blue and gold, looking out into a garden stocked with flowers and arbutus trees, quite different from any that were to be found in Persia.

'Princess,' observed the young man, 'till now I had always believed that Persia could boast finer palaces and more lovely gardens than any kingdom upon earth. But my eyes have been opened, and I begin to perceive that, wherever there is a great king he will surround himself with buildings worthy of him.'

'Prince,' replied the Princess of Bengal, 'I have no idea what a Persian palace is like, so I am unable to make comparisons. I do not wish to depreciate my own palace, but I can assure you that it is very poor beside that of the King my father, as you will agree when you have been there to greet him, as I hope you will shortly do.'

Now the princess hoped that, by bringing about a meeting between the prince and her father, the King would be so struck with the young man's distinguished air and fine manners, that he would offer him his daughter to wife. But the reply of the Prince of Persia to her suggestion was not quite what she wished.

'Madam,' he said, 'by taking advantage of your proposal to visit the palace of the King of Bengal, I should satisfy not merely my curiosity, but also the sentiments of respect with which I regard him. But, Princess, I am persuaded that you will feel with me, that I cannot possibly present myself before so great a sovereign without the attendants suitable to my rank. He would think me an adventurer.'

'If that is all,' she answered, 'you can get as many attendants here as you please. There are plenty of Persian merchants, and as for money, my treasury is always open to you. Take what you please.'

Prince Firouz Schah guessed what prompted so much kindness on the part of the princess, and was much touched by it. Still his passion, which increased every moment, did not make him forget his duty. So he replied without hesitation:

'I do not know, Princess, how to express my gratitude for your obliging offer, which I would accept at once if it were not for the recollection of all the uneasiness the King my father must be suffering on my account. I should be unworthy indeed of all the love he showers upon me, if I did not return to him at the first possible moment. For, while I am enjoying the society of the most amiable of all princesses, he is, I am quite convinced, plunged in the deepest grief, having lost all hope of seeing me again. I am sure you will understand my position, and will feel that to remain away one instant longer than is necessary would not only be ungrateful on my part, but perhaps even a crime, for how do I know if my absence may not break his heart?

'But,' continued the prince, 'having obeyed the voice of my conscience, I shall count the moments when, with your gracious permission, I may present myself before the King of Bengal, not as a wanderer, but as a prince, to implore the favour of your hand. My father has always informed me that in my marriage I shall be left quite free, but I am persuaded that I have only to describe your generosity, for my wishes to become his own.'

The Princess of Bengal was too reasonable not to accept the explanation offered by Prince Firouz Schah, but she was much disturbed at his intention of departing at once, for she feared that, no sooner had he left her, than the impression she had made on him would fade away. So she made one more effort to keep him, and after assuring him that she entirely approved of his anxiety to see his father, begged him to give her a day or two more of his company.

In common politeness the prince could hardly refuse this request, and the princess set about inventing every kind of amusement for him, and succeeded so well that two months slipped by almost unnoticed, in balls, spectacles and in hunting, of which, when unattended by danger, the princess was passionately fond. But at last, one day, he declared seriously that he could neglect his duty no longer, and entreated her to put no further obstacles in his way, promising at the same time to return, as soon as he could, with all the magnificence due both to her and to himself.

'Princess,' he added, 'it may be that in your heart you class me with those false lovers whose devotion cannot stand the test of absence. If you do, you wrong me; and were it not for fear of offending you, I would beseech you to come with me, for my life can only be happy when passed with you. As for your reception at the Persian Court, it will be as warm as your merits deserve; and as for what concerns the King of Bengal, he must be much more indifferent to your welfare than you have led me to believe if he does not give his consent to our marriage.'

The princess could not find words in which to reply to the arguments of the Prince of Persia, but her silence and her downcast eyes spoke for her, and declared that she had no objection to accompanying him on his travels.

The only difficulty that occurred to her was that Prince Firouz Schah did not know how to manage the horse, and she dreaded lest they might find themselves in the same plight as before. But the prince soothed her fears so successfully, that she soon had no other thought than to arrange for their flight so secretly, that no one in the palace should suspect it.

This was done, and early the following morning, when the whole palace was wrapped in sleep, she stole up on to the roof, where the prince was already awaiting her, with his horse's head towards Persia. He mounted first and helped the princess up behind; then, when she was firmly seated, with her hands holding tightly to his belt, he touched the screw, and the horse began to leave the earth quickly behind him.

He travelled with his accustomed speed, and Prince Firouz Schah guided him so well that in two hours and a half from the time of starting, he saw the capital of Persia lying beneath him. He determined to alight neither in the great square from which he had started, nor in the Sultan's palace, but in a country house at a little distance from the town. Here he showed the princess a beautiful suite of rooms, and begged her to rest, while he informed his father of their arrival, and prepared a public reception worthy of her rank. Then he ordered a horse to be saddled, and set out.

All the way through the streets he was welcomed with shouts of joy by the people, who had long lost all hope of seeing him again. On reaching the palace, he found the Sultan surrounded by his ministers, all clad in the deepest mourning, and his father almost went out of his mind with surprise and delight at the mere sound of his son's voice. When he had calmed down a little, he begged the prince to relate his adventures.

The prince at once seized the opening thus given him, and told the whole story of his treatment by the Princess of Bengal, not even concealing the fact that she had fallen in love with him. 'And, Sire,' ended the prince, 'having given my royal word that you would not refuse your consent to our marriage, I persuaded her to return with me on the Indian's horse. I have left her in one of your Highness's country houses, where she is waiting anxiously to be assured that I have not promised in vain.'

As he said this the prince was about to throw himself at the feet of the Sultan, but his father prevented him, and embracing him again, said eagerly:

'My son, not only do I gladly consent to your marriage with the Princess of Bengal, but I will hasten to pay my respects to her, and to thank her in my own person for the benefits she has conferred on you. I will then bring her back with me, and make all arrangements for the wedding to be celebrated to-day.'

So the Sultan gave orders that the habits of mourning worn by the people should be thrown off and that there should be a concert of drums, trumpets and cymbals. Also that the Indian should be taken from prison, and brought before him.

His commands were obeyed, and the Indian was led into his presence, surrounded by guards. 'I have kept you locked up,' said the Sultan, 'so that in case my son was lost, your life should pay the penalty. He has now returned; so take your horse, and begone for ever.'

The Indian hastily quitted the presence of the Sultan, and when he was outside, he inquired of the man who had taken him out of prison where the prince had really been all this time, and what he had been doing. They told him the whole story, and how the Princess of Bengal was even then awaiting in the country palace the consent of the Sultan, which at once put into the Indian's head a plan of revenge for the treatment he had experienced. Going straight to the country house, he informed the doorkeeper who was left in charge that he had been sent by the Sultan and by the Prince of Persia to fetch the princess on the enchanted horse, and to bring her to the palace.

The doorkeeper knew the Indian by sight, and was of course

aware that nearly three months before he had been thrown into prison by the Sultan; and seeing him at liberty, the man took for granted that he was speaking the truth, and made no difficulty about leading him before the Princess of Bengal; while on her side, hearing that he had come from the prince, the lady gladly consented to do what he wished.

The Indian, delighted with the success of his scheme, mounted the horse, assisted the princess to mount behind him, and turned the peg at the very moment that the prince was leaving the palace in Schiraz for the country house, followed closely by the Sultan and all the court. Knowing this, the Indian deliberately steered the horse right above the city, in order that his revenge for his unjust imprisonment might be all the quicker and sweeter.

When the Sultan of Persia saw the horse and its riders, he stopped short with astonishment and horror, and broke out into oaths and curses, which the Indian heard quite unmoved, knowing that he was perfectly safe from pursuit. But mortified and furious as the Sultan was, his feelings were nothing to those of Prince Firouz Schah, when he saw the object of his passionate devotion being borne rapidly away. And while he was struck speechless with grief and remorse at not having guarded her better, she vanished swiftly out of his sight. What was he to do? Should he follow his father into the palace, and there give reins to his despair? Both his love and his courage alike forbade it; and he continued his way to the palace.

The sight of the prince showed the doorkeeper of what folly he had been guilty, and flinging himself at his master's feet, implored his pardon. 'Rise,' said the prince, 'I am the cause of this misfortune, and not you. Go and find me the dress of a dervish, but beware of saying it is for me.'

At a short distance from the country house, a convent of dervishes was situated, and the superior, or scheih, was the doorkeeper's friend. So by means of a false story made up on the spur of the moment, it was easy enough to get hold of a dervish's dress, which the prince at once put on, instead of his own. Disguised like this and concealing about him a box of pearls and diamonds he had intended as a present to the princess, he left the house at nightfall, uncertain where he should go, but firmly resolved not to return without her.

Meanwhile the Indian had turned the horse in such a direction that, before many hours had passed, it had entered a wood close to the capital of the kingdom of Cashmere. Feeling very hungry, and supposing that the princess also might be in want of food, he brought his steed down to the earth, and left the princess in a shady place, on the banks of a clear stream.

At first, when the princess had found herself alone, the idea had occurred to her of trying to escape and hide herself. But as she had eaten scarcely anything since she had left Bengal, she felt she was too weak to venture far, and was obliged to abandon her design. On the return of the Indian with meats of various kinds, she began to eat voraciously, and soon had regained sufficient courage to reply with spirit to his insolent remarks. Goaded by his threats she sprang to her feet, calling loudly for help, and luckily her cries were heard by a troop of horsemen, who rode up to inquire what was the matter.

Now the leader of these horsemen was the Sultan of Cashmere, returning from the chase, and he instantly turned to the Indian to inquire who he was, and whom he had with him. The Indian rudely answered that it was his wife, and there was no occasion for anyone else to interfere between them.

The princess, who, of course, was ignorant of the rank of her deliverer, denied altogether the Indian's story. 'My lord,' she cried, 'whoever you may be, put no faith in this impostor. He is an abominable magician, who has this day torn me from the Prince of Persia, my destined husband, and has brought me here on this enchanted horse.' She would have continued, but her tears choked her, and the Sultan of Cashmere, convinced by her beauty and her distinguished air of the truth of her tale, ordered his followers to cut off the Indian's head, which was done immediately.

But rescued though she was from one peril, it seemed as if she had only fallen into another. The Sultan commanded a horse to be given her, and conducted her to his own palace, where he led her to a beautiful apartment, and selected female slaves to wait on her, and eunuchs to be her guard. Then, without allowing her time to thank him for all he had done, he bade her repose, saying she should tell him her adventures on the following day.

The princess fell asleep, flattering herself that she had only to relate her story for the Sultan to be touched by compassion, and to restore her to the prince without delay. But a few hours were to undeceive her.

When the King of Cashmere had quitted her presence the evening before, he had resolved that the sun should not set again without the princess becoming his wife, and at daybreak proclamation of his intention was made throughout the town, by the sound of drums, trumpets, cymbals, and other instruments calculated to fill the heart with joy. The Princess of Bengal was early awakened by the noise, but she did not for one moment imagine that it had anything to do with her, till the Sultan, arriving as soon as she was dressed to inquire after her health, informed her that the trumpet blasts she heard were part of the solemn marriage ceremonies, for which he begged her to prepare. This unexpected announcement caused the princess such terror that she sank down in a dead faint.

The slaves that were in waiting ran to her aid, and the Sultan himself did his best to bring her back to consciousness, but for a long while it was all to no purpose. At length her senses began slowly to come back to her, and then, rather than break faith with the Prince of Persia by consenting to such a marriage, she determined to feign madness. So she began by saying all sorts of absurdities, and using all kinds of strange gestures, while the Sultan stood watching her with sorrow and surprise. But as this sudden seizure showed no sign of abating, he left her to her women, ordering them to take the greatest care of her. Still, as the day went on, the malady seemed to become worse, and by night it was almost violent.

Days passed in this manner, till at last the Sultan of Cashmere decided to summon all the doctors of his court to consult together over her sad state. Their answer was that madness is of so many different kinds that it was impossible to give an opinion on the case without seeing the princess, so the Sultan gave orders that they were to be introduced into her chamber, one by one, every man according to his rank.

This decision had been foreseen by the princess, who knew quite well that if once she allowed the physicians to feel her pulse, the most ignorant of them would discover that she was in perfectly good health, and that her madness was feigned, so as each man approached, she broke out into such violent paroxysms, that not one dared to lay a finger on her. A few, who pretended to be cleverer than the rest, declared that they could diagnose sick people only from sight, ordered her certain potions, which she made no difficulty about taking, as she was persuaded they were all harmless.

When the Sultan of Cashmere saw that the court doctors could do nothing towards curing the princess, he called in those of the city, who fared no better. Then he had recourse to the most celebrated physicians in the other large towns, but finding that the task was beyond their science, he finally sent messengers into the other neighbouring states, with a memorandum containing full particulars of the princess's madness, offering at the same time to pay the expenses of any physician who would come and see for himself, and a handsome reward to the one who should cure her. In answer to this proclamation many foreign professors flocked into Cashmere, but they naturally were not more successful than the rest had been, as the cure depended neither on them nor their skill, but only on the princess herself.

It was during this time that Prince Firouz Schah, wandering sadly and hopelessly from place to place, arrived in a large city of India, where he heard a great deal of talk about the Princess of Bengal who had gone out of her senses, on the very day that she was to have been married to the Sultan of Cashmere. This was quite enough to induce him to take the road to Cashmere, and to inquire at the first inn at which he lodged in the capital the full particulars of the story. When he knew that he had at last found the princess whom he had so long lost, he set about devising a plan for her rescue.

The first thing he did was to procure a doctor's robe, so that his dress, added to the long beard he had allowed to grow on his travels, might unmistakably proclaim his profession. He then lost no time in going to the palace, where he obtained an audience of the chief usher, and while apologising for his boldness in presuming to think that he could cure the princess, where so many others had failed, declared that he had the secret of certain remedies, which had hitherto never failed of their effect.

The chief usher assured him that he was heartily welcome, and that the Sultan would receive him with pleasure; and in case of success, he would gain a magnificent reward.

When the Prince of Persia, in the disguise of a physician, was brought before him, the Sultan wasted no time in talking, beyond remarking that the mere sight of a doctor threw the princess into transports of rage. He then led the prince up to a room under the roof, which had an opening through which he might observe the princess, without himself being seen.

The prince looked, and beheld the princess reclining on a sofa with tears in her eyes, singing softly to herself a song bewailing her sad destiny, which had deprived her, perhaps for ever, of a being she so tenderly loved. The young man's heart beat fast as he listened, for he needed no further proof that her madness was feigned, and that it was love of him which had caused her to resort to this species of trick. He softly left his hiding-place, and returned to the Sultan, to whom he reported that he was sure from certain signs that the princess's malady was not incurable, but that he must see her and speak with her alone.

The Sultan made no difficulty in consenting to this, and commanded that he should be ushered in to the princess's apartment. The moment she caught sight of his physician's robe, she sprang from her seat in a fury, and heaped insults upon him. The prince took no notice of her behaviour, and approaching quite close, so that his words might be heard by her alone, he said in a low whisper, 'Look at me, princess, and you will see that I am no doctor, but the Prince of Persia, who has come to set you free.'

At the sound of his voice, the Princess of Bengal suddenly grew calm, and an expression of joy overspread her face, such as only comes when what we wish for most and expect the least suddenly happens to us. For some time she was too enchanted to speak, and Prince Firouz Schah took advantage of her silence to explain to her all that had occurred, his despair at watching her disappear before his very eyes, the oath he had sworn to follow her over the world, and his rapture at finally discovering her in the palace at Cashmere. When he had finished, he begged in his turn that the princess would tell him how she had come there, so that he might the better devise some means of rescuing her from the tyranny of the Sultan.

It needed but a few words from the princess to make him acquainted with the whole situation, and how she had been forced to play the part of a mad woman in order to escape from a marriage with the Sultan, who had not had sufficient politeness even to ask her consent. If necessary, she added, she had resolved to die sooner than permit herself to be forced into such a union, and break faith with a prince whom she loved.

The prince then inquired if she knew what had become of the enchanted horse since the Indian's death, but the princess could only reply that she had heard nothing about it. Still she did not suppose that the horse could have been forgotten by the Sultan, after all she had told him of its value.

To this the prince agreed, and they consulted together over a plan by which she might be able to make her escape and return with him into Persia. And as the first step, she was to dress herself with care, and receive the Sultan with civility when he visited her next morning.

The Sultan was transported with delight on learning the result of the interview, and his opinion of the doctor's skill was raised still higher when, on the following day, the princess behaved towards him in such a way as to persuade him that her complete cure would not be long delayed. However he contented himself with assuring her how happy he was to see her health so much improved, and exhorted her to make every use of so clever a physician, and to repose entire confidence in him. Then he retired, without awaiting any reply from the princess.

The Prince of Persia left the room at the same time, and asked if he might be allowed humbly to inquire by what means the Princess of Bengal had reached Cashmere, which was so far distant from her father's kingdom, and how she came to be there alone. The Sultan thought the question very natural, and told him the same story that the Princess of Bengal had done, adding that he had ordered the enchanted horse to be taken to his treasury as a curiosity, though he was quite ignorant how it could be used.

'Sire,' replied the physician, 'your Highness's tale has supplied me with the clue I needed to complete the recovery of the princess. During her voyage hither on an enchanted horse, a portion of its enchantment has by some means been communicated to her person, and it can only be dissipated by certain perfumes of which I possess the secret. If your Highness will deign to consent, and to give the court and the people one of the most astonishing spectacles they have ever witnessed, command the horse to be brought into the big square outside the palace, and leave the rest to me. I promise that in a very few moments, in presence of all the assembled multitude, you shall see the princess as healthy both in mind and body as ever she was in her life. And in order to make the spectacle as impressive as possible, I would suggest that she should be richly dressed and covered with the noblest jewels of the crown.'

The Sultan readily agreed to all that the prince proposed, and the following morning he desired that the enchanted horse should be taken from the treasury, and brought into the great square of the palace. Soon the rumour began to spread through the town, that something extraordinary was about to happen, and such a crowd began to collect that the guards had to be called out to keep order, and to make a way for the enchanted horse.

When all was ready, the Sultan appeared, and took his place on a platform, surrounded by the chief nobles and officers of his court. When they were seated, the Princess of Bengal was seen leaving the palace, accompanied by the ladies who had been assigned to her by the Sultan. She slowly approached the enchanted horse, and with the help of her ladies, she mounted on its back. Directly she was in the saddle, with her feet in the stirrups and the bridle in her hand, the physician placed around the horse some large braziers full of burning coals, into each of which he threw a perfume composed of all sorts of delicious scents. Then he crossed his hands over his breast, and with lowered eyes walked three times round the horse, muttering the while certain words. Soon there arose from the burning braziers a thick smoke which almost concealed both the horse and princess, and this was the moment for which he had been waiting. Springing lightly up behind the lady, he leaned forward and turned the peg, and as the horse darted up into the air, he cried aloud so that his words were heard by all present, 'Sultan of Cashmere, when you wish to marry princesses who have sought your protection, learn first to gain their consent.'

It was in this way that the Prince of Persia rescued the Princess of Bengal, and returned with her to Persia, where they descended this time before the palace of the King himself. The marriage was only delayed just long enough to make the ceremony as brilliant as possible, and, as soon as the rejoicings were over, an ambassador was sent to the King of Bengal, to inform him of what had passed, and to ask his approbation of the alliance between the two countries, which he heartily gave.

6

The Story of the Fisherman

There was once a very old fisherman, so poor, that he could scarcely earn enough to maintain himself, his wife, and three children. He went every day to fish betimes in the morning; and imposed it as a law upon himself not to cast his nets above four times a day. He went one morning by moonlight, and coming to the seaside, undressed himself, and cast in his nets. As he drew them towards the shore, he found them very heavy, and thought he had a good draught of fish, at which he rejoiced within himself; but perceiving a moment after, that instead of fish, there was nothing in his nets but the carcass of an ass, he was much vexed. When the fisherman, vexed to have made such a sorry draught, had mended his nets, which the carcass of the ass had broken in several places, he threw them in a second time; and, when he drew them, found a great deal of resistance, which made him think he had taken abundance of fish; but he found nothing except a basket full of gravel and slime, which grieved him extremely. 'O Fortune!' cried he in a lamentable tone, 'be not angry with me, nor persecute a wretch who prays thee to spare him. I came hither from my house to seek for my livelihood, and thou pronouncest death against me. I have no trade but this to subsist by; and, notwithstanding all the care I take, I can scarcely provide what is absolutely necessary for my family.'

Having finished this complaint, he threw away the basket in a fret, and washing his nets from the slime, cast them the third time; but brought up nothing except stones, shells, and mud. Nobody can express his dismay; he was almost beside himself. However, when the dawn began to appear, he did not forget to say his prayers, like a good Mussulman, and afterwards added this petition: 'Lord, thou knowest that I cast my nets only four times a day; I have already drawn them three times, without the least reward for my labour: I am only to cast them once more; I pray thee to render the sea favourable to me, as thou didst to Moses.'

The fisherman, having finished his prayer, cast his nets the fourth time; and when he thought it was time, he drew them as before with great difficulty; but, instead of fish, found nothing in them but a vessel of yellow copper, which by its weight seemed to be full of something; and he observed that it was shut up and sealed, with a leaden seal upon it. This rejoiced him: 'I will sell it.' said he, 'at the foundry, and with the money arising from the produce buy a measure of corn.' He examined the vessel on all sides, and shook it, to see if what was within made any noise, but heard nothing. This, with the impression of the seal upon the leaden cover, made him think there was something precious in it. To try this, he took a knife, and opened it with very little trouble. He presently turned the mouth downward, but nothing came out, which surprised him extremely. He set it before him, and while he looked upon it attentively, there came out a very thick smoke which obliged him to retire two or three paces away.

The smoke ascended to the clouds, and extending itself along the sea and upon the shore, formed a great mist, which, we may well imagine, did mightily astonish the fisherman. When the smoke was all out of the vessel, it reunited itself, and became a solid body, of which there was formed a genie twice as high as the greatest of giants. At the sight of a monster of such unwieldy bulk, the fisherman would fain have fled, but he was so frightened that he could not go one step.

'Solomon,' cried the genie immediately, 'Solomon, great prophet, pardon, pardon; I will never more oppose thy will, I will obey all thy commands.'

When the fisherman heard these words of the genie, he recovered his courage, and said to him, 'Proud spirit, what is it that you say? It is above eighteen hundred years since the prophet Solomon died, and we are now at the end of time. Tell me your history, and how you came to be shut up in this vessel.'

The genie, turning to the fisherman with a fierce look, said, 'You must speak to me with more civility; you are very bold to call me a proud spirit.'

'Very well,' replied the fisherman, 'shall I speak to you with more civility, and call you the owl of good luck?'

'I say,' answered the genie, 'speak to me more civilly, before I kill thee.'

'Ah!' replied the fisherman, 'why would you kill me? Did I not just now set you at liberty, and have you already forgotten it?'

'Yes, I remember it,' said the genie, 'but that shall not hinder me from killing thee: I have only one favour to grant thee.'

'And what is that?' said the fisherman.

'It is,' answered the genie, 'to give thee thy choice, in what manner thou wouldst have me take thy life.'

'But wherein have I offended you?' replied the fisherman. 'Is that your reward for the good service I have done you?'

'I cannot treat you otherwise,' said the genie; 'and that you may be convinced of it, hearken to my story.

'I am one of those rebellious spirits that opposed the will of Heaven: all the other genii owned Solomon, the great prophet, and submitted to him. Sacar and I were the only genii that would never be guilty of a mean thing: and, to avenge himself, that great monarch sent Asaph, the son of Barakhia, his chief minister, to apprehend me. That was accordingly done. Asaph seized my person, and brought me by force before his master's throne.

'Solomon, the son of David, commanded me to quit my way of living, to acknowledge his power, and to submit myself to his commands; I bravely refused to obey, and told him I would rather expose myself to his resentment than swear fealty, and submit to him, as he required. To punish me, he shut me up in this copper vessel; and to make sure that I should not break prison, he himself stamped upon this leaden cover his seal, with the great name of God engraven upon it. Then he gave the vessel to one of the genii who submitted to him, with orders to throw me into the sea, which was done, to my sorrow.

'During the first hundred years' imprisonment, I swore that if anyone would deliver me before the hundred years expired, I would make him rich, even after his death: but that century ran out, and nobody did me the good office. During the second, I made an oath that I would open all the treasures of the earth to anyone that should set me at liberty; but with no better success. In the third, I promised to make my deliverer a potent monarch, to be always near him in spirit, and to grant him every day three requests, of what nature soever they might be: but this century ran out as well as the two former, and I continued in prison. At last, being angry, or rather mad, to find myself a prisoner so long, I swore that if afterwards anyone should deliver me, I would kill him without mercy, and grant him no other favour but to choose what kind of death he would die; and, therefore, since you have delivered me to-day, I give you that choice.'

This tale afflicted the poor fisherman extremely: 'I am very unfortunate,' cried he, 'to have done such a piece of good service to one that is so ungrateful. I beg you to consider your injustice and to revoke such an unreasonable oath; pardon me, and heaven will pardon you; if you grant me my life, heaven will protect you from all attempts against yours.'

'No, thy death is resolved on,' said the genie, 'only choose how you will die.'

The fisherman, perceiving the genie to be resolute, was terribly grieved, not so much for himself as for his three children, and the misery they must be reduced to by his death. He endeavoured still to appease the genie, and said, 'Alas! be pleased to take pity on me, in consideration of the good service I have done you.'

'I have told thee already,' replied the genie, 'it is for that very reason I must kill thee.'

'That is very strange,' sad the fisherman, 'are you resolved to reward good with evil? The proverb says, "He who does good to one who deserves it not is always ill rewarded." I must confess I thought it was false; for in reality there can be nothing more contrary to reason, or to the laws of society. Nevertheless, I find now by cruel experience that it is but too true.'

'Do not lose time,' replied the genie, 'all thy reasonings shall not divert me from my purpose; make haste, and tell me which way you choose to die.'

Necessity is the mother of invention. The fisherman bethought himself of a stratagem. 'Since I must die then,' said he to the genie, 'I submit to the will of heaven; but, before I choose the manner of death, I conjure you by the great name which was engraven upon the seal of the prophet Solomon, the son of David, to answer me truly the question I am going to ask you.'

The genie finding himself bound to a positive answer trembled, and replied to the fisherman, 'Ask what thou wilt, but make haste.'

The genie having thus promised to speak the truth, the fisherman said to him, 'I wish to know if you were actually in this vessel. Dare you swear it by the Great Name?'

'Yes,' replied the genie, 'I do swear by that Great Name that I was; and it is a certain truth.'

'In good faith,' answered the fisherman, 'I cannot believe you. The vessel is not capable of holding one of your feet, and how is it possible that your whole body could lie in it?'

'I swear to thee, notwithstanding,' replied the genie, 'that I was there just as thou seest me here. Is it possible that thou dost not believe me after this great oath that I have taken?'

'Truly, I do not,' said the fisherman; 'nor will I believe you unless you show it me.'

Upon which the body of the genie was dissolved, and changed

itself into smoke, extending itself as formerly upon the sea and shore, and then at last, being gathered together, it began to re-enter the vessel, which it continued to do by a slow and equal motion in a smooth and exact way, till nothing was left out, and immediately a voice said to the fisherman, 'Well, now, incredulous fellow, I am all in the vessel; do not you believe me now?'

The fisherman, instead of answering the genie, took the cover of lead, and speedily shut the vessel. 'Genie,' cried he, 'now it is your turn to beg my favour, and to choose which way I shall put you to death; but it is better that I should throw you into the sea, whence I took you: and then I will build a house upon the bank, where I will dwell, to give notice to all fishermen who come to throw in their nets to beware of such a wicked genie as thou art, who hast made an oath to kill him that shall set thee at liberty.'

The genie, enraged, did all he could to get out of the vessel again; but it was not possible for him to do it, for the impression of Solomon's seal prevented him. So, perceiving that the fisherman had got the advantage of him, he thought fit to dissemble his anger. 'Fisherman,' said he, in a pleasant tone, 'take heed you do not do what you say, for what I spoke to you before was only by way of jest, and you are to take it no otherwise.'

'Oh, genie!' replied the fisherman, 'thou who wast[16] but a moment ago the greatest of all genii, and now art the least of them, thy crafty discourse will avail thee nothing. Back to the sea thou shalt go. If thou hast been there already so long as thou hast told me, thou mayst very well stay there till the day of judgment. I begged of thee, in God's name, not to take away my life, and thou didst reject my prayers, I am obliged to treat thee in the same manner.'

The genie omitted nothing that might prevail upon the fisherman. 'Open the vessel,' said he; 'give me my liberty, I pray thee, and I promise to satisfy thee to thy heart's content.'

'Thou art a mere traitor,' replied the fisherman, 'I should deserve to lose my life if I were such a fool as to trust thee. I am afraid you will treat me as a certain Greek king treated the physician Douban. Listen, and I will tell you.'

The Story of the Greek King and the Physician Douban

In the country of Zouman, in Persia, there lived a Greek king. This king was a leper, and all his doctors had been unable to cure him, when a very clever physician, called Douban, arrived at his court.

This physician had learned his science in Greek, Persian, Turkish. Arabic, Latin, Syriac, and Hebrew books; and besides that, he was an expert philosopher, and fully understood the good and bad qualities of all sorts of plants and drugs. As soon as he was informed of the king's distemper, and understood that his physicians had given him over, he clad himself in the best robes he could procure, and found means to present himself before the king. 'Sir,' said he, 'I know that all your majesty's physicians have not been able to cure you of the leprosy, but if you will do me the honour to accept my services, I will engage to cure you without potions or external applications.'

The king listened to what he said, and answered, 'If you are able to perform what you promise, I will enrich you and your posterity, and, besides the presents I will make you, you shall be my chief favourite. Do you assure me, then, you will cure me of my leprosy, without making me take any potion, or applying any external medicine?'

'Yes, sir,' replied the physician, 'I promise success, through God's assistance, and to-morrow I will make trial of it.'

The physician returned to his quarters, and made a mallet, hollow within, and at the handle he put in his drugs. He made also a ball in such a manner as suited his purpose, with which, next morning, he presented himself before the king, and, falling down at his feet, kissed the ground.

The physician Douban then rose up, and, after a profound reverence, said to the king that he judged it meet for his majesty to take horse, and go to the place where he was wont to play at polo. The king did so, and when he arrived there, the physician came to him with the mallet, and said to him, 'Sir, exercise yourself with this mallet, and strike the ball with it until you find your hands and your body in a sweat. When the medicine I have put up in the handle of the mallet is heated with your hand it will penetrate your whole body, and as soon as you perspire you may leave off the exercise, for then the medicine will have had its effect. As soon as you return to your palace, go into the bath, and cause yourself to be well washed and rubbed; then go to bed, and when you rise to-morrow you will find yourself cured.'

The king took the mallet and struck the ball, which was returned by the officers that played with him. He struck it again, and played so long that his hand and his whole body were in a sweat, and then the medicine shut up in the handle of the mallet had its operation, as the physician said. At this the king left off playing, returned to his palace, entered the bath, and observed very exactly what his physician had prescribed him.

He was very well after it, and next morning, when he arose, he perceived, with equal wonder and joy, that his leprosy was cured, and his body as clean as if he had never been attacked by that disease. As soon as he was dressed he came into the hall of audience, where he ascended his throne, and showed himself to his courtiers, who, eager to know the success of the new medicine, came thither betimes, and, when they saw the king perfectly cured, all expressed great joy. The physician Douban entered the hall, and bowed himself before the throne, with his face to the ground. The king, perceiving him. called him, made him sit down by his side, showed him to the assembly, and made him eat alone with him at his table.

Towards night, when he was about to dismiss the company, he caused the physician to be clad in a long, rich robe, like those which his favourites usually wore in his presence, and ordered him two thousand sequins. The next day and the day following he continued his favour towards him; in short, the prince, thinking that he could never sufficiently acknowledge his obligations to the able physician, bestowed every day new favours upon him.

But this king had a grand vizier, who was avaricious, envious, and naturally capable of all sorts of mischief. He could not see without envy the presents that were given to the physician, whose other merits had already begun to make him jealous, and therefore he resolved to lessen him in the king's esteem. To effect this he went to the king, and told him in private that he had some advice to give him which was of the greatest concern. The king having asked what it was, 'Sir,' said he, 'it is very dangerous for a monarch to put confidence in a man whose fidelity he has never tried. Though you heap favours upon the physician Douban, your majesty does not know but that he may be a traitor, and have come to this court on purpose to kill you.'

'From whom have you heard this,' answered the king, 'that you dare to tell it to me. Consider to whom you speak, and that you are suggesting a thing which I shall not easily believe.'

'Sir,' replied the vizier. 'I am very well informed of what I have had the honour to represent to your majesty; therefore do not let your dangerous confidence grow to a further height. If your majesty be asleep, be pleased to wake, for I once more repeat that the physician Douban did not leave the heart of Greece, his native country, nor come here to settle himself at your court, except to execute the horrible design which I have just now hinted to you.'

'No, no, vizier,' replied the king, 'I am certain that this man, whom you treat as a villain and a traitor, is one of the best and most virtuous men in the world, and there is no man I love so much. You know by what medicine, or rather by what miracle, he cured me of my leprosy. If he had a design upon my life why did he save me? He needed only have left me to my disease. I could not have escaped it, my life was already half gone. Forbear, then, to fill me with unjust suspicions. Instead of listening to you, I tell you that from this day forward I will give that great man a pension of a thousand sequins per month for life. Nay, though I were to share with him all my riches and dominions, I should never pay him enough for what he has done for me. I perceive it to be his worth which raises your envy; out do not think that I will be unjustly possessed with prejudice against him.'

'I am very well assured,' said the vizier, 'that he is a spy sent by your enemies to attempt your majesty's life. He has cured you, you will say, but, alas! who can assure you of that? He has, perhaps, cured you only in appearance, and not radically. Who knows but that the medicine he has given you may, in time, have pernicious effects?'

The Greek king, who had by nature very little sense, was not able to see through the wicked design of his vizier, nor had he firmness enough to persist in his first opinion. This conversation staggered him. 'Vizier,' said he, 'thou art in the right. He may be come on purpose to take away my life, which he could easily do by the very smell of some of his drugs. We must consider what is proper for us to do in this case.'

When the vizier found the king in such a mood as he wished, 'Sir,' said he, 'the surest and speediest method you can take to secure your life is to send immediately for the physician Douban, and order his head to be cut off as soon as he comes.'

'In truth,' said the king, 'I believe that is the way we must take to put an end to his design.' When he had spoken thus, he called for one of his officers, and ordered him to go for the physician, who, knowing nothing, came to the palace in haste.

'Do you know,' said the king, when he saw him, 'why I sent for you?'

'No, sir,' answered he, 'I wait till your majesty be pleased to inform me.'

'I sent for you,' replied the king, 'to rid myself of you by taking your life.'

No man can express the surprise of the physician when he heard the sentence of death pronounced against him. 'Sir,' said he, 'why would your majesty take my life? What crime have I committed?'

'I am informed on good authority,' replied the king, 'that you came to my court only to attempt my life, but to prevent you I will be sure of yours. Give the blow,' said he, to the executioner, who was present, 'and deliver me from a perfidious wretch, who came hither on purpose to assassinate me.'

When the physician heard this cruel order, he readily judged that the honours and presents he had received from the king had procured him enemies, and that the weak monarch had been imposed on. He repented that he had cured him of his leprosy: but it was now too late. 'Is it thus,' replied the physician, 'that you reward me for curing you?' The king would not hearken to him, but a second time ordered the executioner to strike the fatal blow. The physician then had recourse to his prayers: 'Alas! sir,' cried he, 'prolong my days, and God will prolong yours; do not put me to death, lest God treat you in the same manner.'

The Greek king, instead of having regard to the prayers of the physician, cruelly replied, 'No no; I must of necessity cut you off, otherwise you may take my life away with as much art as you cured me.' The physician melted into tears, and bewailed himself for being so ill rewarded by the king, but prepared for death. The executioner bound up his eyes, tied his hands, and was going to draw the scimitar.

Then the courtiers who were present, being moved with compassion, begged the king to pardon him, assuring his majesty that he was not guilty of the crime laid to his charge, and that they would answer for his innocence; but the king was inflexible, and answered them so as they dared not say any more on the matter.

The physician, being on his knees, his eyes bound, and ready to receive the fatal blow, addressed himself once more to the king: 'Sir,' said he, 'since your majesty will not revoke the sentence of death, I beg, at least, that you would give me leave to return to my house, to give orders about my burial, to bid farewell to my family, to give alms, and to bequeath my books to those who are capable of making good use of them. I have one which I would particularly present to your majesty: it is a very precious book, and worthy to be laid up very carefully in your treasury,' 'Well,' replied the king, 'why is that book so precious?' 'Sir,' said the physician, 'because it contains an infinite number of curious things; of which the chief is that when you have cut off my head, if your majesty will take the trouble to open the book at the sixth leaf, and read the third line of the left page, my head will answer all the questions you ask it.' The king, being curious to see such a wonderful thing, deferred his death till the next day, and sent him home under a strong guard.

The physician put his affairs in order: and the report having spread that an unheard of miracle was to happen after his death, the viziers, emirs, officers of the guard, and, in a word, the whole court, repaired next day to the hall of audience, that they might witness it.

The physician Douban was soon brought in, and advanced to the foot of the throne, with a great book in his hand: then he called for a basin, upon which he laid the cover that the book was wrapped in, and presented the book to the king. 'Sir,' said he, 'take that book, if you please. As soon as my head is cut off, order that it be put into the basin upon the cover of the book; as soon as it is put there, the bleeding will stop: then open the book, and my head will answer your questions. But sir,' said he, 'permit me once more to implore your majesty's clemency; for God's sake grant my request, I protest to you that I am innocent.' 'Your prayers,' answered the king, 'are in vain; and, were it for nothing but to hear your head speak after your death, it is my will that you should die.' As he said this, he took the book out of the physician's hand, and ordered the executioner to do his duty.

The head was so dexterously cut off that it fell into the basin, and was no sooner laid up on the cover of the book than the bleeding stopped. Then, to the great surprise of the king and all the spectators, it opened its eyes, and said, 'Sir, will your majesty be pleased to open the book?' The king opened it, and finding that one leaf was as it were glued to another, he put his finger to his mouth that he might turn it with the more ease. He did so till he came to the sixth leaf, and finding no writing in the place where he was bidden to look for it, 'Physician,' said he to the head, 'there is nothing written.'

'Turn over some more leaves,' replied the head. The king continued to turn over, always putting his finger to his mouth, until the poison, with which each leaf was imbrued, came to have its effect; all of a sudden he was taken with an extraordinary fit, his eyesight failed, and he fell down at the foot of the throne in violent convulsions.

When the physician Douban, or rather his head, saw that the poison had taken effect, and that the king had but a few moments to live, 'Tyrant,' it cried, 'now you see how princes are treated who, abusing their authority, cut off innocent men. Soon or late God punishes their injustice and cruelty.' Scarcely had the head spoken these words when the king fell down dead, and the head itself lost what life it had.

After telling the story, the fisherman said to the genie who was still in the vessel, 'Notwithstanding the extreme obligation thou wast under to me for having set thee at liberty, thou didst persist in thy design to kill me; I am obliged in my turn, to be as hard-hearted to thee.'

'My good friend fisherman,' replied the genie, 'I implore thee once more not to be guilty of such cruelty; consider that it is not good to avenge oneself, and that, on the other hand, it is commendable to return good for evil.'

'No,' said the fisherman, 'I will not let you out. I am just going to throw you to the bottom of the sea.'

'Hear me one word more,' cried the genie. 'I promise to do thee no hurt; nay, far from that, I will show thee how thou mayest become exceedingly rich.'

The hope of delivering himself from poverty prevailed with the fisherman.

'I might listen to you,' said he, 'were there any credit to be given to your word. Swear to me by the Great Name that you will faithfully perform what you promise, and I will open the vessel. I do not believe you will dare to break such an oath.'

The genie swore to him, and the fisherman immediately took off the covering of the vessel. At that very instant the smoke came out, and the genie having resumed his form as before, the first thing he did was to kick the vessel into the sea. This action frightened the fisherman.

'Genie,' said he, 'what is the meaning of that? Will you not keep the oath you just now made?'

The genie laughed at the fisherman's fear, and answered: 'No, fisherman, be not afraid; I only did it to please myself, and to see if thou wouldst be alarmed at it; but to persuade thee that I am in earnest, take thy nets and follow me.' As he spoke these words, he walked before the fisherman, who took up his nets, and followed him, but with some distrust. They passed by the town, and came to the top of a mountain, from whence they descended into a vast plain, and presently to a great pond that lay betwixt four hills.

When they came to the side of the pond, the genie said to the fisherman, 'Cast in thy nets and catch fish.' The fisherman did not doubt of catching some, because he saw a great number in the pond; but he was extremely surprised when he found that they were of four colours—white, red, blue, and yellow. He threw in his nets, and brought out one of each colour. Having never seen the like, he could not but admire them, and, judging that he might get a considerable sum for them, he was very joyful.

'Carry those fish,' said the genie, 'and present them to the sultan; he will give you more money for them than ever you had in your life. You may come every day to fish in this pond; and I give you warning not to throw in your nets above once a day, otherwise you will repent it. Take heed, and remember my advice.' Having spoken thus, he struck his foot upon the ground, which opened and swallowed up the genie.

The fisherman, being resolved to follow the genie's advice exactly, forebore casting in his nets a second time, and returned to the town very well satisfied with his fish, and making a thousand reflections upon his adventure. He went straight to the sultan's palace.

The sultan was much surprised when he saw the four fishes. He took them up one after another, and looked at them with attention; and, after having admired them a long time, he said to his first vizier, 'Take those fishes to the handsome cook-maid that the Emperor of the Greeks has sent me. I cannot imagine but that they must be as good as they are fine.'

The vizier carried them himself to the cook, and delivering them into her hands, 'Look,' said he, 'here are four fishes newly brought to the sultan; he orders you to dress them.' And having so said, he returned to the sultan his master, who ordered him to give the fisherman four hundred pieces of gold of the coin of that country, which he accordingly did.

The fisherman, who had never seen so much cash in his lifetime, could scarcely believe his own good fortune. He thought it must be a dream, until he found it to be real, when he provided necessaries for his family with it.

As soon as the sultan's cook had cleaned the fishes, she put them upon the fire in a frying-pan with oil; and when she thought them fried enough on one side, she turned them upon the other; but scarcely were they turned when the wall of the kitchen opened, and in came a young lady of wonderful beauty and comely size. She was clad in flowered satin, after the Egyptian manner, with pendants in her ears, a necklace of large pearls, bracelets of gold garnished with rubies, and a rod of myrtle in her hand. She came towards the frying-pan, to the great amazement of the cook, who stood stock-still at the sight and, striking one of the fishes with the end of the rod, said, 'Fish, fish, art thou in thy duty?'

The fish having answered nothing, she repeated these words and then the four fishes lifted up their heads all together, and said to her, 'Yes, yes; if you reckon, we reckon; if you pay your debts, we pay ours; if you fly, we overcome, and are content.' As soon as they had finished these words, the lady overturned the frying-pan, and entered again into the open part of the wall, which shut immediately, and became as it was before.

The cook was greatly frightened at this, and, on coming a little to herself, went to take up the fishes that had fallen upon the hearth, but found them blacker than coal, and not fit to be carried to the sultan. She was grievously troubled at it, and began to weep most bitterly. 'Alas!' said she, 'what will become of me? If I tell the sultan what I have seen, I am sure he will not believe me, but will be enraged.'

While she was thus bewailing herself, in came the grand vizier, and asked her if the fishes were ready. She told him all that had happened, which we may easily imagine astonished him; but, without speaking a word of it to the sultan, he invented an excuse that satisfied him, and sending immediately for the fisherman, bade him bring four more such fish, for a misfortune had befallen the other ones. The fisherman, without saying anything of what the genie had told him, but in order to excuse himself from bringing them that very day, told the vizier that he had a long way to go for them, but would certainly bring them to-morrow.

Accordingly the fisherman went away by night, and, coming to the pond, threw in his nets betimes next morning, took four such fishes as before, and brought them to the vizier at the hour appointed. The minister took them himself, carried them to the kitchen, and shut himself up all alone with the cook: she cleaned them and put them on the fire, as she had done the four others the day before. When they were fried on one side, and she had turned them upon the other, the kitchen wall opened, and the same lady came in with the rod in her hand, struck one of the fishes, spoke to it as before, and all four gave her the same answer.

After the four fishes had answered the young lady, she overturned the frying-pan with her rod, and retired into the same place of the wall from whence she had come out. The grand vizier being witness to what had passed said, 'This is too surprising and extraordinary to be concealed from the sultan; I will inform him.' Which he accordingly did, and gave him a very faithful account of all that had happened.

The sultan, being much surprised, was impatient to see it for himself. He immediately sent for the fisherman, and said to him, 'Friend, cannot you bring me four more such fishes?'

The fisherman replied, 'If your majesty will be pleased to allow me three days' time, I will do it.' Having obtained his time, he went to the pond immediately, and at the first throwing in of his net, he caught four fishes, and brought them at once to the sultan. The sultan rejoiced at it, as he did not expect them so soon, and ordered him four hundred pieces of gold. As soon as the sultan had received the fish, he ordered them to be carried into his room, with all that was necessary for frying them; and having shut himself up there with the vizier, the minister cleaned them, put them in the pan upon the fire, and when they were fried on one side, turned them upon the other; then the wall of the room opened, but instead of the young lady there came out a black man, in the dress of a slave, and of gigantic stature, with a great green staff in his hand. He advanced towards the pan, and touching one of the fishes with his staff, said to it in a terrific voice, 'Fish, art thou in thy duty?'

At these words, the fishes raised up their heads, and answered 'Yes, yes; we are; if you reckon, we reckon; if you pay your debts, we pay ours; if you fly, we overcome, and are content.'

The fishes had no sooner finished these words than the black man threw the pan into the middle of the room, and reduced the fishes to a coal. Having done this, he retired fiercely, and entering again into the hole of the wall, it shut, and appeared just as it did before.

'After what I have seen,' said the sultan to the vizier, 'it will not be possible for me to be easy in my mind. These fish without doubt signify something extraordinary.' He sent for the fisherman, and said to him, 'Fisherman, the fishes you have brought us make me very uneasy; where did you catch them?'

'Sir,' answered he, 'I fished for them in a pond situated between four hills, beyond the mountain that we see from here.'

'Know'st thou that pond?' said the sultan to the vizier.

'No, sir,' replied the vizier, 'I never so much as heard of it: and yet it is not sixty years since I hunted beyond that mountain and thereabouts.'

The sultan asked the fisherman how far was the pond from the palace.

The fisherman answered that it was not above three hours' journey.

Upon this, there being daylight enough beforehand, the sultan commanded all his court to take horse, and the fisherman served them for a guide. They all ascended the mountain, and at the foot of it they saw, to their great surprise, a vast plain, that nobody had observed till then, and at last they came to the pond which they found really to be situated between four hills, as the fisherman had said. The water of it was so transparent that they observed all the fishes to be like those which the fisherman had brought to the palace.

The sultan stood upon the bank of the pond, and after beholding the fishes with admiration, he demanded of his emirs and all his courtiers if it was possible that they had never seen this pond, which was within so little a way of the town. They all answered that they had never so much as heard of it.

'Since you all agree,' said he, 'that you never heard of it, and as I am no less astonished than you are, I am resolved not to return to my palace till I know how this pond came here, and why all the fish in it are of four colours.' Having spoken thus he ordered his court to encamp; and immediately his pavilion and the tents of his household were pitched upon the banks of the pond.

When night came, the sultan retired to his pavilion and spoke to the grand vizier by himself.

'Vizier, my mind is very uneasy; this pond transported hither; the black man that appeared to us in my room, and the fishes that we heard speak; all this does so much excite my curiosity that I cannot resist the impatient desire I have to satisfy it. To this end I am resolved to withdraw alone from the camp, and I order you to keep my absence secret.'

The grand vizier said much to turn the sultan from this design. But it was to no purpose; the sultan was resolved on it, and would go. He put on a suit fit for walking, and took his scimitar; and as soon as he saw that all was quiet in the camp, he went out alone, and went over one of the hills without much difficulty. He found the descent still more easy, and, when he came to the plain, walked on till the sun rose, and then he saw before him, at a considerable distance, a great building. He rejoiced at the sight, and hoped to learn there what he wanted to know. When he came near, he found it was a magnificent palace, or rather a very strong castle, of fine black polished marble, and covered with fine steel, as smooth as a looking-glass. Being highly pleased that he had so speedily met with something worthy of his curiosity, he stopped before the front of the castle, and considered it attentively.

The gate had two doors, one of them open; and though he might have entered, he yet thought it best to knock. He knocked at first softly, and waited for some time. Seeing nobody, and supposing they had not heard him, he knocked harder the second time, and then neither seeing nor hearing anybody, he knocked again and again. But nobody appeared, and it surprised him extremely; for he could not think that a castle in such good repair was without inhabitants. 'If there is nobody in it,' said he to himself, 'I have nothing to fear; and if there is, I have wherewith to defend myself.'

At last he entered, and when he came within the porch, he called out, 'Is there nobody here to receive a stranger, who comes in for some refreshment as he passes by?' He repeated the same two or three times; but though he shouted, nobody answered. The silence increased his astonishment: he came into a very spacious court, and looked on every side, to see if he could perceive anybody; but he saw no living thing.

Perceiving nobody in the court, the sultan entered the great halls, which were hung with silk tapestry; the alcoves and sofas were covered with stuffs of Mecca, and the porches with the richest stuffs of India, mixed with gold and silver. He came afterwards into a magnificent court, in the middle of which was a great fountain with a lion of massive gold at each corner; water issued from the mouths of the four lions, and this water, as it fell, formed diamonds and pearls, while a jet of water, springing from the middle of the fountain, rose almost as high as a cupola painted after the Arabian manner.

On three sides the castle was surrounded by a garden, with

flower-pots, fountains, groves, and a thousand other fine things; and to complete the beauty of the place, an infinite number of birds filled the air with their harmonious songs, and always stayed there, nets being spread over the trees, and fastened to the palace to keep them in. The sultan walked a long time from apartment to apartment, where he found everything very grand and magnificent. Being tired with walking, he sat down in a room which had a view over the garden, and there reflected upon what he had already seen, when all of a sudden he heard lamentable cries. He listened with attention, and distinctly heard these sad words: 'O Fate! thou who wouldst not suffer me longer to enjoy a happy lot, and hast made me the most unfortunate man in the world, forbear to persecute me, and by a speedy death put an end to my sorrows. Alas! is it possible that I am still alive, after so many torments as I have suffered?'

The sultan, touched at these pitiful complaints, rose up, and made toward the place whence he heard the voice; and when he came to the gate of a great hall, he opened it, and saw a handsome young man, richly dressed, seated upon a throne raised a little above the ground. Melancholy was painted on his looks. The sultan drew near, and saluted him; the young man returned him his salute, by a low bow with his head; but not being able to rise up, he said to the sultan, 'My lord, I am very sure you deserve that I should rise up to receive you, and do you all possible honour; but I am hindered from doing so by a very sad reason, and therefore hope you will not take it ill.'

'My lord,' replied the sultan, 'I am very much obliged to you for having so good an opinion of me: as to your not rising, whatever your excuse may be, I heartily accept it. Being drawn hither by your complaints, and distressed by your grief, I come to offer you my help. I flatter myself that you would willingly tell me the history of your misfortunes; but pray tell me first the meaning of the pond near the palace, where the fishes are of four colours. What is this castle? how came you to be here? and why are you alone?'

Instead of answering these questions, the young man began to weep bitterly. 'How inconstant is fortune!' cried he, 'She takes pleasure in pulling down those she had raised up. Where are they who enjoy quietly their happiness, and whose day is always clear and serene?'

The sultan, moved with compassion, prayed him forthwith to tell him the cause of his excessive grief. 'Alas! My lord,' replied the young man, 'how can I but grieve, and my eyes be inexhaustible fountains of tears?' At these words, he lifted up his gown, and showed the sultan that he was a man only from the head to the waist, and that the other half of his body was black marble.

The sultan was strangely surprised when he saw the deplorable condition of the young man. 'That which you show me,' said he, 'while it fills me with horror, so excites my curiosity that I am impatient to hear your history, which, no doubt, is very extraordinary, and I am persuaded that the pond and the fishes have some part in it; therefore I beg you to tell it me. You will find some comfort in doing so, since it is certain that unfortunate people obtain some sort of ease in telling their misfortunes.'

'I will not refuse you this satisfaction,' replied the young man, 'though I cannot do it without renewing my grief. But I give you notice beforehand, to prepare your ears, your mind, and even your eyes, for things which surpass all that the most extraordinary imagination can conceive.

The Story of the Young King of the Black Isles

'You must know, my lord,' he began, 'that my father Mahmoud was king of this country. This is the kingdom of the Black Isles, which takes its name from the four little neighbouring mountains; for those mountains were formerly islands: the capital, where the king, my father, had his residence, was where that pond now is.

'The king, my father, died when he was seventy years of age; I had no sooner succeeded him than I married, and the lady I chose to share the royal dignity with me was my cousin. Nothing was comparable to the good understanding between us, which lasted for five years. At the end of that time I perceived that the queen, my cousin, took no more delight in me.

'One day I was inclined to sleep after dinner, and lay down upon a sofa. Two of her ladies came and sat down, one at my head, and the other at my feet, with fans in their hands to moderate the heat, and to hinder the flies from troubling me. They thought I was fast asleep, and spoke very low; but I only shut my eyes, and heard every word they said.

'One of them said to the other, "Is not the queen much in the wrong not to love such an amiable prince as this?"

"'Certainly," replied the other; "for my part, I do not understand it. Is it possible that he does not perceive it? "

"'Alas!" said the first, "how would you have him perceive it? She mixes every evening in his drink the juice of a certain herb, which makes him sleep so soundly that she has time to go where she pleases; then she wakes him by the smell of something she puts under his nose."

'You may guess, my lord, how much I was surprised at this conversation; yet, whatever emotion it excited in me, I had command enough over myself to dissemble, and pretended to awake without having heard one word of it.

'The queen returned, and with her own hand presented me with a cup full of such water as I was accustomed to drink; but instead of putting it into my mouth, I went to a window that was open, and threw out the water so quickly that she did not notice it, and I put the cup again into her hands, to persuade her that I had drunk it.

Soon after, believing that I was asleep, though I was not, she got up with little precaution, and said, so loudly that I could hear it distinctly, "Sleep, and may you never wake again!"

'As soon as the queen, my wife, went out, I got up in haste, took my scimitar, and followed her so quickly, that I soon heard the sound of her feet before me, and then walked softly after her, for fear of being heard. She passed through several gates, which opened on her pronouncing some magical words; and the last she opened was that of the garden, which she entered. I stopped there that she might not perceive me, and looking after her as far as the darkness permitted, I perceived that she entered a little wood, whose walks were guarded by thick palisades. I went thither by another way, and slipping behind the palisades of a long walk, I saw her walking there with a man.

'I listened carefully, and heard her say, "I do not deserve to be upbraided by you for want of diligence; you need but command me, you know my power. I will, if you desire it, before sunrise, change this great city, and this fine palace, into frightful ruins, which shall be inhabited by nothing but wolves, owls, and ravens. If you wish me to transport all the stones of those walls, so solidly built, beyond the Caucasus, and out of the bounds of the habitable world, speak but the word, and all shall undergo a change."

'As the queen finished these words, the man and she came to the end of the walk, turned to enter another, and passed before me. I had already drawn my scimitar, and the man being nearest to me, I struck him on the neck, and made him fall to the ground.

I thought I had killed him, and therefore retired speedily, without making myself known to the queen, whom I chose to spare, because she was my kinswoman.

'The blow I had given was mortal; but she preserved his life by the force of her enchantments; in such a manner, however, that he could not be said to be either dead or alive. As I crossed the garden, to return to the palace, I heard the queen cry out lamentably.

'When I returned home, being satisfied with having punished the villain, I went to sleep; and, when I awoke next morning, found the queen there too.

'Whether she slept or not I cannot tell, but I got up and went out without making any noise. I held my council, and at my return the queen, clad in mourning, her hair hanging about her eyes, and part of it torn off, presented herself before me, and said, "Sir, I come to beg your majesty not to be surprised to see me in this condition. I have just now received, all at once, three afflicting pieces of news."

'"Alas! what is the news, madam?" said I.

'"The death of the queen my dear mother," answered she; "that of the king my father, killed in battle; and that of one of my brothers, who has fallen down a precipice."

'I was not ill-pleased that she made use of this pretext to hide the true cause of her grief. "Madam," said I, "I am so far from blaming your grief that I assure you I share it. I should very much wonder if you were insensible of so great a loss. Mourn on, your tears are so many proofs of your good nature. I hope, however, that time and reason will moderate your grief."

'She retired into her apartment, and gave herself wholly up

to sorrow, spending a whole year in mourning and afflicting herself. At the end of that time she begged leave of me to build a burying place for herself, within the bounds of the palace, where she would remain, she told me, to the end of her days. I agreed, and she built a stately palace, with a cupola, that may be seen from hence, and she called it the Palace of Tears. When it was finished she caused the wounded ruffian to be brought thither from the place where she had caused him to be carried the same night, for she had hindered his dying by a drink she gave him. This she carried to him herself every day after he came to the Palace of Tears.

'Yet with all her enchantments she could not cure the wretch. He was not only unable to walk and to help himself, but had also lost the use of his speech, and gave no sign of life but by his looks. Every day she made him two long visits. I was very well informed of all this, but pretended to know nothing of it.

'One day I went out of curiosity to the Palace of Tears to see how the queen employed herself, and going to a place where she could not see me, I heard her speak thus to the scoundrel: "I am distressed to the highest degree to see you in this condition. I am as sensible as yourself of the tormenting pain you endure, but, dear soul, I constantly speak to you, and you do not answer me; how long will you be silent? Speak only one word. I would prefer the pleasure of always seeing you to the empire of the universe."

'At these words, which were several times interrupted by her sighs and sobs, I lost all patience, and, showing myself, came up to her, and said, "Madam, you have mourned enough. It is time to give over this sorrow, which dishonours us both. You have too much forgotten what you owe to me and to yourself."

"'Sir,' said she, "if you have any kindness left for me, I beseech you to put no restraint upon me. Allow me to give myself up to mortal grief, which it is impossible for time to lessen."

'When I saw that what I said, instead of bringing her to her duty, served only to increase her rage, I gave over, and retired. She continued for two whole years to give herself up to excessive grief.

'I went a second time to the Palace of Tears while she was there. I hid myself again, and heard her speak thus: "It is now three years since you spoke one word to me. Is it from insensibility or contempt? No, no, I believe nothing of it. tomb! tell me by what miracle thou becamest the depositary of the rarest treasure that ever was in the world."

'I must confess I was enraged at these words, for, in short, this creature so much doted upon, this adored mortal, was not such an one as you might imagine him to have been. He was a black Indian, a native of that country. I say I was so enraged that I appeared all of a sudden, and addressing the tomb in my turn, cried, "O tomb! why dost not thou swallow up this pair of monsters?"

'I had scarcely finished these words when the queen, who sat by the Indian, rose up like a fury. "Cruel man!" said she, "thou art the cause of my grief. I have dissembled it but too long; it is thy barbarous hand which hath[17] brought him into this lamentable condition, and thou art so hard-hearted as to come and insult me.'

'"Yes," said I, in a rage, "it was I who chastised that monster according to his deserts. I ought to have treated thee in the same manner. I repent now that I did not do it. Thou hast abused my goodness too long."

'As I spoke these words I drew out my scimitar, and lifted up my hand to punish her; but she, steadfastly beholding me, said, with a jeering smile, "Moderate thy anger." At the same time she pronounced words I did not understand, and added, "By virtue of my enchantments, I command thee immediately to become half marble and half man." Immediately I became such as you see me now, a dead man among the living, and a living man among the dead.

'After this cruel magician, unworthy of the name of a queen, had metamorphosed me thus, and brought me into this hall, by another enchantment she destroyed my capital, which was very flourishing and full of people, she abolished the houses, the public places and markets, and reduced it to the pond and desert field, which you may have seen; the fishes of four colours in the pond are the four sorts of people, of different religions, who inhabited the place. The white are the Mussulmans; the red, the Persians, who worship fire; the blue, the Christians; and the yellow, the Jews. The four little hills were the four islands that gave the name to this kingdom. I learned all this from the magician, who, to add to my distress, told me with her own mouth these effects of her rage. But this is not all; her revenge was not satisfied with the destruction of my dominions, and the metamorphosis of my person; she comes every day, and gives me over my naked shoulders an hundred blows with an ox-goad, which makes me all over gore; and, when she has done, she covers me with a coarse stuff of goat's hair, and throws over it this robe of brocade that you see, not to do me honour, but to mock me.'

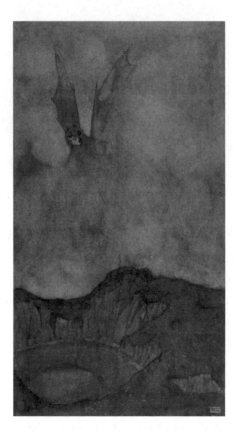

After this, the young king could not restrain his tears; and the sultan's heart was so pierced with the story, that he could not speak one word to comfort him. Presently he said: 'Tell me whither this perfidious magician retires, and where may be the unworthy wretch who is buried before his death.'

'My lord,' replied the prince, 'the man, as I have already told you, is in the Palace of Tears, in a handsome tomb in form of a dome, and that palace joins the castle on the side of the gate. As to the magician, I cannot tell precisely whither she retires, but every day at sunrise she goes to see him, after having executed her vengeance upon me, as I have told you; and you see I am not in a condition to defend myself against such great cruelty. She carries him the drink with which she has hitherto prevented his dying, and always complains of his never speaking to her since he was wounded.'

'Unfortunate prince,' said the sultan, 'never did such an extraordinary misfortune befall any man, and those who write your history will be able to relate something that surpasses all that has ever yet been written.'

While the sultan discoursed with the young prince, he told him who he was, and for what end he had entered the castle; and thought of a plan to release him and punish the enchantress, which he communicated to him. In the meantime, the night being far spent, the sultan took some rest; but the poor young prince passed the night without sleep, as usual, having never slept since he was enchanted; but he had now some hope of being speedily delivered from his misery.

Next morning the sultan got up before dawn, and, in order to execute his design, he hid in a corner his upper garment, which would have encumbered him, and went to the Palace of Tears. He found it lit up with an infinite number of tapers of white wax, and a delicious scent issued from several boxes of fine gold, of admirable workmanship, all ranged in excellent order. As soon as he saw the bed where the Indian lay, he drew his scimitar, killed the wretch without resistance, dragged his corpse into the court of the castle, and threw it into a well. After this, he went and lay down in the wretch's bed, took his scimitar with him under the counterpane, and waited there to execute his plan.

The magician arrived after a little time. She first went into the chamber where her husband the King of the Black Islands was, stripped him, and beat him with the ox-goad in a most barbarous manner. The poor prince filled the palace with his lamentations to no purpose, and implored her in the most touching manner to have pity on him; but the cruel woman would not give over till she had given him an hundred blows.

'You had no compassion,' cried she, 'and you are to expect none from me.'

After the enchantress had given the king, her husband, an hundred blows with the ox-goad, she put on again his covering of goat's-hair. and his brocade gown over all; then she went to the Palace of Tears, and, as she entered, she renewed her tears and lamentations; then approaching the bed, where she thought the Indian was: 'Alas!' cried she, addressing herself unawares to the sultan; 'my sun, my life, will you always be silent? Are you resolved to let me die, without giving me one word of comfort. My soul, speak one word to me at least, I implore you.'

The sultan, as if he had waked out of a deep sleep, and counterfeiting the language of the Indians, answered the queen in a grave tone, 'There is no strength or power but in God alone, who is almighty.'

At these words the enchantress, who did not expect them, gave a great shout, to signify her excessive joy. 'My dear lord,' cried she, 'do I deceive myself? Is it certain that I hear you, and that you speak to me?'

'Unhappy wretch,' said the sultan, 'art thou worthy that I should answer thee? '

'Alas!' replied the queen, 'why do you reproach me thus?' 'The cries,' replied he, 'the groans and tears of thy husband, whom thou treatest every day with so much indignity and barbarity, hinder me from sleeping night and day. I should have been cured long ago. and have recovered the use of my speech, hadst thou disenchanted him. That is the cause of the silence which you complain of.'

'Very well,' said the enchantress; 'to pacify you, I am ready to do whatever you command me. Would you have me restore him as he was?'

'Yes,' replied the sultan, 'make haste and set him at liberty, that I be no more disturbed with his cries.'

The enchantress went immediately out of the Palace of Tears; she took a cup of water, and pronounced words over it, which caused it to boil, as if it had been on the fire. Then she went into the hall, to the young king her husband, and threw the water upon him, saying, 'If the Creator of all things did form thee so as thou art at present, or if He be angry with thee, do not change. But if thou art in that condition merely by virtue of my enchantments, resume thy natural shape, and become what thou wast before.'

She had scarcely spoken these words, when the prince, finding himself restored to his former condition, rose up freely, with all imaginable joy, and returned thanks to God.

Then the enchantress said to him, 'Get thee gone from this

castle, and never return here on pain of death!'

The young king, yielding to necessity, went away from the enchantress, without replying a word, and retired to a remote place, where he patiently awaited the success of the plan which the sultan had so happily begun.

Meanwhile the enchantress returned to the Palace of Tears and, supposing that she still spoke to the black man, said, 'Dearest, I have done what you ordered.'

The sultan continued to counterfeit the language of the blacks. 'That which you have just now done,' said he, 'is not sufficient for my cure. You have only eased me of part of my disease; you must cut it up by the roots.'

'My lovely black man,' replied she, 'what do you mean by the roots?'

'Unfortunate woman,' replied the sultan, 'do you not understand that I mean the town, and its inhabitants, and the four islands, which thou hast destroyed by thy enchantments? The fishes every night at midnight raise their heads out of the pond, and cry for vengeance against thee and me. This is the root cause of the delay of my cure. Go speedily, restore things as they were, and at thy return I will give thee my hand, and thou shalt help me to rise.'

The enchantress, filled with hope from these woids, cried out in a transport of joy, 'My heart, my soul, you shall soon be restored to health, for I will immediately do what you command me.' Accordingly she went that moment, and when she came to the brink of the pond, she took a little water in her hand, and sprinkling it, she pronounced some words over the fishes and the pond, and the city was immediately restored. The fishes became men, women, and children; Mahometans, Christians, Persians, or Jews; freemen or slaves, as they were before; every one having recovered his natural form. The houses and shops were immediately filled with their inhabitants, who found all things as they were before the enchantment. The sultan's numerous retinue, who had encamped in the largest square, were astonished to see themselves in an instant in the middle of a large, handsome, and well-peopled city.

To return to the enchantress. As soon as she had effected this wonderful change, she returned with all diligence to the Palace of Tears. 'My dear,' she cried, as she entered, 'I come to rejoice with you for the return of your health: I have done all that you required of me; then pray rise, and give me your hand.'

'Come near,' said the sultan, still counterfeiting the language of the blacks. She did so. 'You are not near enough,' said he, 'come nearer.' She obeyed. Then he rose up, and seized her by the arm so suddenly, that she had not time to discover who it was, and with a blow of his scimitar cut her in two, so that one half fell one way, and the other another. This done, he left the carcass at the place, and going out of the Palace of Tears, he went to look for the young King of the Black Isles, who was waiting for him with great impatience. 'Prince,' said he, embracing him, 'rejoice; you have nothing to fear now; your cruel enemy is dead.'

The young prince returned thanks to the sultan in such a manner as showed that he was thoroughly sensible of the kindness that he had done him, and in return, wished him a long life and all happiness. 'You may henceforward,' said the sultan, 'dwell peaceably in your capital, unless you will go to mine, where you shall be very welcome, and have as much honour and respect shown you as if you were at home.'

'Potent monarch, to whom I am so much indebted,' replied the king, 'you think, then, that you are very near your capital?'

'Yes,' said the sultan, 'I know it; it is not above four or five hours' journey.'

'It will take you a whole year,' said the prince. 'I do believe, indeed, that you came hither from your capital in the time you speak of, because mine was enchanted; but since the enchantment is taken off, things are changed. However, this shall not prevent my following you, were it to the utmost corners of the earth. You are my deliverer, and that I may show you that I shall acknowledge this during my whole life, I am willing to accompany you, and to leave my kingdom without regret.'

The sultan was extremely surprised to learn that he was so far from his dominions, and could not imagine how it could be. But the young King of the Black Islands convinced him beyond a possibility of doubt. Then the sultan replied, 'It is no matter: the trouble of returning to my own country is sufficiently recompensed by the satisfaction of having obliged you, and by acquiring you for a son; for since you will do me the honour to accompany me, as I have no child, I look upon you as such, and from this moment I appoint you my heir and successor.'

The conversation between the sultan and the King of the Black Islands concluded with the most affectionate embraces; after which the young prince was totally taken up in making preparations for his journey, which were finished in three weeks' time, to the great regret of his court and subjects, who agreed to receive at his hands one of his nearest kindred for their king.

At last the sultan and the young prince began their journey, with a hundred camels laden with inestimable riches from the treasury of the young king, followed by fifty handsome gentlemen on horseback, well mounted and dressed. They had a very happy journey; and when the sultan, who had sent couriers to give notice of his delay, and of the adventure which had occasioned it, came near his capital, the principal officers he had left there came to receive him, and to assure him that his long absence had occasioned no alteration in his empire. The inhabitants came out also in great crowds, received him with acclamations, and made public rejoicings for several days.

On the day after his arrival, the sultan gave all his courtiers a very ample account of the events which, contrary to his expectation, had detained him so long. He told them he had adopted the King of the Four Black Islands who was willing to leave a great kingdom to accompany and live with him; and as a reward for their loyalty, he made each of them presents according to their rank.

As for the fisherman, since he was the first cause of the deliverance of the young prince, the sultan gave him a plentiful fortune, which made him and his family happy for the rest of their days.

THE END

Notes

1. from where
2. to that place
3. to this place
4. do I have
5. have
6. will
7. you
8. you
9. your
10. are
11. up to this place or point
12. to what place
13. from that place
14. your
15. no
16. were
17. has

一千零一夜

Preface to the Chinese Translation
中文譯本序

從前，在古代中國和印度之間，傳說有一個薩桑王國，統治者蘇丹名叫山魯亞爾，他治理國政深得人民的愛戴。有一天，他打獵回來，發現王后竟然另有所歡，在花園中和一個侍從嬉戲作樂，他一怒之下，把男女兩個一起殺了。從此他成了痛恨女性的暴君，實行瘋狂的報復。他下令每天要獻一個少女進宮，當夜和她成親。這些不幸的少女在後宮只做了一夜王后，第二天一早就被人拖出去殺了。

這樣連續三年，這暴君都是今天新娶了王后，明天就把她殺了。京城裏到處聽到百姓的哭喊聲，有好些人家帶着女兒逃走了。終於有一天，宰相找遍全城，也搜索不到一個少女。第二天如果沒有少女獻進宮去，暴君一定會大發雷霆，宰相簡直不敢想像會有怎樣的災禍落到自己頭上。他回到家裏，心事重重。

宰相有兩個女兒，山魯佐德是大女兒的芳名，小女兒叫敦亞佐德。山魯佐德多才多藝，不僅博覽詩書，熟知歷代的傳說，還有極好的口才。

那天她看到父親回家悶悶不樂，便上前問父親有甚麼心事。宰相說出了他面臨着天大的災禍，不知道怎麼辦才好。他女兒聽了當即說道："就把我獻給蘇丹吧，我願意犧牲自己，去拯救那許多穆斯林女兒。"

宰相慌忙勸告女兒，千萬不能冒這生命危險。誰知她已打定主意，怎麼也不聽從父親的勸阻，說道：“請爸爸不要見怪，我已拿定了主意。如果你只知道愛你的女兒，不肯同意我的請求，那我只好自己進宮去把我獻給蘇丹了。”

最後，那做父親的拗不過女兒的決心，無可奈何地聽從了女兒的主意。他心裏雖然悲痛，卻立即去叩見蘇丹，說是第二天晚上他將把自己的女兒獻給他為妻。

蘇丹聽說宰相願意犧牲自己的親生女兒，十分驚奇，問道：“你怎麼捨得把女兒獻進宮裏來呢？”

“陛下，”宰相回答道，“這是她自願的呀。等待着她的悲慘命運嚇不倒她。她只要這份榮譽：做陛下的一夜王后，並不顧惜自己的生命。”

“不過你千萬不要弄錯了，大臣，”蘇丹說道，“第二天我交山魯佐德到你手裏的時候，我就要你親手處死自己的女兒。如果你辦不到，那麼我發誓，你自己的命也保不住了。”

“陛下，”宰相回答道，“雖說她是我的女兒，我一定服從王上，親手執行你的命令。”

宰相回到家中，山魯佐德感謝父親按照她的意願去做。可是看到父親愁容滿面，就安慰他道，她希望他不會因為把女兒嫁給了蘇丹而後悔莫及。相反，她希望他為了按照女兒的話去做，而有理由在以後的日子感到高興。

山魯佐德用心打扮了一番，好去見蘇丹；但是在離開家之前，她把妹妹敦亞佐德叫到一邊，對她說道：

“好妹妹，有一件事事關重大，我需要你的幫助，請你千萬不要拒絕我。父親就要領我到蘇丹跟前去了，你不必為我擔驚受怕，但是你要用心聽好我現在跟你說的話。

"我到了蘇丹跟前之後，我要求他准許你第二天一早就來看我。讓我在被處死之前，我們姐妹兩人再見一面，待上一兩個鐘，然後我再和你訣別。要是我得到了恩准，像我所希望的那樣，那麼你記住，你要在天亮之前的一小時就來叫醒我，這樣跟我說道：'姐姐，你醒過來了沒有？求求你啦，在天亮之前，趁我們還沒分離，快給我講一個有趣的故事吧——你不是經常給我講故事的嗎？你肚子裏好聽的故事多着呢。'於是我就馬上開始給你講一個故事。我只希望憑着我那些故事能把這個京城從恐怖中拯救出來。"

敦亞佐德答應姐姐她一定按照姐姐指點她的話做去。

安息的時分已到，宰相就把山魯佐德送進宮裏，又引領她到蘇丹的臥房裏，於是他就告退了。這時只剩下蘇丹和她兩人在一起，蘇丹吩咐山魯佐德撩起面紗來。那君主看見今夜的這一個新娘長得這麼秀麗，心裏高興極了；可是又看見她掉下兩滴淚珠，就問她為甚麼要哭。於是山魯佐德回答道："陛下，我有一個妹妹，我們兩人彼此相親相愛。我希望她能夠得到恩准，今天晚上讓她就在這裏過夜，讓我也好和她見最後一面，跟她告別。不知陛下能不能賞給我這樣一個機會，讓我表一表姐妹的情誼，這樣我就是死也安心了。"

蘇丹應允了她的請求，派人傳喚敦亞佐德，她應召而至。那一夜，蘇丹和山魯佐德同睡在高大的牀上，敦亞佐德睡在牀腳邊的一條席墊上。

在天亮還有一小時的光景，敦亞佐德果真按照姐姐的囑咐，來到大牀邊，呼喚道："好姐姐，時間不多了，我們馬上就要分手了，求求你啦，快給我講一個好聽的故事吧。唉！這是我最後一次享受聽你講故事的快樂了。"

山魯佐德並沒有直接回答妹妹，卻先轉過臉來向蘇丹請示："不知陛下能容許我滿足我那妹妹的請求嗎？"

"很好，你就給你妹妹講個故事吧。"

於是山魯佐德叫妹妹坐在她身邊，又轉身面對着蘇丹，開始講她的故事了。

直到天大亮了，她的故事還沒講完，蘇丹正聽得津津有味，急於想知道故事的最後結局，心想：且待聽完了故事再處死她也不遲。誰知道第二天的大天亮，故事又正是講到緊要關頭，於是暴君又下不了決心下令處死她。

就這樣，一個故事接着一個故事講下去，反正山魯佐德肚子裏的故事多着呢，她又把故事講得那麼有聲有色，娓娓動聽，蘇丹簡直聽得入迷了，因此始終捨不得處死她。她一夜又一夜，接連講了一千零一夜的故事。蘇丹終於受到感化，回心轉意，改變了他過去憎恨女性的反常心理，放下屠刀，深深愛上了他那無比聰明美麗的王后。後來蘇丹和山魯佐德相親相愛，白頭偕老。

阿拉伯民族愛講故事，善於把人生的經驗、智慧、哲理編織在故事中。講着講不完的故事，終於喚回了蘇丹的人性和愛心的山魯佐德，實際上是阿拉伯民族智慧、才華的美麗的化身。

她那許多帶有神話色彩、生動有趣的故事從八世紀起就流傳在中亞一帶，包括非洲埃及的民間故事。大約在十六世紀出現了彙編成集的《一千零一夜》(舊譯《天方夜譚》) 定本。其中最著名的一些故事已是家喻戶曉。像《阿里巴巴與四十大盜》、《神燈》、《仙巴歷險記》、《神馬》等等，都是情節曲折生動，想像豐富瑰麗，或者發揚勇敢冒險的精神，或者歌頌忠貞純潔的愛情。對於善良機智、挺身和惡勢力鬥爭的下層社會人民，給予了高度的讚揚。這些名篇都已收入了我們這一精選本。

　　《一千零一夜》是阿拉伯古典文學中的瑰寶，也可說是世界文學寶庫中光彩鮮豔的珍品，為各個地區的人民所喜愛。

　　　　　　　　　　　　　　　　　　　　方平

1
阿里巴巴與四十大盜

從前在波斯的一個城鎮裏，住着兩兄弟，哥哥叫卡西姆，弟弟叫阿里巴巴。父親很窮，沒給他們留下甚麼家產。那做哥哥的娶了一個有錢的老婆，生活就闊起來，成為當地的大商人。那弟弟呢，卻娶了一個跟他一樣窮苦的女子，因此只得靠到山林中去打柴，養活妻子和孩子。他把砍下的柴分裝在三頭驢子背上，運到鎮上去叫賣。

有一天，阿里巴巴在林子中砍柴，遠遠望見空中捲起一團塵土，好像在漸漸地向前移來。他留神觀看，過了片刻，就有一匹匹奔馬在揚起的塵土中顯現出來。他懷疑來了一幫強盜吧，就慌忙捨下驢子，爬上了一株大樹，躲進濃密的樹陰裏，好暗中觀察究竟是怎麼一回事。

阿里巴巴在暗中點數得很清楚，這一隊人馬共有四十條漢子。他們奔馳到這一片林子，就勒住馬頭跳了下來，各自把馬繫在樹邊，餵一些草料；接着就把沉甸甸的馬褡褳從馬背上取下，全都跟隨在他們的頭目後面。只見那頭目向阿里巴巴躲藏的地方走來，來到一塊大岩石面前站住了，大聲喊道："芝麻芝麻，把門打開！"說也奇怪，那頭目的話音剛落，那塊大岩石頓時打開一扇石門。那許多漢子就一個接一個走了進去，最後進去的是他們的頭目。等他一進去，那石門隨即就自動關上了。

那一幫強盜在石窟裏待了好長時間，躲在樹上的阿里巴巴始終不敢動彈一下。

最後，石門再次打開，那一幫人又一個接一個地走出石窟。這一回是那個頭目走在前面，看着他的三十九個弟兄從他面前經過，都走了出來；於是只聽得他喊道："芝麻芝麻，把門關好！"石門應聲而關。接着，他們都跳上了馬背，那頭目看到大夥兒都準備好了，就帶着這支隊伍，沿着來時的路奔馳而去了。

阿里巴巴目送着他們，直到連影都望不見了，還在樹上躲了好大一會，這才壯着膽子從樹上爬下來。他撥開灌木叢，走近那塊大岩石，記起剛才那個頭目所唸的咒語，就照着他的聲調嚷道："芝麻芝麻，把門打開！"果然，那扇石門又應聲而開了。

阿里巴巴本來以為那石窟一定又黑暗又潮濕，他完全沒有料到那裏邊竟是又明亮又高又寬敞，他舉起手來還碰不到上面的石頂呢。石窟的頂部有一道裂縫，天光就穿過這裂縫瀉下來。裏面堆積着許許多多糧食啊，色彩富麗的綢包裹啊，一匹匹織錦花緞啊，名貴的地毯啊，一大堆一大堆金條和銀錠啊。眼前令人目眩神迷的景象，使他猜想這一定不是只由一幫強盜佔有，而是前後經過好幾幫強盜繼承下去，才能在這個石窟裏積聚起這麼多金銀財寶。

阿里巴巴勇敢地走進石窟，趁沒有人看見，盡他所能，把好多袋金幣搬出了石窟，藏在筐子裏，上面再蓋些木柴，讓驢子馱着。他裝載完畢，就走到石門前，唸了關門的咒語"芝麻芝麻，把門關好！"於是石門應聲關上了。

阿里巴巴趕着驢子，往市鎮而去，等回到家裏，他隨即關上大門，扔掉遮蓋馱籃的木柴，拿着筐子走進屋內，叫他妻子快來看今天他帶回來甚麼東西。他把三筐金幣全都倒在她面前，鋥亮的金光叫她眼睛都睜不開了。她心裏不由得起了驚慌，這麼多的錢莫非是丈夫偷來、搶來的嗎？阿里巴巴把當天發生的事情全都對她說了，說完之後，又再三叮囑她，這件事千萬不能泄露出去。

那妻子這才打消了滿腹疑慮，明白她家已交上好運了，便歡天喜地地計數起眼前那麼一大堆金幣來。

"親愛的，"阿里巴巴說道，"你就是不懂得這件事該怎麼辦，看你現在計數起金幣來了，你怎麼數也數不過來。讓我趕緊去挖個大坑，把金子埋起來吧。一刻也不能耽誤呀。"

"你說得對，丈夫，"她回答道，"不過我們總得心中有個數，我們究竟弄來了多少金幣，最好是確切些，所以我想去向鄰居借一桿秤來，趁你在挖坑的時候，我先把金子稱一下。"

阿里巴巴的妻子於是來到卡西姆的家裏。恰好他不在，所以她開口向卡西姆的妻子借秤。那大嫂問她秤要大的還是小的，她說要小的秤，講明用完就還。那大嫂一口答應了，請她稍候一會。

但是她心裏在嘀咕，阿里巴巴窮得要命，他要借秤去稱些甚麼樣的穀子呢。於是她想出了一個主意，在秤盤的底上塗上一層牛脂，這才把秤借給弟媳婦，嘴裏故意說道："真對不起，叫你久等了，我找了半天才把秤找到了。"

阿里巴巴的妻子借到了秤，趕回家去把一大堆金幣一盤盤稱起來，等到她把金子全都稱完，她丈夫也快把坑挖好了。她喜氣洋洋地告訴丈夫他們總共有多少金子。阿里巴巴着手把金子埋進泥裏，她呢，趕忙到大嫂家去還秤，免得嫂子抱怨久借不還，可是卻沒有注意到有一小枚金幣粘着在秤盤的底上了。

"大嫂，"她一邊説，一邊把秤還給她，"你看，我並沒有借去多少時候，現在物歸原主，我非常感謝你的好意。"

阿里巴巴的妻子轉身走了之後，卡西姆的妻子立即翻過秤盤，看到有一小枚金幣粘在上面，這使她大吃一驚，而且妒火中燒。

她説："甚麼！難道阿里巴巴有那麼多金子，已經數不過來，只能用秤來稱斤兩嗎？"

等到卡西姆回到家的時候，他的妻子就迎上去説道："我知道你一定自以為很有錢了吧，那你可大大弄錯啦。阿里巴巴家裏藏的錢不知比你多上多少倍呢！他不像你，一五一十地數錢，他用秤來稱金子。"

卡西姆給弄得莫名其妙，要她把話説得清楚些。於是她把事情經過都告訴了丈夫：她是使用了怎樣一個計謀才發現這個祕密的；又把那枚從秤盤底上掰下來的金幣拿給他瞧。這已是一枚很古老的金幣，他們誰都説不清這是哪一個王朝鑄造的錢幣。

卡西姆娶了那富有的女人以後，就再沒有當阿里巴巴是弟弟，而且忽視了他。現在，他聽着這些話，瞧着那枚金幣，並不為他那窮兄弟交了好運而高興，卻跟他妻子一樣，妒火中燒。這一夜他睡也睡不好，第二天日出前，就找他弟弟去了。

"阿里巴巴，"他一進門就嚷道，"瞧你，裝出一副窮模樣，原來私下卻在稱金子呢。這就是我妻子從秤盤底下發現的一枚金幣。"

阿里巴巴立即知道這件事再也掩蓋不過去了，只怪他妻子又蠢又粗心，讓兄嫂兩個看出了破綻。事情落到這個地步還有甚麼辦法可想呢？於是他只得把昨天的前後經過都如實說出來，還表示願意從他得到的金子中拿出一份來送給哥哥，務必請哥哥替他保守這個祕密。

　　"果然不出我所料！"他的兄長傲慢得真夠受，"可是我非得確切知道不可：那許多金銀財寶藏在哪裏，如果我想親眼去瞧瞧，該怎麼去法，你都得跟我交代清楚。否則我就到官府去告發你，那時你不僅再也弄不到金子銀子，就連已經到手的也保不住了。而我呢，告發有功，倒可以得到一大筆賞金呢。"

　　阿里巴巴把真情實況都跟哥哥說了，就連進出石窟的咒語也告訴了他。

　　第二天，太陽還沒升起，卡西姆早已起身，準備妥當，趕着十頭驢子，運着十個大箱子，向山林出發了。不久，他就來到了那個山頭，根據他弟弟提供的線索、那株樹和其他的標誌，他找到了那塊大岩石。於是他唸起咒語來："芝麻芝麻，把門打開！"石門應聲而開，等他一跨進石窟，石門就隨即關上了。他向石窟四處張望一下，真是吃驚不小，只見到處堆積着那麼多眼花繚亂的金銀，比他聽到阿里巴巴那一番話所想像的還要多得多。於是他立即動手把一袋袋金子搬到石門邊，可是他的情緒太興奮了，只想着這下子他可發大財啦，竟把最重要的開門的咒語忘個乾淨，再也想不起來。他只會急得亂嚷："麥子，把門打開"，卻忘掉了是"芝麻"。任他怎麼嚷，怎麼求，那石門根本不理睬他。

　　卡西姆做夢也沒有想到他會落進這麼糟糕的局面。他知道大禍臨頭了，嚇得直哆嗦。他拼命想把那句開門的咒語回憶起來，誰知他的頭腦早已成了一團亂麻，哪裏能回想得起來！他把那些壓在他肩膀上沉甸甸的袋子都扔在地上，魂不附體地在石窟中來回轉着，一眼也不看一下他周圍的那許多金銀財寶。

將近中午時分，那幫強盜恰好有事，回石窟來了。還沒來到那大岩石，他們先遠遠望見了卡西姆的一羣驢子，驢子背上都裝着一個大箱子。他們知道發生了甚麼情況，立即催馬加鞭，奔馳到石窟。他們趕走了驢子，這羣驢子穿過森林走到很遠，遠得轉眼間就離開了他們的視線。他們手持着軍刀，直走到門前。頭目唸出正確的咒語，門隨即打開。

關在石窟裏邊的卡西姆聽到外邊傳來一陣馬蹄聲，知道一定是那幫強盜來了，他不趕快逃出去就沒命了；所以一看到石門打開，就直衝出去，正好和強盜頭目撞個滿懷。雖然他摔下了頭目，但可憐他始於逃不過其他的大漢。他這條老命就此送在他們的刀鋒底下。

那些大漢先檢查了石窟，找到卡西姆搬到洞口，且準備放在驢子上的所有一袋袋金幣，又把它們搬回原處，並發覺已有好些財寶被人偷盜了。於是他們商量了一番，猜測卡西姆進入石窟後，找不到方法離開，卻想像不到他從哪裏得知開門的咒語。他們決定把卡西姆的屍體宰成四塊，兩塊掛在門左邊，兩塊掛在門右邊，誰膽敢闖進石窟來盜寶，這就是警告！他們做完這事，離開了石窟，又騎馬趕路，去襲擊過路的駱駝商隊了。

到了晚上，卡西姆的老婆還沒看見丈夫回來，她心神不定，奔到阿里巴巴的家裏，説道："好兄弟，你的哥哥一早就到山林裏，他要辦的事你也明白，可現在天已經黑了，還不見回來，我只怕出了甚麼事啦。」

阿里巴巴安慰嫂子不必驚慌，想必哥哥為了避人耳目，準備夜深人靜才進城來。

卡西姆的老婆考慮到丈夫要把行動保持得愈低調愈好，就信服了妹夫所說的話。回家後，她不曾合上眼睛，直至半夜。她又急又悔恨，不該使用心計去刺探弟弟家的私事。她一整晚也在哭泣；第二天一清早，就趕到了阿里巴巴家裏，放聲大哭。

阿里巴巴勸了嫂子一番，帶着他三頭驢子立即出發去找卡西姆。他一路來到石窟附近，既不見人，也不見驢子，卻在石門邊發現了一攤血跡，嚇了他一大跳，這決不是甚麼好兆頭啊。他唸了咒語，跨進石門，第一眼看到的就是掛在兩邊的他哥哥的屍體，叫他心驚膽戰。他讓一頭驢子載着屍體，上面遮蓋了一些木柴，另外兩頭驢子載着從石窟裏取來的好幾袋金幣，上面也蓋着一些木柴。然後，他關上門就離開了。快要走出林子的時候，他就停下步伐，直到天黑以後再繼續趕路回家。來到家中，他把那兩頭運載着金幣的驢子趕到院子中，交給妻子去把筐子卸下來，他自己趕着另一頭驢子到嫂子家去了。

給阿里巴巴開門的是一個聰明懂事、辦事可靠的年輕女奴，名叫莫吉娜。他進入院子，把筐子從驢背上卸下之後，就把莫吉娜拉到一邊，輕聲說道：「我現在跟你說的話，你半個字也不能泄漏出去啊。你主人的屍體就裝在筐子裏，我們一定要把他當作壽終正寢似的安葬入土。這件事就交給你了，相信你一定能辦好。」

阿里巴巴幫忙把屍體放到屋內，再三提醒莫吉娜要妥妥當當地辦好事情，才騎着驢子回去。

翌日清晨，莫吉娜已出現在藥鋪子裏，說是要買一劑給昏迷不醒的病人吃的藥。藥鋪老闆問你家誰得病了。她長歎一聲，說是她的好東家卡西姆病倒了，他水米不進，連說話也不能了。

黃昏時分，她又來到了藥鋪子裏。只見她眼淚汪汪，要藥鋪老闆給凶多吉少的病人服的藥水。

"唉！"她說道，"只怕這瓶藥水不會比昨天那劑藥更有效，可憐的好東家，他這條命只怕難保了。"

再說那天裏，鄰居們只看見阿里巴巴和他的妻子在卡西姆家和他們自己家來回出出進進，忙了一天，又是滿臉愁容。因此，到了晚上，卡西姆家裏傳出了他老婆和莫吉娜的一片哭喊聲，誰也不感到奇怪。莫吉娜逢人便說："想不到她主人竟一病不起！"第二天一大清早，莫吉娜就趕到一個叫做姆達法的皮匠那裏，向他問了聲好，塞了一個金幣在他手裏，說道："巴巴姆達法，請你快收拾你的鑽子針線，跟着我走；可是我得先跟你講明了瞭，我得把你的眼睛蒙起來，才能把你領到一個地方去。"

那老皮匠聽了這話，不免有些猶豫，"哎呀，"他回答道，"你這是要我做甚麼違背良心的事嗎？要我以後見不得人嗎？"

"罪過啊！真主不容許我要你做見不得人的事！"那女子說道，一邊又塞了一個金幣在他手裏，"你儘管放心好了，快跟着我走吧。"

說完，莫吉娜掏出手帕，把皮匠的雙眼蒙住了，讓他跟着她來到主人家裏。接着她又引着皮匠進入了停放東家屍體的房裏（她早已把四塊屍體拼湊在一起），這才給那皮匠解開手帕，說道："巴巴姆達法，你快些把這四塊屍體縫在一起，等做完了，我再給你一塊金幣。"

皮匠做完了事，她又蒙上他的雙眼，當真又給了他一枚金幣，同時叮囑他這件事千萬不能跟別人說起；於是領着他走了好一程路，來到了剛才蒙起他眼睛的地方，莫吉娜這才解下手帕，放他自己回去。這女子怕他會在她後面偷偷盯梢，所以看着他一路往皮匠攤走去，直到望不見了，這才放心回家。

莫吉娜回家後用熱水洗乾淨屍體，同時阿里巴巴燃點了香，再以傳統儀式給屍身穿上葬禮衣服，這樣就可以準備出殯、落葬了。出殯的時候，莫吉娜從清真寺請來了阿訇和助手。四個鄰居扛着棺材走在前面，後面跟隨着阿訇，一路上唸着經文。莫吉娜是死者的奴隸，戴着頭巾，跟在阿訇的後面，她一邊走一邊哭，淚流滿面。在這支隊伍最後面的是阿里巴巴，由一些鄰居陪同着。卡西姆的寡婦則留在家中，左鄰右舍的婦人們按照當地的風俗，陪着她一起哭泣，一時間這周圍一帶只聽得一片哭泣聲，好不傷心。

卡西姆死於非命這件慘事就這麼瞞過了人們的耳目，只有阿里巴巴、卡西姆的寡婦和莫吉娜知道真相。如此多的妙計，城內的人不但毫不知情，而且沒有起一絲疑心。三四天後，阿里巴巴在大白天把自己家裏的東西往嫂子家搬，到了夜深人靜，才悄悄地把從石窟裏取得的金幣運到她家裏。他做好住過去的準備，於是公開宣佈和嫂子結婚。這在當時本是很通常的事，而且先前已說好，所以並沒引起別人的議論。至於卡西姆的店鋪，他交給自己的長子打理。

又過了幾天，那幫強盜回到了他們在山林裏的石窟。他們跨進石門就大吃一驚，掛在兩邊的屍體已不見了，接着又發現少了幾個裝金子的麻袋。那頭目說道："我們的祕密被人發現了。屍體移走了，金子不見了，這顯然說明我們殺的那個人有同謀。要是我們不把那個人查出來幹掉他，那麼我們積聚起來的這麼多金銀財寶就保不住了。你們覺得呢，我的小伙子？"

他手下的那一幫強盜都認為這番話說得太對了。

"要查出那個人是誰、住在哪裏，"頭目接下去說道，"唯一的辦法是派你們當中最有膽識和最機靈的人到市鎮上去，假扮成旅客和外地人，打聽一下城裏有沒有談論我們殺的那個人。事關重大，為免被人欺騙，我把話說清楚，誰要是出去打聽卻一無結果，即使只是判斷錯誤，那是不能輕易便宜他，甚至要他的性命。"

有一個強盜當場霍地站起身來，說道："我此去如果打聽不出甚麼來，那麼我甘願聽候處罰。為了我們大夥的事，我豁出自己的一條命，我認為這是給自己的臉上增添了光彩。"

那頭目和那許多強盜都稱讚他是一條好漢，於是那個強盜化裝了一番，讓人再也認不出他來，就出發了。他來到城鎮，東走西逛，留心觀看。無意之間來到了皮匠攤，那裏總是比任何店鋪早營業。

那老皮匠坐在一條長凳上，手拿着一把鑽子，正要動手做事。那強盜上前去和他打個招呼，看見他已上了年紀，就說道："老人家，你一早就做事了嗎？像你這樣的年紀，眼力還是那麼好嗎？現在光線又不怎麼好，你照樣能補補縫縫嗎？"

"別說了，"老皮匠回答道，"即使年紀大，但視力好得不得了。前幾天我在一個人家把幾塊屍體縫合在一起，光線比現在還暗呢。"

"幾塊屍體！"那強盜故意大驚小怪地叫了起來。"你是說把幾塊裹屍布縫合在一起吧？"

"不是裹屍布，是這麼回事，"老皮匠說道，"可是這回事我一句也不能跟你多說甚麼。"

"說實話，"那強盜說道，"我並不想打聽你的祕密，不過我倒是很想去看看那幢房屋——就是把你叫去做那稀奇事情的那個人家。"說罷，他塞給了老皮匠一個金幣，這樣，他的話對方就聽進去了。

"就算我願意討個好，照你的話去做，"老皮匠說道，"我也辦不到呀。我一路上去，一路下來，都是被人蒙住眼睛，領着走的呀。"

"好吧，"那強盜說道，"你被人蒙住眼睛領着走的時候，也許多少還記得一些路程吧。這樣吧，讓我就在同一個地方把你的眼睛紮起，然後我跟着你，兩個人一起走。俗話說，皇帝不差餓兵，我這裏再給你一個金幣，你就照我的話去做吧。"

這兩枚金幣對老皮匠可真有些力量，把老皮匠的心打動了。他看了很久手上的金幣，不發一語，最後掏出錢包，把它們放進去。

他說道："不知道我還記不記得那段路程，不過既然你來求我，我就盡我的力試一下吧。"

說罷，老皮匠站起身來，把強盜引到莫吉娜原來蒙上他的眼睛的地方。

"我就是在這裏給蒙住了雙眼，於是我的臉轉向這一個方向，"他說道。

那強盜已準備好一條手帕，蒙住他的眼睛，於是一半是跟着他，一半是領着他，一起走去，直到老皮匠停下腳步。他正好停在卡西姆的住宅面前，現在是阿里巴巴在當家。那強盜先用手裏的粉筆在那個人家悄悄地畫了個記號，然後再替那皮匠解去手帕；於是又問他，這是誰家的宅子。那老皮匠回說，他不是這裏附近的居民，所以說不上來。

那強盜覺得從老皮匠那裏再打聽不出甚麼來，就謝過了他出的力，放他回皮匠攤去了。那強盜自己則回山林去，滿以為他已立下了大功呢。

強盜和老皮匠走了不多一會之後，莫吉娜有事從家裏外出，她回來的時候看到了強盜在門上所做的記號。

她站定了想道：這個記號有甚麼用意呢？莫非有人要謀算我家主人嗎？不管是好是壞，反正防備一着總是不錯的。

於是她也拿了一支粉筆，在東邊兩三家門上、西邊兩三家門上都照式照樣畫了一個記號，卻不在主人和女主人面前提起有這回事。

那強盜辦了這事，立即趕回去向頭目報告，他已經查訪到了那個人家；於是當場決定大夥兒悄悄進城去，伺候機會，下手殺死他們的仇人。誰知來到那裏，那個充作嚮導的強盜傻了眼，只見一排並列着好幾家房屋，家家門上都畫了同一個記號。他再也認不出自己的記號畫在哪一家門上了。

"去他媽的，"強盜頭目說，"這事辦得糟透了，我們只好回頭走，白來這一次。你別給我活在這世上了。"他們回到了大本營後，馬上幹掉了那個不稱職的嚮導。

強盜中又有一個自願到市鎮上去走一趟。他也同樣由老皮匠領路，來到了卡西姆的家門口，他比上一個強盜做事仔細，用紅粉筆揀門上不會被人注意到的地方畫了一個記號，於是趕回去報信了。

可是莫吉娜的眼睛十分尖利，那個記號並沒能逃過她的注意；於是她又像上一次那樣，在鄰居家門上畫了同樣的記號。

強盜回到大夥兒那裏後，稱讚自己所採取的方法，認為這是區分阿里巴巴的住宅與其他房屋的可靠方式；頭目和所有人都認為這次必定會成功。但是，當他們進城後，強盜和頭目走在街頭時，卻遇上同樣的困難。頭目被激怒了，那個強盜則感到非常困惑。

那一幫強盜第二次進城又失敗了，這一回更把那強盜頭目氣壞了，他下令把那第二個嚮導押回去，進入了山林，立即把他幹掉了。

那強盜頭目眼看費了這許多周折，又殺了兩個部下，事情卻一無進展，心中很是焦急，決定親自去走一趟。

他也由那個老皮匠領路，來到卡西姆家門口。這一回他並不做甚麼記號，只是在宅子前來回轉着，直到他把周圍的環境都記住在心裏，這才趕回山林。

他十分滿意這回的行動，掌握了想知道的事情，回到樹林去。他手下的那幫強盜都聚在石窟裏盼望他。他一跨進石窟就宣佈："伙計們，這一回我們的仇人逃不了啦！"

於是他把自己打定的主意說了一遍，大夥兒都說這主意好，就聽從他的吩咐，到各處村子裏買了十九頭驢子，三十八個很大的罐子，有一壇盛滿了油，其餘都是空的。

他們忙了兩三天，一切準備就緒，於是十九頭驢子馱着一個裝滿罐油的罐子和三十七個各自躲進一個強盜的罐子，由強盜頭子帶領，一起出發。他們進入市鎮，天色正好暗下來了。那頭目趕着一隊驢子，穿過大街小巷，來到了阿里巴巴家的門口。他本想叩門找主人說話，恰好阿里巴巴吃罷晚飯，正坐在門口散散心。那強盜頭目讓他的一隊驢子停了下來，上前說道：“我是一個油商，這許多油都是我從老遠的地方販運來的，準備明天拿到市場去出賣。現在天色已晚，我在這裏人地生疏，不知哪裏可以住宿，請問是否可以就讓我在府上耽擱一夜，那我是感激不盡了。”

雖然阿里巴巴原是在樹上看到過這個強盜頭目，但是這時卻沒有認出他來，竟說歡迎歡迎，讓他和他的一隊驢子進入了他的宅子。同一時間，當驢子卸下時，阿里巴巴還叫來僕人，以安置牠們在馬廄，餵飼牠們。他又吩咐莫吉娜準備晚飯，款待這位過路的商人。

他們吃完晚飯後，阿里巴巴向莫吉娜說：“明天一早我會去洗澡，你去準備我的浴巾，交給阿大拉（那是奴隸的名字），並在我回來時烹煮好肉羹。”之後，他就上牀睡覺。

與此同時，這強盜頭目去察看一下他那些罐子，悄悄來到院子裏，從這一個壇走到那一個壇，跟躲在裏面的強盜一個個都說了話：“一聽到我從窗內扔出石子來，你們馬上一齊從壇裏爬出來，我很快就趕來和你們集合在一起。”

這樣關照之後，他就回到自己的房裏，隨即把燈火吹滅了，以免引人注目。他和衣而睡，這樣就隨時可以行動。

這時候莫吉娜正在爐灶邊準備第二天的早飯，恰好燈油燒光了，宅子裏既沒有多餘的油，也沒有蠟燭，莫吉娜不知怎麼辦才好；可是肉羹是非燒好不可的。阿大拉看她為此發愁，說道："別急，你到院子裏去，那裏有好多罐子，都裝滿了油，你只消拿一點出來就夠用了。"

莫吉娜感謝他出了個好主意，於是拿着一個油瓶，到院子裏去了。她走近第一個罐子時，只聽見裏邊有人悄悄地問："時間到了嗎？"

如果不是莫吉娜，換了別的女奴，忽然發現罐子裏裝的不是油，是人，一定會嚇得大聲直叫起來，那後果就不堪設想了。可是莫吉娜不是尋常的女奴可比，她知道在這一緊急關頭，必須保持冷靜的頭腦，要是不趕快拿出對付的辦法，只怕阿里巴巴一家，以及她自己，就要大禍臨頭了。於是她從一個罐子走到另一個罐子，壓低着嗓子，一一回答他們的問話："時間還沒到，不過快了。"直至來到了當真是裝油的罐子。

就這樣，莫吉娜發現主人引了三十八個強盜到屋來，而假裝成油商的人是他們的頭目。她趕緊把油灌滿了自己的油壺，急忙回到廚房，點亮了燈盞，拿起一隻大油壺，再趕到院子裏，用罐子裏的油灌滿了大油壺，在灶膛裏生起熊熊烈火。一等到油燒得沸滾，就悄悄來到院子裏，把熱油往一個個罐子裏灌，躲在裏邊的三十七個強盜就這樣被她一個個都消滅了。

莫吉娜真是個又勇敢又機智的女子，她神不知鬼不覺地做完了這件了不起的事，就提着一個空壺回廚房去了。她熄滅了燒得好旺的烈火，只留下一點小火熬肉羹。她把燈也吹滅了，但不去睡覺，只是靜悄悄地在開向院子的窗邊守望着，看有甚麼動靜。

她在窗邊守候了沒有多少時候，那邊強盜頭目行動起來了。他打開窗戶，看不見光，聽不到聲音，發現屋內沒有人醒着，於是扔了一塊石子到院子中，等待了一會，卻不見一點動靜。他又扔了一塊石子，再扔一塊，卻仍不見反響。他這一下子慌了，趕緊溜出房外，來到院子中。他在每一個罐子裏發現一個屍體，在最後那一個油罐子裏又發現已沒有油了，於是他猜想到他手下的那幫弟兄是怎樣死於非命的。他的復仇計劃徹底完蛋了，真叫他氣壞了。可是咬牙切齒也沒用，他無可奈何，只得撬開了院門的鎖，衝進花園，翻過園牆，逃命去了。

莫吉娜在窗邊看得一清二楚，她打敗了那幫強盜，保衛了主人的家，心裏十分高興，於是她上牀睡覺去了。

第二天，阿里巴巴一早起身，洗澡去了，後面跟着一個奴僕，家裏發生了甚麼事他還一點不知道呢。

他洗澡回來，太陽已升起了。他看到那許多袋子和驢子都在那裏，那個過路的商人卻獨自走了，感到好不奇怪。於是他問莫吉娜，是誰開的院門，那商人為甚麼一早獨自走了。

"好主人，"她回答道，"願真主保佑你和你一家人吧。你要知道這究竟是怎麼一回事，那只消勞駕跟我走一趟，我有東西給你看，那時你就會完全明白了。"

阿里巴巴於是跟着莫吉娜來到了院子。她請主人先看看第一個罐子裏邊是否裝着油。阿里巴巴往裏邊一望，只見蜷縮着一個人，嚇得倒退一步，失聲叫了起來。

「不必害怕，」莫吉娜說，「你看到的這個傢伙既不會傷害你，也不會傷害別人。他已經死了。」

「哎呀，莫吉娜！」阿里巴巴嚷道，「你要我看的就是這個嗎？快告訴我吧，這究竟是怎麼一回事？」

「我這就說，」莫吉娜回答道，「你不要嚇成這樣，千萬不能讓左鄰右舍聽到甚麼風聲。事關重大，一定要保守祕密！其餘那些罐子你也一一都查看一下吧。」

於是阿里巴巴一隻罐子又一隻罐子看過去，最後來到了那裝油的罐子，卻看到那個罐子裏面沒有油，而是空空如也；他一動不動地站在那裏，只是一會看看那些個罐子，一會看看莫吉娜，害怕得一句話都說不出來。

最後，他總算鎮靜了一些，就問莫吉娜：「那麼那個商人又怎麼樣了呢？」

「商人！」莫吉娜回答道，「我正要告訴你：他究竟是甚麼人，他又怎麼樣了。」於是她把事情的經過前前後後地，從門上做暗號直到那三十七個強盜在罐子裏送了命，全都說了一遍。

阿里巴巴這才知道，原來莫吉娜做了那麼多事，他感動極了，嚷道：「是你救了我的性命，我要報答你，給你自由，你不再是奴隸了——但是這個還不夠，我還要酬謝你。」

於是阿里巴巴帶着奴隸阿大拉在花園盡頭掘了一條又深又長的溝，把那許多強盜全埋了。接着又把那許多袋子、鋼刀藏了起來；後來阿里巴巴又設法把那許多驢子陸續賣掉了。

再說那強盜頭目，獨自一人逃回了山林，好不淒涼，他簡直害怕踏進那石窟，因為處處叫他觸景生情。可是他發誓此仇必報，決不跟阿里巴巴善罷甘休，因此一計不成又想出了一計。他返回城鎮，找了個地方住宿，扮成一個絲綢商，逐漸將各式各樣的貨物和細麻布從石窟運送到住所，且用盡一切必要的方法掩飾這些物品運來的地方。他在卡西姆的店鋪（阿里巴巴的兒子在叔叔死後就住在那裏）的對面租了一個鋪位，運來了不少上好的絲綢，以整理好這些商品。

他改名換姓，自稱"柯吉亞・霍沙英"。身為新來者，他按照習俗，對鄰近的所有商人都極為客氣和殷勤。阿里巴巴的兒子是第一個和他交談的人，柯吉亞・霍沙英着力嘗試與他熟起來。他搬來後的兩三天，阿里巴巴來見他的兒子，強盜頭目立即認出了他，很快就弄清楚對面那個小伙子是誰家的兒子。自此，就存心和他結交，經常送他禮物，請他吃飯，想方設法地討好他。

阿里巴巴的兒子想到人家待他這麼殷勤，很過意不去，便去對父親說，要父親準備酒席，回請那絲綢商。

阿里巴巴非常樂意請客，當即答應了。他說道："兒子，明天是星期五，這一天，像柯吉亞・霍沙英這樣的大商人和你自己的商店都關門，那麼請你陪同他來我家造訪。我會吩咐莫吉娜準備晚餐。"

到了第二天，阿里巴巴的兒子陪同柯吉亞・霍沙英來赴宴。說也奇怪，那強盜頭目來到阿里巴巴的家門口，報仇雪恨的機會終於來到了，他心裏卻退縮起來，想要轉身便走。可是這時候阿里巴巴從裏面出來迎客了，他向那個絲綢商表示感謝，承蒙他這麼厚愛自己的兒子，因此特地設宴招待，務必請他賞光。

"大爺，"柯吉亞‧霍沙英回答説，"我十分樂意，可惜我起過誓，不吃放了鹽的東西[1]。在這種情況下，我怎麼能到府上來吃飯呢。"

"如果只為了這個緣故，請別為這事操心，"阿里巴巴回答道，"首先，我的麵包沒有放鹽。至於我們今晚將要吃的餚菜，我會去關照廚子，燒菜時不要放鹽。所以，請你一定要留下來，我去去就回來。"

阿里巴巴果真來到廚房，命令莫吉娜不要在當晚的餚菜下鹽，並趕快多做兩三碟蔬菜燉肉片，確保裏面不放鹽。

莫吉娜總是遵從主人的命令，但聽到這樣奇怪的要求，覺得很詫異。

她問道："這個不吃鹽的奇怪人是誰？你的晚飯放這麼久，都要變壞了。"

"別生氣，莫吉娜。"阿里巴巴回答，"他是一個誠實的人，因此按我的要求行事吧。"

莫吉娜勉強服從，儘管有些不情願。她很想去看看那個不肯吃鹽的奇怪人；因此，她幫阿大拉把一道道菜送到酒席上，一眼就認出了柯吉亞‧霍沙英就是那個強盜頭目，即使他喬裝起來。她仔細地打量他，察覺到他的衣服底下藏有匕首。

"我絲毫沒有感到驚訝，"她對自己説，"這個壞人是主人的最大敵人。他當然不吃鹽，因為他打算暗殺他；但是我會阻止他的。"

那強盜分明來意不善，眼看阿里巴巴一家又要大禍臨頭，莫吉娜決心再一次從危險中救出主人。她想出了一個大膽果斷的主意，好不讓壞人陰謀得逞。當阿大拉把水果甜品端上餐桌，將它與酒和玻璃杯放在阿里巴巴面前之後，莫吉娜就回到自己的房裏，換了一身舞女的服裝，戴上一個很漂亮的面罩，腰際又束了一條鍍銀的帶子，在腰帶裏暗暗插了一把尖刀。她打扮妥當後，走出房間對阿大拉說：“你去把手鼓拿來，我們兩個好給主人和賓客助興。”

於是阿大拉一路上打着手鼓，引領着莫吉娜來到大廳。莫吉娜踏進大廳，就在門口恭恭敬敬地行了個禮，請求主人容許她為今晚的宴會跳舞助興。

“來吧，莫吉娜，”阿里巴巴說，“讓柯吉亞‧霍沙英看看你能做甚麼，以便他告訴我們他對你的表現有何看法。”

莫吉娜得到賓主的同意，就翩翩起舞了。阿大拉在旁邊打着手鼓配合，還唱着歌。柯吉亞‧霍沙英眼看着那個舞女只是在他面前轉來轉去，心中在嘀咕：只怕動手報仇雪恨的大好機會被耽誤了。可是，他希望，要是現在錯過了目標，就藉此機會與父子二人保持友好的來往，以便下次實現目標。因此，儘管他本來希望阿里巴巴拒絕觀看跳舞，但他假裝熱切期待表演，順着主人的心意，大大讚賞舞蹈，這叫主人稱心滿意。

莫吉娜表演了幾套舞蹈，動作、身段又輕捷又優美，後來她從腰際拔出刀子來，只見她越跳越興奮，越轉越快，一會揚起尖刀，好像在自衛，一會刀尖對準自己的胸口，好像要直刺下去似的，真使人眼花繚亂。最後，她從阿大拉手裏奪過手鼓來，一手拿刀，一手把小鼓翻過來，就像那些賣藝人向周圍看客討賞錢那樣，把翻轉的手鼓伸向了阿里巴巴。

阿里巴巴在手鼓裏放進了一枚金幣,他的兒子也同樣放進了一枚金幣。於是莫吉娜來到了貴賓的面前。柯吉亞‧霍沙英從懷裏掏出一個錢袋,他正要把錢袋投進手鼓裏,莫吉娜眼明手快,就在這時,舉起拿在右手的尖刀,一刀子猛扎下去,直刺進對方的胸膛,那刀尖埋得很深,這倒霉的傢伙當場死去。

阿里巴巴和他的兒子看到此情此景,嚇得目瞪口呆。

過了一會,父子兩人大聲嚷道:"該死的賤丫頭!你這是做甚麼?你是要毀了我,毀了我們一家嗎?"

"不是要毀了你,是為了要救你!你自己瞧吧,"莫吉娜說着,解開了那個自稱絲綢商人的外衣,果然裏邊藏着一把尖刀,"你設宴招待的是甚麼貴賓呀?你請來的是敵人!請好好地看看他那張臉吧,你會認出來,他就是那個喬裝改扮的油販子,也就是那四十個強盜的頭目。你沒有忘了吧,他不願意吃你家裏的一粒鹽。你還能說他不是你兇惡的敵人,而是心地善良的客人嗎?在我看見他之前,當你說你有這樣一個賓客,我就懷疑他。我知道是他,你現在明白我的懷疑並非沒有根據。"

阿里巴巴聽了莫吉娜這番話,又看到眼前的光景,頓時明白過來:原來這是莫吉娜再一次救了他的命,不由得感激萬分地說道:"莫吉娜,上一回我給你自由,你不再是我家的女奴了;不過當時我說過,這還不夠,我還要繼續酬謝你。現在我要讓你看到,我說這話是真心誠意的。我準備這樣表示我的感謝:我認你做我的兒媳婦。"

說罷,阿里巴巴又轉過身來跟他兒子說道:"孩子,我選莫吉娜做你的妻子,我相信你不會拒絕吧。那個柯吉亞‧霍沙英巴結你，和你拉關係，他存心不良，想借個機會向我下毒手呀。他殺害了我，也不會放過你，連你也殺了，他才算解了恨，報了仇。你要知道，你娶了莫吉娜為妻，就是娶了我家的救命恩人，也是你的救命恩人為妻呀。"

他的兒子不會違背父親，而且他本來就喜歡莫吉娜，一口答應了這門親事。過了幾天，阿里巴巴就為兒子和莫吉娜舉行盛大的婚禮，辦了豪華的酒席，宴請諸親好友，有跳舞有唱歌，十分熱鬧。獲邀請的朋友和鄰居對婚姻的真正動機一無所知，而且那些不熟悉莫吉娜優秀品格的人稱讚阿里巴巴為人慷慨善良，為此他心滿意足。阿里巴巴很怕四十個強盜中還有兩名還活在世上，所以整整一年，沒有敢走近那石窟。

可是一年過去了，那兩個強盜始終不露面，從不曾來找他麻煩；於是阿里巴巴來到石窟前面，唸了開門的咒語"芝麻芝麻，把門打開"，走進石窟，那裏並沒有一點跡象表明最近有人來過。這時候阿里巴巴知道，他是世上唯一掌握這石窟祕密的人。他心裏的高興可想而知，他的運氣真是太好了。他騎馬回城的時候，從那取之不盡的寶窟裏拿走了儘可能多的金銀財寶。後來阿里巴巴把兒子帶到了石窟裏，把那祕密交給了他，他又把這個祕密傳給了他的後代。阿里巴巴的子孫都很珍惜他們的好運氣，從不驕奢淫逸，所以他們這一族始終繁榮昌盛，受到人們的尊敬。

2

阿拉丁與神燈

當年有個破落的裁縫名叫馬斯塔斯，在中國的一個繁華大省城居家過日子。他有妻有兒，一家三口，但他很窮，每日的勞動工作只能勉強支撐他自己和家庭的生活。

他的獨子取名阿拉丁，是個粗心懶散的小傢伙。他不聽父母話，一大清早就出門，整天和同齡的淘氣鬼在街頭和公眾地方嬉戲玩耍。

阿拉丁長大得可以學門像樣的手藝時，他父親把他帶到自家店鋪，教他拿起了針線。但是，父親把他留下來工作的心力全是徒勞的。他爹才走出鋪子或是剛招呼主顧，他就跑到那些歇腳的園林裏去找不三不四的小傢伙。馬斯塔斯訓斥他，但阿拉丁就這麼吊兒郎當，不聽管教，他爹眼睜睜看着他走下坡路，心裏好不難過，幾個月後終於得病歸天了。

這一下阿拉丁可不用再害怕老父了，這個小流氓變得無法無天，想怎麼就怎麼，一天天學壞。他沒日沒夜地蕩在外面，只有吃飯才回家。混來混去不覺到了十五歲。一天，他和一班豬朋狗友正在街頭玩耍，一位過路的出家人停住腳步，上上下下打量起阿拉丁。

這出家人是位神巫，從非洲遠道而來，他能猜會算，神通廣大，他的魔力可拔移高山，以山推山。

端詳一番之後，他喃喃自語："我需要的正是這後生子；為了尋找他，我才離鄉背井。"他把另一個小鬼拉到一邊，打聽阿拉丁的姓名，他爹是誰，生活過得怎麼樣。他把阿拉丁家中的底細摸得一清二楚，於是走到小傢伙面前，領着他從那夥人裏走開。他問道："我說孩子啊，你可是那裁縫馬斯塔斯的兒子？"

"是啊，大人，"阿拉丁回了話，"可我爹早就不在了。"

一聞此言，非洲人便雙手摟着阿拉丁的脖子，一個勁地親吻着他，兩汪眼淚直往下流，說道："我是你叔叔，你值得尊敬的父親是我的親兄弟。我一眼看到你，馬上就認出了你，你這神氣明擺着是我兄弟的兒子。"

話音剛落，他便從錢包裏掏出十來塊碎金送給阿拉丁，問了問他母親的住處。後生子比劃着把他家的地段告訴了他，神巫聽罷便説："這點小意思交給你媽，並向她請安。對她説你叔叔回鄉了，天主保佑的話，我明天去看望她。就説我想會會她，看看我兄弟在世時的光景，還要到他的墳上去看看。"

得了十文小錢，阿拉丁好不快活，直奔回家去見母親。

"娘，"他嚷嚷開了，"兒有喜事相告。我是不是有個叔叔？他走江湖回來了，囑咐我給您請安。"

"你莫是在尋娘的開心吧，孩兒？"那婦人發話了，"他是哪一門的叔伯啊？你從哪輩子起有了個叔叔呀？"

"你怎麼能説我沒有叔叔伯伯活在世上？"阿拉丁頂嘴了，"那人正是我爹的兄弟。他又是抱我，又是親我。一聽到我爹已經歸天便號啕大哭起來。他親口叮囑我把他回鄉的消息稟告你呢。"

"這話對了，孩兒，"母親接着話茬道，"你是有過一個叔叔。可他去世了，再沒聽説過甚麽別的叔伯。"

次日一早，摩爾神巫就離開下處，在大街小巷東走西轉，尋那阿拉丁的行蹤，真是眼皮底下一刻也離不開人影。不一會發現他和那羣頑童正在街頭玩耍，神巫三步併作兩步，走到跟前摟着親了親他，又給了兩枚銀幣。

"快去交給你媽。勞她弄點晚飯，就説叔叔今晚要去做客。再指給我看一遍，上你家該怎麼走。"

"歡迎光臨，大人，"阿拉丁回過話，指明了路，便拿着錢回到母親那裏。

"叔叔要來吃飯，"他轉告母親。

母親連忙來到街市，大包小包的食品酒菜買了好些。又向左鄰右舍央借了盤盤罐罐，開始燒鍋做飯。天色一暗她便對阿拉丁説："飯菜備齊了，兒啊，沒准你叔叔摸不清路。出去瞧瞧，要是碰見了就給他帶路。"

阿拉丁正待去接叔叔，傳來了敲門聲。他跑去開門，摩爾神巫已站在門檻，旁邊的腳夫拎着沉甸甸的瓜果禮酒。阿拉丁領他進了屋裏。摩爾人打發了腳夫之後，便向老婦打恭作揖，眼淚汪汪地懇求她把丈夫生前坐慣的地方指給他看看。阿拉丁的母親就手一指，他頓時雙腿屈跪，連連磕頭。

"天可憐見，兄弟啊！我的手足，"他哭哭啼啼道。"喪兄之痛怎麼能彌補啊！"他就這般長吁短歎地哀哭不已，直到寡婦確信了他真的是老叔爺。後來見他傷心得死去活來，便輕輕扶他站起來，哭泣道："你別哭了，我説叔爺。要不然會傷了身子的！"

她拿好言好語勸他，讓他坐下。三人坐定之後，摩爾人開口了。

"我的好嫂子，您莫見怪，兄弟活着的時候您竟沒見過我，互不相識。掐指算來，自我出門漂泊遠方，已有四十個年頭了。我跑遍了印度、波斯，還有阿拉伯；又去了埃及，在開羅小住了一陣子，那裏可是天下的奇觀。末了我長途跋涉走到摩洛哥的內地，一落戶便是三十個春秋。有一天我枯坐半晌，胡思亂想開了，牽掛起家鄉兄弟。思念之情難以自禁，想起身在離家萬里之外的異鄉，不免叫人心碎。無時無刻不在惦記他，這才橫下心來不顧路途遙遠，返回故里。我常自言自語，我這人命苦。離鄉背井，從唯一的兄弟身邊跑開，要流落到何年哪月啊？乘真主還沒把我招去，拿定主意去找兄弟吧！誰能保得住不出意外？禍福無常啊！要是合眼以前不能再見上兄一面，那才真是太痛心了。說不定他還沒米下鍋哩。謝天謝地，我算是富起來了。走吧，看看兄弟。他落難時幫上一把。

"這麼一想，我便興沖沖地打點行裝準備上路。唸完《古蘭經》開頭的幾節經文，我就騎馬出發了。途中吃盡苦頭，歷經艱險，托真主的福，我總算回到老家了。這些都不去提它了。前天我在街上轉悠，正巧看見阿拉丁和小朋友們戲耍。我認出是姪兒，高興得心裏怦怦直跳，一肚子心事全都忘光。不想他卻告訴我可憐的兄弟早已歸天，我傷心得差點昏過去。當時我的悲痛他大概對你說了。還有阿拉丁這麼個姪兒，可以寬寬我的心。常言說得不錯：有了兒女就是死了還活在人間。"

這一番話勾起老婦對往事的回憶，不免又要淚水汪汪，摩爾神巫一見此情，便把話頭一轉，面向阿拉丁，心想這下可得手了。

"孩兒，你可學得手藝了？"他問道，"阿拉丁，你做甚麼工作來養活你母子兩口呢？"

阿拉丁腦袋一耷拉，做娘的便代他回話："唉，就別過問阿拉丁學手藝的事吧！老天爺啊，他真不懂事。我還沒見過比他更不中用的孩子。一天到晚跟着街頭的二流子遊手好閒。就是他把老子活活氣死了，我也快去了。我無日無夜地圍着紡車拼命地幹，掙得兩個飯錢。我說叔爺，當着你的面，我是不說瞎話的，他只有吃飯才進屋，別的時間連個影兒也不見。我早就想着把他攆出家門，讓他自己去找飯吃。我上了年歲，沒有氣力折騰自己，老想着卻是做不到。"

"這哪像話，姪兒，"摩爾人朝着阿拉丁數落開了，"你這樣放肆下去不走正道，就不怕人恥笑嗎？像你這般聰明伶俐、體面人家出來的後生可不許學壞啊！叫老人家做生活來供養你，旁人會說話的。你長大了，可以自謀生路了。感謝真主，家鄉出了不少能工巧匠。想學哪一行就認準了，我會幫襯你的。來日你成人了就有本事吃飯了。你若是不愛你爹的手藝，喜歡學哪一門，拿定了主意，我會盡力幫忙的。"

阿拉丁並沒接嘴，摩爾人肚裏明白他還是貪玩，便又說道："別慪氣了，好姪兒。你要是不肯學手藝，也沒有甚麼關係。我給你開個門面，備齊了呢絨綢緞，過不多久就會成為城裏有名的生意人了。"

聽到這裏，阿拉丁笑逐顏開：眼看自己就要當上衣冠楚楚的商人了。他對摩爾人笑嘻嘻地點頭同意了這個主意。

「既然我説的合你的意，姪兒，你想經商，自己開爿店，好吧，像個男子漢的樣子，身價變了，搞出點名堂來。明天我帶你上街，買套掌櫃的漂亮衣服。然後再為你找個合適的店鋪。」

這門親眷剛剛相認便出手大方，阿拉丁的母親不免另眼看待，真心實意地連聲道謝，叮嚀兒子再不要遊手好閒，凡事多聽叔叔的話。説完便端上美酒佳餚；三人邊吃邊喝，摩爾人和阿拉丁聊起了生意經。此時夜色深沉了，摩爾人説好次日清早再來，便告辭回去歇宿了。

當夜那阿拉丁樂得合不上眼。天一亮便有人敲門，老婦人起身應門，看見來領兒子的摩爾人正站在外邊。阿拉丁忙不迭快步迎客，向他叔叔請安，吻他的手背。這出家人牽着他的手一起逛街市去了。兩人踏進一家款式齊備的衣店，要看一身考究的衣服。店老大取來了幾件華麗的外裝，摩爾人讓阿拉丁挑一套自己頂中意的。一見叔叔如此氣派，阿拉丁喜不自禁地選中一套盛裝，摩爾人當下付了賬。他又把阿拉丁帶入澡堂，兩人洗洗身子精神一爽，阿拉丁穿上新衣瞧着自己儀表堂堂的時行打扮，心裏美滋滋的。他喜上眉梢，連連吻着叔叔的手背，感激叔叔解囊相助。

説話間，摩爾人已把阿拉丁領到買賣興隆的去處，讓他看看經商人家在店裏做生意的門道。

「我説姪兒，你就要當店老大了，和這班掌櫃的一樣身份。此地你要勤走動、跟他們混熟才好。」

他將城中繁華之處、朱門樓閣、廟宇寺院一一指點告訴阿拉丁，晌午時分又請他進了飯莊，這裏上菜的盤碟一應俱是銀器。

兩人大吃大喝，不覺已經酒酣飯飽。摩爾人帶着阿拉丁觀光蘇丹的廳殿和附近一帶的園林。過後又來到他下榻的客商旅店，請客吃飯，這樣便可讓大家見見他姪兒的面。

天色一暗，他親自把阿拉丁送回他母親那裏。一眼看到兒子通身老闆氣派，這苦命的婦道人家快活得歡天喜地，她左一聲託福，右一聲託福，實在感恩不盡。

"叔爺啊，"她說道，"你真是好心人，叫我怎麼報答你喲。"

"好嫂子，"摩爾人回話說，"我沒有出力，豈敢承謝。阿拉丁就是我自己的兒子；我本該盡到做父親的責任。不必再為他的將來擔心了。"

"感謝真主，皇天有眼，"老婦驚呼道，"你是有福的人啊，兄弟！看在我這老臉上，你要活到長命百歲，我這沒爹的孩兒才有你的照拂。他呀，還說不定偏偏就服你，變得像個人樣，對得起你一片好意。"

"阿拉丁不是小孩了，"摩爾人說，"他已是懂事的大人了。我一心一意指望他能繼承父業，這樣對您老人家也是個安慰。哦，對了，我只好打聲招呼。明天星期五店家關門，我答應的事情完不成了。開張門面要等到後天。我明天過來帶阿拉丁去城外逛逛花園。他可以結識一些常去那裏的商人和頭面人物。"

說完，摩爾人便回客棧休息去了。

這一宵阿拉丁心花怒放，想着自己運氣來了，好事接二連三地來臨。第二天他早早起牀，一聽見敲門便蹦蹦跳跳地跑去接他叔叔。出家人摟抱着他親了幾下，對他說："乖姪兒，我今兒讓你開開眼界，你自小還沒見到過呢。"

轉眼工夫，他兩人攜手同行，走出城門，遊至茂林修竹亭館峥嶸之處。阿拉丁以前不曾見過這番氣象，走過一座座高大的府宅，高興得直嚷起來。他們信步而至，漸漸離城遠了，都有幾分倦意。於是進了一個美麗的花園，尋了個清澈見底的泉水瀉地好去處，坐下來歇歇腳。四周的黃銅獅像燦爛耀眼，有如金子。摩爾人解開行囊，拿出一包瓜果點心。

"快吃吧，姪兒，你該餓了，"他說。

兩人一起吃了點心，又休息了一會之後，摩爾人便叫阿拉丁站起來，和他往前再走一段。他們走遍了一座座花園，來到郊野，一座大山擋在面前。

"這是上哪一方去，叔叔？"阿拉丁問道，他從來沒走過這麼遠的路，"那些花園都溜達完了，沒甚麼可遊覽的了，只有大山在前。我們回城吧，我走得累壞了。"

"孩子，做個男子漢，"摩爾人開口道，"我想再領你去看看一個林苑，那裏的風光比你剛才看到的更勝一籌。天底下的帝王還拿不出這樣漂亮的花園呢。"

摩爾人為了給阿拉丁解悶，便滔滔不絕地講起奇奇怪怪的各種故事，最後他們來到神巫事先定下的去處。正是要找到此地他才長途跋涉從摩洛哥前往中國。

"我們一路尋訪的就是這塊地方，"摩爾人說，"坐下喘口氣。真主在天，我這就給你看幾件少見的寶貝，凡人俗眼是從未見過的。"

他答應讓小傢伙憩息片刻，過後吩咐道："該起來了，阿拉丁，你去拾些乾樹枝和碎木塊，我們便好生個火。然後你就會看到那稀世奇物，我是為了它才把你帶到這裏的。”

阿拉丁心下納悶，不知叔叔有甚麼主意，一時顧不得疲倦，走進草木叢中去找幹樹枝條。他撿了一大堆，抱至長者跟前。神巫隨即點燃枯枝，等到火光融融的時分，他打開一個隨身帶來的小盒子，從中攝了一把沉香撒入火堆，嘰嘰咕咕唸起咒言。霎時間天空一片昏暗，大地震動起來，在他眼前裂開，露出一塊厚實的雲石，上面放着一個銅環。小傢伙一見此狀渾身戰慄，想拔腿就跑；但是摩爾人如果少了阿拉丁的幫忙就永遠得不到他獵求的東西，便一把抓住他，撩起拳頭往他臉上狠狠搋了一下，差點打落他的牙齒。阿拉丁跟跟蹌蹌直往後退；他失去了知覺，後來摩爾人才用巫術使他清醒過來。

“叔叔，我怎麼啦，要搋你的打？”阿拉丁啜泣着問道。

“不打不成器啊，孩子，”摩爾人口氣溫和地教訓起來。“我既是你叔叔，跟你爹是手足，你就得聽我的。你要是照我的話去做，會比世上皇帝更有錢。現在把我的吩咐聽仔細了。你也看清楚了，我的神力巫術能打開地府之門。在那雲石下面藏着珍寶，除了你，別人休想打開；惟獨你能夠掀起石磐，沿着底下的石階往下走。我的話你照辦，我們就可平分埋在那裏的財富。”

阿拉丁聽着神巫的話驚歡不置，剛才搋的那一拳和撲簌簌的眼淚全拋至腦後了。

“叔叔，告訴我如何行動吧，我一定聽話，”他大聲道。

摩爾人走到他面前親親他。“姪兒，”他說，“我說你比親骨肉還乖。我又無別的親戚，你是我唯一的繼承人。我是為你才辛辛苦苦遠道而來；我最大的心願便是看你成為體面的大富翁。過去，你抓牢那個銅環往上拉。"

"可我力氣不夠，一人拉不起來。叔叔你幫我一下。"

"不行，姪兒，"摩爾人説。"我一插手就一無所獲，前功盡棄。你去試試就知道舉手之勞便可掀起來。對你説了別人移不動，只有靠你。抓牢銅環，拉的時候報出你自己和你父母的名字。"

阿拉丁迸足全身氣力依那神巫的吩咐去拉。石磐居然不費吹灰之力便在他手下移開了；他坐在旁邊看到下面是個地窖，拾級而下便是入口。

"可得留神，阿拉丁，"摩爾人喝道。"我怎麼説你就怎麼做，不可大意。先進洞穴，走到頭便是一座大廳，共分四間。你在每間屋裏會看見四件金製容器和其他黃金白銀財寶。你切莫停下來，當心別碰着容器和牆壁，就連長袍的下擺也不能擦過。要是一碰着，你馬上就變成了黑石頭。走進第四間屋子，你就會發現另一道門，推開便是一座果樹亭亭如蓋的花園。這裏你再報出一家三口的姓名，和進去時一樣。走了五十來步又有一層三十級左右的樓梯，通向一個平台。你在那平台上將找到一盞吊燈。取下來後把燈油倒盡，藏在胸口。別怕弄髒衣服，那燈油原不是日常的燈油。出來的時候可以在樹叢裏轉一圈，愛吃甚麼水果自己儘管摘。"

吩咐完了，摩爾人取下一隻指環戴在阿拉丁的手指上。

"小伙子，這只指環可以祛邪化險，只是我剛才的話你要照辦。堅強些，別猶豫，不要害怕。你現在是大人了，不是小孩了。過一會你就成為大富翁了。"

於是阿拉丁跳進洞穴，他果真發現四間屋子裏各有四件金製容器。他牢記着摩爾人的指點，一步一步躡手躡腳穿過屋子來到花園。又從這裏爬上樓梯走近平台。都是遵照摩爾人的叮囑去做。吊燈到手後他回到花園，這下子才敢停住腳步，望着一片果樹和枝頭小鳥，聽見牠們鳴聲啾啾，像是在歌頌造化。樹上果實纍纍，五色繽紛，有雪白的，鮮紅的，嫩綠的，乳黃的，色彩可豔麗啦。阿拉丁小小年紀，並不知道這些全是珍珠鑽石，紅寶石綠寶石，國王也從未擁有過那麼多的珠寶。他採了一些，只當是並不值錢的彩色玻璃。他就是喜愛它們光彩熠熠，正午的陽光燦爛奪目，可是它們更加明媚耀眼。阿拉丁採了又採，口袋裏塞得鼓鼓囊囊，後來連衣襟裏也裝滿了。到後來他全身沉甸甸的再也放不下了，這才趕緊走出四間屋子，還算細心沒有碰着金製容器。他趕緊爬着樓梯來到了洞口。可是那最後一級偏偏又高，身上太重他爬不動了。

　　“叔叔，”他扯開了嗓門，“把手給我，拉我出來。”

　　“先把那盞燈遞給我，”摩爾人回答道，“你的腰都給壓彎了。”

　　“現在不行呀，”阿拉丁說，“伸手拉我一把吧，我一上來你就拿到燈了。”

　　這神巫一心一意要把那盞燈歸為己有，又急不可待地提出他的要求。阿拉丁呢，全身的東西壓得他動彈不得，掏不出燈，自然沒法子先把燈交出來。阿拉丁磨磨蹭蹭可使摩爾人脾氣上來了，獨吞臟物原是他的本意，這時他大發雷霆，奔向燒得正旺的火堆，又扔了好些沉香，大呼了一聲咒語。那雲石板立刻移合成原樣，大地又將洞穴封閉起來，阿拉丁留在地下出不來了。

　　瞧吧，我起先交代過了，摩爾人其實是生客，根本不是阿拉丁的叔叔。他是從遙遠的摩洛哥內地來到此處的邪惡神巫，這個非洲人精通當地人都聽說的妖術。他自幼便好玩妖術魔法，四十年來他琢磨的就是魔法和占卜，終於有一天他聽說遠在天邊的中國某個城市藏着無數的金銀財寶。連國王也從沒積聚過那麼多財富。他還打聽到其中有盞神燈，誰要是獲得神燈，他的財富和威力便可超過天底下的任何一位君王。不過只有一個本地人方能打開這些寶藏的大門，他就是出身貧寒名叫阿拉丁的小伙子。神巫信以為真，便起程前往中國。雖然路途漫漫，風吹雨打，他還是找着了阿拉丁，到達了這塊埋藏珍寶的地方。可是他白忙了這些日子，於是決計把阿拉丁活活埋葬，這樣一來小傢伙和神燈都休想從地下鑽出來。他的美夢落空之後，他打消了尋寶的念頭，垂頭喪氣地返回非洲。摩爾人就不再細說了。

　　言歸正傳。阿拉丁眼見大地就要把他覆蓋起來，不免發急地大聲呼救，央求叔叔伸手拉他爬出洞穴。他再三呼叫都毫無反應，他明白自己上當了，摩爾人不是他的叔叔。逃出去是完全沒有指望了，他哭哭啼啼地走下石階，底下黑燈瞎火的，他摸着路朝花園走。但是原來靠魔力打開的那扇大門此刻又借着魔力關閉上了。他回到洞口，絕望地癱坐在石階上。他枯坐了三天三夜，點滴未進，最後心想這下活不成了。他又泣不成聲地抽搭起來，祈求真主為他解圍，雙手扭成一團，感到山窮水盡了。這時他冷不防擦動一下指環，那是摩爾人給他的護身符。剎那之間，他的面前出現了一個巨大的漆黑的魔鬼，個子高大猶如所羅門的一個精靈。

"主人，我在此恭候。你的奴僕靜聽吩咐。你想要甚麼請説，誰戴着我主子的指環，我就是誰的奴僕。"

一見神怪出現，阿拉丁心裏驚恐不已。但是想起了摩爾巫士的話，他重新產生了希望，鼓足勇氣。

"你既是指環的奴僕，我就命你把我帶回到地面上去。"

話才脱口，大地便向兩邊裂開，他發現自己正好站在雲石塊的那個位置。他在伸手不見五指的黑暗之中待了幾天，一時受不了刺眼的光線，過了許久才張開雙眼。他環顧四周，竟然看不見洞穴和入口的痕跡，他目瞪口呆了。他已認不出這塊地方，只見巫士的火堆燃盡後的焦灰還在。遠遠望去，城中燈火在一片園林中閃爍發光，他不禁喜悦非常，快步向前。他由衷地感謝真主使他脱險獲救了。

阿拉丁到家時周身無力，又餓又累，兩眼一花，摔倒在母親腳下。老人自兒子離開後一天到晚傷心落淚。現在她手忙腳亂地幫兒子恢復知覺：往他臉上灑水，又把香味撲鼻的草藥拿給他聞。他剛緩過氣來便討吃的東西。

"娘，我可餓壞了，"他説。"弄點吃的吧，我有三天沒吃沒喝了。"

他母親把家裏能找到的吃食都端在他面前，他吃飽喝足之後有點精力了，便訴説起來："知道了吧，娘啊！這自稱是我叔叔的人原來是個摩爾巫士，是個心懷鬼胎的騙子，是個大魔鬼。他滿口應承，不過是想毀了我。他説得動聽，我們都蒙在鼓裏，真不敢想像。娘，你聽我説他都做了些甚麼。"

阿拉丁一五一十從頭到尾把他跟摩爾人的歷險經過告訴母親。

聽完後，阿拉丁母親連連搖頭。"我早該清楚這老混蛋不是你叔叔，他是個偽君子，是個不信真主的人，"她說。"祝福神明吧，是真主把你從他的奸詐、欺騙中解救出來的。"

她輕聲細語地寬慰兒子。阿拉丁已是三宵不曾合上一眼了，這時呼嚕呼嚕酣睡起來。第二天快吃中飯時他才醒來。睜開眼來，他又向母親討吃的。

"嗐，孩子啊！"她歎了口氣說，"連饅頭皮兒也沒了。你昨天把所有的東西都吃完了。先別着急。我紡好了一些棉紗；我這就上街賣掉，得了錢給你買點吃的回來。"

"棉紗先放着吧，娘，"阿拉丁說道，"將帶來的那盞燈拿給我。我去賣掉，管保比您的棉紗值錢。"

阿拉丁的母親取過燈來，看到髒得很，便說："把它洗乾淨擦得光亮些，可以多賣幾個錢。"

她用水攪拌了一把黃沙，慢慢洗擦起來。可她一觸到燈罩，一個兇神惡煞的龐然大物忽然出現在她面前，對她說道："有何吩咐，當家人？我是你的奴僕，也是燈的主人的奴僕：我等都是燈的奴僕。"

老婦初次看見如此模樣的神物，不禁萬分驚恐，不敢作聲；她張口結舌，暈倒在地。阿拉丁曾在帶指環的洞穴裏見過這神怪，這時聽到他和母親說話，連忙奔去相助，從母親手中搶過神燈。

"燈奴，"他發話道，"我肚子空空。弄些個可口的吃食來。"

神怪當下無影無蹤，眨眼之間又從天而降，頭上頂着純銀的貴重托盤，上面裝着十二小碟鮮嫩肴肉，一對銀製酒杯，兩瓶清醇的陳酒，還有雪白的饅頭。他把東西放在阿拉丁面前又隱身而去了。一見母親仍躺在地板上不省人事，阿拉丁便朝她臉上灑着玫瑰露，又給她聞聞濃郁的香水。母親清醒過來之後，他便說："娘，您起來吧。我們坐下來好好享受一頓，這美食是大恩大德的真主為我們準備的。"

阿拉丁母親一見碩大的銀製托盤，大為詫異。"是哪一位慷慨施惠的恩人發覺我們在受窮捱餓呢？"她驚呼道，"難得他這麼好心腸，真是感激不盡！恐怕蘇丹聽說我們落難遭罪，賜來這盤食物吧。"

"娘，"阿拉丁答道，"哪有閒工夫問東問西啊！快起來一起吃吧。已經餓壞了。"母子兩人坐在托盤邊，津津有味地一飽口福。阿拉丁的母親今生今世還沒嘗過這般鮮美的食品，可以端上國王的餐桌了。他們也不知道這只托盤是稀世珍品還是家常雜物，反正是從未看見過的東西。兩人直到吃不下了才停住，還有好些剩餘，足夠他們當晚和明天三頓的飯菜。於是他們站起來洗洗手，又坐着閒聊開了。

"兒啊，"母親說道，"你怎麼對付那神怪的，快講給我聽。感謝真主，好一頓佳餐，我們都已吃飽了，別再找藉口說你肚子叫了。"

於是阿拉丁便把母親暈過去之後所發生的一切訴說一遍。

"絲毫不假，"受了驚的老婦這才發話。"神怪向凡人顯靈，可我卻不曾見過。救你出洞的肯定就是這個神怪。"

"不是的，娘啊，"阿拉丁答道。"又是一個。在你眼前現形的原是那盞燈的神怪。"

"怎麼回事哦，孩子？"她又問道。

"這個神怪模樣不同。另外一個是指環的奴僕；你剛才見到的只服從你手裏拿的那盞燈。"

聽到此處，老人家大驚失色。"兒啊，"她大叫一聲，"你是喝我的奶長大的，所以求你行行好，快扔掉那盞燈和那指環。我害怕極了，再也不敢看到這些神怪。何況跟他們打交道可不是安分守己的事。蒙受真主祝福的先知告誡我們要對神怪加以提防。"

"娘，兒是該多聽你的話，"阿拉丁忙說，"可我捨不得跟這盞燈和這指環分手。您親眼看到，我們餓肚子的時候，多虧這燈出了大力。我走進地洞時，那摩爾騙子並未叫我拿那些金銀財寶，雖說四間屋子堆得滿滿的。這可別忘了。他偏偏就讓我為他拿那盞燈；他一定知道它價值連城。不然的話，他哪會受這份罪，大老遠的從本鄉本土來此尋找它；再說，我不肯交給他，他又為何把我關在地洞裏呢？所以我們得守着這盞燈，好生保管它，有了它，我們再也不會餓肚子缺吃少用了。還有，不可讓街坊看見。那指環呢，我也不能沒有它。若不是它招來神怪，我肯定在地下悶死了，活活死在金銀堆裏。你說我能從手指上取下來嗎？天曉得今後我會碰到甚麼麻煩災難呢？這隻指環準能救我一命。你既然討厭它，我且藏起來，這樣你就再也看不見了。"

"孩子，那好吧，"母親同意了，"你看着辦吧。我可和它們決不扯上關係，更不想再瞧見那副怕人的樣子。"

接着兩天，母子兩人吃着那神怪送來的飯菜。吃完之後，阿拉丁從魔盤裏拿了個菜盤上街去了。到了市場，有個猶太銀匠迎面而來，他比魔王還要狡猾。阿拉丁並不知道那個菜盤是足銀的，便順手給他看貨；銀匠端量一番，忙把小主顧拉到背靜之處，他又裏裏外外看個究竟，結果發現是成色上好的純銀，但他心裏沒底：阿拉丁可知道它是貨真價實的？還是個好糊弄過去的傻蛋？

"少爺，您要甚麼價？"銀匠先問了一句。

"你該清楚它值多少，"阿拉丁回話利落。

一聽對答靈活，銀匠沒了主意要付給他多少。他起初想只給個銅子，又怕阿拉丁興許識貨。後來打算拿出一筆整數，但暗忖說不定阿拉丁並不知道銀盤的價值。末了他從兜裏摸出一個金幣交給阿拉丁。瞧見是塊金子，阿拉丁一把奪來，一溜煙地飛跑而去。銀匠於是明白小孩不知這菜盤值錢，真後悔竟花掉一兩金子。

阿拉丁奔到饅頭店，換了現錢，買些麵點。過後他便跑回家把饅頭和找頭交給母親。

"娘，"他說，"缺甚麼你就去買回來吧。"

母親就上街添置了一些少不了的東西。他們從此不愁吃飯的事了。錢一用光，阿拉丁便到市場賣掉盤子，因此那精明的銀匠老頭低價買下了十二隻菜盤，他本想壓價，可是頭一回既然付了一個金幣，他又生怕那樣的話，小孩會脫手給別人。等到十二隻菜盤全賣掉了，阿拉丁決定出讓那銀製托盤。這只盤子又大又沉，他便把那做銀器生意的老頭找到家中讓他看貨估價。銀匠一見是特大號的便付給他十個金幣，這筆數目足夠母子兩口開銷好些日子哩。

錢一用完，阿拉丁便取出神燈，剛去洗擦，又是那個神怪出現在他面前，說道："主人，要些甚麼請吩咐。我是您的奴僕，誰握着這盞燈，我便是誰的奴僕。"

"快去拿盤食品來，跟你上次送來的東西一樣。我餓了。"

神怪隱形片時，轉眼工夫端着托盤回來了。盤數樣數一件不多，一樣不少。阿拉丁事先打過招呼，他母親離家回避一下，因此不會再和神怪照面。但她回來看見裝滿銀器的托盤，聞到香味撲鼻，頓時歡天喜地，讚不絕口。

"娘，快瞧瞧！"阿拉丁嚷道。"你還讓我把燈扔掉呢。無價之寶啊，看到了吧。"

"真主在上，他將善有善報！"老婦應道。"不過我反正是不想再看到那神怪。"

她和兒子坐定下來又美美地飽餐一頓。沒吃完的剩飯留到次日。菜盤見底了，阿拉丁便拿一隻塞進袍子裏，出去找那老頭準備賣給他。可是說來湊巧，他沿着市場緩緩行走的時候又路過一家店鋪，老闆是個誠實的金匠，心地純良，買賣公平，大家都是知道的。老闆招呼他，把他叫住了。

"後生家，你帶甚麼貨來啦？"他問道。"常見你經過這裏跟一個猶太人談生意。你出手給他幾樣東西，我都看在眼裏了。今天又捎來甚麼打算賣給他吧？他一定發現你容易上鈎啊！你要賣掉甚麼，就拿來看看，我可以向真主擔保，甚麼貨甚麼價，一塊錢也不會少的。"

阿拉丁便遞過盤子，金匠接過手放上秤盤。

"你賣給他的盤子都是這麼大小的嗎？"老人詢問道。

"是啊，"阿拉丁告訴他。

"你得了多少錢？"金匠又問道。

“一隻盤子一個金幣，”阿拉丁實話相告。

“好一個黑心鬼，”金匠失聲叫道，“他就這麼坑害真主的僕人們！後生家，要知道這奸商耍了人還把你當成大笨蛋。這盤子是純銀的，起碼值七十個金幣。若是這個價你願意賣，這些金幣就是你的了。”

金匠如數點清之後，阿拉丁接過金子，感激老人一片好心。到了時候，他又把其餘的菜盤以同樣價格賣給了他。於是阿拉丁和母親的手頭漸漸富裕起來，可他們還是過着小康日子，從不亂花錢講甚麼排場。

阿拉丁眼下不再終日東遊西蕩了，過去的三朋四友也不相往來，成天留在城中市場裏，專和體面人物大小商賈交談。他還走訪金匠和珠寶商店家，一坐半天，察看那首飾買賣。不久他就心裏明瞭，他從寶庫裏帶出來的各色“果實”不是五彩或透明玻璃，而是些勝過國王財產的寶石。他走遍了市場上的首飾鋪子，仔仔細細摸了底，發現那些寶石還比不上他手頭最不起眼的。這下他就時常出入首飾店，想和那些人熟悉熟悉，從中打聽行情。怎麼買進怎麼出脫，進出價格多少，他都問得一清二楚，天長日久他就有譜了，甚麼首飾便宜，甚麼首飾昂貴。

一日他偶然上市去看首飾，半路聽見大街小巷都在傳命：“當朝皇帝陛下降旨：傳喻全體臣民關閉店門，在家回避。巴德爾·阿·菩德公主，蘇丹之女，是日欲赴浴場。無視此令者格殺勿論。”

一聞頒發此令，阿拉丁情不自禁地極想一睹蘇丹女兒的儀容，原來老老少少無不稱她婀娜多姿。他左思右想怎麼才能看上一眼，終於認定了最好是躲在浴室門後，這樣公主進去時可以領略她的花容月貌。他毫不猶豫，徑直跑向浴場，藏在一堵大門背後，這裏誰也發現不了。此時公主已經離宮，策馬緩行，觀賞着各處景色。她在浴場門前停下。她邊走邊揭去了面紗；她的臉龐豔如朝陽，神采煥發，可與明珠媲美。

“果不其然，”阿拉丁喃喃自語。“她真是造化的奇跡啊！老天爺竟誕生了這般豔麗動人的女兒！”

阿拉丁目不轉睛地望出了神，恍恍惚惚；他眼花繚亂，愛慕之心油然升起。他常聽人議論巴德爾・阿・菩德怎麼美麗，不過他原以為天下女子都和他母親一個長相呢。他六神無主地踱回家去。母親見狀，不安地詢問起來，可他偏不吭氣。送來飯菜，他也不肯動筷子。

“你怎麼啦，孩子？”她忙問道。“可是不舒服？還是有甚麼事不順心？快對娘説，兒啊，你行行好吧。”

“讓我清靜會兒，娘，”他説。

母親一個勁地盯着他，最後他只好吃了幾口，就軟綿綿地倒在牀上，無精打采地癡想了一夜，次日整天還是這樣。眼見他行為反常，老婦大為不安，於是又盤問起來。她道：“要是頭疼腦熱的，跟我説了好去找大夫。現在城裏有位阿拉伯大夫，是蘇丹派來的。人人都誇他醫道好。我去請來給你看看好嗎？”

“我沒害病，”阿拉丁回答説。“我身體很好。只是我以前總以為女人家跟你長得一個模樣。可昨天巴德爾・阿・菩德公主去浴場，我看見她了。看得真真切切，她進去的時候掀開了面紗。望着她的臉蛋，她那嫻雅的風姿，我便心旌飄搖，魂不附體地愛上了她。除非去懇求蘇丹國王，讓他同意把女兒嫁給我，不然我就坐立不安。”

聽完這番話，母親心想他是發瘋了。

“真主保佑，我的兒啊！”她驚叫一聲。“你怕是昏頭了。行啦，快放明白些，不要瘋頭瘋腦了。”

“我可沒瘋，娘，”阿拉丁說道。“憑你怎說，我主意已定。不能娶到美人巴德爾·阿·菩德，我就無法安寧。她是我的心肝寶貝。我決計向她父親求親。”

“別說胡話，求求你啦！”老婦人喝道。“街坊若是聽到這話，會說你神鬼附體了。不要異想天開。哼，誰敢向蘇丹提這門親事？就算你膽大妄為，又想讓誰為你說媒呢？”

“娘，有你在，還有甚麼旁人可以替我說親啊？”他頂了一句。“我最信得過的人不就是你嗎？勞駕你親自去說情提親吧！”

“真主可不許我這麼做！”她嚷道。“你以為我也腦子發熱了吧？敢情你不知天高地厚。孩子啊！你爹是城裏再窮不過的裁縫，我又不是大家閨秀。你怎能妄想得到蘇丹的公主？她父親只肯把她嫁給權勢門第都高攀得上的名門望族的王子。”

“這些我都思量過了，娘，”阿拉丁耐性聽罷之後說道。“甚麼情形都動搖不了我的決心。您若疼愛我這個兒子，求您做件好事，成全了我。不要讓我見閻王去；娶不到心上人，我就沒命了。娘，別忘了我是您的兒啊！”

“不錯，”老婦泣不成聲地說，“我是做娘的，就你一個孩子。我一心盼望的便是看到你討個媳婦，看到你快快活活，娘才高興。你想成家，我就替你找一個家境相當的女子。可是別人問起你做甚麼生意，有多少家底，娘不好回話啊！連對我們這樣沒身份的窮人家，我都開不了口，豈敢向國王討那獨養女兒呢？開開竅吧！孩兒。甚麼人想娶她？竟是裁縫的兒子！哼，我敢肯定，一提這事，咱娘兒兩人就完了；弄得不好還有送命的危險。再說，我怎麼能厚着臉皮不顧一切地開這個口呢？我如何接近蘇丹國王？詢問起來，叫我怎麼回話？人家恐怕當我是瘋婆娘哩。就算讓我拜見蘇丹，我拿甚麼進貢呢？兒呀，我知道蘇丹十分慈悲，從未把兩手空空和含冤抱屈的百姓打發走了事；我也知道他把恩惠施給大家。但是他的庇護只賜予那些有資格的人和奉侍左右舉止高貴的人。孩子，你倒說說，你為蘇丹和王室效過力沒有，你配享受這種恩寵嗎？我再說一遍，沒有一個向蘇丹求情的，不在他腳下獻上一份厚禮。你有甚麼禮品能夠進貢奉獻的呢？”

“娘，你說的一點不假，”阿拉丁答道。“問我拿得出甚麼貢品嘛，我可以送他一樣東西，天下的君主還不曾得到過。我從寶庫裏帶回的那些五顏六色的‘果實’便是無價的首飾，我原以為它們是玻璃和水晶的呢。世上的國王休想佔有。我這些日子常和珠寶商接觸，才打聽到它們是價值巨萬的寶石。您想看看是真是假，就拿個大瓷盤來，讓您開開眼吧。我保管帶上這樣的禮物，託您的事便可馬到成功。別錯看了這些值錢的飾物。我常見那些商人開價極大而賣的寶石並不值錢，跟我手裏的珠寶是不能比的。”

老婦人將信將疑地起身取來一個大瓷盤，放在阿拉丁面前。他把藏好的那些珠寶飾物拿出來，靈巧地擺滿了一盤子。母親望着色彩繽紛的寶石，不覺眼花繚亂了。

"娘，瞧見了吧？"阿拉丁對目瞪口呆的婦人說。"還能找到比這更華貴的禮品進貢蘇丹嗎？沒問題，他會盛情接待，把您視為上賓的。別磨磨蹭蹭了，拿上瓷盤進宮去吧。"

"那好，孩子，"她答道，"我承認你的貢品是稀世珍寶。天下有誰會這麼冒冒失失地站在蘇丹面前向他提親？他若問我有何要求，我就會心裏發怵，七上八落說不出話來。就算真主保佑，我斗膽訴說你的意思，人家準以為我老糊塗了，連笑帶罵把我趕出宮門。再說，咱娘兒兩人說不定還有殺身之禍哩。好吧好吧，為着你，我只得捨着這副老臉去走一趟。不過孩子，要是蘇丹開顏賞臉，問起我你的身份收入，我該如何稟告才是啊？逢到這種情況，人們都會提出這一個問題來的；可不，恐怕還是他的第一個問題呢。"

"見到這些燦燦發光的珠寶，蘇丹肯定不會再這樣問你了，"阿拉丁說道。"不要怕這怕那地瞎擔心事了。大膽去一趟，把這些寶石送給他。別忘了我有盞燈，想要甚麼它都會弄來。如果蘇丹提你所說的問題，神燈會教我怎樣回答。"

他們一直談到深更半夜。天一亮阿拉丁的母親便起來梳洗好，準備拜見蘇丹，不再是那樣顧慮重重了。她明白這盞神燈可以呼風喚雨，無所不能。阿拉丁不許她泄漏祕密，於是她用一塊漂亮的披巾包住寶石盤，踏上了進宮的路程。

老婦來到大廳，朝拜的人還沒到齊。她看着大臣和一些達官顯貴步入蘇丹的殿堂。不一會，王公大臣、文武百官，還有王室要人擁滿了大廳。蘇丹駕到，眾臣便斂氣屏息，肅然靜立。蘇丹升坐王位，擺擺手讓大家入座，各就各位。

陳情訴狀者——被召喚到王座跟前，每樁案子都酌情裁決；但是時間有限，多數官司無法受理。阿拉丁的母親雖說來得比旁人早，卻無人理睬她，也沒人肯領她拜見蘇丹。臣子完事之後，蘇丹便退席了。老婦只得作罷回家。阿拉丁一見母親帶回寶石盤，心想總是出了岔子。他並不盤問，讓母親進屋之後把前前後後敘述了一遍。

"感謝真主，兒啊，"她終於開口了。"我今兒壯起膽子進了朝拜大廳，儘管我和許多人一樣，沒能跟蘇丹說上話。可我不害怕了。真主允許的話，我明天再去見他。"

阿拉丁一見誤事便來氣了，可母親幾句話說得他又高興起來，安心盼望着。第二天上午母親又帶上盤子來到蘇丹的宮殿，卻發現聽政廳大門關着。打聽下來才知道國王每週僅有三天聽政，因此她只好回家。

此後她就天天進宮，看到大廳敞開着，便無可奈何地站在那裏，直到王上聽政完畢之後她才往回走。別的日子她總見大門關着。一連七天她照去不誤，在最後一次聽政結束的時候，國王原來就注意到她每次必到，此刻眾臣紛紛離宮了，他便對大臣說："六七天來我見那老婆子每日進宮，外衣裏還藏着甚麼。她有何請求？"

"陛下，婦人家心眼兒小，"大臣稟告道。"恐怕此人就是要來告她丈夫或是家裏的人。"

這話卻是搪塞不了國王的。他吩咐大臣等她如果下次再來，把她帶入寢宮。

"遵命，陛下，"大臣連連作揖。

次日，國王又見阿拉丁母親和前幾天一樣滿面倦容站立在聽政堂。

"昨天跟你說的便是此人，"他告訴大臣。"即刻把她傳來，我瞭解一下，好讓她如願以償。"

大臣立即起身，便把阿拉丁母親領到蘇丹御前。她忙跪倒在地，連稱萬壽無疆，榮華千古。

"婦人，"國王道，"見你多次來到聽政廳，佇立許久一無所求。你的請求說給我聽，自當欽准。"

阿拉丁的母親又向蘇丹祝福跪拜，然後說道："偉大的國王，懇求您答應饒恕我的冒失，然後我才敢提出要求，但願我這非分之請沒有冒犯陛下。"

蘇丹素來大度包容，他一口應諾，命左右退下，這樣她就無所顧忌了。只有宰相留下，國王面對阿拉丁母親說道："婦人，講吧，真主保護你。"

"大王，"她說，"求您寬恕。"

"真主寬大為懷，"他答道。

"陛下，我有個兒子，叫阿拉丁，"老婦開始說。"有一天他聽見傳旨，大家不得出門，因為巴德爾·阿·菩德公主要去浴場。兒子一聞此訊就切望瞧上一眼；他躲在浴場大門背後，公主進去時他看見了。他一見鍾情，以後一直神魂不定。他讓我來向陛下求情，同意把公主嫁給他。我千方百計也無法打消他這個心事。他說是如果得不到心上人就沒有命了。請求大王開恩，原諒我們母子的放肆。"

聽完之後，蘇丹和善地笑道：“告訴我那個包裹你帶了甚麼東西。”

阿拉丁的母親察覺到蘇丹沒有動怒，便解開披巾，把裝滿首飾的瓷盤呈獻上去。頓時殿堂光華熠熠，宛如被吊燈和五顏六色的火炬照亮了。國王盯着這些貢品，看得目瞪口呆，這樣耀眼奪目，碩大無比，這樣形狀美觀的珠寶真是少見啊！

“我還未曾看到過像這樣的首飾！”他驚歎起來。“我的財寶中沒有一塊寶石能比得上。宰相，你以為如何？見過這樣的稀世珍品嗎？”

“從未見過，陛下，”宰相附和道。“怕是就連最小的，你的全部財寶中也找不着。”

“那麼你是不是這樣認為：送禮的這位青年更有資格向我女兒求婚了？”蘇丹問道。宰相一聞此言大為不安，一時答不上話。原先國王曾把公主許諾給他的公子。

他稍停片刻，壯起膽子說道：“想來您一定胸懷海量，允許臣提醒陛下，您已將公主許給我的兒子。因此祈求陛下寬限三個月，真主保佑的話，讓他找到比這份嫁妝更加貴重的聘儀。”

蘇丹肚裏明白，不論宰相還是天下最富裕的君主都無法找到一份嫁妝可以抵得上他收下的這份厚禮。但他不願得罪大臣，於是同意宰相提出的期限。

“到你兒子那裏去告訴他，我的女兒將屬他。只是要過三個月才能舉行婚禮，有大小事情要一一籌辦呢。”國王對老婦人說道。

阿拉丁的母親叩謝不已，然後喜不自禁地慌忙趕回家去。阿拉丁看見她沒有把盤子帶回來，又發現她滿面春風，心想是個吉兆。

"真主保佑，"他叫了起來，"娘，你給我捎來了好消息吧。但願那些珠寶獲得了蘇丹的歡心；他以禮相見，聽了你的說媒。"

母親便告訴他蘇丹收禮不勝歡賞的情景。

"他應諾公主歸你，"她又說。"可是宰相耳語了幾句，然後他說要過三個月才能舉辦婚禮。兒啊，我擔心的是宰相使點子，要蘇丹改變主意。"

雖說拖了好幾天，阿拉丁聽說蘇丹許了願，真是歡天喜地。他連連感激母親一番苦勞。

"娘，我向真主起誓，"他說，"我像是死人，您又使我活了過來。要感謝真主啊！現在我肯定是世上最闊氣最福氣的人了！"

在那兩個月裏，阿拉丁耐着性子計算着日子，再過多久大喜的日子就要來臨了。一天傍晚母親出去買油，走在街上發覺店家統統關門，全城張燈結綵，四處通明。家家戶戶窗口懸掛鮮花燭燈，廣場上兵士雲集，手持火把的達官貴人個個騎在馬上。老婦看傻了眼，踏進一爿開張的油店，買完東西，問起為甚麼外面這樣熱鬧。

"咳，好嫂子！"店主回答道。"想必你是從外地來的吧，你還不知道今兒是巴德爾‧阿‧菩德公主和宰相公子的成婚之夜。公子即刻就要從浴場出來，這些官兵要護送他進宮，蘇丹的女兒正等候着呢。"

阿拉丁的母親頓時心裏發冷。她心事沉重地回到家中，不知該怎麼把這壞消息透給兒子。

"孩兒，"她一進門便說，"大事不妙。怕你聽了會十分傷心。"

"娘，甚麼消息呀？"阿拉丁性急地問道。

"唉，國王對你言而無信。宰相公子就在今晚要和公主成親哩。你看，我早就擔心宰相會使國王改變主意的！我對你說過，在國王接受你的求婚之後，他湊在國王的耳邊嘀咕了幾句。"母親答道。

"那你怎麼知道宰相兒子今晚要娶公主呢？"

母親便把在城裏看到的種種情景描述了一遍。阿拉丁聽得有這樣的事，火冒三丈；幸而一會他想起了神燈，便又鎮定下來。

"等着瞧吧，娘，"他說，"我看宰相公子今夜未必能享受洞房的歡樂。先不談它。快去做飯吧。我要到房裏去動動腦筋該怎麼辦才好。依我說，還是有希望。"

飯後，阿拉丁把自己關在屋裏，鎖上房門，取出神燈擦了一下。神怪立刻顯形，說道："要甚麼請吩咐。我是你的奴僕。"

"好生聽着，"阿拉丁說。"我向蘇丹求親，要娶公主。他許諾我三個月後和她成婚。但他言而無信，馬上要把公主嫁給宰相公子。婚禮就在今晚舉行。你如果是神燈的可靠的奴僕，我命你一見新郎新娘雙雙躺在牀上，就立即把他們帶到我家。其餘的事由我處理。"

"遵命，"神怪答應道。"還要我做些甚麼？"

"現在沒事了，"阿拉丁說。

神怪隱身消失了，阿拉丁走到母親屋裏坐下來和她聊天。他估計神怪該回來了，便又把自己關進房裏。不一會神燈的奴僕果然帶來了剛剛上牀的一對新人。阿拉丁心花怒放了。

"把這條可憐蟲帶走，"他對神怪喝道，"讓他睡在儲藏室裏。"

神怪馬上帶走宰相公子，把他放進那裏，對他吹了一口氣，他就動彈不得，十分可憐。神怪回到阿拉丁房裏。

"主人，還要甚麼？"他問道。"您說了我一定照辦。"

"早上再來，"阿拉丁說。"那時你可以把他們帶回王宮了。"

"是，"神怪回了話便隱沒了。

阿拉丁簡直不敢相信這一切真的實現了。這裏只剩下他和公主兩個，他一刻也沒有因為渴望之情而喪失理智，雖說他滿懷激情地愛慕着她。

"絕頂美麗的女子，"他說，"不要以為把您帶到這裏，我會玷辱您的清白；真主不容許我這麼做。這樣安排只是為了不讓旁人得到您，因為令尊大人許下諾言，您應是我的新娘。不必驚慌；在這裏您不會受到絲毫傷害。"

公主忽然發現自己留在這麼個黑沉沉陰慘慘的地方，聽到阿拉丁的話，她害怕極了，不知道該怎樣回答。過了一會阿拉丁起身脫下衣服，上牀去躺在她身旁，中間放了把不帶鞘的寶劍。公主受了驚，一宵沒睡。宰相公子躺在密室裏動彈不得，自然更不好過。

第二天清早，不等阿拉丁擦燈神怪又走了進來。

"主人，"他說，"吩咐吧，我樂意從命。"

"去把新娘新郎帶回蘇丹的王宮。"

眨眼工夫，神怪就辦完了差使。他將宰相的公子放在公主的身邊，送回王宮；他動作神速，驚恐萬狀的一對新人連送走他們的是誰也沒看清。神怪剛剛放下他們就消失了，這時蘇丹進來看視女兒。這可苦了宰相的公子，在密室裏一夜過得好不淒涼，他剛想在被窩裏暖和暖和，聽到蘇丹駕到，他一骨碌跳下牀來穿上衣服。

蘇丹在女兒眉心親了一下，道聲早安。問起她和丈夫是否情投意合。她卻臉帶哀色地望着父親，一聲不吭。他一連問了好幾遍，公主仍是一言不發。最後他怒氣衝衝地離開新房，來到王后面前告訴她女兒舉止反常。

"陛下，"王后想讓他息怒，便說，"剛過了新婚之夜，新娘十有八九總不免顯得羞羞答答。言語別說重了。很快她就會和以前一樣談吐自如的。此刻完全是出於害羞穩重，才不肯開口。我這就去看她。"

一邊說着，王后穿戴完了，過去探望女兒。她來到公主房裏，在她眉心輕輕一吻，說聲早安。可是公主還是一言不發。

"發生了甚麼怪事，才使她如此神不守舍，"王后暗自思忖。"甚麼事這麼傷心呀，女兒？"她忙問。"出了甚麼事，講吧。我來此看望你，祝你早安，你竟會不理我。"

"母后，您別生我的氣，"公主抬起頭來說，"原諒女兒剛才失禮。求您允許我說說我目前的處境。我昨夜過得多麼可憐啊！我們一同上牀便有人來 —— 我們看不清是誰 —— 把我們連人帶牀搬到一個破破爛爛、昏昏暗暗的骯髒地方。"

公主把昨夜前前後後發生的一切對王后訴說了一遍。

"今天一早，"她繼續說道，"把我們帶走的那個人又把我們帶回到這間臥室。他剛放下我們走了，父王就進了門；我害怕極了，張口說話的勇氣也沒有了。要是因此引起他的不快，求您把發生的事向他說明一下，這樣他也許不會怪罪我，而寬恕我的無禮。"

"好寶貝！"王后驚叫起來。"切記此事不可告訴旁人。人家會說蘇丹的女兒變瘋了。算你聰明，沒有把這一切告訴你父王。一字別提，我先告誡你。"

"母后，但我沒瘋呀！"公主說道。"我跟你說的是真事。不信的話，去問問我丈夫吧。"

"孩子，該起牀了，"王后發話了，"不要再去胡思亂想。穿好衣服，過去觀看全城上下為你舉行的喜慶活動。外邊鑼鼓喧天，歌聲四起，你去聽聽。處處張燈結綵，你去瞧瞧，都在慶賀你的大喜日子哩。"

王后說完便召來侍女，她們伺候她穿衣打扮。然後王后回到蘇丹御前，告訴蘇丹說女兒做了噩夢，求他不要動怒。她接着悄悄地把宰相兒子叫來進行盤問。

"陛下，您說的事我並不知道呀，"他答道，害怕說了實話會失去新娘。王后這時確信公主是由於噩夢中了邪，再不就是產生了幻覺。喜慶活動熱鬧了一天，宮內歌舞喧鬧，器樂伴奏。王后、宰相、公子千方百計地使宴席熱熱鬧鬧，跟新娘逗趣兒，希望驅散她的憂愁。可是他們所做的一切都是徒勞，新娘仍是悶悶不樂，腦子裏轉來轉去還是昨夜發生的事情。說真的，宰相公子在暗室裏過了一夜，吃的苦頭比公主還多哩。但他一口否認，寧肯忘掉所受的委屈，因為他唯恐會一旦失去新娘和這椿親事給他帶來的榮華，因為人人都羨慕他的好運，娶了菩德公主這麼個尊貴顯赫而又花容月貌的女子。

這天阿拉丁出去觀望了城裏宮內的歡樂氣象，心裏暗暗發笑；他聽人談起宰相公子已是名滿天下，做了蘇丹的駙馬，他來日前程無量，阿拉丁更是竊笑不已。

"全是蠢貨！"他自忖道。"你們還不知道他昨天夜裏吃了甚麼苦呢。"

一到天黑，阿拉丁又進屋拂拭起神燈。神怪顯形了，阿拉丁便命令他今夜在新郎靠近新娘之前再把這一對連人帶牀搬到這裏來。神燈的奴僕應聲而去，一會就完成了任務。他照樣把公子關進暗室，新郎又是呆若木雞。阿拉丁又起身取劍，放在他和公主之間，一夜睡在她身邊。天亮之後，神怪又照樣連人帶牀運回宮中。阿拉丁看到他的計謀一步步實現，心裏真是高興。

蘇丹早上醒來，首先想到去看望女兒，瞧瞧她的舉止神色可還像昨日一樣。他馬上爬起來披上衣服，往菩德公主臥室走去。一聽到房門打開，宰相的公子跳下牀來忙整理衣冠，夜裏受了寒，兩排肋骨疼得快要裂開了。蘇丹走到女兒跟前，掀開羅帳，吻了吻她的眉心，祝她早安。他問起她一夜可好，誰知女兒又眉頭緊蹙，臉色陰沉地望着他，就是不吭氣。她茫然沮喪，已經陷入了絕望的境地。她的沉默使得蘇丹很生氣。他頓時明白女兒有事瞞着他。

"女兒，你受了甚麼驚？"他怒吼一聲，拔出劍來。"快如實說來，不然我這就劈下你的腦袋。你竟然對父王如此無禮，對你說話，你卻一字不吐。"

公主一見父王在她面前舞起劍來嚇得直打哆嗦。

"父王，求您千萬不要動怒，"她抬頭答道。"這兩夜我是怎麼熬過來的，您要是聽了，就會寬恕我憐惜我。我從小知道您是最疼愛女兒的慈父。"

於是她把這兩夜的情形細細訴說給蘇丹聽。

"好吧，父王，"她接着又說，"您若是想弄清我說的可是實話，就請問問我的丈夫吧。他會原原本本稟告您的。他被人帶走後的情況，他被關在哪裏，我都不清楚。"

女兒的訴說使蘇丹深為動容，雙眼飽含着淚花。他把寶劍套入鞘內，輕柔地吻過公主，說道："孩子，你為何不早點告訴我，否則昨夜我便可保護你不致受驚了。不必害怕；你起牀吧，別再去想這些怕人的事。今夜我派人在你臥室四周守夜，你就不會有任何危險了。"

蘇丹回到房內，立刻召見宰相。

"此事該怎麼說？"宰相一到御前，他便喝道。"恐怕令郎已把他和新娘經歷的怪事告訴你了吧？"

"陛下，我這兩天沒有見過兒子，"宰相回了話。

國王便把公主的遭遇說了一遍。

"你去問問令郎，"他又吩咐道，"把前後經過弄個水落石出。我的女兒八成是嚇得魂不守舍，究竟出了甚麼事她並不清楚；不過我還是信以為真的。"

宰相便把兒子叫來，詢問他蘇丹所說的可是真實情況。

"真主有眼，菩德公主是不會撒謊的，"新郎忙說。"她講的都是實話。這兩夜對於我們兩個都是一場噩夢，哪裏談得上洞房花燭夜。我的情況更糟。非但沒能和新娘同牀共枕，我整夜被鎖在暗室裏，一片漆黑，臭氣熏人，可怕極了。我的肋骨凍得發痛，像要裂開似的。"他把事情經過詳詳細細地敍述給宰相聽。

"父親大人，求求您了，"他最後說，"向蘇丹說個情，解除這門親事吧。我明知能做蘇丹的駙馬是無上榮幸，更何況我對公主一往情深。可是這兩夜的折磨我再也受不了啦。"

宰相聽到這番話，十分煩惱。他原先朝思暮想，希望兒子能高攀上蘇丹的女兒，這樣一來他就成了朝中的顯宦。他面臨着難題，不知該如何行動。退掉這門婚事真叫他傷心透了，他本來是動足了腦筋一心一意成全兒子的。

"先別着急，孩子，"他終於開口了。"看看今夜情況再說。我們在新房周圍派兵守護。不要過於魯莽地放棄這份難得的榮耀，除你之外，別人還休想得到哩。"

宰相扔下兒子，回到蘇丹面前稟告他公主說的事一點不假。

"既然如此，"蘇丹笑逐顏開，說道，"我在此宣佈取消這門親事。"他立刻下令中止慶典，解除婚約。

國王突然變卦，城中的老老少少聞訊都十分詫異，瞧見宰相和公子垂頭喪氣一臉慍色走出王宮，大家更是面面相覷。接着便紛紛打聽出了甚麼事，好端端的婚姻怎麼就吹了。可是誰也不知底細，只有那阿拉丁樂不可支，他的擺佈原是人們想不到的。

卻說國王早已忘記他對阿拉丁母親的許諾。三個月過去了，阿拉丁又打發母親去要求蘇丹實現自己的誓言。於是老婦人再度進宮。她一踏進聽政廳，國王便認出了她。

"進貢珠寶的那個婦人又來了，"蘇丹面對宰相說道。"我答應過她三個月之後把女兒嫁給她兒子。你去把她帶來相見。"

宰相便領她來到御前，阿拉丁的母親匍伏在地，歌頌一番之後，蘇丹問她有何請求。

"陛下，"她說，"您曾把菩德公主許給我的兒子阿拉丁，現在三個月已到期了。"

蘇丹茫然不知如何答覆是好，一眼可以看出這老婦人分明一生窮困，臣民中算得最寒微的小戶人家了。可是她進貢的聘禮確確實實是無價之寶。

"你有何高見？"他悄悄地向宰相討主意。"是有此事，我對她許過願。可是他們明明是低賤人家，怎麼能讓人瞧得起呢。"

宰相失了面子懷恨在心，眼下又醋意十足，暗自思忖："我的兒子都沒有這福氣，這號窮鬼還配娶公主？"

"陛下，"他回答道，"小事一樁。我們自然要教訓這個無名小子；您是一國之主，要把公主下嫁給一個不知天高地厚的暴發戶，門第不配。"

"那該如何回絕他呢？"蘇丹又問。"我答應過他。國王說話可得當真啊！"

"我看嘛，"宰相說道，"您要求他進貢四十個足金的盤子，裝滿珠寶，個個都要像他上次送來的一般大小。再叫四十個女奴把金盤端來，還要四十個奴僕護送進宮。"

"真主在上，宰相，你真是足智多謀，"蘇丹應道。"這一下可把他難倒了。我們從此擺脫他的糾纏了。"

然後，蘇丹轉向阿拉丁的母親說道："去告訴你兒子，我遵守諾言。等他送上一份像樣的嫁妝，就舉行婚禮。要他準備四十個足金的盤子，裝滿珠寶，跟你上次的貢品一模一樣，派四十個女奴連同四十個奴僕一起送來。你的兒子如果送得起這份聘禮，公主就屬他了。”

阿拉丁的母親默默無言地退下，神情沮喪地往家走去。

“我這苦命的孩子上哪裏去弄到這些金盤珠寶呢？”她一邊心裏盤算一邊搖頭。“就算他再去一趟寶庫，把魔樹上的珠寶全部拿來——我並不當真相信他有這能耐，就算他辦得到吧——這四十個女奴加上四十個奴僕又怎麼可能從天而降呢？”老婦人左思右想，拖着步子回到家中。阿拉丁正在東張西望等着她哩。

“孩子啊，”她一進門便歎氣道，“我不是跟你説過別打菩德公主的主意嗎？我不是提醒過你這門親事輪不到我們老百姓家嗎？”

“快講講是怎麼回事，”阿拉丁粗聲大氣地説。

“蘇丹很和氣地接見了我，”她告訴他説，“我看王上對你倒有些意思。和你過不去的是那可惡的宰相。我向蘇丹提起他許下的諾言，他便同宰相合計。這壞東西鬼頭鬼腦嘀咕了幾句。王上過後就給了我回話。”

她把蘇丹要求多少嫁妝告訴了阿拉丁。

“阿拉丁，王上現在等候回話呢。我們還能給他甚麼回話呢。”她又道。

“娘喲，你盡想這些個嗎？”阿拉丁應道，哈哈笑了。

“你以為這是萬萬辦不到的事吧！現在快搞點吃的去，一會，真主開恩，您就會親眼看到我的回答了。蘇丹同你一樣；料想我沒這個本事。不是我誇口，他提的要求算不了甚麼。燒飯去吧，把一切都交給我吧。”

母親立起身子，上街買下飯的菜去了。在這時候，阿拉丁走進自己的屋裏，拿出神燈拂擦起來。神怪馬上又出現了，説道："主人，有何指示？"

"蘇丹有意把女兒嫁給我，"阿拉丁告訴他説。"不過我得進貢四十個足金的盤子，每一個淨重十斤，還要把珠寶裝得滿滿的，珠寶大小跟那寶庫花園裏的一樣。這些金盤非得由四十個女奴捧去。還要四十個奴僕陪伴同行。你快去照辦，不可誤事。"

"遵命，"神怪應道。

説完，神燈的奴僕便無影無蹤了。不到片刻他帶來了四十個女兒家，每人都由一位相貌端正的奴僕伴陪着；個個女孩頭上頂着堆足了稀世寶石的金盤。神怪領着她們走至主人面前，問道還有甚麼差事他可以效力。

"此刻無事，還要甚麼我會叫你的。"阿拉丁回答説。

神怪又不見了。阿拉丁的母親買好東西回家，看看滿屋子都是婢女奴僕，驚歎不已。

"莫非這一切都是神燈鬼使神差？"她失聲叫道。"但願真主為我的阿拉丁保管好這件神物！"

她還來不及掀開面紗，就聽阿拉丁説："娘，時間一刻也不能耽擱。必須在他回後宮之前先把他要的嫁妝送去。現在就走。這下子他大概會清楚知道他要的東西我都可以給他，而且還能多給些。到時候他會明白過來是上了宰相的當，他會看到那些藉口是難不倒我的。"

於是阿拉丁站起來推開家門，讓母親領着一婢一奴，雙人成行地魚貫而出，一會摩肩接踵佔了半條街。來往行人瞧見這樣的氣派場面，個個停住腳步，嘖嘖讚歎起女子的絕色天姿，她們身着金光閃閃的袍子，衣袍上的珠寶連最不起眼的也值個十萬八萬。人們又都盯住她們頭上的金盤，看到灼灼閃亮，十分璀璨。隻隻金盤都勝似朝陽，一條條鑲着金邊嵌着寶石的頭巾蓋在金盤上面。

阿拉丁母親在前率領着浩浩蕩蕩的一支隊伍穿街走巷，路人立刻簇擁上來，一邊驚歎一邊呼喊，熱鬧非凡。這時眾婢奴行至王宮，嫋嫋婷婷逶迤步入花柳園亭。一見此情此景，太監侍女讚不絕口，他們一輩子還未曾見過這樣的場面。尤其那許多絕色美女，就是一個隱士也會為之心旌搖盪。不過太監侍女都是大家出身的體面人；他們再瞧瞧女子們一身華麗衣袍，頭上頂着金碧輝煌的托盤，更是驚奇不已。金盤光芒四射耀眼奪目，他們幾乎睜不開雙眼。

宮中侍者忙去稟報蘇丹，王上聞訊後便命即刻帶進來。阿拉丁的母親便領着眾婢女來到御前，一齊恭恭敬敬地行了朝拜的禮節，於是放下托盤，掀去蓋在上面的飾巾，個個雙手交叉地佇立着。蘇丹一見婢女舉止十分嫻雅，容貌漂亮得難描難畫，心下不禁歎為奇觀。再看到金盤上堆滿了令人目眩的寶石，蘇丹不覺發起怔來。一天之內，連人帶物如數進貢，這可真叫他啞口無言。少時，蘇丹便叫婢女將金盤送至菩德公主房內。這時阿拉丁的母親走到王座前面説道："陛下，這些聘儀見不得人，實在不能和公主的身份相配，公主那麼高貴，應該獻上更多的珍寶才對。"

"你現在有甚麼話要説嗎？"蘇丹又向宰相輕聲問道。"他這麼快就拿得出如許財寶，還有甚麼話可説的呢？難道他還不配做我的駙馬、娶我的女兒為新娘嗎？"

眼睜睜望着這花團錦簇的厚禮，宰相比蘇丹更加愕然，心裏頓生妒忌；一看到國王對阿拉丁的彩禮這麼滿意，越發懷恨在心。

"大王，"他狡猾地説道，"天底下的所有財富都及不上菩德公主的一顰一笑。這份彩禮豈可與令愛同日而語？大王把它看得太重了。"

蘇丹知道宰相的這番話是出於醋心，他便對阿拉丁的母親説道："告訴你兒子我收下了他的彩禮。朕言而有信。我的女兒將成為他的新娘。讓他進宮來吧，我好見見他。他會受到隆重接待的。婚禮就定在今晚。只是叫他快快進宮。"

老婦想着兒子前程無量，心裏樂開了花，她一陣風似地奔回家去把這喜事告訴阿拉丁。她一離宮，國王便來到公主的閨閣，吩咐女奴們將金盤首飾搬至房內，讓公主瞧瞧。公主見到碩大的珠寶和美貌的女奴，連連讚歎；聽説一切都是由新的郎君饋贈的，馬上喜上眉梢。父王看到她不再沒精打采面帶愁容，自然十分高興。

"孩子，你中意這份彩禮嗎？"他問道。"我看准了，這位後生做你丈夫要比那宰相兒子來得合適。真主開恩，你和他將會幸福美滿的。"

且説阿拉丁一見母親興沖沖地回到家裏，他明白大功告成了。

"讚美真主！"他喊了出來。"我的心願總算實現啦！"

"開心了吧，孩子，"老婦人也亮起嗓門道，"你這下稱心如意了。蘇丹收下彩禮，公主要做你的新娘了。喜事就在今晚辦。王上已經當着眾人的面宣佈你為他的女婿，他要你即刻進宮晉見。感謝真主，我算完事了。"

阿拉丁親親母親的手心，打從心裏感激她老人家。他回到自己房裏，取出神燈拂拭了一下。神怪顯形了，說道：“奴才在此，有何吩咐？”

　　“神燈的奴僕，命你把我帶到天下氣派最大的浴場，再弄一身鑲金嵌寶、連世上的國王都沒有穿過的衣服。”

　　“遵命。”

　　於是神怪便把阿拉丁背在肩上，一眨眼就來到一個連國王皇帝也從未見過的浴場。浴場是用瑪瑙和雪花石砌成的，裏外裝飾着精彩的圖畫，令人目不暇給。穹形的白色浴場裏一派寧靜，世上的凡夫俗子從不曾闖進去過。神燈的奴隸領着阿拉丁進入內廳，這裏的四壁都綴滿了首飾珠寶，有個凡人模樣的神怪替他洗擦身子。過後阿拉丁又跟着回到外間的更衣室，原來的衣服不見了，他看到一身華麗的衣冠，神怪端來了美酒咖啡，郁香飄來沁人心脾。杯酒下肚，他頓覺神清氣爽。忽然間一班奴僕進來為他打扮一番，抹上香水。

　　讀者知道，那阿拉丁原是個窮裁縫的兒子；可目前人人見了只當是哪個顯赫的王子。真主有回天之力，同時卻又依然故我，多麼神妙啊！

　　這時神怪已將阿拉丁送至家中。

　　“主人，您可還要些甚麼？”

　　“嗯，還要四班隨從，兩班騎馬在前開路，兩班騎馬在後護衛。號衣、馬、刀劍一齊備好。隨從要華冠盛妝，馬要有馬衣馬飾。再弄一匹進得了皇上馬廄的千里馬，一應馬具都要用金銀首飾綴飾。此外準備四萬八千個金幣，每個隨從帶上一千金幣，快去快回，一切都得在我進見蘇丹之前安排停當。最後，好好挑選十二個絕色侍女，着上豔服麗妝，陪我母親進宮；每個侍女攜帶一身皇后才配得上的華服。"

"遵命。"

神怪隱身而去，頃刻之間就把阿拉丁所要的都帶回來了。他手中牽着的是走遍阿拉伯也找不着這樣軒昂的好馬，還配金光熠熠的馬鞍馬具。阿拉丁立即喚來母親，讓她領着十二個侍女；再遞給她一套出入王宮的華服。他又打發一個隨從去探問蘇丹可離開後宮了。隨從閃電般地速去速回，報告道："主人，王上等候着呢。"

阿拉丁一躍上馬，眾多隨從前呼後擁，紛紛跨馬。他們緩緩行進，不斷將大把大把的金幣散擲給前來圍觀的人羣。阿拉丁看上去儀表堂堂神采奕奕，叫那天下最堂皇的王公都自歎不如。如此排場全靠了神燈的威力；誰佔有了神燈，就擁有了美女，財富，知識。老老少少無不驚歎阿拉丁的慷慨賞賜；阿拉丁人才出眾，舉止文雅，氣宇昂然，使人人驚歎。他們讚頌仁慈的真主造就出一個這般高貴的生靈，大家一起拜伏在他足下為他祈福。儘管他們都知道阿拉丁原是寒磣的衣匠兒子，可誰也不眼紅他：人們眾口一詞說他合該有這福分。

這時蘇丹已經召集一朝顯貴，通報他們婚禮就要舉行。他命令百官恭候阿拉丁光臨，列隊迎迓。他將藩侯眾相、太監、富翁、將領全部請來。他們都站在宮門前面迎候。不一會，阿拉丁駕到，正欲下馬，蘇丹早就安排好一位藩侯快步上前。

"大人，陛下之意您騎馬入宮，到了聽政廳再下馬。"

眾朝臣便走在前面開道，行至聽政廳時有人過來抓住馬鐙，還有幾個在兩邊保駕，餘者拉着他的手扶他下馬。於是藩侯和高官們引領入廳，他一走近王座，剛要在地毯上拜倒行禮，蘇丹就離席擁抱着他吻了一下，請他坐在右首。阿拉丁祝王上萬歲，為他祈福。

"陛下，承您厚愛，將令愛賜臣為妻，我本是無名百姓，如許殊榮愧不敢當。我祈求真主永葆王上安然無恙。王上，我接受這份非凡的恩寵，感激之情無以言表。在此僅央求陛下賜予我一方土地，我要建造一所配得上菩德公主的宮殿。"

國王看到阿拉丁一身王室打扮，光彩照人，深為詫異。他凝神注視，見他文質彬彬，風度翩翩，又大為稱歎。接着又驚訝地打量起他身邊伺立的英俊魁梧的隨從。正在這時，阿拉丁的母親由十二位亭亭玉立的女奴擁進宮來，她穿着華貴，好不氣派，恍若王后，更使國王大出所料。阿拉丁口齒伶俐，談吐不俗，蘇丹和舉座的人都歎服不置。只有心懷嫉妒的宰相氣急敗壞。蘇丹聽罷阿拉丁一番言語，又見他風度優雅，舉止莊重，不免又擁抱着吻了一下。

"賢婿，十分遺憾，朕與你今日才得相見，都是天數所定啊！"

蘇丹隨後便命樂師奏樂；他挽着阿拉丁的手，領他步入大殿，婚禮筵席已經張羅就緒。蘇丹入席後，請阿拉丁在他右首就坐。滿朝的達官顯貴王公諸侯也各依序坐下。一時樂曲飄揚，歡聲笑語在大殿裏回蕩不已。席間，蘇丹和阿拉丁一邊談話一邊打趣，阿拉丁應對自如，妙語不斷，彷彿他出身王室，終日和帝王同席共遊。閒聊久了，蘇丹益發覺得他才識超人。

宴席終了，國王又下令傳司儀和證婚人進來。他們即刻為阿拉丁和公主修好婚書。儀式一完畢，阿拉丁便起身告辭，蘇丹卻止住了他。

"賢婿，上哪裏去？"他嚷道。"來賓尚未退席，宴慶還沒散。婚書還筆跡未乾呢。"

"陛下，我打算為菩德公主建造一座和她門第相稱的宮殿。只有了此心願我才能迎娶公主。真主保佑，我迫不及待，要將宮殿儘早落成。儘管我一心盼望和公主一起享受新婚的歡樂，可我還得首先完成眼前應該完成的事。我想借此證明對於公主的深情厚誼。"

"看上哪塊地方，儘管由你挑，我的孩子，"蘇丹說道，"不過依我之意，最好宮址就在附近，建在王宮前面的寬敞廣場上。"

"如能在陛下附近安家，那是最稱我的心意也沒有了。"

說完他就辭別蘇丹，騎上駿馬，回家了，一路上觀者如堵，不斷為他發出掌聲喝彩聲。他才進家門，便走入自己屋裏擦拭神燈。

"主人，有何吩咐？"神怪出現在他面前請示道。

"有件要緊的事要你去辦。希望你在蘇丹的王宮前面為我造座宮殿，越快越好。這建築必須是天下君王從未見過的奇觀。然後配就宮內用具擺設，一切都要富麗堂皇安逸舒適。"

"遵命。"

神怪無蹤無影了。拂曉之前，他回來稟告阿拉丁說："主人，大功告成了。請您動身去瞧瞧宮殿。"

阿拉丁剛站起來，神燈的奴僕眨眼工夫已把他送至宮殿。阿拉丁放眼望去，恍入奇境。宮殿裏裏外外皆由碧玉大理石、鑲磚青石砌成。神怪引他進入寶庫，只見各種各樣的金銀珠寶堆積如山，價值連城。接着領他來到膳廳，滿眼盡是金銀器皿，有盤碟水壺、杯具匙盆。神怪又帶阿拉丁到廚房，原來罎罎罐罐一應炊具也是金銀製品。他們從這裏穿入另一間屋室，阿拉丁發現成箱成箱的華麗衣裝、金線織繡、花團錦簇的中國和印度絲綢堆了一房間。神怪還引他到另外幾間上房轉了一圈，房內珠寶琳琅滿目，形容不盡。最後阿拉丁被帶入馬廄，一頭頭良種駿馬就連帝王君主也休想拿得出。隔壁的雜物間裏放着昂貴的馬鞍韁繩，上面裝飾的珍珠首飾十分精緻。所有這些物器都是一夜之間製成的。

阿拉丁目瞪口呆，難以置信，眼前的奇觀就是帝王做夢也想不到。宮殿裏侍從婢女來往不絕，哪怕足不出戶的隱士見了這般美貌麗人兒也會神魂顛倒。不過環顧四周，妙不可言的還得算殿宇的圓頂，開着二十四扇窗戶，嵌鑲着紅綠相間的寶石。其中一扇窗戶卻安裝得歪歪斜斜，這是阿拉丁的要求，原來他想給蘇丹出個難題，讓他來修整一下。阿拉丁左瞧右望，好一派富麗氣象，他不禁眉開眼笑，轉身對神燈的奴僕説道：「甚麼都有了，只缺一樣東西，我忘提了。」

「説吧，馬上可以辦到。」

「還要一張金線織成的厚實的錦緞地毯，從這裏一直鋪到蘇丹的王宮，這樣菩德公主便可在上面走路，用不到踩着地面了。」

神怪消失了，一剎那之間就回來稟告：「主人，您的要求得到了允准。」説罷，他就帶着阿拉丁去看看，果然一條五彩繽紛的地毯從他的宮苑一直鋪到王宮。於是神怪又將阿拉丁送回家中。

次日清晨，蘇丹醒來，推開臥房的窗戶向外望去。他瞥見王宮前方有座高樓。他揉揉雙眼，睜開再看了一眼。高樓聳立在他眼前，好一座雄偉華麗的大廈，令人望而興歎。一條地毯從門檻鋪至王宮的台階。宮門前的守衛，以及每個人見了無不驚訝。此時宰相進入國王房內，看到拔地而起的殿宇和如此氣派的地毯，也看得眼花繚亂。

"真主可以作證，古今帝王還不曾造得起這麼宏偉壯觀的宮殿。"他們齊聲驚叫起來。

"阿拉丁和公主門當戶對，這下你該心服了吧？"蘇丹轉身向宰相問道。"這般輝煌的高樓你親眼看見了，如此非凡的富麗氣象超過了一切奇思異想。"

"陛下，"宰相醋意十足地答道，"若非神差鬼使，這座大廈休想建成。就是世上最有錢的大富翁也無法在一夜之間造起一座宮殿。"

"我真不懂你，"蘇丹喝道。"怎麼你總把阿拉丁往壞處想。你這不是在忌妒他嗎？我賜予他這塊土地，同意他替小女建造一座宮殿，你是在場聽見的。送得起那麼多首飾的彩禮，他自然能在一夜之間建立一座宮殿。"

宰相看到國王十分喜愛阿拉丁，不會對他產生反感，於是謹慎地閉上了嘴，不再多話。

再說阿拉丁打量時機成熟，可以進宮了，於是他又拂拭神燈，對着神怪說道："我現在要去蘇丹的宮廷了；婚宴定在今日。希望你能送來一萬金幣。"

神怪剎那間變出了一萬金幣。阿拉丁立刻起身上馬，眾多隨從前後保駕揚鞭策馬。一路上阿拉丁把金幣散發給眾人。一見他這般輕財好施，個個都頂禮膜拜起來。不一會，他已行至王宮附近。朝臣門吏連忙入稟報國王阿拉丁駕到。蘇丹出宮迎接，一面擁抱一面親吻，攜手領他步入大廳，請他坐在自己的右首。此時全城上下張燈結綵，宮內樂師唱歌奏樂，一派喧鬧。

蘇丹降旨婚宴開始。他和阿拉丁及一朝臣子盡興酣飲。不只是宮內大家歡天喜地，蘇丹治下的臣民，不論名門望族還是黎民百姓，都一起同喜，歡慶盛典。地方官員不遠萬里來到朝廷，親臨阿拉丁的婚禮，觀光喜慶的熱鬧，蘇丹心下不勝驚歎，阿拉丁的母親當初衣衫襤褸進宮求見，她的兒子卻是腰纏萬貫。再說那些貴賓參觀了阿拉丁的宮殿，人人都歎為觀止，這樣氣派的寓所居然一夜落成了。他們全都拜伏在他腳下高呼：「願真主保佑他幸福長壽！」

酒席上賓主已經盡興，阿拉丁欠身向蘇丹告辭。他跨上坐騎，由侍從們陪同，回到自己的宮殿，準備與新娘見面。大路兩旁的觀者不斷地為他祝福，阿拉丁信手抓起金幣擲給眾人。一到家，他先坐在會客廳歇息。他喝完果子露，便命令上上下下的男女奴僕準備迎接新娘。午後天氣涼爽，驕陽已近平西，蘇丹下了聖旨：眾臣百僚在王宮對面的閱兵場上各就各位。於是他們一擁而出，蘇丹也不例外。阿拉丁立刻加入行列，跨上坐騎。阿拉伯所有的駿馬沒有一匹堪與牠的雄姿媲美。他快馬加鞭，環繞廣場飛馳起來，騎術的嫻熟使四周的人相形見絀。菩德公主從窗口瞧見了他。阿拉丁眉清目秀，身手不凡，公主一見鍾情，為之傾倒。各路騎手表演完畢之後，蘇丹和阿拉丁便各自回宮了。

掌燈時分，羣僚顯貴一起過訪阿拉丁，邀他同去沐浴，於是他們浩浩蕩蕩地來到王室浴場。他洗完澡，抹上香水，換了一身更加華貴的裝束，在長官衛兵的護送下騎馬回家。四個執事手握利劍分走左右，當地的居民，本國和外國的人民手持燭燈，敲鑼打鼓，吹笛奏笙在前面開道。到了宮殿，他下馬行至客廳，和眾官坐下來休息。僕人端來了果露點心，陪同他的隨從男女不計其數，現在都伺候開了。阿拉丁一聲令下，僕人們又走出宮門向人羣拋撒金幣。

蘇丹從閱兵場回宮之後，馬上降旨：宮內所有人員一起出動，將菩德公主送至阿拉丁的宮殿。衛隊朝臣聞聲而動；男僕女婢個個手執燭燈，遮天蓋地的大隊人馬簇擁着公主來到新郎宮中。阿拉丁的母親緩步走在一邊，達官貴人和一朝臣子的妻室走在前面。公主的身後跟着阿拉丁送給她的四十八個婢女，每人舉着琥珀手柄的火炬，金製燭台個個都是鑲珍嵌寶的。眾婢女帶她走進閨房，替她穿好新娘禮服，打扮得花枝招展，領她來到丈夫房裏，阿拉丁的母親做了陪客。過了片刻阿拉丁來了，他掀開她的面紗，做婆婆的驚訝地端量着嫵媚動人天姿絕色的公主。新房四處金光閃爍，金製吊燈綴滿了紅綠寶石，老婦又是一陣讚歎。宮殿裏外如此富麗堂皇，菩德公主觀看之際，驚奇之心並不亞於阿拉丁的母親。不一會開筵設席了。他們對酌慢飲，尋歡作樂。有八十名女奴，懷裏各抱着樂器，輕撥絲弦，彈起妙曲。菩德公主完全陶醉於樂曲聲中，不覺放下酒杯，出神地聽着。阿拉丁則頻頻敬酒，一對新人眉飛色舞傾訴衷腸。這樣的一個勝境良宵就連亞歷山大皇帝畢生也未曾躬逢。宴席一散，殘桌收去，阿拉丁情不自禁地起身扶着新娘進了新房。

　　次日清早，阿拉丁穿上管家為他預備的一套盛裝。他喝了幾
口咖啡便命隨從備馬，於是就和一班人馬行至蘇丹王宮。蘇丹馬
上站起來歡迎他，如同親生子女一般熱和，擁抱親吻過後，讓他
坐在右首。國王和宮內羣宦紛紛向他道喜，祝他快樂。早餐用畢，
阿拉丁向蘇丹發出了邀請："父王，今日可能驚動御駕賞光，和令
愛菩德公主共進午餐？敬請朝中顯宦王公陪同陛下一起貴臨。"

　　蘇丹欣然接受，立刻下令所有內侍隨同赴宴，接着便和阿拉
丁並駕齊驅，前往剛落成的宮殿。一進大門，蘇丹就盛讚這座用
碧玉瑪瑙修砌的大廈。這樣奢侈富麗雄偉壯觀的景象使他見了之
後目瞪口呆。

　　"足下有何見教？"蘇丹得意地衝着宰相挖苦了一句。"今生
今世可曾見過如此氣派的殿宇？這裏見到的金銀首飾，天底下最
大的君主可拿得出來嗎？"

　　"陛下，"宰相答道，"如此奇跡是世間一切國王都沒有本事
創造的。普天之下所有的人也建造不起這樣的宮殿。根本找不
到勝任這項工作的石匠。我已對陛下說過，唯有魔法才能創造出
來。"

　　可是國王心裏明白他是出於嫉妒才這麼說的。"算了吧，宰
相，你這樣說的用意我是清楚的。"蘇丹怫然作色道。

　　說罷，蘇丹走到宮殿的高聳圓頂下方，一見全部窗槅都是用
五彩寶石砌起的，他真是無比驚訝。他圍繞着走了一圈，這些耗
資巨萬的奇觀令他目眩眼花，但他馬上瞧見了阿拉丁存心安排的
窗口上的一處漏洞。

"嗨嗨，美中不足的窗口，你還沒完工呢！"蘇丹望着破綻說道。然後他又向宰相問道："窗櫺安得不齊整，道理在哪裏？足下知道嗎？"

"恐怕是因為陛下催着阿拉丁快些成親，他來不及裝修吧。"

阿拉丁剛才去告訴新娘父王駕到了，現在回來聽到蘇丹向他提出這個問題。

"陛下，婚禮是臨時決定舉行的，石匠時間不夠了。"

"那麼我倒是樂意由我親自來完工。"

"真主保佑陛下千古榮華。說來這也是對令愛宮殿的一個紀念。"

蘇丹於是傳喚加工首飾金器的匠人，吩咐下人從庫房裏取來各式要用的金器首飾。不到半晌，一批匠人來到御前，蘇丹便命他們完成那扇窗口的裝飾。

大家正在動工的時候，菩德公主出來迎接父王了。一見女兒滿面春風，蘇丹高興地抱住她親了一下，父女二人往閨房走去，上下內侍跟了一大羣。不覺已到午飯時分，僕人專為蘇丹、菩德和阿拉丁備了一席，另替宰相等人備了一桌。國王在女兒女婿中間坐下，舉杯下筷之間一迭連聲地誇讚滿桌的佳餚和各色精美的菜盤。八十個容貌標致光彩映人的女奴亭亭玉立，美如天仙。她們調和樂器之後，撥動琴弦，奏起了美妙的音樂。眾多賓客傳杯換盞，開懷縱飲。用罷午宴之後，大家來到隔壁的客廳，眾奴僕端上了鮮果甜食。

蘇丹這時過來視看匠人的活計，他想瞧瞧他們的手藝可比得上宮殿的玲瓏剔透。國王行至那扇窗口，大失所望地發現一巧一拙相去太遠了，和整個天衣無縫的圓頂毫不相稱。他們稟告國王，庫房裏所能找到的奇石珍寶全都搬來了，但還是不夠用。國王又降旨要人打開國庫，由他們任意選取；如果仍然缺少，就動用阿拉丁進貢的首飾。匠工們立刻依命辦事，可是後來看到所有這些寶石還不夠裝飾半扇窗楣。蘇丹一見此狀，又下令將諸侯望族家中的全部寶石統統拿來。匠工們用上這些，卻還是數目不足。

第二天上午，阿拉丁來到匠工中間，看到他們連半扇窗楣還沒裝飾完畢，於是讓他們馬上停工，把所有寶石如數歸還物主。匠工們遵命辦理，再去把阿拉丁的吩咐稟報蘇丹。

"他怎麼跟你們說的？為甚麼不讓把那扇窗戶裝好？你們做好的窗子他怎麼又拆毀了呢？"蘇丹詰問道。

"奴才不知，陛下，"他們齊聲答道。

蘇丹立刻傳人備馬，不一時來到女婿的宮殿。這時阿拉丁已把匠工全打發走了，他進入自己的房裏拂拭起神燈。神怪顯形後說："有何示下？奴才一定效勞。"

"我要你安好那扇沒完工的窗戶。"

"您的意旨立刻照辦。"

神怪消失了，霎時回來報告說："主人，完工了。"

阿拉丁爬上圓頂看到所有的窗戶都完美無瑕了。正在查看的時候，太監前來告訴他國王駕到。阿拉丁連忙下來相迎。

"賢婿，你為甚麼要這麼幹呀？"蘇丹一見面便大聲嚷道。"你怎麼不讓匠工們裝飾好那扇窗楣，留下了一個美中不足之處？"

"大王，留下一處沒完工，原是我的要求，我並非沒有本事完成它，我也不願意在一座美中不足的宮殿裏迎接陛下。或許陛下樂意上來看看現在還有甚麼不圓滿的地方。"

蘇丹拾階而上，來到圓頂之處。他環顧左右，十分詫異地發現窗櫺已經完工了。他抱住阿拉丁親吻起來。

"賢婿，好個傑作啊！匠工們要花上幾個月才能完成，你卻只用了一個晚上。真主在上，你是天底下無與倫比的人物了。"

"真主保佑陛下萬壽無疆！你的僕人當不起這樣的讚美。"

"賢婿，何必過謙呢？哪個首飾匠也完不成的事你卻一下子完成了。"

蘇丹走下扶梯，過去探望菩德公主，看到女兒在金碧輝煌的新居生活幸福，不禁喜形於色。他在女兒房間小憩片刻便回宮去了。

從此以後，阿拉丁每日進城，眾多隨從在他的坐騎前面向路人拋擲金幣。男女老少，不論本國百姓還是異邦來客，無不心嚮往之，人人都稱道他慷慨大方，熱心佈施。他不斷地濟貧救窮，親手散發錢財。不久，他便四海揚名了；名門貴族時常成為他的席上食客，不論名位高下，個個都發誓效忠。公主的愛慕之心更是與日俱增。她不時想起真主大發善心，在和宰相公子經歷一番噩夢之後救了她的性命，將她交給了自己真正的丈夫阿拉丁。

阿拉丁的聲譽在人們心目中日益增進，大家更加愛戴他了。當時有些叛軍正向蘇丹國境逼來，國王於是召集軍隊，任命阿拉丁為統帥。阿拉丁率兵馳騁戰場，舞劍殺敵，他奮不顧身地驍勇作戰，直衝敵陣。一場血戰接踵而來，他和部下把叛軍打得落花流水，東逃西竄。阿拉丁的軍隊獲得了不少戰利品。在一片凱旋聲中班師還朝。全城上下一派節日氣象,準備迎接阿拉丁。蘇丹親自出朝相迎,慶祝他旗開得勝;在一片歡騰聲中,蘇丹擁抱了阿拉丁。然後他和女婿回到阿拉丁的家中。菩德公主見了丈夫心花怒放,親吻了他的眉心,便拉他進了閨房。不一會,國王來看他們,三人一起坐下喝了些飲料。蘇丹降下聖旨:舉國上下都要張燈結綵,慶賀阿拉丁的戰功。此時在三軍將士和全體百姓的眼中,天上只有真主,地下只有阿拉丁,阿拉丁輕財好施,挺身救國,而且騎術高強,一股英雄氣概,因此比起往日,人們更是敬愛三分。

再說那摩爾巫士。他把阿拉丁關閉在地窖裏,料想他活不成了,自己一路兼程回到本國。終日唉聲歎氣,心想吃了這許多苦,費了九牛二虎之力,原來可以穩穩到手的神燈卻成了一場空歡喜。夢寐以求的肥肉剛剛到嘴,轉眼間又不翼而飛了,想到這裏,氣得他只是把阿拉丁詛咒。

"小混蛋埋在地下早沒命了,這是好事。神燈留在寶庫還是不會出岔子,我說不定還能弄到手。"巫士時常這麼自寬自慰。

有一天他想探明阿拉丁的生死和神燈的確切位置,於是撒開流沙來扶乩。巫士擺開架勢,把前前後後各種圖形逐一標出,認認真真過目一遍,卻看來看去不知神燈的下落。他一氣之下,又抓了一把流沙撥弄一番,想吃準小傢伙已經死了,可是寶庫裏竟無他的屍體。不久他風聞到阿拉丁還在人世,不禁火冒三丈。他恍然大悟,阿拉丁一定逃出了地窖,獲得了神燈。他過去出入虎穴,歷經磨難,為的就是這盞神燈啊!他心中暗想:"這該死的小壞蛋倒是隨手就得到了。他要是發現了神燈的魔力,現在就變成數一數二的大富翁了。我非得想個辦法毀了他。”

巫士再次撒散流沙，仔仔細細察看圖形。他終於發現阿拉丁手中的錢財堆積如山，而且和蘇丹的女兒結了婚。他醋勁兒發作，暴跳如雷，陷入了瘋狂，於是巫士跳起身來，立時三刻就動身上路，往中國去了。

他跋山涉水，經過千辛萬苦，總算到了京都，找了個客棧安頓下來。阿拉丁就住在城裏，因此巫士到處聽見人們在談論阿拉丁那座雄偉壯麗的宮殿。他歇息了半個時辰，換了一身打扮，穿街走巷閒逛起來。不論他路過哪裏，耳邊只聽得眾人紛紛誇讚阿拉丁宮殿好不氣派，他的翩翩風采和英俊的儀表；人人稱道他的豪舉和美德。有個人正在說阿拉丁的好話，摩爾人便走上前去打聽道：“好伙計，你捧得這麼高的人究竟是誰啊？能告訴我吧？”

“哎！先生，想來您准是個外地來的生人，”那人答道。“就算新來乍到，難道您就一點沒聽人說起阿拉丁王爺嗎？他大名鼎鼎，誰不認識他呀！他的宮殿是天下一大奇觀。您居然一無所聞，連阿拉丁這個名字也不曾聽到過，這是怎麼搞的？願真主使他安享殊榮，幸福快樂！”

“我十分想觀光那座宮殿。能勞駕您給我指路嗎？我是初到此地。”摩爾人乘機說道。

“哦，願意效勞。”那人說罷便走在他前面，把他帶到阿拉丁的宮殿。

巫士望着這座高樓，心裏馬上明白了那是全仗神燈的魔力建造的。

"哼，"他暗自思忖，"我要他落入我的圈套，這該死的衣匠子弟過去是一頓晚飯錢也撈不到。如果天意幫忙，我會叫他傾家蕩產，讓他老娘再去紡紗織線。"

巫士懷着滿肚子的怨恨和嫉妒，回到了客棧，又取出占卜的木盒。他撒開流沙，結果發現了神燈藏匿的地方。原來它就在宮裏，阿拉丁並沒有隨身帶着。這一下他高興極了，失聲叫道："現在我要幹這事輕鬆多了，我自有辦法弄到這神燈。"

他離開下處，走到一個銅匠跟前對他説："請你打造幾盞銅燈。假如你手腳快些，工錢不會少給。"

"好説好説，"銅匠一口應承下來。一會就動手做了起來。

工作做完了，摩爾人並不討價還價，付了工錢，拿起銅燈回到落腳之處。他把東西放進一隻籃子，沿着街巷集市轉悠，嘴裏吆喝着："誰要舊燈換新燈，快來吧！"

眾人聽着他的喝聲，都在訕笑他。"這人準是瘋了，"大家你言我語説開了。"誰會這麼東奔西走，去拿新燈換舊燈呀？"

頓時一大羣人緊跟在後面，好些頑皮的孩子跟着起哄，摩爾人走到哪裏，他們也跑到哪裏。摩爾人旁若無人地只管自己走路，不覺已經來到阿拉丁宮殿的前面。他放開嗓門，一聲比一聲喊得響亮。一羣小孩卻連連不斷地叫喚："瘋子來嘍！瘋子來嘍！"偏巧公主留在圓頂大廳裏，她聽見了街上的喧鬧聲，於是便差了一個婢女出去看個究竟。婢女上街一瞧，只見一條漢子嚷嚷着："誰要舊燈換新燈，快來喲！"小孩們一個勁地嘘他滾開。

婢女回來告訴女主人説："公主，大門外面有個老頭在喊甚麼'誰要舊燈換新燈，快來喲！'小孩們在拿他取笑呢。"

公主一聽這麼個奇怪的交易，也覺得好笑。且說阿拉丁把神燈擱在自己房裏，忘了上鎖。有個婢女無意之間看到了，此時便說：“公主，主人的房裏有盞舊銅燈。我們取來交給老頭，看看他可當真換個新的，好嗎？”

“那就給我拿來吧，”公主點了頭。

菩德公主哪裏知道這燈和它的魔力，她更不知道正是這個玩意給阿拉丁帶來了大宗大宗的錢財。她現在不過是想弄個明白，摩爾人怎麼會鬼迷心竅用新燈調換舊燈。

婢女走入阿拉丁的房裏，取來了舊燈交給公主。公主派管家的太監出去換盞新燈回來。太監奉命把那盞舊的遞給摩爾人，換回了一盞新的送給公主。菩德公主左看右看，發現果然是嶄新的，笑口大開，說那老頭真笨。

且說那摩爾人一眼認出了神燈，他連忙藏進長衫的胸袋，把籃子裏剩下的幾盞銅燈順手扔給一班戲弄他的小流氓。巫士飛奔而去，徑直出城，來到一片不見人煙的曠野。他等着夜幕降臨。天黑之後，他才掏出神燈來拂拭。神怪頓時出現在他面前，說道：“奴僕在此，主人。有何吩咐？”

“神燈的奴僕，我命令你把阿拉丁的宮殿連同裏面的所有家當統統搬起來，再帶上我，一起運送到非洲我的國家去。我的故鄉你知道在哪裏；你就使宮殿坐落在花園庭院之中。”“遵命。你先閉起眼睛再睜開，就會發現你連人帶物都在故土了。”

話音一落，大功告成了。剎那間，摩爾人和阿拉丁的宮殿，還有宮中的一切財寶，全部輕而易舉地搬到了非洲。不在話下。

現在回過頭來再說蘇丹和阿拉丁。國王次日起牀之後，像他平日的習慣一樣，推開窗戶眺望對面公主的宮殿。可是他只見一大片空空蕩蕩的場地，又是從前的光景。他大大地吃了一驚，茫然若失。他揉揉雙眼又看了一遍，怕是睡眼惺忪。瓊殿玉宇突然間片瓦不見，他弄不明白怎麼會消失得無影無蹤。絕望之際他雙手緊摀，老淚縱橫，因為他還不曉得女兒的下落。蘇丹立即召見宰相。宰相聞命趕到，一見蘇丹萬分悲傷便驚呼起來：“願真主保佑陛下不致中邪！怎麼會看到王上如此心碎？”

“你還蒙在鼓裏？”蘇丹詰問道。

“憑着真主起誓，我一無所知，”宰相回了一句，“不明底細。”

“這樣説來，你沒有朝阿拉丁的宮殿望上一眼嗎？”蘇丹愀然作色道。

“是這樣。宮門還沒開哩。”

“難怪你不明真相，”蘇丹泣不成聲地説道，“請你從窗口瞧個仔細，看看哪裏還有阿拉丁的宮殿，你説是宮門緊閉着呢。”

宰相走向窗口，往阿拉丁的高樓大廈望了一眼。只見滿目荒涼，朱樓畫棟已是一掃而空。宰相見此出人意表的景況呆住了，他回到蘇丹跟前。

“哼，你該清楚我怎麼會傷心了吧？看得見阿拉丁的宮殿嗎？虧你説得出是宮門未開哩。”

“大王，我三番五次稟告陛下，宮殿也罷，婚事也罷，從頭到尾都是妖術作怪。”

“阿拉丁在何處？”蘇丹勃然大怒道。

“打獵去了，”宰相答道。

蘇丹當即下令派上一批官兵前去捉拿阿拉丁，説是要套上手銬腳鐐帶至御座跟前。於是眾多官兵一躍上馬，執行命令去了。他們遇到了阿拉丁，對他說道："老爺，驚動您了。蘇丹命令我們給你套上手銬腳鐐去見他。請多多擔待。我們遵照聖旨辦事，不敢違命。"

阿拉丁一聽此話如雷轟頂，原來他不知就裏。這時他面對一班官兵說道："諸位兄弟，你們可知道蘇丹如何會下這道命令的？我自知清白無辜，不曾忤上，也未對國家犯罪。"

"老爺，我們哪裏知道！"

"那麼你們就執行命令吧，"阿拉丁說完跳下馬來。"所有臣民必須服從王上。"

官兵們一陣忙亂，將他套上鐐銬，押送回京。且說城中百姓一見阿拉丁落到這個地步，馬上心裏明白了，蘇丹要他的腦袋。大家本是愛戴他，所以黑壓壓站了一街子的人，個個手持棍棒，握住刀劍，緊跟着他，想看看會出甚麼事。

這班官兵將阿拉丁帶至王宮面稟國王，蘇丹當即下令刑吏斬首。眾民一聞此令，便關閉了所有宮門，並向蘇丹發出一道警告，說是："如果阿拉丁受到半點傷害，我們此時此刻就當着你和宮裏人的面，摧毀宮室。"

宰相進來把奏摺交給蘇丹。

"陛下，此命一下，我等就完了。不如饒了阿拉丁一命，不然後果可怕得很。臣民們愛戴阿拉丁勝似我等。"

在這時候刑吏攤開墊子，讓阿拉丁跪下。他蒙上阿拉丁的眼睛，在他身邊走過三圈，等着國王的最後命令。蘇丹只見臣民們聚在宮門周圍，人聲鼎沸，包圍了四面宮牆，就要爬上城牆，好摧毀這座王宮。他連忙下令刑吏住手，吩咐傳令的人出宮向眾人宣佈國王已經饒恕了阿拉丁。

阿拉丁被解除了鐐銬，走到蘇丹面前説道："陛下，您既然開恩饒我一命，央求您明示我犯了甚麼罪過，觸怒了王上。"

"好個奸賊，"蘇丹怒喝道，"竟敢佯裝不知你的罪過？"他又轉向宰相道："帶他到窗口去看看，現在哪裏還有他的宮殿！"

宰相引着阿拉丁走近窗口，阿拉丁往外朝着宮殿的方向望去。他只見一片淒涼光景，人煙消失，玉宇瓊樓沒有一點影蹤。他瞠目結舌地回到御前。

"看到甚麼了？"蘇丹發問道。"你的宮殿呢？我的女兒呢？她是我的心肝寶貝，我只有她一個孩子啊！"

"大王，此事我一點不知道，也不清楚出了甚麼事。"

"你聽仔細了，阿拉丁，我暫且不將你處死，要你去解開這個謎團，把我的女兒找回來。找不着她就別回來見我。要是你不能帶她回宮，我立誓要親自砍掉你的腦袋。"

"遵命，陛下，只求您寬限四十天。如果我不能按時帶她來見您，就聽憑處置，斬了我的頭也可以。"

"那好吧，我准你四十天期限。不過你切莫以為能夠逃出我的手掌。你就是騰雲駕霧，我也能把你拿獲。"

眾人總算見到了阿拉丁，個個都歡天喜地。阿拉丁走出王宮，自己還能活着出來，心中怎麼能不高興；但是剛才的一切使他丟了面子，況且他的冤家對頭又是趾高氣揚，他不覺垂頭喪氣了。一連兩天他心灰意懶地在城中東走西逛，該做些甚麼也沒主意，虧得還有幾個朋友私下給他捎些吃的喝的。他也顧不得東南西北，無意間走入一片荒地，於是越走越遠，來到一條河邊。他擔驚受怕，心意煩亂，不抱一星半點的盼頭，也許不由自主地就會投河輕生了。好在他誠心誠意地信仰真主，於是提醒自己真主是獎懲分明的，他並未自殺，而是跪倒在河岸邊進行祈禱。他雙手捧起河水，按照儀式規矩擦洗手指。他正巧拂拭了摩爾人給他的那個指環。一個神怪當下就顯形了，他說：“我在這裏。奴才站在主人跟前。有何吩咐？”

阿拉丁一見神怪就手舞足蹈，驚叫起來：“指環的奴僕，把我的愛妻、殿堂和宮中一切人物財寶快快送還。”

“大人，您的要求我無能為力，那是燈奴範圍的事。”“好吧，既然你此事辦不到，那就把我帶走，讓我在自家殿堂的附近停下，不論它在天涯海角。”

“主人，奴才當依命行事。”

說完，神怪一手把他托起，轉眼工夫便將他放在那座宮殿附近，妻子的閨房就在前面。這裏地處非洲。此時夜色深沉，他看到了自己的宮殿，不覺就無憂無慮，轉悲為喜了。阿拉丁充滿希望地向真主祈禱，祝願自己在絕望之後還能破鏡重圓。他陷入了沉思，驚歎起法力無邊的神威——正是上蒼把指環賜予他，如果沒有指環的奴僕助他一臂之力，他就走投無路了。阿拉丁心裏一樂，就把那重重心事拋至腦後。三四天來他焦急萬分，悲痛欲絕，不曾合過眼；此刻他四肢舒展，睡倒在宮殿邊上的一棵大樹下。原來現在的宮殿坐落於城外，四處都是花草叢生之地。

雖說不安的思緒依然縈繞於他的腦海，阿拉丁還是在樹下酣睡起來，直到破曉時分，鳥語陣陣把他驚醒了。他爬起身來，走到不遠的一條流向城裏的河邊，洗過手，擦完臉，又唸起早晨的祈禱。過後，他回到原處，坐在菩德公主的閨房窗下。

公主自從和父王、丈夫分離以來，落入了可惡的巫士的魔掌，她終日傷心流淚，不吃不喝。可是無巧不成書，那天清早一個婢女進房給她着衣，打開窗子，瞧見阿拉丁坐在下邊，她喜出望外地對女主人呼叫起來。

"公主，公主，這不是我家老爺阿拉丁嗎？他正坐在下面呢！"

菩德公主衝向窗口，一對別離的情侶立刻認了出來，相互招呼，快活得瘋了一般。

"上來呀，快點！"公主叫道。"從邊門進來。巫士此刻不在這裏。"

婢女奔到樓下，打開一道邊門，阿拉丁徑直跑進妻子的閨房。兩人又哭又笑，撲向對方的懷抱，忘情地親吻起來。

"菩德，你先要告訴我，我出城游獵時留在我房裏的那盞銅燈弄到哪裏去了？"他們剛坐下阿拉丁就問道。

"嘻，親愛的！偏偏就是那盞燈讓我們倒霉了。"

"前前後後都講給我聽吧。"

菩德便把用舊燈調換新燈的經過和後來發生的一切從頭到尾講了一遍。

"第二天早上，"她又說道，"我們突然發現來到這個國家。那個欺騙我們的對我說一切都是靠他的魔法和那盞燈的威力完成的。他還說自己是非洲的摩爾人，我們目前在他的故鄉。"

"這個惡魔打算怎麼對待你呢？"菩德講完之後阿拉丁問道。"他對你說了些甚麼？他在你身上打甚麼主意？"

"他每日來看我一次，想方設法博取我的歡心。他要我忘掉你，把他當作我的愛人。他說蘇丹已經讓你人頭落地了，還說你本是窮人家出身，你的財富全得之於他。他一心想討我的喜歡，但他得到的只有沉默和眼淚。他從未聽到我對他說一句好話。"

"現在告訴我，他把神燈放在哪裏？"阿拉丁又問道。

"他總是隨身帶着，"菩德答道。"燈他是一刻也不離身的。但有一回他從長袍裏掏出來給我看過。"

阿拉丁聽了這話十分高興。

"菩德，你聽着，"他說道，"現在我打算出去一趟，換身衣服再回來。看到我化了裝不要受驚。派個婢女守在剛才那道暗門口，這樣我一回來她就好放我進門。我已想到一個妙計來殺死這個專做壞事的巫士。"

說罷，阿拉丁便走出了宮殿。他動身往城裏的方向去了。沒走幾步他就在路上碰見一個農夫。

"好兄弟，我們兩人換一身衣服吧。"他說。

農夫不肯；阿拉丁一把抓住他，非讓他脫下衣服，自己套在身上，把自己華貴的長袍回送給他。阿拉丁繼續趕路。到了城裏，他走到專賣香料的街市，買了一劑迷魂藥。他回到宮殿，從暗門走入菩德的房裏。

"且聽我說，"阿拉丁對公主說道，"你穿上一身漂漂亮亮的長袍，戴上首飾，不要愁眉苦臉的樣子。摩爾人回來時，高高興興地笑臉相迎。請他和你一起用飯，假裝你已忘掉丈夫和父親，深深地愛上他了。讓他取來紅酒，喜氣洋洋地祝他身體健康。三杯下肚之後，就把這劑藥倒在杯裏，再斟上一杯。他一喝下去，便會仰天躺倒，像個死人一樣。"

"這可難住我了，"公主答道。"可是要想擺脫那個可恨的惡魔，只好這樣做了。殺死這種人自然是不犯法的。"

阿拉丁和公主飽餐一頓，填滿了肚子。他起身飛快地離開了宮殿。

菩德喚來貼身女僕，她替公主梳洗過了，抹上香水，給菩德穿上最艷麗的衣服。過了片時，摩爾人進來了。看到公主換了新裝，心裏好不高興，一見公主又是笑臉相迎，自然更是喜出望外。此刻已是垂涎三尺了。菩德便拉他坐在自己的身邊。

"親愛的，你要是喜歡，"她溫柔地說道，"今晚就到我房裏來，我們兩人一起吃飯吧。我已傷心到頭了，就算長年累月坐着哭個不停，阿拉丁也決不會起死回生的。你昨天說的話我前思後想過了。我的父親蘇丹和我生離死別，八成是在悲痛之中處決了他。這話我信。因此你見我變了一個人，不必大驚小怪。我主意已定，往後你就是我的心上人和知己，你替代了阿拉丁，我現在只有你一個人了。讓我們今宵相聚，一起吃頓飯，喝上幾盅。我特別想嘗一口你們非洲的美酒，說不定比我家鄉的酒更加醇香可口。我這裏還有些家鄉的酒，可我更想喝點你們的酒。"

摩爾人看到菩德對他大顯熱情，一舉一動格外輕快，以為她再也不想阿拉丁了。於是他心裏大喜，說道："寶貝，你的願望我當然會百依百順。我家裏有一桶非洲好酒，我埋在地下已有八年了。我這就去取，我們可以喝個痛快。天一黑我就到你身邊來。"

菩德還想哄他一回，便說："心愛的人兒，不要把我孤零零的丟下。派個僕人去拿酒來吧，你好好坐在我身旁，有你作伴我才開心哩。」

「好太太，酒桶藏的地方只有我一人知道。我去去就來。」摩爾人回話道。

一邊說着他已離去，不上一會他拎着一大瓶酒回到房裏。

「我的心肝，偏勞你了。」

「瞧你説的，寶貝。為你效勞是你賞臉啊！」

菩德走到桌前，和他一同坐下，開始吃飯了。公主要來一杯，女僕便替她斟滿，再給摩爾人倒了一杯。他們嘻嘻哈哈地互祝健康，菩德一面機智伶俐地拿花言巧語來迷惑他。摩爾人酒後豪興大發，早把萬事忘得一乾二淨，不存一點戒心，以為公主是真心實意的，哪裏明白她這番情意不過是叫他送命的一個圈套罷了。他們喝完之後，他已是醉醺醺的了，菩德説道：「我們國家有個習慣，不知你們這裏怎麼樣？」

「那是甚麼習慣呢？」

「飯後情侶要飲交杯酒。」

她説完便拿起摩爾人的酒杯，為自己滿上一杯；接着她又讓女僕把杯子遞給他，裏面的酒已摻上了迷魂藥。女僕一點不動聲色，因為宮殿裏的男女僕人都盼着他早死，同公主齊心合力地對付他。那摩爾人接過交杯酒後神魂蕩漾，公主這番柔情蜜意已使他得意忘形，他想像自己就是當年不可一世的亞歷山大大帝。

「我的心肝，」菩德忸忸怩怩地把手放在摩爾人的手掌心裏，「我們兩人交過杯了，現在飲下這杯酒吧。」

菩德接過他的杯子一飲而盡；她走到摩爾人跟前，在他臉上親了一下。受寵若驚的摩爾人也想學她的樣，他把酒杯舉到嘴邊一口乾了，哪裏察覺酒中放了東西。他頓時便滾倒在地，四肢朝天，一副死人模樣，酒杯也從手中落下。菩德喜壞了，左右女僕連奔帶跑到了宮殿的門口，讓主人阿拉丁進來。

阿拉丁三腳兩步來到妻子的房裏，見她坐在桌旁，摩爾人一動不動地躺倒一邊。他笑逐顏開地把菩德抱在懷裏連連稱她幹得好。

"你先和僕人們進裏面臥室去，讓我一個人待會兒，事情還沒完哩。"

大家出去之後，阿拉丁隨即鎖好房門，走到摩爾人跟前，把手伸進他的胸口，從長袍裏掏出神燈。這時他拔出劍來劈下了摩爾人的腦袋。幹掉了仇人，他擦拭起神燈，神怪立刻出現了，說道："主人，奴才在此，奴才在此。你想要甚麼？"

"我命令你把這座宮殿抬起來，將它安放在原來的地方，就是中國王府的前面。"

"主人，奴才遵命照辦。"

阿拉丁進了裏屋，坐在妻子身邊，彼此親熱了一會。此時神怪已把宮殿搬到先前的地址，前面便是蘇丹的王宮。阿拉丁吩咐女僕們搬來飯桌，他和公主吃了一頓豐盛的晚餐，彼此都心滿意足了。他們兩人飯後又走進飲酒的廂房，兩人對飲作樂，酒興漸漸發作，睡意都上來了。

第二天一早阿拉丁起牀，喚醒了公主。女僕們進來給菩德梳妝打扮，阿拉丁也整好衣冠。兩口子都盼着早些見到蘇丹。

再說蘇丹。他放掉阿拉丁之後，還是為失去了女兒傷心不已；他日夜都在為菩德哭泣，就像一個傷心的女人。因為他就只有這麼一個孩子。每日天亮，剛一下牀，他就朝原先阿拉丁宮殿的方向張望，不停地涕泣，直到淚水哭幹了，眼皮兒哭疼了。這天早上他像往常一樣，起來推開窗戶向外眺望——眼前赫然出現一座高樓。他再揉眼細看，目不轉睛，那是阿拉丁的宮殿，沒錯！他立即吩咐備馬，趕到女婿的住所。

阿拉丁看着御駕漸漸走近，他下樓來到廣場中央恭迎國王，然後扶住蘇丹，領他走進公主的閨閣。菩德一見父王駕到，萬分高興。蘇丹緊緊抱住女兒，父女二人淚水交流，接着蘇丹問起她一切可好。

"父王，我一直心如死灰，昨天見到了丈夫，我才打起了精神。他把我從摩爾巫士的魔掌裏搭救出來，走遍天下再也找不到比他更下流的壞蛋了。要不是多虧了阿拉丁，我就逃不出他手裏，您這輩子也就休想再見到女兒啦。一來離開了您的身旁，二來和丈夫天各一方，我經不起這樣的悲痛，一天瘦似一天。我一定要好好報答阿拉丁，他是我的救命恩人啊！"

菩德又把遭難的經過敍述了一遍。她告訴蘇丹摩爾人先把自己喬裝成賣燈的小販，後來她又拿丈夫的舊燈調換了一盞新燈。

"隔了一夜，父王，"她接着說，"我們發現整個宮殿和宮裏的人已經在非洲了。換燈的時候我並不知道舊燈神通廣大，後來阿拉丁來看我們，想出條妙計對付摩爾人，我們才逃脫出來。沒有丈夫來救命，那壞蛋就要無禮了。阿拉丁交給我一劑迷魂藥，我把它拌在酒裏給他喝了。酒一落肚，他便摔倒在地，像斷了氣的人一樣。這時阿拉丁衝了進來，也不知他怎麼着了，反正一眨眼我們回到自己國家了。"

"陛下,"阿拉丁說,"我進去之後看到他已昏昏沉沉躺在那裏失去了知覺,就叫菩德公主和女僕們進裏屋去。她們走後,我蹲在摩爾人旁邊,伸到他的胸口掏出了神燈,菩德告訴我這燈他是隨身帶着的。然後,我召來神燈的奴僕,命令他把宮殿搬回原處。陛下,您要是不信的話,請過來看看那可惡的摩爾人吧。"

國王跟阿拉丁過去看到了摩爾人。他當即下令把屍首抬出去燒掉。他一面擁抱阿拉丁,一面說道:"賢婿,我委屈你了,原諒我吧。都是那壞心眼的巫士讓你中計吃苦了。我的過錯也許能得到寬恕,因為我嘗到了喪女之痛。比起我的王國,我的獨生女兒更加可貴。你也知道天下父母是多麼愛他們的子女;我愛我的女兒又更甚一層,菩德原是我唯一的寄託。"

"大王,"阿拉丁答道,"您並未委屈我,我也沒有得罪陛下。一切都是那該死的摩爾人的不是。"

蘇丹降旨:全城上下粉飾一新。於是大街小巷鋪陳一番,百姓聞訊之後歡騰雀躍,國王還叫傳令官告諭大家,這一天定為喜慶日,舉國百姓要慶祝一個月,紀念菩德公主和阿拉丁駙馬的歸來。

雖說這該死的巫士屍首已經付之一炬,骨灰也隨風飄去,阿拉丁卻並沒有十分太平。那個惡棍還有一個更壞的兄弟,同樣精通巫術占卜,真是應了古話:難兄難弟,一對活寶。兩人各居一方,專使些歪門邪道,都是詭計多端,不安好心。偏巧有一日這個巫士心血來潮,要打聽分手多年的兄弟的情況。他便撒開流沙,畫些圖形,細細地端詳。他突然心涼了半截,原來兄弟不在人世了。他再次撒開流沙，想弄清楚兄弟死亡的經過和地點。他終於發現兄弟不明不白地死在中國一個名叫阿拉丁的後生手裏。他馬上爬起來打點行裝準備上路。他在途中翻山越嶺，穿過荒地平原，歷經數月到了中國，不久便進京了。他在客商落腳的下處歇息了半晌，然後便上街走訪，千方百計要為死去的兄弟報仇。他走進街市上的一家茶館。這裏十分寬敞，客人三五成羣，有的在扔骰子，有的走雙陸，還有的在下象棋。他在一張桌子跟前坐了下來，聽見旁邊桌子的人在議論一個叫做法娣瑪的聖女，她在城外一間幽室裏修道，每月進城兩趟；她妙手回春，醫道非凡，遠近無人不知。

"這下總算有門了，"摩爾巫士自言自語道。"真主保佑的話，靠着這個女人我就能實現我的計策了。"

他轉向那些熱心讚美聖女的客人，向一位詢問道："老兄，這個聖女是誰啊？她住在何處？"

"唷，伙計，"這人叫了一聲。"法娣瑪的奇跡居然還有人不曾聽說過？可見你是生客了。她禁食多年，一心修道，菩薩心腸，你才頭一回聽人誇讚她？"

"您說對了，我是外鄉人，"摩爾人答道。"昨晚上我才到此地。就請您談談這位賢良婦人的奇跡吧，再告訴我她的住址。我走了背運，想去求她唸唸經，也許真主肯為我排憂解難。"

這人便將聖女法娣瑪的奇跡和美德一一道來。說完便攙住摩爾人的手，領他走到城郊，把通向小山頂上一個窨洞的小路指點給他，說是法娣瑪就住在那洞裏。摩爾人感謝此人的一番好意，然後又回到下處去了。

事有湊巧。第二天法娣瑪就進城來了。摩爾人一早出門，發現街上擠滿了人。他上前打聽為甚麼如此熱鬧，原來聖女站在人羣中間。那些有病痛的人把她圍了個水泄不通，人人求她祝福唸經；她的妙手所觸之處百病皆除。摩爾人一步也不遠離，直到她返回山洞。他等着天黑之後，走進一家酒肆，喝下一大盅烈酒，徑直往法娣瑪的山洞走去。到了洞裏，只見她已睡熟，墊的是塊草席。他輕手輕腳走過去，悄沒聲兒的就坐在她肚子上，拔出匕首，怪嚇人的大吼一聲。法娣瑪猛地張開眼睛，她呆住了：眼前一個摩爾漢子正蹲坐在她胸口，手握匕首就要下毒手了。

　　"給我聽着！"他嚷道。"你要敢吐一個字叫出聲來，我這就宰了你。快爬起來照我說的去做。"

　　他又向她擔保，只要服從他就不會遭到傷害。說完便扶她站了起來。

　　"你先跟我換身衣服。"

　　她就把身上穿的、頭上戴的、臉上披的全交給了他。

　　"現在，往我臉上塗些油膏，臉色看上去要跟你一模一樣。"

　　老婦走到角落取出一罐油膏，放一些在手心裏，搽在他臉上，終於和她自己的臉色分辨不出了。她把拐棍也給他了，還教他走路時如何使用，下山進城後該做些甚麼。末後再將念珠套在他頭頸裏，遞給他一面鏡子，說道："你瞧！哪裏看得出你我是兩個人啊。"

　　摩爾人一照鏡子，活脫是老婦的模樣。他一達到目的就背信棄義了。他要了一根繩子，她剛拿來，摩爾人便一把掐住她的脖子，勒緊繩子，直到她斷了氣。他把屍體拖出洞口，扔進一個坑裏。然後他到山洞裏又睡了一大覺。

天一亮他就起來趕路進城。他在阿拉丁宮殿的前方站停下來。人們紛紛圍住了他，都以為他是聖女法娣瑪。他完全學她的樣，把手放在病人身上，大唸經文。菩德聽見街上鬧鬧哄哄的，便叫僕人出去看個究竟。太監轉了一圈，回來報告說："公主，是聖女法娣瑪在行醫，她可是手到病除哦。你要是有這意思，我就請她進來，沒準兒你還託她的福哩。"

"去帶她過來。我早已聽人說起她的奇跡和德行，自然很想見到她。"菩德說道。

太監便將偽裝成法娣瑪的摩爾巫士領入宮內。一走到公主面前，他便主動唸了一大段經文，祝她延年益壽。人人都信了他就是聖女本人。菩德起身相迎，寒暄了幾句，讓他坐在身邊。

"法娣瑪太太，"菩德說道，"我真想和你朝夕相處，這樣既託你福，又能學到你的虔誠和善良。"

巫士一聽正中下懷。但他不露半點破綻，說道："公主，老婦人受慣了窮。長年累月生活在荒山野地。像我這樣的出家人哪配住進君主的王宮呀！"

"別為這事犯愁，"公主說道。"我讓人給你騰出一間屋子歸你用，你可以清清靜靜地唸經。這裏總比山洞強些，你可以好好地敬奉真主。"

"公主，我不敢違命。公主王孫的言語是不可違背的。我只求您許我飲食起居都在自己房裏，沒有人來打擾。我不講究吃的。每日請人送兩個饅頭一杯清水，這已是讓您破費了。肚子餓了，我會在房裏吃的。"

狡猾的摩爾人提出這個要求，原來是害怕吃飯時掀起面紗他那一臉鬍子會洩漏天機。

"不必操心，"菩德答應了，"遵照你的意思就是了。我現在帶你去看看房間。"

公主起身領着這個喬裝改扮的巫士來到她派給聖女專用的屋子。

"法娣瑪太太，"她説，"這裏歸你用。沒人打擾，安安靜靜的。"

摩爾人道過謝，為她祈福。菩德接着又帶他看了二十四扇窗檽的珠寶圓頂，問他造型可美觀。

"真主有眼，我説閨女啊，這實在漂亮極了，"摩爾人道。"天下再找不到這樣的好所在。可依我看少了一樣東西。"

"那是甚麼呀？"公主詢問道。

"一種叫做大鵬的鳥蛋，"巫士答道，"要是把它懸掛在圓頂中央，這大廳就成了名副其實的天下奇觀了。"

"這是甚麼鳥，上哪裏能找到蛋呢？"公主問道。

"這鳥奇大無比，公主，"摩爾人答道。"它形狀碩大，力氣也大，爪子能握住駱駝、大象一起飛翔。卡夫山上多半能發現這種鳥。要建造這座宮殿的人才能為你搞到一個鳥蛋。"

到了開飯時分。女僕們鋪開桌面，菩德便請客人一起用餐。巫士辭謝一番，回屋自顧自去吃了。

晚上，阿拉丁游獵回宮了。菩德過去招呼他，阿拉丁抱着她親了幾下。一見她神色不安，像有心事，忙問她是怎麼回事。

"好好的呢，"她説。"我總想宮裏應有盡有，不缺甚麼了。

就是珠寶圓頂上如果懸掛一個大鵬的蛋，那這座宮殿便是舉世無雙的了。"

"就這麼點事，"阿拉丁答道，"再便當不過了。我的乖乖，別愁眉苦臉的。想到要甚麼儘管說出來，我馬上就弄來，哪怕是藏在一團漆黑的大山洞裏的東西。"

阿拉丁離開了妻子，走進自己房裏取出神燈，剛一拂拭，神怪便出現了，說道："您要甚麼？"

"你去弄個大鵬的蛋來，把它掛在圓頂中央。"

可是一聽此話，神怪就緊皺起眉頭。

"忘恩負義的人類！"他暴跳如雷。"我和神燈其他的奴僕都是隨叫隨到，你還不知足啊？你竟然開口要我把眾奴僕的女管家找來，讓她吊在圓頂中央供你取樂嗎？你和公主真該燒成灰，讓風飄走。不過你們兩人都不知道這是犯忌的，招來的後果你們也不知道，所以饒了這一回。該怪的不是你。禍首是那為非作歹的巫士，他是原來那個摩爾人的兄弟。這人現在就住在你宮殿裏，他化裝成聖女法娣瑪。他把她弄死在山洞裏，然後披上了她的衣裝。他到這裏來是為他死去的兄弟報仇。就是他調唆你的妻子提出這麼個要求。"

話音未落，神怪便隱身而去了。

阿拉丁聽了這番話如雷轟頂，手腳嚇得直打哆嗦。可他一會就鎮靜下來了。他回到公主跟前說是頭疼，因為他也知道聖女的醫道是出了名的。公主於是派人上去叫法娣瑪，只消讓她的手放在他頭上，阿拉丁的頭就不痛了。

"法娣瑪馬上就能醫好你的頭疼，"她說。

"誰是法娣瑪？"阿拉丁問道。

菩德告訴他已請聖女法娣瑪進宮和自己作伴。這時摩爾人走入房裏，阿拉丁起身相迎，一點不露聲色，把他當成真正的法娣瑪。他行過禮便説："法娣瑪太太，請您開開恩吧。您是手到痛除，久仰大名了。我的頭現在疼得厲害哩。"

可惡的摩爾人簡直以為自己聽錯了，他再盼望不過的就是阿拉丁這句話了。他走到阿拉丁旁邊，把一隻手放在他頭上，另一隻手從長袍裏摸出一把匕首要殺阿拉丁。不過阿拉丁早有戒備，他立刻抓住摩爾人的手，奪下兇器，刺入了他的胸膛。

"唷！你下了毒手，真可怕啊！"驚慌失措的公主失聲大叫。"你殺死了法娣瑪，難道就不怕真主的懲罰嗎？她是個有德行的出家人，她的奇跡是舉世公稱的呀！"

"你聽我説，"阿拉丁應道，"我殺死的這個壞蛋並不是法娣瑪，卻是暗害她的人。他是那個用妖術把你弄到非洲去的摩爾巫士的兄弟。他來到我們國家想出這些鬼點子。先害死了法娣瑪，又化裝成她的樣子，他是來找我算帳的，因為他兄弟死在我的手裏。正是他花言巧語哄你要個大鵬的蛋，想借此弄得我家破人亡。你要不信的話，就來看看我殺死的究竟是甚麼人。"

阿拉丁撕開摩爾人的面紗，菩德只見是個長了一臉鬍子的男人，於是真相大白了。

"親愛的，"她説，"我這是第二次差點送了你的命。"

"別説這話，菩德，"阿拉丁説。"為了你這雙美麗的眼睛，你降臨在我身上的一切我都甘心情願地認命了。"

菩德緊緊摟住阿拉丁的脖子，親吻着他。

"你就那麼珍惜我的感情？我卻辜負了你的深情厚誼，我要向你坦白。"她喃喃地説。阿拉丁便把她抱在懷裏，親吻她，兩人更加恩愛了。

正在此時蘇丹駕到了。他們兩個你言我語説開了，最後又把巫士的屍體指給他看。蘇丹下令把壞人燒成灰燼，和他兄弟一個下場。

阿拉丁和公主從此以後平平安安地過着快樂的生活。蘇丹一去世，他繼承了王位，大公無私地治理王國。他獲得了全體臣民的敬愛。

3

仙巴歷險記

仙巴第一次航海

年輕的時候，我從父親手裏繼承了一筆遺產，但我揮霍無度，很快就花掉了一大半；後來我終於認識到自己的無知：像我這樣揮霍無度，就是有一座金山也會坐吃山空的呀，更何況我在揮霍錢財的時候花去的時間比金錢更有價值，沒有甚麼比老來受窮更為可悲的了。我決心痛改前非，而且說幹就幹：我把家裏的東西全都賣掉，加上花剩下的那一點父親的遺產，湊合起來做了跑買賣的本金。

我帶着錢到了巴索拉，跟幾個商人合資包了一條船，就從那裏出海了。

我們經波斯灣往東印度去。我第一次嘗到了暈船的滋味，但我很快就適應了。

在航行中我們經過了幾座島嶼，出售或交換我們的貨物。有一天，我們正鼓帆順風往前行駛，突然風平浪靜，我們的船在一座稍稍露出海面的小島前打住了。小島鬱鬱蔥蔥，就像一塊草坪。船長命令下帆，讓願意上島的乘客自便，我也跟着上去了。就在我們玩得高興的時候，小島突然搖晃了起來，我們覺得腳下劇烈地震動了一下。

留在船上的人覺察到島上發生了地震，立即叫我們回船，否則我們全都難逃厄運；可是，我們腳下的所謂小島，其實是一條鯨魚的背。那些機敏的人都跳進了救生艇，其他的人躍入了大海，朝船游去；只有我還留在"島"上，確切地說，是留在鯨背上；這時鯨魚潛入水面，我剛抓住一塊生火用的木板，那巨大的傢伙就消失在浪谷底下。風漸漸大了起來，船長決定抓緊時間開船，帶着已經上船的人揚帆而去，留下我聽憑海浪發落。我整整一天一夜泡在海裏，隨時都有葬身魚腹的危險。第二天早晨，我精疲力竭，萬念俱灰，幸運的是一個激浪把我沖上了一座小島。

儘管我四肢乏力，但還是拼命往前爬，想找一些可以充飢的藥草或水果，我不僅找到了充飢的東西，還幸運地找到了一溪清水。吃飽喝足了，我力氣大增，開始在島上張望。走近一塊美麗的平地，看見一匹馬兒在吃草。我躡手躡腳地朝牠走去，驚喜交加，渾身顫抖，不知前面等着我的是凶是吉。走近一看，我發現那是一匹拴在柱子上的牝馬；正在我為牠的美麗而傾倒的時候，耳邊響起一個人的聲音，只見那人正朝我走來，問我是甚麼人。我向他講了我的經歷，他聽後拉着我的手，把我領進一個洞，我發現那裏還有一些人，我們彼此都很驚奇。

他們給了我一些吃的東西，我邊吃邊問，他們到這不毛之地來做甚麼，他們回答說，這島是米哈雷吉國王統治的，他們是他的奴僕，他們每年這個季節都上這裏來，讓米哈雷吉國王的母馬和上岸來的海馬配種。他們把馬拴起來，就像我剛才看見的那樣，因為他們一聽到母馬的嘶鳴，就得立刻把海馬趕回去，否則的話，海馬准會把母馬撕得粉碎。等母馬一受孕，他們就趕馬回去，這樣生出來的小公馬，叫做海公馬，專門留出來供國王使用。他們説，明天就是他們預定要回去的日子，要是我遲一天上島的話，肯定就沒命了，他們住得很遠，沒有人引路別想找到他們住的地方。

就在他們跟我説話的時候，海馬躍出了水面，就像他們剛才告訴我的那樣，立即朝母馬衝去。眼看着牠就要將那些母馬撕得粉碎，但是那些僕人們齊聲大吼，海馬只好作罷，重新躍入大海。

第二天，他們牽着馬、帶着我回到這個島國的首府。我們一到那裏，他們就把我介紹給了國王，國王問我是誰，怎麼會到他的屬地來的；我一一回答了他的問題，他對我的不幸表示了同情。他下達命令，要對我精心照料，滿足我的一切要求。

我認識了一些跟我一樣做生意的人。我特別注意尋找外國商人，一方面是為了打聽一些巴格達的情況，另一方面也是希望能夠找到可以和我結伴回家的人，因為米哈雷吉島國的首府在海岸線上，有一個美麗的港口，每天都有世界各地的船隻穿梭往返。

有一天，我正站在港口邊，看見一條船朝岸邊駛來。船員們把錨拋下後，就開始卸貨，岸上的貨主們把貨物往倉庫裏搬。我無意間朝那些包裹瞥了一眼，卻發現其中一些包裹上寫着我的名字。我仔細一檢查，認出正是我在巴索拉帶上船的那些東西。我還認出了那位船長；不過，我肯定他以為我已經死了，所以就走上前去，問他道："這些包裹是誰的？"

他回答説："是一個叫仙巴的巴格達商人，搭我的船時帶上來的。有一天，我們的船駛近一座小島，至少看起來像是一座小島，他和其他一些乘客上島去了。其實那根本不是甚麼島，而是一條巨大的鯨魚，正躺在水面上睡覺。有個人在鯨背上點火煮食，鯨魚被燙醒了，在大海裏翻騰起來。鯨背上的人大多淹死了，其中就有這個不幸的仙巴。這些包裹是他的，我決定把它們賣掉，以後若有機會碰到他家裏的人，我可以把賺到的錢交給他們。"

"船長，"我說，"我就是仙巴，你以為我死了，其實我還活着；這些包裹是我的財產和貨物。"

船長聽我這麼一說，驚叫起來："天啊！我該相信誰呀！這世上再也沒有甚麼人可以相信了！我是親眼看見仙巴淹死的；我船上的乘客們也親眼看見的，可你竟然這麼肯定地說你就是仙巴？初看起來你倒像個正派人，沒想到竟是個騙子，想把不屬你的東西佔為己有。"

"耐心點，船長先生，"我說，"請你耐心聽我説！"於是，我就把如何得救，如何遇見米哈雷吉國王的僕人並被帶進王宮的事，一五一十地告訴了船長。

船長聽得目瞪口呆，但他很快就相信我不是個騙子，因為他船上的一些乘客也認出了我，並祝賀我死裏逃生。最後他自己也認出了我，他一把抱住了我，驚喜地說："感謝上帝，你大難不死，必有後福。這是你的東西，你拿去吧。"我從心底裏感謝他，欽佩他的高尚行為。

我從包裹裏選出最珍貴的東西，作為獻給米哈雷吉國王的禮物。國王已經知道我的不幸經歷，他為我有這些珍貴、罕見的寶物感到驚奇，問我是從哪里弄來的。我向他講了我重新找回財物的經過，國王屈尊降貴地向我道賀，為我欣喜。他接受了我的禮物，回贈我更加貴重的東西。以後幾天，我第一次做起生意，用剩下來的貨物換了這個國家裏的一些產品，有蘆薈、檀香木、樟腦、肉豆蔻、丁香、辣椒和生薑。做完了生意，我就告別了這個國家，乘上原來的那條船，回家了。

仙巴第二次航海

昨天我有幸告訴諸位，在經歷了第一次航海，回到家裏後，我決定在巴格達安享餘年。可是我心裏那個舊念頭又復萌了，我要去領略異國風光，走海路跑買賣。我備好了貨物，約了幾位信得過的商人，準備第二次出海。我們上了一條好船，祈禱真主保佑，開始了航行。

我們經過了一座又一座小島，帶去的貨物賣出了好價錢。一天我們登上一座果樹覆蓋的小島，誰知島上一片荒涼，渺無人煙。我們在草坪上，在滋潤草坪的溪水邊散步；我們幾位同伴采水果、摘鮮花，聊以自娛。我掏出隨身帶着的酒和食物，坐在小溪邊涼爽的樹蔭底下吃喝起來。我吃飽喝足了，倦意漸漸襲來，不知不覺地就睡着了。也不知睡了多久，反正醒來時船已不在眼前。我嚇壞了，跳起來尋找我的同伴，但他們全都走了；我遠遠看見船兒正揚帆而去，轉眼就沒了影兒。

陷入這麼令人沮喪的境地，當時我的心情各位不難想像。我一次又一次地責怪自己：我怎麼這麼傻呀，雖然我生性愛冒險，可有了第一次的航海經歷，照理也該滿足了呀；但是現在後悔又有甚麼用呢。看來只好聽天由命了。我爬上一棵大樹，朝四處打量，看看可會發現甚麼給我帶來希望的東西。我朝大海望去，那裏除了無垠的海水，就是灰濛濛的天空。我又朝島上看看，咦，看見了一個白色的東西。我連忙下樹，收拾起吃剩的食物，朝那東西走去。

走近一看，是一個圓球，再走近一點，用手一摸，軟乎乎的。我繞着它兜了一圈，看看有沒有進口，但沒找到，這圓球很滑，我幾次努力爬上去，都滑了下來。它的圓周約有五十步幅。

這時太陽已快落山；天色突然暗了下來，像是有一片烏雲遮沒了天空。我被這變化嚇了一跳，等到發現那片所謂的烏雲原來是一隻碩大無朋的鳥在我頭頂盤旋時，我更是嚇得魂飛魄散。我想起曾聽水手們說過有一種大怪鳥，兇猛異常，看來那個引起我注意的白色大圓球肯定就是這隻大怪鳥下的蛋了。果然不錯，眨眼工夫那大鳥就降落在圓球上，好像坐在上面。這時我靈機一動，有了主意：我悄悄地朝那鳥蛋湊過去，來到一隻鳥爪跟前；這鳥爪粗得像根大樹幹。我用頭巾把我綁在了鳥爪上，但願第二天早晨這鳥起飛時能把我帶出這個荒島。我的計劃成功了。第二天破曉，大怪鳥振翼起飛，牠把我帶到好高好高，地面上的東西都看不清了；然後，牠猝然下降，我差點昏了過去。大怪鳥一落地，我就迅速給自己鬆綁。就在我鬆綁後的一刹那，牠"嗖"地朝一條其長無比的蛇撲去，一口咬住牠，振翼而去。

大怪鳥把我帶到的是一個很深的山谷，四周是聳入雲端的高山、插翅難飛的峭壁。我真是劫數難逃了，剛離開荒島，又落入死谷，雖然換了個地方，死神卻一刻也沒放鬆我。

我沿着山谷察看，發現遍地都是鑽石，有些大得驚人，我仔細查看，倒也有趣，一時竟忘記了憂愁和不幸。但我很快發現遠處有一些東西不僅破壞了我的興致，而且叫我毛骨悚然。

原來前面盤臥着一條條巨蛇，就連最小的一條也能輕易地一口吞下一頭大象。白天，牠們藏在洞穴裏躲避牠們的天敵大怪鳥，只有在晚上才出來活動。我整個白天就在山谷裏四處探察，找着機會便休息片刻；太陽落山後我躲進一個安全的小洞，洞口又低又窄，我搬來一塊大石頭堵住洞口，既可防止巨蛇襲擊，又能讓一縷陽光射進洞裏。

我吃了一點東西，清晰地聽見巨蛇出洞的聲音。那嘶嘶的巨大響聲讓我毛髮悚立。各位不難猜出，這一晚我沒有睡好覺。

東方發白，蛇羣退去。我戰戰兢兢地出洞，說老實話，儘管我腳下淨是鑽石，可我一點沒起貪心。我找了個地方坐下來，吃完了僅有的一點食物，儘管一想到那些可怕的蛇，心就怦怦地跳個不停，難以鎮定，但抵不住昨天一夜未睡，壯着膽子躺了下來。

就在睡意蒙矓之際，一件東西掉在我身邊，砰的一聲巨響驚醒了我。睜眼一看，好傢伙，竟是一大塊鮮肉，緊跟着峭壁上又接二連三地滾下來許多肉。

以前我常聽水手和其他人講起鑽石谷，講起商人們獲取這些珍貴鑽石的方法，我總覺得那是胡說。現在我總算相信這是真的了。獲取鑽石的辦法是這樣的：商人們在老鷹孵小鷹的時候爬上山谷四周的高山。他們事先切好大塊的肉，扔進山谷，把鑽石粘住。這裏的老鷹比別的地方更大更有力，牠們咬住肉塊，飛到峭壁頂上喂小鷹。商人們奔到鷹巢，發出各種響聲，嚇走老鷹，取下粘在肉塊上的鑽石。

本來我認定無論如何跑不出這個山谷了，我把它當成了我的墓地；但現在看見這些肉塊，想起了水手們的故事，我急中生智，又有了辦法。

我先撿了一些最大的鑽石，塞進我裝食物的包裹，然後挑了一塊最大的肉，用頭巾把它緊緊綁在我的身上。我就這樣躺在地上，緊緊抓着裝鑽石的包。

我躺了沒多久，一羣老鷹就從天而降，各自叼起一塊肉就飛走了。一隻最健壯的鷹衝向綁在我身上的肉，叼起來朝牠的巢穴飛去。商人們齊聲吶喊，嚇走了老鷹，然後，其中一位商人走上前來，一看見我，嚇得驚叫起來。但他馬上就鎮定下來，問我是怎麼上這裏來的，並跟我爭起鑽石，說那是他的財產。

"要是你知道我是用了甚麼辦法才到這裏來的，"我說，"你就只會可憐我，而不會生我的氣了。你且息怒，我不僅給自己拿了鑽石，也為你拿了一份。我的鑽石比他們全部加起來的還要值錢。我在山谷裏挑選了一些最好的，裝進了這個包裹。"

我邊說邊讓他看我的包。我話音剛落，另外一些商人發現了我，擁上前來，吃驚地圍住了我，我向他們講了我的經歷後，他們更是一迭連聲地嘖嘖稱奇。

他們把我領到他們的住處，看見我的鑽石，一個個都羨慕不已，說他們從沒見過這麼好、這麼大的鑽石。他們每個人都有一個睡覺的地方，我就和其中一位合住；為了表示謝意，我請他在我的包裹任意挑選，要多少拿多少。但他只拿了一顆，而且是最小的，我讓他再拿一些，別怕我發火，他拒絕了。"不要了，"他說，"有這麼一顆我就很滿足了，有了它，我再也不用冒險航海去碰運氣了。"

商人們已經在那裏留了幾天，現在他們覺得到手的鑽石已夠多了，第二天我們就一起離開了那裏，越過蛇羣出沒的高山；幸運地躲過了牠們的侵襲。我們一路平安地來到最近的港口，從那裏登船到了羅哈島，我在那裏用鑽石換了一些很值錢的貨物。我們又去了其他一些島嶼，最後回到了巴索拉，又從巴索拉回到了巴格達。我回家後做的第一件事就是把我歷經艱險所換來的許多錢分送給窮人，還剩下許多，我盡情享用，但我從來不做為富不仁的事情。

仙巴第二次航海的故事到此結束了。他又讓人拿來一百個金幣，送給欣巴德，並邀他第二天再來聽他講第三次航海的故事。

客人們回家了，第二天又按時來到仙巴家，腳夫欣巴德也來了，他幾乎忘記了他是個窮人。他們在桌旁坐下；酒足飯飽後，仙巴講起他第三次航海的故事。

仙巴第三次航海

我冒着生命危險換來了財產，過上了舒適的生活，很快就忘記了兩次航海中遇到的危險；但我正當年富力壯的時候，對這種平淡無奇的生活感到厭倦了，也不管將會遇到甚麼樣的災難，帶着一大批貨物從巴格達到了巴索拉。又在那裏和其他一些商人登船出海去了。這次我們的航程很長，經過了好多港口，買賣興隆，得利很多。

有一天，我們正在寬闊的大海上航行，遇上了一場狂風，使我們沒法憑藉天體測算方位。狂風一連颳了好幾天，把我們趕近一座小島，船長真想避開那座島，可我們萬般無奈，只得在那裏拋錨。船帆落下後，船長告訴我們說，這一帶和鄰近一些島嶼上住着野人，他們會襲擊我們。船長又說，雖然他們都是些侏儒，但我們千萬別想抵抗他們；因為他們人多勢眾，要是我們失手打死了他們中的一個，他們就會像蝗蟲一樣朝我們湧來，把我們搗成肉醬。

船長一番話，說得水手們一個個心驚肉跳，我們很快就發現船長所言不虛。我們看見不計其數的可怕的野人朝我們衝來，他們身高不過兩英尺，滿頭紅髮。他們飛身躍入大海，朝我們的船游來，一下子就把船團團圍住了。緊跟着，他們往船上爬，動作敏捷麻利，兩腳幾乎就沒沾船邊，轉眼工夫就佔領了甲板。

各位可以想像當時我們的情形：不敢自衛，甚至不敢跟他們講話，無力防止迫在眉睫的危險。他們解開船帆，割斷錨索，把船拖上岸，然後命令我們下船；他們把我們押到他們來的那個小島。任何航海人都像避瘟神一樣地躲避這座島，為甚麼呢，說來叫人傷心，你們馬上就會聽到；但是我們偏偏不走運，被帶到了這裏，只好聽天由命了。

我們離開海岸，進入小島深處，看見一些水果和藥草，就吃了起來，我們知道早晚得做刀下冤鬼，但都想儘量多活些時間。走着走着，我們看見遠處有一座大房子，我們轉身朝那裏走去。那是一座雄偉的宮殿，我們推了推烏木雙扇門，門開了。我們走進庭院，迎面看見一個帶門廊的大房間，房間一邊是一大堆死人骨頭，對面有許多烤肉鐵杷。見到這副景象，我們嚇得直打哆嗦，倒在地上，好久爬不起來。

太陽下山了；就在我們可憐巴巴地癱在地上的時候，突然砰的一聲巨響，房門打開了，一個面目可憎、像棵棕櫚樹一樣高大的黑人進了房間。他腦門中間一隻獨眼閃閃發光，像正在燃燒的煤塊一樣通紅；他的門牙又長又尖，露出在嘴巴外面，嘴巴大得像馬嘴巴一樣，下嘴唇耷拉到胸前；他的耳朵可以跟大象耳朵匹敵，垂在肩上，又長又曲的指甲尖如鷹爪。猛一見到這麼個可怕的巨人，我們都嚇得昏死了過去，久久回不過神來。

我們好不容易醒了過來，看見那巨人坐在門廊下，那隻敏銳的獨眼緊盯着我們。他發現我們醒了過來，便走上前來，伸出手抓住我的頭，把我轉了個圈，就像屠夫擺弄羊頭一樣。他仔仔細細地檢查過我後，發現我很瘦，簡直像皮包骨頭，就放了我。他又把我的同伴一個個仔細檢查過，我們的船長最胖，那巨人就像我逮麻雀一樣一隻手抓住他，另一隻手抓起一根烤肉鐵杷從他身上穿過，然後點起一堆大火，把船長烤了起來，烤熟了，就進內室裏把他當晚飯吃了。

巨人吃飽了，又回到門廊下，倒頭便睡，鼾聲如雷。他一覺睡到大天亮，而我們整夜提心吊膽，片刻不得安眠。那巨人醒來後便出去了，把我們留在宮殿裏。

我們估計他走遠了，便開始叫起苦來，昨天晚上因為怕吵醒巨人，我們整整憋了一夜沒敢吱聲。現在宮殿裏盡是我們的呻吟聲。儘管我們人不少，我們共同的敵人只有一個，卻誰也想不出辦法來殺死他，救出我們自己。但是，不管這是件多麼困難的事情，我們必須馬上採取行動。

我們設想了許多行動措施，但決不定到底採用哪一個；於是，我們決定聽從真主的旨意，這一整天，我們走遍小島，像剛上島時那樣，看見植物和水果抓來就吃。到了晚上，我們想找個過夜的地方，但是沒有找到，只好又留在宮殿裏。

那巨人準時回來，把我們的一個同伴當他的晚飯。吃好後倒頭鼾睡直到天亮，然後像第一天一樣起來，出去。我們的處境實在不妙，有幾個同伴甚至想，與其在這裏被可怕的妖魔生唻，不如跳海；他們還勸其他人效法他們，但有一個同伴説："自殺是犯禁的；即使真主允許自殺，我們何不齊心協力消滅這個吃人的妖魔呢，這樣豈不更好？"

我已想好一個對付那巨人的辦法，這時便乘機向我的患難兄弟透露了出來，大家一致贊同。"朋友們，"我接着説，"你們知道海岸上有許多木頭。你們聽我吩咐，我們紮幾隻木排，紮好後就藏起來，一找到機會就能用上。同時，大家開始實行我先前説的辦法，除掉那個巨人。如果我的計謀成功，我們就可以耐心地等在這裏，直到有船兒經過，我們就能上船離開這個要命的小島；如果我們失敗了，我們就把木排推下海，坐木排走。"

大家一致同意我的意見，我們很快紮了幾隻木排，每只木排可以坐三個人。

傍晚時分我們回到宮殿，轉眼工夫那巨人也回來了。我們又有一個同伴做了他的晚飯。但我們很快就報了仇。他吃完了可怕的人肉晚餐後，像往常一樣倒頭便睡。一聽見他的鼾聲，我們中九個最大膽的人加上我自己，每人拿起一根鐵抛，把尖頭燒燙，一齊刺進他的眼睛，把他刺瞎了。

巨人疼得嗷嗷大叫。他突然跳了起來，伸出雙臂朝四處亂摸，想要抓住我們，出他這口惡氣，但是，幸運得很，我們都及時地跑到他的腳踩不到的地方，躺在地上。他實在抓不到我們，只好摸到了門，哇哇地叫着，出去了。

我們立即跟着巨人出了宮殿，跑到藏木排的海岸邊。我們把木排推入大海，準備等到天亮後就登上木排，為的是怕會有人給巨人領路來抓我們；不過我們希望如果到天亮他還沒來，如果他那響遏行雲的痛叫聲停息了，我們就可以認為他死了；那樣的話，我們就可以留在島上，直到能找着更安全的航海的辦法。可誰知，太陽剛一露頭，我們就看見了那個兇惡的敵人，兩個差不多跟他一樣高大的人為他領路，還有許多人在他們前面快速奔跑。

一見這副情景，我們拔腿就朝木排上跑，儘快地把木排撐離海岸。那些巨人一看我們跑了，連忙撿起大石塊，朝海邊奔來，甚至跳進海裏，直到海水齊腰的地方，把石塊朝我們扔來，他們扔得準極了，除了我坐的那個之外，所有的木排都被砸沉了。這樣，只有我和另外兩個同伴逃了出來，其他人全都淹死了。

我們拼命地撐着木排，轉眼工夫石塊就砸不到我們了。

我們來到了大海上，在風浪裏顛簸，隨時都有被大海吞沒的危險，弄得我們整整一天一夜驚魂不定；但第二天，我們時來運轉。一個巨浪把我們沖上了一座島，我們欣喜若狂地爬了上去。我們找到了鮮美的水果，飽食了一頓，很快就從精疲力竭的狀態中恢復過來。

夜色降臨，我們到海灘邊睡覺，但很快就被一陣巨響驚醒，睜眼一看，唰的一下冷汗就出來了，只見一條長如棕櫚的巨蛇正朝我們撲來，沒等我們回過神，牠一口就咬住了我的一個同伴，儘管他拼命掙扎，還是被牠吞了下去。

另一位同伴和我拔腿就跑。"真主啊！"我驚叫，"我們甚麼時候才能消災解難啊！昨天我們還在慶倖從兇惡的巨人和風浪之中逃了出來，今天又遇到了同樣可怕的危險。"

我們走着走着，看見了一棵大樹，打算就在那上面過夜，希望那裏不會有危險。我們吃了點水果，天快黑時爬到了樹上。誰知轉眼就聽見了嘶嘶的聲音，一條巨蛇來到了樹下，順着樹幹往上爬，一口吞下了我的同伴，游走了。

我在樹上直待到天亮，下來時已經跟死人差不多了；說真的，我總覺得我會落得跟我同伴一樣的命運。

我拾了許多小木柴和荊豆，紮成一個個柴捆，繞樹放了一個大圈，又紮了一些十字架，蓋在我的頭上。夜晚來臨時，我就躲在這個圈子裏，坐在地上，沮喪而又聊以自慰地想：為了活命，我已使出了全部的力量。那條蛇又來了，牠想把我也吞掉，可是我紮的柴捆築起了一道圍牆，巨蛇不能如願。牠整夜盯着我；天終於亮了，巨蛇退去，但是直到太陽出來，我才戰戰兢兢地走出我的堡壘。

巨蛇一步不離地盯着我，害得我整夜不敢合眼，加上我紮了那麼多的柴捆，實在精疲力竭了，與其這麼一次次擔驚受怕，倒不如死了痛快。我朝大海奔去，想就此結束我的生命；但是真主可憐我，就在我即將跳海的一刹那，我看見遠處有一條船。我用盡全身力氣叫了起來，解開頭巾拼命揮舞，希望引起船上人的注意。算我走運，水手們都看見了我，船長放了只救生艇接我上船。

我一上船，船上的商人和水手們就迫不及待地問我怎麼會到那個孤島上去的；我向他們述說了發生的一切，他們為我的九死一生表示慶賀；他們猜想我一定餓了，拿出最好的東西來給我吃，船長看我的衣服破了，就慷慨地把他的衣服送給了我。

我們在海上逗留了很久，上過幾座島；最後我們登上了薩拉哈島，商人們從船上卸下貨物，在島上出售或交換。有一天，船長把我叫去，對我說："兄弟，我這裏有一些貨物，是很久前一位搭船的商人的。這位商人死了，我想把它們估個價，將來有機會碰到他的家人時，可以把錢交給他們。"他說的那些東西已堆在甲板上，他向我指點說："喏，就是這些東西；我想請你照料並負責出售，你可以照慣例拿到酬金。"我答應了，並感謝他給我一個幹活的機會。

一位船員把貨物登上貨主們的名字；在登到船長派我照管的貨物時，他問該寫誰的名字。船長說："你就寫航海人仙巴。"

我聽見有人竟叫得出我的名字，非常激動，仔細一看，這位船長就是我第二次航海時搭乘的那條船的船長，當時我在島上的小溪邊睡着了，他沒等我就開船走了。我一開始並沒有認出他，他的外貌跟我上次見到時判若兩人。他以為我已經死了，難怪他沒有認出我。

"船長，"我對他說，"這些貨物的貨主叫仙巴嗎？"

"是的，"船長回答說，"他叫仙巴；是巴格達人，在巴索拉搭上我的船。有一天，他登上一座小島去取淡水，不知甚麼緣故，被落下了。直到四個小時後，我們才發現他沒有上船，當時風很大，我們沒法返回去。""你認為他死了嗎？"我説。"肯定死了，"船長回答説。

"好吧，那就請你睜大眼睛吧，"我嚷道，"好好看看，被你留在孤島上的仙巴就在你面前。"

船長聽我這麼一説，立即直愣愣地盯着我，仔仔細細地打量過我後，終於認出了我。"謝天謝地！"他一把抱住了我，"我太高興了，能有機會彌補我的過失。這是你的貨物，我小心地保存着，每到一個港口就要估估價，現在我把它們還給你。"

我們從薩拉哈島到了另一個島，我在那裏買了丁香、桂皮和別的香料。經過長途航行，我們終於回到了巴索拉，從巴索拉回到了巴格達，我帶回了不計其數的錢財，給了窮人許多，又買了大量的土地。

仙巴第三次航海的故事到此結束。他又給了欣巴德一百個金幣，邀他明天再來赴宴，仙巴保證接着講他第四次航海的故事。欣巴德和別的客人們告辭而去，第二天他們準時赴約。晚飯過後，仙巴繼續講他的歷險經過。

仙巴第四次航海

第三次航海回來後，雖然日子過得悠閒自在，無憂無慮，但總覺得有點美中不足，總想着再到海上去冒一次險。我實在太愛做生意、太愛冒險了，斟酌再三，到底還是下定了決心：再去闖它一回。我安排妥當事務，備足了緊俏的貨物，便朝波斯出發，我經過波斯的幾個省份，最後到達一個港口，在那裏上了船。我們停靠過幾個大陸國家，又到過幾個東方島國；但是有一天，我們突遭暴風襲擊；帆被撕成碎片，船像脫韁之馬，撞上沙灘，粉身碎骨。許多船員葬身海底，貨物被海浪沖走。

我總算萬幸，跟幾個商人和船員一起抓住了一塊船板；一股巨流把我們沖上一座島嶼。我們找到一些水果、一股清泉，吃飽喝足了，力氣大增，就地躺下睡了一覺。

第二天早晨，太陽初升，我們離開了海岸，朝小島深處走去。我們發現了一些人家，就朝那裏加快了腳步。我們剛走近，就見一大羣黑人擁來，包圍了我們，使我們成了俘虜。他們嘀咕了一陣，好像在瓜分我們，隨後就各自領着我們到他們家去。

我跟五個同伴被帶到一戶人家。主人讓我們坐下，給我們一種藥草，做着手勢要我們吃下。我的同伴飢不擇食，想都沒想就狼吞虎咽地吃了起來，我一看，那些抓我們的人自己都沒有吃，心裏頓時起了疑心，知道這東西吃下去凶多吉少，所以我碰都沒碰；幸虧我有先見之明，不多一會，我就發現同伴們一個個失去了知覺，說起胡話來。而後，黑人們給我們吃椰子油煮的米飯；我的同伴們對自己的行為已經失去了控制，見了這米飯便不要命地吃了起來。我跟着吃了一點。

黑人們先給我們吃的草藥就像迷魂湯，它使我們忘卻在這種不幸的處境裏可能會產生的悲傷，而米飯則是為了把我們養胖。他們是些食人生番，想把我們養胖了供他們美餐。我的同伴們成了這種可怕的習俗的犧牲品，因為他們已經失去了理智，看不到厄運正等着他們。而我呢，不但沒有像我的同伴們那樣長胖，反而越來越瘦。我拿起飯來就想着要死，心裏就覺得害怕，所以這飯吃下去非但不補，反而有害，我很快就瘦得皮包骨頭了，到頭來卻反而因禍得福，因為那些黑人吃完了我的同伴們後，決定把我留下來，等我甚麼時候身上有肉了再吃。

在這同時，我得到了很大的自由，幾乎沒人注意我的行動。終於有一天，我找到一個機會，離開了那個黑人家，逃走了。我一連氣走了七天，時時留心着避開看上去有人家居住的地方，充飢解渴全靠椰子。

第八天，我來到了海邊；看見一些白人在摘辣椒，這裏到處都是辣椒。他們一看見我就朝我走來，用阿拉伯話問我從哪裏來。

重聞鄉音，我高興極了，爽快地回答了他們的問題。

我一直跟他們住在一起，直到他們摘夠了辣椒。他們邀我搭上他們的船，我們很快到達另外一座島，這裏就是他們的家。我的救命恩人們帶我晉見他們的國王，一個賢明的君主。他耐心地聽我講述了我的冒險經歷，聽得他瞠目結舌；他命人給我換上新衣服，吩咐手下人好好照料我。這個島國人口稠密，各種商品應有盡有。我在這新的地方生活得悠閒自在，忘卻了前些天的不幸，慷慨的君主對我體貼入微，使我樂而忘返。說真的，我就像是他最大的寵兒。

我發現一件很奇怪的事情：這裏的每一個人 —— 連國王也不例外 —— 騎馬時都不用馬鞍、韁繩或馬鐙。有一天我冒昧地詢問國王陛下他們為甚麼不用這些東西；他回答說，他從來沒有聽說過我提到的這些東西。

我立即找到一個工匠，給了他一個鞍架的樣品，叫他照樣做一個。他做好後，我親手給它包上鑲銀嵌金的皮，裏面塞進頭髮。而後我請一位鎖匠照我給的樣子做了一個馬嚼子，幾副馬鐙。

我把這些東西獻給了國王，並用他的一匹馬做了試驗；於是國王騎上他的駿馬，這些馬具使他非常高興，為了表示對我的感謝，他給了我許多禮物。接着，我又做了幾個馬鞍送給一些大臣和王室的主要官員，他們回贈我珍貴、精緻的禮物，我還給城裏的首富們做了幾個馬鞍，這樣一來我聲名大振。

我時常出入王宮，有一天，國王對我說："仙巴，我愛你；我知道，我的大臣們凡是認識你的都很敬重你。我有一個請求，你千萬不要拒絕。"

"哦，國王陛下，"我回答說，"對於陛下我唯命是從，豈有拒絕之理。陛下對我具有無上的權力。"

"我希望你娶親，"國王說，"這樣就能把你留在我的屬地裏，以免你重回故鄉。"我不敢違拗國王的命令，他賜給我一位王室裏的女子：高貴、秀麗、富有、賢淑。婚禮過後，我住進了妻子的家裏，和她生活了一段日子，我們相敬如賓，和睦融洽。但我對這種處境並不滿意，一心想着只要找到機會就逃掉，重回巴格達。

就在我想着逃跑的時候，一位和我很熟的鄰居的妻子生病死了。我上門去安慰他，發現他痛不欲生，我就對他說："願真主保佑你長壽。"

"天啊！"他回答說，"我最多只能再活一個小時了。"

"哦，"我說，"別這麼悲觀絕望；我還想享受好多年你我之間的友誼帶給我們的樂趣呢。"

"我從心底裏祝願你長壽，"他說，"可是我，死神已在向我招手，今天我就要跟我妻子一起下葬；我們這個島上的老祖宗們留下這麼一個習俗：妻子死了，丈夫要為她殉葬；同樣，丈夫死了，妻子也要為他殉葬。多少年來，這個習俗原封不動地保存着，每個人都遵守這個規矩。甚麼也救不了我啦。"

聽着他的話，我頭皮一陣陣發麻，心裏充滿恐懼；天底下竟有這種野蠻、古怪的習俗。這時，他的親戚、朋友和鄰居們前來安排葬禮。他們給屍體穿上盛裝，這是她生前婚禮上穿的，又給她佩戴上所有的珠寶飾件，然後，他們把屍體放在一隻停屍架上，一行人朝外走去。丈夫身穿喪服，緊跟在妻子的屍體後面，親戚們也都跟在後面。他們走向一座高山，爬上山頂，有幾個人動手搬起一塊大石板，底下露出一個深坑，屍體連同華貴的衣服和飾件一同放進深坑。這時，丈夫告別了親友，毫不抗拒地任人將他放上停屍架，他身邊放了一桶水、七隻小麵包；然後，像他的亡妻一樣，他也被放入深坑。這座山綿延數十里，直伸向海邊，這個坑很深。葬禮結束後，那塊大石板又蓋了上去，那些人就下山了。這場葬禮使我感觸很深，我情不自禁地向國王説起我對這件事的看法。

"哦，國王陛下，"我説，"貴國用活人陪葬的奇怪習俗令我不勝驚訝；我走洋過海，到過不少國家，從未聽説過這麼殘酷的規矩。"

"你説我該怎麼辦呢，仙巴？"國王回答説，"這是一條法規，各個階層的人都要遵守，連我都不能例外。要是我的王后先我而死，我就要為她陪葬。"

"陛下，恕我冒昧，請問如果是外來的人，是否也要遵守這個習俗呢？"

"當然，"國王回答說，"只要他們在這個島上結婚成家，就不能例外。"

我憂心忡忡地回到家。要是妻子比我先死，我不就得為她陪葬了嗎？一想到這事，我沒精打采，茶飯不思。誰知不久我的擔心竟成了事實；妻子害了一場重病，沒幾天就去世了。對我來說，被活埋跟被生番活剝一樣可怕；但我不得不遵守習俗。國王表示他要親臨葬禮，全部廷臣隨侍左右；城裏的大戶人家出於對我的尊敬，也要出席我的葬禮。

葬禮準備停當，我妻子的屍體穿上盛裝，佩戴上珠寶飾物，放在停屍架上，送葬的隊伍出發了。作為這出可怕的悲劇中的主角，我熱淚盈眶，緊跟在妻子的屍體後面，悲歎自己不幸的命運。在到達那座高山前，我向送葬的人們發出了懇求同情的呼籲。我先是請求國王，又請求在我身邊的廷臣，請求他們可憐可憐我。

"你們應該考慮，"我說，"我是外來人，不必遵守你們這種殘酷的法律，而且我在自己的國家裏另有妻子兒女。"我自以為這幾句話說得語調悲愴，催人淚下，但看來誰也沒受感動；相反，送葬的人趕緊把屍體放進了深坑；緊跟着我也被放上停屍架，身邊放着一桶水和七隻麵包。最後，葬禮結束了，儘管我發出可憐的哀號，他們還是蓋上了大石板。

我下到坑底，借着外面射進來的一絲微弱的亮光看清了這個地穴。這是個很大的山洞，約有五十腕尺深。我聞到一股刺鼻的臭味，是從四周已腐爛的屍體上發出的。我甚至覺得自己聽見了歎息的聲音，是最近淪為犧牲品的人發出的。停屍架在洞底一放下來，我立即走下來，屏住呼吸，走到離屍體遠遠的地方。我躺了下來，躺了很久，放聲痛哭了一場。然而，死神並沒有因此把我從這恐怖的居所釋放出來；對生存的渴望還在我心裏滋生，促使我想方設法延長生命。我摸索着走到我的那個停屍架前，儘管裏面越來越黑，我還是摸到了麵包和水，吃了起來。

我靠着這些東西活了幾天，但不久東西吃完了，我作好了死的準備。正當我聽天由命的時候，突然聽見我頭頂上的石板被搬開了。一具屍體、一個活人被放下來。死者是個男人。一個人到了山窮水盡、走投無路的地步時，自然只能依靠暴力來維持生命。那個陪葬的女人下來後，我走近她的停屍架停放的地方，等到上面的大石板又蓋上了，我操起一根大骨頭，對準那個不幸的女人的頭部，狠狠地給了她兩三下。她暈了過去，或者確切地說，是我打死了她。我採取這個毫無人性的行動，是為了奪取她帶下來的水和麵包。現在我又能多活幾天了。當我把這點東西又吃光的時候，又有一個死去的女人和陪葬的男人送了下來，我照樣打死了那個男人；也算我走運，那段日子城裏死人很多，我總是用同樣殘酷的辦法獲取我的食物，所以，我在深坑裏倒也沒有斷過頓。

有一天，我剛結果了一個不幸的女人，突然聽見了腳步聲，還聽見了好像是呼吸的聲音。我朝着聲音傳來的方向走去，途中又聽見了呼吸聲，比剛才更響，我恍惚看見一樣東西從我面前逃開。我緊追那飛舞的影子，它不時地停一下，等我走近時又飛開了。我緊追不捨，追了很遠很遠，最後我看見一點亮光，像個星星在閃爍，我朝着這點亮光往前走，前面豁然開朗，只見岩石上有一個出口，足以讓我通過。

這個發現使我大喜過望，我停下腳步，讓激動的心情平靜下來，然後鑽出洞去，發現已來到了海邊。當時我那欣喜的心情，各位不難想像；我簡直不敢相信這是真的。當我確信這是事實，我的知覺沒有捉弄我時，我才明白，我在洞裏聽見其聲音並跟蹤它的那個東西，一定是生活在海裏、常到那個洞裏吞食屍體的動物。

我回到洞裏，把所有停屍架上的珍珠瑪瑙、金銀飾物——一句話，我在黑暗中所能摸到的一切值錢的東西——都收攏來，全部帶到海邊。我把它們打進幾個包裹裏，放到一個拿起來方便的地方，只等機會到來便把它們運走。

兩三天後，將近黃昏時，我發現港口那裏有一艘船朝我這裏駛來。我揮動頭巾，拼命叫喊。他們聽見了我的喊聲，放下一隻小艇來接我。水手們問我倒了甚麼霉，怎麼會困在這個地方，我回答說，兩天前我被海水沖到岸上，幸虧我的貨物全在。總算走運，那些人沒有細想我的話是否可信，倒是對我的回答很滿意，他們讓我帶着包裹上了小艇。

我們到了船上，船長對我被沖上海岸的事情毫不懷疑。

我終於平安到達巴格達，還帶回大量的財寶。為了感謝真主的保佑，我拿出許多錢來，捐助清真寺，救濟窮人。此後我天天和親友歡聚，吃遍山珍海味，享盡榮華富貴。

仙巴第四次航海的故事結束了。他照樣給了欣巴德一百個金幣，並邀請他以及其他人第二天再來吃晚飯，聽他講第五次航海的故事。第二天，大夥兒都到齊後，圍桌而坐，吃罷晚餐，仙巴開始講他第五次航海的故事。

仙巴第五次航海

　　幸福快樂的生活很快使我忘記了曾經遇到過的危險；然而，這些歡樂並不能使我得到完全的滿足，我不久又打定了主意，要去進行第五次航海冒險。我備好了貨物，從陸路運到最近的港口。這回我不再相信任何船長，乾脆自己掏錢造了一條裝備齊全的船。船一造好，我就裝上貨物，準備啟程；由於我的貨物裝不滿這條船，我就接受了幾個商人帶着貨物來搭船，這些商人來自各個不同的國家。

　　迎着第一陣涼爽的海風，我們升起船帆，出海了。在海上走了很久，第一次停泊在一座孤島前，我們在島上發現一個大怪鳥的蛋，就像我前兩天講到的那隻一樣大，已經快孵出小鳥來了，牠的喙已快啄破蛋殼。搭我船的商人們用斧子砸破了蛋，把剛成形的怪鳥劈成一塊一塊，放在火上烤起來。我曾認真地勸告他們，不要動那隻蛋，可他們根本沒聽。

　　他們剛吃完烤怪鳥肉，就見兩塊巨大的烏雲從遠處飄來。船長見多識廣，立即明白那是甚麼，大聲叫道，不好啦，怪鳥的爸爸媽媽來了。他向我們發出警告：儘快上船，躲開這迫在眉睫的危險。我們聽從了他的勸告，立即上船升帆。

　　兩隻大怪鳥飛過來，發出可怕的叫聲，及至看見牠們的蛋被打碎、小鳥被劈成碎塊，叫聲便更加使人恐怖。牠們決意報復。只見牠們飛回到牠們剛才來的高山，消失在山巒裏；我們乘這機會拼盡全力把船開走，以免任何不幸落到我們頭上。

　　牠們很快就回來了，我們看見每只大怪鳥的爪子裏都捧着塊大石頭。牠們飛臨船上，在空中盤旋，其中一隻把石頭扔了下來。虧得我們的舵手技術高超，突然把船往旁邊一駕，沒讓石頭砸着我們。但石頭擦着我們的邊掉進了海裏，把船砸出一個大洞，我們幾乎看見了海底。不幸的是，另一隻大怪鳥把石頭不偏不倚地砸在我們的船上，把船砸成了碎片。水手和乘客不是被砸死就是被淹死。我也沉到了水下。我浮出水面時，幸運地抓住了一塊船板。我兩隻手交替划水，始終騰出一隻手來抓着這塊船板，我終於游到了一座島嶼跟前。海岸很陡，但我奮力爬上海灘，踏上了小島。

我坐在草地上休息。恢復了疲勞後，站起來朝海島裏面走去，探看四周。這裏好似一座芬芳四溢的花園。到處可見美麗的果樹，有些樹上的果子還是生的，有些已經成熟，晶瑩明亮的溪水蜿蜒流淌。我用噴香的水果充飢，又用誘人的溪水解渴。

夜色降臨了，我揀了個地方，在草地上躺下來。但我每次睡不到一個小時就要醒一醒，後來我乾脆睜着眼睛，大半個夜晚都用來悲歎自己的命運，責怪自己做事冒失，明明已經擁有足以使自己安度餘年的一切，卻偏偏貪心不足，還要出來冒險。我越想越傷心，甚至動起自殺的念頭；但是白天又來了，使人歡樂的陽光驅散了我的憂愁。我爬起來，壯着膽子走進樹叢裏。

我往島子裏走了不遠，看見一個看來非常衰弱的老頭，坐在一條小河的岸上。我走過去，向他致意；他只是稍微點一點頭，算是回答。我問他在做甚麼，可他沒有回答，而是示意我背他過河，表示要去摘些水果。

我以為他只要我幫他這個忙，就背起他趟過河去。到了對岸，我蹲下身子，示意他下來；可是，這個看來如此衰弱的老頭，不僅沒有下來，反而雙腿輕捷地一躍，騎上了我的脖子，穩穩地坐在我的肩膀上。他惡狠狠地卡着我的喉嚨，幾乎令我窒息；我大驚失色，昏了過去。

那老頭卻不管這一切，依然騎在我脖子上，只是把手稍稍鬆開了一點，正好讓我呼吸。我多少蘇醒了些，他撩起一腳踢在我肚子上，又用另一隻腳踢我的腰部，迫使我站起來。他就這麼騎着我，在樹底下摘果子，邊摘邊吃，還強迫我一起吃。整整一天他都沒放過我；晚上我想好好睡一覺，他也在我身邊躺下，始終卡着我的脖子。天一亮他就弄醒了我，逼我起來，走路，時時用腳踢我。想想看吧，我整天馱着這個老頭，根本別想逃跑。

有一天，我偶爾發現樹上掉下幾隻葫蘆。我拾起一隻大的，洗乾淨，把幾串葡萄的汁擠進去，這個島上到處都是葡萄。葫蘆裏裝滿了葡萄汁，我把它藏在一個地方，幾天後，我又跟老頭回到了藏葫蘆的地方。我嚐了嚐葫蘆裏的葡萄汁，呵，已經變成了醇酒，幾口下肚，我立刻就把這些天來馱老頭的痛苦給忘了。我力氣倍增，勁頭十足，一邊走一邊連唱帶舞。

那老頭一看這飲料竟有這樣的功效，便示意我讓他嚐嚐；我把葫蘆遞給他，他一嚐便欲罷不能，一口氣喝了個精光。濃烈的酒味直衝他腦門，他很快就醉了，唱了起來，並在我肩上左右搖晃。我發現他卡着我脖子的手已放鬆，便把他啪的一下摔了下來，他一動不動地趴在地上。我抱起一塊大石頭砸死了他。

終於幹掉了這個老頭，我很高興；我朝海邊走去，在那裏碰見了一些人，他們把船停在這裏，上島找淡水。他們看見我並聽我講了我的奇遇，非常驚訝。

"你落入了'海上老人'的手裏，算是第一個沒有被他卡死的人。他在這座島上卡死了許多人，這座島因此而出名。在這裏上島的水手和商人，除非身強力壯，否則誰也不敢往裏走。"

他們把這個情況告訴了我，而後帶我上船，船長聽説了我的遭遇，對我深表同情。他命令升帆開船。沒過幾天，我們就來到一座大城市的港口，這座城裏的房子都是石頭砌的。

船上有一位商人對我很友好，請我和他作伴，領我住進專供外國商人住的船艙。他給了我一個大麻袋，然後把我介紹給這城裏的一些人，他們也都背着麻袋。他請他們帶我去摘椰子，並對我説：

"跟他們去吧，看他們怎麼做，你跟着做就是了；別離開他們，要不你會有生命危險的。"

他給了我一天的食物，我就跟着新朋友們出發了。

我們到達一個大樹林，裏面全是椰子樹，又高又直，樹幹滑溜溜的，根本沒法爬上去摘果子。我們打算用竿子把椰子打下來，用麻袋在下面接着。進入樹林，我們看見一大羣大大小小的猴子，一看見我們就全都溜走，敏捷麻利地爬到了樹上。跟我一起去的商人們撿起石子兒使勁朝猴子扔去，有些猴子已爬到了最高的樹枝上。我也跟着扔石頭，而且很快就發現這些猴子把我們的辦法學了過去，它們摘下椰子朝我們扔來，那舉動明顯流露出氣惱和蔑視。我們用這樣的計謀很快就把椰子裝滿了麻袋，看來只有這個辦法才行。

我們滿載而歸，回到了城裏，那個派我到樹林裏的商人收購了我摘的椰子。我一連又去了幾天，摘到許多椰子，換得大筆金錢。

商人們把椰子裝上船，開走了。我等着下一艘船。不一會船就進港了，也是來裝椰子的。我把摘來的椰子全都運上船，船快起錨時，我告別了那位對我有恩的商人。

我們的船開到了科馬里島。我把所有的椰子換了蘆薈；然後，我像別的商人一樣，辦了個採珠場，僱了許多潛水員。我很快就收集到許多又大又美的珍珠，我帶着這些珍珠興高采烈地上了船，平安到達巴索拉，從那裏返回巴格達。我把帶回來的蘆薈和珍珠賣了一大筆錢。和前幾次出海歸來時一樣，把十分之一的錢財施捨給窮人，用各種各樣的娛樂來恢復旅途的疲勞。

仙巴講完了，又給了欣巴德一百個金幣，欣巴德和其餘的客人告辭而去。第二天，富裕的仙巴家重擺宴席，主人像前幾次一樣盛情款待了客人之後，講起他第六次航海的故事。

仙巴第六次航海

朋友們，我相信你們一定覺得奇怪，我幾次航海獲得了這麼多的珠寶，怎麼還會受命運之神的誘惑，再去航海冒險呢。我剛起這個念頭的時候，自己也覺得驚訝。肯定是命運之神看我休息了一年，要我第六次到那變幻無常的海上去冒險。

這次我沒走波斯灣，而是穿過波斯和印度的幾個省份，到達一個港口，在那裏上了一條好船，船長打定主意要作一次長途航行。這次航行的距離確實夠長的，而且非常不幸，因為船長和舵手迷失了航向，不知該往哪裏駛。最後他們終於弄清了我們所處的位置；但是這個發現並不能使我們高興，因為船長突然離開了他的崗位，放聲痛哭起來，我們全都驚呆了。他把頭巾扔在甲板上，扯鬍子捶腦袋，像發瘋似的。我們問他為甚麼這麼傷心，他回答說："我不得不告訴你們，我們正面臨着極大的危險。一股激流在把船迅速向前推進，不出十五分鐘我們就要葬身海底了。祈禱真主把我們從這可怕的危險中拯救出來吧，除非真主可憐我們，否則我們是在劫難逃了。"

船長說完，下令落帆；但是繩索斷了，船像脫韁野馬，完全失去了控制，一股急流把它沖向一塊岩礁，船嘩啦啦地被撞成了碎片，幸虧我們手腳麻利，及時搬下了食物和最值錢的一部分貨物。

我們集中在岸上，船長說："這是真主的旨意。我們要在這裏為自己掘墓了，大傢伙兒這就互道永別吧；這是一個非常荒涼的地方，凡是被海水沖到這裏來的人從來沒有生還過。"船長的話更使我們傷心。

原來我們是在一座山的山腳下，這座山是一個長形大島的一側。海灘上覆蓋着船骸；到處可見一堆堆的屍骨，面對這副景象，我們相信，許許多多人在這裏丟了性命。海岸上堆着不計其數、各種各樣的貨物，簡直令人難以相信。

在任何別的地方，常可看見眾多的小河流入大海；而這裏，卻有一條很大的淡水河從海裏分離出來，穿過一個黑黝黝的山洞，沿海岸流淌，那個山洞的洞口又高又大。這地方最顯著的特點是，那座山上佈滿紅寶石、水晶和別的珍貴的寶石。這裏還有一種瀝青或叫柏油似的東西，從岩石上滴落到海裏，魚兒吃了這種東西，又把它吐出來，這時它就變成了龍涎香，海浪又把它沖上海岸。

要完整地形容這個地方，我只要說這麼一句話：任何船隻，一旦來到一定距離內，難免不被拖到這裏來。要是海上起風，風就助長激流的威勢，誰都沒有辦法逃脫；要是風從陸上颳來，高山會擋住它的勢頭，這樣一來，激流就會肆虐，把船隻沖到岸上，把它撞成碎片，就像我們的船一樣。更糟糕的是，這座山很陡，根本別想爬到山頂，也沒有其他任何逃脫的辦法。

我們留在岸上，垂頭喪氣，只等着送命。我們把食物平分了，這樣誰先把食物吃完，誰就先完蛋，誰吃得省，誰就能多活些日子。

有些人先死了，其他人掩埋了他們。最後我懷着淒涼悲痛的心情，掩埋了我的最後一個同伴；因為我不但吃得節省，而且，我還曾偷偷地藏起一部分食物，沒讓我的同伴們知道。但是，儘管這樣，當我掩埋完最後一個同伴時，我的食物也所剩無幾了，我想也許我很快就會跟他去的。

但是，真主依然可憐我，鼓勵我到那條隱沒在山洞裏的河邊去。我非常仔細地打量着小河，產生了這樣一個念頭：這條在地底下流淌的河，一定會通到外面重見亮光的地方。於是我設想，如果我有一個木排，它也許會載着我，把我帶到有人煙的地方。即使我被淹死，那也不過是換個死法而已；但如果事情正好相反，我平安地走出這個要命的地方，那就不僅逃脫了像我同伴那樣的死亡的厄運，而且還可能有機會再發一次財。

有了這樣的念頭，我勇氣倍增，賣力地紮起木排來。海岸上有的是厚木板和粗纜索，我把它們撿來，紮緊，做成了一個結實的框架。木排做成後，我把許多紅寶石、綠寶石、龍涎香、水晶以及一些金銀裝了上去。我把東西堆好，使木排保持平穩，然後就登上木排，用兩支小槳划起來；我順着激流奮力划槳，把生命託付給了真主。

木排一進入山洞，我立即陷入一片黑暗之中，激流載着我向前，但我辨不清它的流向。我就在這伸手不見五指的山洞裏漂流了好幾天，在這些天裏，不到實在支持不住的時候，我決不吃東西；但是，儘管我這樣節省，食物還是吃完了。於是我就睡覺，也不知睡了多久，反正我醒來時，嚇了一跳，只見我已來到一個空曠的地方，靠近一條河的河岸，我的木排被拴在河岸上，我四周圍着一大羣黑人。我站起來向他們致意；他們跟我說話，可我一句也聽不懂。

這時我欣喜若狂，簡直不敢相信自己醒着。最後我確信自己不是在做夢，就用阿拉伯話大聲地說：

"祈求萬能的主吧，他會來幫助你們。閉上你們的眼睛，在你們睡着的時候，真主會賜給你們好運。"

一個聽得懂阿拉伯話的黑人聽見我這麼說，便走近我，說："兄弟，見了我們別害怕；我們住在這裏，今天我們到這條河來，是要挖渠引水，澆灌我們的田地。我們發現激流載着甚麼東西，就連忙奔到岸邊來看個究竟，結果就看見了這只木排；我們中的一個弟兄馬上跳下河去，把木排拖到了岸邊。我們把它拴住了，等着你醒來。你的經歷一定很有趣，請你給我們講講，好嗎。告訴我們，你從哪裏來。"

我請他先給我點吃的，並保證說，只要讓我吃飽了，一定滿足他們的好奇心，把我的來歷原原本本地告訴他們。

他們給了我幾種肉食，我狼吞虎咽地吃了起來，吃飽之後，就把我遇到的一切告訴了他們。他們一個個聽得目瞪口呆，嘖嘖稱奇。

我一說完，他們的翻譯就對我說，我的故事讓他們吃驚，我必須到王宮去，把我的歷險經過向國王再講一遍，因為這些事兒太不尋常了，只有讓本人來複述才夠味兒。

我回答說，我隨時聽候他們的吩咐。黑人們便去找馬。很快就找來一匹；他們把我扶上馬，有幾個人走在我旁邊，為我領路，還有一些身強力壯的人從水裏抬起木排，連同那上面的一袋袋寶石一起扛在肩上，跟在我們後面。

這座島叫塞倫第，我們一起進了城，黑人們帶我晉見了他們的國王。我走近御座，用印度人的禮節向他致意：跪在他的腳跟前，親吻地面。國王倒也平易近人，他讓我起來，要我坐在他身邊，他先問我叫甚麼名字；我回答說，我叫仙巴，因為好幾次在海上航行，所以得了個綽號：航海人；而後我又說，我是巴格達人。

國王很驚奇："那你怎麼會到鄙國來的呢？你從哪裏來？"

我把真實情況對國王和盤托出；就像我告訴你們的一樣；他很高興，命令把我的歷險經過用金字寫下來，保存在他王國的檔案室裏。這時，木排抬來了，裝寶石的口袋也當着他的面打開。他對蘆薈和龍涎香讚不絕口，而對紅寶石和綠寶石更是愛不釋手，他可從來沒有過這麼值錢的寶貝。

我發現他滿心喜悦地審視着我的無價之寶，便跪在他面前，冒昧地説："國王陛下，不僅我是你的奴僕，就是我木排上的一切也都聽憑你處置，但願陛下肯賞臉，收下我這點小小的禮物。"

國王微微一笑，回答説，他不想掠人之所好，我的東西他不能要；他不但不要我的東西，而且還要為我錦上添花；等我離開他的王國時，他要讓我知道他的慷慨大方。聽了他的話，我感激涕零，從內心裏祈求真主保佑他國泰民安。

他吩咐他的一位臣子招待我，又指派了他的幾個僕人供我使喚。那個臣子和那些僕人們都忠實地履行職責，把我裝寶石的包裹全都運到了我下榻的地方。我每天準時進宮向國王請安，其餘的時間就瀏覽市容。

塞倫第島正處在赤道下，因此白天和黑夜一樣長。這座主要的城市位於一個美麗的山谷的頂端，在島子中央一座山腳下，這座山是全世界最高的；從需要三天航程的海面上看這座山，只有朦朧一片。我奮力攀登，來到了亞當從天堂被逐後所住的地方；我很想再接再厲，登上山頂。最終還是半途而廢了。

我回到城裏，請求國王開恩，允許我返回故國，他慨然應允，並從金庫中拿出一份豐厚的禮物要我收下；當我去向國王辭行時，他又交給我一份禮物，比第一份更貴重，並讓我帶一封信給我們的大教長 [2]，國王説："我請你把這封信和這份禮物轉交給哈里發哈龍·拉希德，並向他表示我的友好情意。"

我畢恭畢敬地接過禮物和信，並向國王保證：既蒙陛下信任，我當盡心盡力，不負重託。在我登船前，國王叫來與我同行的船長和商人，叮囑他們要盡力照顧好我。

國王的信是寫在一種動物的皮上的，這種動物在當地很罕見，因此它的皮彌足珍貴。皮是黃顏色的，而信本身則是用藍墨水寫的，全文如下：

有千頭大象為其開道；身居屋頂
上萬顆寶石熠熠生輝的王宮，
寶庫裏擁有二萬頂鑲嵌
鑽石之王冠的印度
國王謹致哈里發
哈龍·拉希德

儘管我們的禮物微不足道，但請像兄弟和朋友一樣收下它，要知道我們內心對你的友好情意。我們很高興能有機會向你證實我們的友好情意。我們請求你回贈我們同樣的情意，我們與你地位相等，想來我們的請求不是奢望。謹致兄弟之禮。再見。

這份禮物包括四件東西：第一、一隻用單塊紅寶石製成的花瓶，雕琢成杯狀，半英尺高，一英寸厚，裏面裝滿精緻的珍珠，每顆都有半打蘭[3]重；第二、一塊蛇皮，那條蛇足有金幣粗，蛇皮具有一種特殊功效：睡在它上面可以祛除百病；第三、五萬打蘭最珍貴的蘆薈，另加三十顆樟腦，像阿月渾子的子那麼大；第四、一個貌似天仙的女奴，她的衣服上綴滿珠寶。

船起航了，航程雖長，卻是一路順風，我們抵達了巴索拉，我從那裏回到了巴格達。我一到家，第一件事就是完成國王交託的使命。我帶着國王的信，來到大教長的宮殿門前，身後跟着那個美麗的女奴和幾個家人，他們捧着國王託我轉交的禮物。我向守門人說明來意，立刻被引到哈里發御座前。我匐伏在他腳下，闡明我的使命，呈上國王的信和禮物。

哈里發唸完信，問我塞倫第島的國王是否真的像他信中所說那麼富有、強盛。

我第二次匐伏在地，然後站起來說："大教長，我敢向你保證，塞倫第國王信中所說句句是實；我親眼見過他的富裕和威嚴。他王宮的輝煌壯麗令人稱羨。如果國王要在大眾前露面，就有一隻御座放在象背上；他坐在象背上，兩邊排列着滿朝文武，大小臣子。他前面坐着一個臣子，手執金矛，御座後面站着一個臣子，握着一根金柱，金柱頂端鑲嵌着一塊半英尺長、一英寸厚的綠寶石。國王前面有千人衛隊為他開道，衛隊身穿嵌金鑲銀的綢衣，騎在裝飾華麗的大象上。

"國王巡幸路上，坐在他前面的臣子不時大聲吆喝：'偉大的國王，印度強大的蘇丹駕到。他的宮殿鑲嵌着十萬顆紅寶石，他擁有兩萬頂鑽石王冠。這是加冕的國王，比索里馬或偉大的米哈雷吉更偉大。'

"他說完這些話後，就輪到站在御座後面的臣子喊話了：'這個偉大的國王一定要死，一定要死，一定要死！'然後，第一個臣子繼續說：'光榮屬不生不死的國王。'"

哈里發對我的敍述很滿意，賜給我一份厚禮，打發我出宮。

仙巴講完了，客人們告辭；欣巴德照例得到一百個金幣。第二天，客人們和腳夫又來到仙巴家，主人講起他第七次航海的故事。

仙巴最後一次航海

第六次航海回來後，我徹底拋棄了再出海冒險的念頭。我的生命的鼎盛時期已過，到了安度餘年的時候了；此外，我經歷了那麼多的危險，一次次死裏逃生，我發誓再也不拿生命去冒險了。因此，我打算平靜、安寧地享幾年福。

有一天，我的一個僕人對我說，哈里發的一個臣子要跟我說話。我離開餐桌去見他。

他說："哈里發命令我告訴你，他想見你。"

我跟他來到王宮，他引我晉見哈里發，我俯伏在他腳下，向他請安。

哈里發說："仙巴，我想請你為我效一次力。你必須帶着我的回信和禮物去見塞倫第國王；承他以禮待我，我理當回敬。"

哈里發的這個命令，對我猶如晴天霹靂。"大教長！"我回答說，"陛下的任何吩咐，我都唯命是從；但是，我懇求陛下體諒我上次航海歸來，疲勞不堪，身體日漸衰竭。我甚至已發過誓，再也不離開巴格達。"

接着我乘機向他講了我一次次的冒險經歷，他倒是耐着性子，仔細聽完了，然後說："我承認，你說的這些事情非同尋常；但是，這並不能成為你拒絕為我出海的理由；只不過是到塞倫第島去跑一趟嘛。完成了我託付你的使命，你就能自由地回來了。但你一定得去，你是個明白人，要知道如果不把這筆人情賬還掉，就大大有損我的尊嚴。"

我看哈里發決心已下，便向他表示願遵命而行。他似乎很高興，給了我一千個金幣作為盤纏。

我在幾天內作好了出發的準備；一接到哈里發託我轉送的禮物和他的一封親筆信，我就踏上通往巴索拉的道路，又從那裏上了船。一路順風地到達塞倫第島，一上島我就找到幾個宮廷大臣，向他們說明來意，請求他們儘快安排我晉見國王。

國王立即召見了我，對我的來訪極為高興。"歡迎你，仙巴，"他說，"自從你離開後，我常記掛你。今天我又看見了你，這是個真主保佑的日子。"

我感謝了國王的善意，然後呈上哈里發的禮物和信，國王非常滿意，高興地收了下來。

哈里發送給他一匹金薄絹，估計價值為一千個金幣，五十件用罕見的料子製作的長袍，一百件白麻布衣服，都是開羅、蘇伊士、亞歷山大出產的最好的料子；一牀深紅色的墊被，還有一牀不同式樣和顏色的墊被。此外，他還送了一隻扁的瑪瑙瓶，有指頭般粗 —— 周圍有一幅淺浮雕，雕着一個人跪在地上，手執弓箭要射一頭獅子；還送了一張鑲金嵌銀的桌子，據說是所羅門王傳下來的。哈里發的信是這樣寫的：

> 承真主賜以王位，繼承已故祖先遺業
>
> 的阿布杜拉·哈龍·拉希德
>
> 以領路的賢明君主之名義
>
> 謹祝強盛、幸福的

蘇丹身體健康

奉讀尊函，殊覺欣喜；根據我們賢者雲集之教法會議的意見，謹回贈區區薄禮。若蒙陛下從中體察我們的一片善意而笑納之，則幸甚矣。再見。

塞倫第國王見哈里發表示了他的友好感情，大為高興。這次召見以後不久，我又請求再次召見，以便向國王辭行，但這次遇到了一些麻煩。最後我終於如願以償，國王見我要走，送了我一份厚禮。我立即揚帆出發，打算返回巴格達，但這次運氣不好，沒有照我希望的那樣早日回家，因為真主另有安排。

在海上航行了三四天後，我們遭到了海盜襲擊，他們輕而易舉地搶佔了我們的船。我們船上有幾個人想反抗，卻送了性命。我跟其餘那些老實順從的人當了奴隸。他們把我們全身衣服剝光，給我們圍上破布，然後把船朝遠處一座島嶼駛去，到了那裏後，我們被賣掉了。

買我的人是個富商，他把我帶回家，給我吃的，又給我穿上奴隸的衣服。

他沒有弄清我的來歷，因此幾天後他問我可會做生意。我回答說，我不是個匠人，而是個商人，那些海盜搶走了我的一切。

"可是你得告訴我，"他說，"你會不會射箭？"

我回答說我年輕時練過，現在也沒完全荒疏。

於是他給了我一張弓，幾支箭，讓我跟他同騎一頭大象，帶着我出城走了幾小時，來到一座大樹林。我們朝樹林裏走了很遠，來到一個地方，那商人停了下來，讓我下了大象。他指着一棵大樹，對我説：

"爬到那棵樹上，看見有大象從樹底下走過就射箭，樹林裏這種動物很多；要是有頭象倒下了，就來告訴我。"

説完後，他給我留下點吃的，就回城裏去了。我通宵守在樹上。

第一個晚上沒遇見大象；但第二天，太陽剛出來，樹林裏就出現了一大羣象。我朝牠們射了很多箭，最終有一頭象倒下了。其餘的都逃走了，我下樹去向主人報告這個好消息。他對我的箭術大加讚賞。特地備了一桌酒席，以示獎勵。然後我們一起回到樹林，我們挖了個坑，把被我射死的那頭象埋了。這是我主人的主意，他要讓象的屍體在土裏爛掉，然後他可以取出象牙。

我連續幹了兩個月，每天都射死一頭象。有一天早晨，我正等候着象羣，突然發現，一大羣象沒有跟往常一樣從樹林裏走過，而是齊聲怒吼着朝我衝來，牠們的腳步震得大地都在搖晃，我可嚇壞了。

象羣來到我藏身的那棵樹旁，把它包圍起來，牠們的鼻子伸得長長的，眼睛緊緊盯着我。我一動不動地注視着這驚人的場面，弓箭不知不覺地從手裏掉了下去。

我的恐懼不是沒有理由的。象羣注視了我一會後，其中最大的一頭用長鼻子圍住了樹幹，猛一用力，把樹連根拔起，扔在地上。我隨着樹一起摔倒在地；但是那頭大象用鼻子把我捲起來，放在牠的背上，我昏迷不醒地趴在那裏。

這個龐然大物領頭，牠的伙伴們跟在後面，牠們成一列縱隊走到一個隱祕的地方。

大象把我放了下來，然後跟牠的伙伴們一起走掉了。

我在那裏等了一會，看看沒別的象羣，就站了起來，發現自己是在一個完全被象牙和象骨覆蓋着的小山丘上。現在我明白了，這是牠們葬身或舉行葬禮的地方，牠們把我帶來是為了讓我看看，既然我射死牠們只是為了要牠們的牙，那我今後別再這麼幹了，儘管到這裏來拿就是。

我沒有在山上久留，而是轉身朝城裏跑去，整整走了一天一夜，終於回到我主人家。

我主人一見到我，就驚叫道："哎呀，可憐的仙巴！我正擔心，不知你出了甚麼事呢。我到過樹林裏，看見一棵連根拔起的樹，你的弓箭掉在地上；我到處找你，沒找到，以為再也見不到你了，心裏難受極了。快告訴我，你到底出了甚麼事，怎麼還活着。"

我把事情經過一五一十地告訴了他，第二天他跟我一起騎一頭大象上山，親眼看見我所說的確屬事實，他喜出望外。我們把儘可能多的象牙裝進口袋，放到了象背上，然後回到了主人家裏。

一到家，主人就對我說："兄弟，你把你的發現告訴了我，我肯定能發財了，所以我不能再把你當成奴隸。願真主保佑你萬事如意！我當着真主的面賜給你自由。樹林裏的象羣每年要殺死許多我們派去找象牙的奴隸。儘管我們總是提醒他們要當心，並教給他們對付大象的辦法，可他們遲早總要上這些大象的當，丟了性命。肯定是真主在保佑你，使牠們獨獨對你表現出憐憫，讓你死裏逃生。這是一個徵兆，說明你受到特別的保護，你是人類的有用之材。你使我獲得意外的收益；至今為止，我們每次搜集象牙都要用許多奴隸的命去冒險，現在，你的發現將使我們全城的人都富起來。我打算給你一份厚禮。我可以讓全城人和我一起使你發財，我準能做到一呼百應，但我覺得這是一種不能分享的樂趣，我要獨自享用。"

對於他的好意，我回答說："主人，願真主保佑你！你給我自由，就是對我的最好報答，我感激不盡；我唯一需要的就是請你同意放我回家。"

"好啊，"他回答說，"季風一起，就會有船來裝象牙。到時候我就給足你盤纏，讓你回家。"

我又一次感謝他給我自由。我留在他家裏，直到颳秋風的季節，在這段時間，我們常到象牙山上去，他的庫房裏裝滿了象牙。城裏其他的商人也都把象牙裝滿了倉庫，因為我的發現早已不是祕密。

最後，船終於來了，我的主人為我挑選了一條船，上面堆放象牙，大部分貨物送給了我。他向真主祈禱，保佑我一路平安，又硬要我收下一些他們國家的珍奇特產。我謝過了他，登上了船。

我們停靠過幾個島嶼，補充了給養。我們的船原來是從印度陸地的一個港口開出的，我們在那裏停了下來。我怕前往巴索拉的海面上有危險，就把船上屬我的那部分象牙拿出來，決定改走陸路。

我把象牙賣了好大一筆錢，買了許多可作禮品的新鮮玩意；這一切準備妥當之後，我加入了一支商人的大篷車隊。我在路上走了很久，吃了不少的苦；但是所有這些疲憊勞累最終到了頭，我高興地回到了巴格達。行裝甫卸，我就進宮晉見哈里發，向他述職。

哈里發說，我去了這麼久，害得他為我擔心，但他始終希望真主不會拋棄我。

哈里發賜給我豐厚的禮物、崇高的榮譽，我滿意地告辭；從那以後，我就整日和家人、親戚、朋友在一起。

仙巴就這樣結束了他第七次，也是最後一次航海的故事；他對欣巴德說：「我說，朋友，你可曾聽說過有誰像我這樣歷經艱險，一次次落入困境？經歷了這麼多的艱難困苦，我難道不該享受舒適、安寧的生活嗎？」

聽完這些話，欣巴德走上前去，親吻他的手，說：「我必須承認，你遇到過可怕的危險；我的不幸與你根本不能相比。你不但應該享受安寧的生活，而且也配擁有這一切財富，你用這些財富做了那麼多的好事，你是那樣的慷慨大方。祝你永遠這樣幸福地生活下去，直到死神降臨！」

仙巴又給了欣巴德一百個金幣。他要欣巴德做他的朋友，放棄腳夫的職業，繼續做他的座上客，這樣他一輩子都會記得航海人仙巴。

4
三姐妹的故事

從前波斯有一位蘇丹，名叫赫諾沙，他經常由他信任的一位宰相陪同着，穿上平民百姓的服裝，走出宮外，在京城裏到處走走，碰到過不少奇遇。

有一次，他經過窮人的居住區，走過一戶人家，只聽得裏面在高聲談話，他走近一步，從窗外張望進去，只見姐妹三個，吃罷晚飯，正坐在沙發上閒聊。聽那大姐所說的一些話，蘇丹就知道她們的話題是個人的願望。

"我的願望是，"那大姐說道，"能夠嫁給蘇丹的麵包師。我有這樣一個丈夫，那麼精美可口的'蘇丹麵包'我想吃多少就能吃多少了。你們兩個的志趣呢？是不是和我一樣高雅？"

那二姐說道，"我但願能嫁給蘇丹的首席廚師，有了這樣一個丈夫，那麼好魚好肉好菜就盡我吃了。可我不想吃甚麼'蘇丹麵包'，因為我知道，在蘇丹的宮裏，這種'蘇丹麵包'是算不得甚麼好東西的。所以你看，我的志趣不是比你高雅嗎？"

那小妹妹長得十分秀麗，舉止優雅，聰明伶俐，她的兩個姐姐都不及她，現在輪到她表達自己的心願了，只聽得她這麼說道：

"兩位姐姐，至於我呢，我但願有一天能嫁給蘇丹，做他的王后娘娘。我要給他生下一個小王子，王子的頭髮半邊是金的，半邊是銀的；他哭喊的時候，流下的眼淚就是一串串珍珠；他向你一笑,那兩片朱紅的小嘴唇就像在和風裏剛綻開的玫瑰花。"

那三姐妹的心願,尤其是三妹的心願使蘇丹感到很大興趣,他決心滿足她們的願望。他回過頭來吩咐宰相把這戶人家的地址記下來,明天帶三姐妹去見他。

第二天,宰相果然引領着三姐妹進宮叩見蘇丹。蘇丹問道:"昨天晚上,你們姐妹談得可高興,每人都吐露了自己的一個心願,還記得有這麼一回事嗎?現在你們得如實告訴我,我要知道你們有些甚麼願望。"

三姐妹完全沒有想到她們私下談心,蘇丹竟會知道了,羞得眼瞼低垂,兩頰通紅,只覺得好不窘人。她們害怕會得罪蘇丹,一句話也不敢説。

蘇丹看到她們心慌意亂,説道:"你們不必害怕,我把你們召喚來並不是要來難為你們。其實你們姐妹的願望我都已經知道了。你們兩個,"他向那大姐、二姐説道,"將要嫁給我的首席麵包師和首席廚師。至於你呢,"他轉向那三妹説,"將會實現你的願望,今晚就做我的妻子。"

按照蘇丹的佈置,三姐妹當天就成婚。三妹嫁給波斯的蘇丹為妻,那婚禮真是一派豪華,喜氣洋溢。大姐二姐的婚禮就不能那麼闊氣了,只能按照她們的丈夫首席麵包師和首席廚師的身分、地位辦事。

大姐和二姐只覺得她們的婚禮比起三妹的婚禮來,差得太遠了,不由得妒火中燒。她們經常在心裏打主意,怎樣在她們的妹妹 —— 現在是她們的王后 —— 身上出這口氣。在表面上,她們卻在王后跟前竭力奉承討好,裝出一副恭恭敬敬的樣子來。

時間過得好快，不久王后生下了一個小王子，長得容貌不凡，真是滿室生光。她把嬰兒交託給兩個姐姐看護。誰知她們兩個起了歹念，把嬰兒包紮好了，裝進一個籃子裏，然後拿起籃子來到王宮附近的一條運河邊，把籃子放進河裏，看着它漂流而去。她們回到宮裏，卻編造出這樣的謊話：王后生下的不是孩子，只是一條小狗。蘇丹聽説了，十分惱怒。

且説那籃子載着小王子，順水漂流，流經了王宮的花園。恰好御花園的總管在運河邊散步，望見河面上漂來了一隻籃子，就把園丁叫來，用一個竹耙，把籃子拉到河岸邊。

園丁從河裏提起籃子交給花園的總管，他看到籃子裏邊裝着一個嬰兒，真是大吃一驚。雖説是剛出世不久的娃娃，已經可以看出長得眉清目秀了。這個總管結婚多年，卻是膝下沒有一子半女，難免感到遺憾，因此他高高興興地抱起嬰兒，回到家中，徑直進入妻子的房裏，説道：

"愛妻啊，我們自己沒有生養孩子，現在真主給我們送一個來了。僱一個奶娘給他餵奶，要小心伺候他，因為我在現在已把他認做我的兒子了。"

過了一年，王后又生下了一個小王子，誰知她那兩個狠心的姐姐又把嬰兒裝在籃子裏，再放進運河裏，任它漂流而去，回來卻揚言：王后生養了甚麼孩子？只是一隻貓罷了。

幸虧王家花園的總管又恰好在運河岸邊散步，他又救起了嬰兒，抱回家中，交給妻子，囑咐她好好照看，就像她照看第一個孩子那樣。

這一回，蘇丹對於王后心中更是不滿了，幸虧他的宰相在旁邊勸說，王后並沒有受到甚麼處分。

又過了一年，王後生下了一個小公主，仍然沒有逃出那兩個壞姐姐的毒手；幸而小公主跟她的兩個哥哥一樣，也是多虧那位仁慈好心的總管，逃出了劫難，得到了很好的照看。

這一回那兩個壞姐姐趕緊去向蘇丹報告，說是王后第三胎生下的哪裏是孩子，一根木條罷了。為了證明她們所說的並非謊言，竟拿出事前準備好的一根木條給蘇丹看。

蘇丹再也受不了這第三次的刺激，他一氣之下，下令在那宏偉的清真寺附近，搭起一個小小的木棚，把王后趕出宮外，關禁在這小木棚裏，好讓她受盡千千萬萬經過此地的行人的恥笑。可憐那王后，從未受過這樣無情的折磨，但是她耐心地忍受着命運的安排。

再說那兩個小王子和小公主。花園的總管夫婦自從收養了這三個漂流來的嬰兒，對他們十分鍾愛，就像是他們的親生父母親。三兄妹漸漸長大，個個都氣度不凡，自有高貴的品德，因此越發博得了老夫婦的歡心。總管給大王子取名"巴曼"，給二王子取名"佩維士"，這都是前朝的蘇丹的名字；又給三公主取名"佩莉佐德"，這也是前朝的許多公主的名字。

兩位王子已經長大，總管特地請了老師來教他們讀書寫字。那公主也是求知心切，渴望讀書，所以總管又請那位老師同時也教導她。

公主天資十分聰明，讀書寫字不在兩位哥哥之下，又會唱歌、彈弄各種樂器。後來兩位王子學習騎馬，她也跟着哥哥，一起學習騎馬、彎弓、投射標槍，在各項競賽中甚至比兩個哥哥還強。

那總管看到他收養的三個孩子個個有出息，他為他們花費的心血和教育費用可說得到了加倍的回報，他真是心花怒放，因此不惜花一大筆錢在京城附近購置了一座別墅，佈置得十分華麗，別墅四周是一大片林苑，豢養着成羣的鹿，這樣，王子、公主隨時可以在自己的林苑裏打獵消遣。

這座住宅佈置得盡善盡美，完工之後，園林總管就去叩見蘇丹，跪倒在他的腳下，説是他伺候陛下多年，現在年老體衰，請求辭職告退。蘇丹同意了他的請求。於是總管帶着他的三個養子女遷居到鄉間新建的住宅去了。

總管的妻子亡故有年，他住到新居不滿半年也得了急病故世了。他死得突然，所以沒來得及跟三個孩子交代一下他們的來歷。

那兄妹三人並不知道自己的身世，認定那總管就是他們的親生父親，因此安葬的時候個個都哀哭一場，表現了子女的孝思。

總管留下了豐厚的家產，因此兄妹三人和睦地過着舒適富裕的日子。他們並沒有甚麼野心想到朝廷上去謀取官職爵位，也好顯赫一番，雖説憑他們的品德才能是很容易得到朝廷的賞識的。

有一天，兩個王子出外打獵去了，只有公主一人在家，園門外來了一個虔誠的老婦人，懇求讓她進入宅內在神龕前祈禱一番。在這住宅附近並無清真寺，所以當初建造大院宅，特地佈置了一個小禮拜堂。現在公主吩咐僕人們把那老婦人帶到小禮拜堂去。

那老婦人唸完禱告之後，又給帶到大廳去見公主。公主詢問了老婦人是哪裏人，要去哪裏等等之後，又問她這一座宅院怎麼樣，她覺得好不好。

"小姐，"那老婦人回答道，"如果你容許我説出心裏的話，那麼恕我直言，這座宅院如果有了三樣寶貝，那就誰家都比不上了——可惜你們沒有。是哪三樣寶貝呢？第一樣，會説話的鳥，牠不同尋常，一張嘴，就把周圍的鳥全都吸引來了。第二樣，會唱歌的樹，每一張葉子都發出不同的樂音，合在一起，就成為一曲永不靜止的美妙和諧的音樂。第三樣是閃閃生光的金黃水；你準備好一個盆，只消滴下一滴金黃水，頓時湧起一滿盆水，中間又噴射出一條水柱，就像是噴泉；這水柱向上噴射個不停，可是盆裏的水永遠不會溢出來。"

"啊，老大娘，"公主嚷道，"我是多麼感謝你！你讓我知道了世界上有這些稀奇的寶貝，這是我過去從來沒聽説的。如果你看得起我，請快告訴我怎樣才能得到這三樣寶貝吧。"

"小姐，"那老大娘回答説，"這三樣寶貝都在同一個地方，就在我們的王國和印度的邊界附近，等待着有人去取寶。去那裏的路就在你家門口，你派人去取寶，只消沿着這條路一直往前走二十天，到了第二十天，碰到第一個人，就上前去問那人：請問能言鳥、唱歌樹、金黃水在哪裏，那個人就會把地點告訴他。"

説完，那老大娘就告別了公主，獨自上路了。

公主一心想要得到這三樣寶貝，不斷地想着這三樣寶貝的好處。她的兩個哥哥打獵回來，看到妹妹低頭不語，好像有重重心事似的，感到十分奇怪，因此很關切地問她有甚麼事。

起初她怎麼也不肯説，後來問急了，她只得這樣説道："我一向總認為父親給我們蓋了這麼一座大宅院，真是盡善盡美，甚麼都不缺少了。到今天我才知道它還缺少三樣寶貝呢：——能言鳥，唱歌樹，金黃水。"

接着，她把那三樣寶貝的稀奇之處形容了一番，於是要求兩個哥哥派一個得力可靠的人去探求那三樣寶貝。

"妹妹，"大王子回答道，"我要親自出發去探求寶貝。請你告訴我寶貝在哪裏，我該朝哪個方向走？我明天就動身。"

第二天早晨，把妹妹託付給二弟照看後，大王子就跳上馬背。二王子和公主跟他擁抱告別，祝他一路平安。臨到兄妹分手之際，公主總覺得放心不下，她哥哥此去一定會遭遇到許多危險，因此說道："哥哥，誰能說得準我今後會不會再看到你！留在家裏別出門去吧！我寧可沒有能言鳥、唱歌樹、金黃水也不願你去冒生命的危險。"

"妹妹，"那兄長看到她一下子擔心成這個樣子，笑着向她說道，"我的主意已經打定了，要我聽從你的勸告是辦不到的事。不過我出去求寶，也許不免會有不測之事，因此我留下一把佩刀給你。這把刀不同尋常，如果你從鞘子中抽出刀身，只見它閃閃生光，跟現在一樣，那說明我安然無恙；如果刀身上血漬斑斑，那麼這就是個信號，我已不在人世了。"

說罷，大王子策馬而去，一路上並沒左顧右盼，而是徑直向印度奔去。

到了第二十天，他看到有一個相貌奇特的老頭兒獨坐在大路邊的樹陰下。他那兩根眉毛像白雪一般，他長長的鬍鬚一直拖到腳背。手指甲和腳趾甲都長得要命。有一頂寬闊的傘遮蓋在他頭上。他的唯一的衣裳就是披在身上的一張席子。原來這是一個苦行僧，在此遁世隱居，冥思苦想，已有許多年，因此成了目前的模樣。

大王子行近苦行僧之後，跳下馬來，按照那個虔誠的老婦人給予公主的指示，上前行了個禮，說道：“願真主保佑你長生不老，好大爺，願你的願望得到實現。”

那苦行僧還了一禮，但是他說的話王子一個字也聽不懂。原來苦行僧的頭髮太長了，遮住了他的嘴，幸而王子隨身帶着一把剪刀，於是他這樣說道：“尊敬的苦行僧，我想跟你談話，可是你的頭髮太長，使我沒法聽懂你的話。我想替你剪掉一些頭髮，你不會見怪吧。”

苦行僧並沒有不許他剪。王子把他的頭髮剪短之後，他發覺苦行僧並不是那麼年老。

“尊敬的苦行僧，”他說道，“可惜我手邊沒有鏡子，否則我就能讓你看到自己是多麼年輕。現在我可以叫你是一個‘人’了，在這之前，誰也不知道叫你甚麼好。”

“哥兒，不管你是誰，”那苦行僧微笑着回答道，“你為我做了好事，我很感謝。請說吧，你要我怎樣來向您表示感激呢。”

“尊敬的苦行僧，”王子回答道，“我出門尋找能言鳥，唱歌樹，金黃水。我知道離這裏不多遠，就有這三樣寶貝，可我就是不知道它們究竟在哪裏？如果你知道我該到哪裏去找，請你給我指一下路吧。”

王子跟他這麼說的時候，那苦行僧的臉色漸漸變了，他雙眼下垂，神情十分嚴肅。他沉默了一會之後，開口說道：

“哥兒，你向我問路，我是知道這條路的。可是你不知道，這條路有多危險。有好多像你一樣有身份又勇敢的年輕人來向我問這條路；可是，我可以告訴你，我從沒看見有哪一個從原路回來過。他們全都死在那裏了。如果你看重自己的生命，那麼聽我的話，快回家去吧。"

"不管你怎麼説，"王子回答道，"反正我是決不改變主意的。既然你知道這條路，那麼我再一次求你，快告訴我吧。"

苦行僧於是取過身邊的一個布袋，伸手從裏面拿出一隻碗來，説道："既然你不願意聽我的勸告，那麼把這只碗拿去吧。你跳上馬背後，就把這只碗往前一扔，碗在前面滾，你在後面跟，就這樣一直到山腳下。等到碗兒停下來了，不滾了，你也從馬背上跳下來，把馬勒放在馬頸上，讓馬兒就站在那裏等你回來。

"你一路上山去，只見左右兩邊都是些很大的黑石塊，耳邊只聽到從四面八方傳來一片喊鬧聲，一百遍、一千遍地在咒罵你，恐嚇你，威脅你。最最重要的是，千萬別回過頭去向後面張望。你一回過頭來，那麼你就立刻變成了一塊黑石頭，像那許許多多在你之前的年輕人一樣，他們都像你一樣來到這裏尋寶，卻一個個都失敗了，變成了一塊塊黑石頭。

"如果你闖過這一關口，你就會看到一隻鳥籠，關在那籠子裏的就是你尋求的那隻鳥兒。你就問牠：'唱歌樹在哪裏？金黃水在哪裏？'牠自會告訴你。我要告訴你的全説了，只是我還想再一次請求你別去冒這個生命的危險吧。"

王子得到了苦行僧的指點，就跳上馬背，恭恭敬敬地告別了苦行僧。於是他把那碗兒往前面一扔，不料那碗兒一路滾去，滾得好快，王子不得不在後面策馬緊追，唯恐跑慢了，望不見那碗兒。

碗兒滾到山腳邊就打住了，王子也從馬背上跳了下來，把馬勒放在馬頸上；他先打量了一下那座高山，果然看到兩邊全是些黑石塊。於是他登上山路，還沒走了四步，耳邊只聽得像雷鳴般地轟響着，也不知道誰在那裏吆喝：

攔住他！

逮住他！

宰了他！

有賊！

你這殺人犯！你這兇手！

一忽兒又聽到一種取笑的聲音："不，不，不要傷害他吧，看這小伙子多漂亮啊，放他過去吧！那籠中的鳥兒在等候他呢。"

儘管他耳邊轟響着一陣陣雷鳴般的聲音，王子還是勇敢、堅定地一步步登上山去。可是到後來那一片喧鬧的吆喝越來越可怕，那王子不由得感到心驚膽戰，他下邊的兩條腿也不由自主地在打戰了。這時候，他已忘了苦行僧的囑咐，想回身逃下山去。他這一回頭，馬上變成了一塊黑石頭。他停歇在山腳下的馬兒也同時變成了黑石頭。

自從王子出發之後，公主在家總是把那把佩刀插在腰帶裏，一天要把刀從鞘裏抽出好幾回，好知道她的哥哥是否平安無恙。

在王子變成黑石頭的不祥的日子裏，公主正在和二王子聊天，她像平時一樣隨手抽出鋼刀來看看，只見有一滴血凝聚在刀尖上，公主嚇得直叫起來：

"哎呀，我的好哥哥呀！都怪我不好！你這條命是害在我手裏的呀！我再也見不到你啦！我為甚麼要聽信那個蠢老太婆的嚼舌頭呀！"

二王子像他的妹妹一樣，為哥哥的死亡而感到傷心，可是他知道，妹妹在內心中還是渴望着那能言鳥，那唱歌樹，那金黃水，便這樣勸慰妹妹道：

"妹妹，我們再怎麼傷心地哭泣，也不能叫哥哥起死回生了。那敬神的老婦人跟你說的那一番話是當真不假的呀，你為甚麼要懷疑啊。哥哥也許是由於甚麼地方不小心，因此送了命。我決定接替哥哥，去尋找這三件寶貝。明天就上路。"

公主再三勸阻二王子，求他快放棄這個念頭，無奈二王子打定主意，怎麼勸他也沒有用。他臨走之前，交給公主一串珠圈，穿着一百粒珍珠，說是她撥弄着這些珍珠，就可以知道他是否安然無恙；如果這些珍珠忽然撥不動了，那麼這就是千真萬確的信號，他已經像大哥一樣，遇到了不測之事了。

二王子趕了二十天路程，於是就跟他的哥哥一樣，在同一個地點遇見了同一位苦行僧，向他提了同樣的問題。那苦行僧同樣警告他此去危險重重，也像勸告大王子那樣，盡力勸他不如回家去吧；還告訴他，不久之前，有一位哥兒，相貌長得跟他很像，也是為了求寶，從這裏路過，可是再不見他回來。

"尊敬的苦行僧，"二王子說道，"你提起的那位哥兒是我的大哥。我知道他已經失去了生命，可是我不知道究竟為了甚麼原因。"

"我能告訴你，"苦行僧回答道，"他像許許多多去求寶的人一樣，已經變成黑石塊了。如果你不聽從我的指點，不比你的哥哥更加小心，那麼同樣的命運就在等待着你。可是讓我再一次勸告你，不如打消了你的主意吧。"

“尊敬的苦行僧，”二王子回答道，“對你的好意我很感謝，可是我不能半途而廢。所以我求你啦，上回你幫助我的哥哥，現在你幫助我吧。”

於是苦行僧遞給了他一隻碗，王子跳上馬背，往前面一扔，緊追着那碗而去了。

那碗兒在山腳停下來之後，二王子跳下馬來，鼓足勇氣，登上山去。可是他走了還不到六步，就聽到身後有人呵斥他：

“給我站住，你這不知天高地厚的小子，竟敢闖到我這裏來了，我要好好地教訓你！”

二王子受人侮辱，怒不可遏，早把苦行僧的指點忘個乾淨，他伸手拔劍，一個轉身想找那個辱罵他的人算賬；他剛回頭看到原來背後空無一人，他和他的馬兒已經變成黑石塊了。

再說公主在家中一天要把珍珠串撥弄好幾遍，只要珍珠能夠撥動她就放心了。在二王子變成黑石塊的那一天，公主也像平常那樣逐一撥弄着一顆顆珍珠；誰知那些珍珠卻一下子撥不動了，這分明是個信號，她的二哥已經失去生命了。

她心中本來早已打定主意，萬一她的二哥也出事了，她該怎麼辦；所以她並沒有只管坐着放聲痛哭，而是立即行動起來。她穿上了她哥哥的衣服，女扮男裝，跳上馬背，沿着哥哥走過的道路出發了。

到了第二十天，她同樣看到了路邊坐着一位苦行僧，問了同樣的問題，得到了同樣的回答，而且聽到了同樣的勸告：千萬不要因為找寶貝而糊裏糊塗地把命送了。公主回答道：

“我如果沒有領會錯你的指點的話，那麼我想要達到目的必須做到這樣兩點：在上山去到鳥籠的路上，切不可被那一片可怕的吆喝聲嚇壞了；其次，切不可回頭張望。我希望我有力量控制自己，一路上不回一下頭，只是勇往直前；至於說到那可怕的吆喝聲，我想請教，是否可以採取預防的手段呢？"

"你打算採用甚麼樣的預防手段呀？"苦行僧問道。

"我想用兩個棉花球塞住我的兩隻耳朵，"公主回答道，"這樣，不管那一片吆喝聲多麼地響，多麼地可怕，我也不至於被嚇得心驚膽戰，失去了控制自己的力量。"

"好朋友，"那苦行僧回答道，"你打算怎麼辦，就怎麼辦好了；不過我還是要勸你千萬不要去冒這個險。"

公主謝過了那苦行僧之後，便騎上馬背，把苦行僧給她的碗兒往前面一扔，跟着碗兒奔去，直到山腳下才停下來。

公主跳下馬背，用棉花球塞住了兩邊耳朵，於是毫不畏怯地登上山去。她聽到了喊叫聲；她越走越高，那喊叫聲越來越鬧，成了一片怒吼。幸虧她早在耳朵裏塞了棉花球，因此這一片可怕的聲響並沒有使她感到緊張或者激動；相反，她對那些粗魯的吆喝，惡毒的謾罵，只是一笑置之。

最後，在雷鳴一般的聲響中，她終於望見了那個籠子和籠中的鳥兒。公主看到鳥籠，更是勇氣百倍，加快步子，直奔過去，她伸手拍拍那鳥籠，說道：

"鳥兒啊，我終於把你找到了，你是再不能從我手裏逃走了。"

她剛把話說完，那一片吼叫聲頓時寂靜了。

於是公主從耳朵裏取出棉花球，只聽得籠中的鳥兒這樣說道：

"好一個勇敢的公主，我的命運是要給人充當奴隸；我與其給別人做奴隸，寧可做你的奴隸，因為你為了要贏得我，表現出那麼大的勇氣。我知道你是誰，你喬裝改扮瞞不過我。過幾天有空的時候，我還有更多的事情告訴你呢。目前，你有甚麼吩咐儘管説吧，我一定完全服從。"

"鳥兒，"公主説道，"我聽説離這裏不遠，有金黃水，具有特殊的性能；你能告訴我到哪裏去找嗎？"

那鳥兒果然指點她在甚麼地方可以找到，原來就在附近。於是公主走到那裏，拿出隨身帶着的一個小銀壺，盛了滿滿一壺金黃水；又回到鳥兒面前，説道：

"鳥兒，我有了金黃水還不夠，我還要唱歌樹，請告訴我吧，我在哪裏可以找到它。"

"你轉過身來，"鳥兒回答道，"就可以看到在你身後有一座樹林，唱歌樹就在這林子裏。你從唱歌樹上折下一根樹枝，把它帶回家中，種植在花園裏。它很快就會在泥土中扎根，要不了多久，就成長為一株高大的樹。"

公主走進林子，就聽到美妙和諧的聲音，她隨着聲音尋去，果然找到了那株唱歌樹。她折下一根樹枝，回到鳥兒面前説道：

"鳥兒，你幫助我找到了兩件寶貝，但我還有要求呢。我的兩位哥哥，因為尋找你，變成了山坡上的黑石塊，快告訴我吧，怎樣才能破除這魔法？"

對於這個問題，鳥兒似乎很不願意回答。公主非要救活她的兩個哥哥不可，否則她也不想活在這人間了。鳥兒這才指點她，只消在她一路下山的時候，在每塊黑石頭上灑一滴金黃水，就能產生奇跡。

公主遵照鳥兒的指點去做，她灑下仙水的每一塊黑石塊都立即重又變成為一個男子漢，或者重又變成為鞍轡俱備的駿馬。在這些恢復原形的男子漢中，有兩位就是她的大哥和二哥。

兄妹在這時相見，真有說不出的高興！公主向她的哥哥，同時也向那許多高貴的青年說明她怎樣搭救他們的經過。於是公主帶頭，率領一隊人馬下山去了。

這支隊伍在回家的途中人數一天比一天減少，因為這些青年本是來自四面八方，不同的國家，所以每逢來到路口，這一位或是那一位青年就向公主告別，踏上通向自己的家園的道路而去了。

兄妹三人回到老家之後，公主就把能言鳥掛在花園裏。那仙鳥剛一調嗓囀鳴，那夜鶯啊，百靈鳥啊，紅雀啊，金翅雀啊，各種各樣的鳥兒就從四面八方飛來了。

公主又把唱歌樹的枝子種在花園裏，這樹枝馬上就在泥土中扎根，而且很快就變成一株大樹，那茂密的樹葉發出一陣陣和諧的音樂聲，就像山上的母樹一樣。

公主又吩咐在花園中安置一個漂亮的大理石盆；她於是把金黃水傾注在這石盆中，只見那仙水不斷在上漲，不多一會就溢滿了這極大的石盆，甚至高出了石盆的邊緣；在石盆中心湧起一注噴泉，足有二十尺高，水珠不斷從高空落下來，卻從不濺落在石盆外邊。

那兩位王子在家休息了幾天，從旅途的疲勞中恢復過來後，就像平時一樣，騎着馬兒出外打獵，作為消遣。這次他們走得很遠，離家有二三十里路。

恰好波斯的蘇丹也在這天出外打獵，也來到了這裏，在一條狹路上碰上了他們弟兄兩人。那兩兄弟慌忙跳下馬來，匍匐在地，向蘇丹致敬。

蘇丹吩咐他們起身之後，又見站在他面前的兩個小伙子長得一表人才，儀態不凡，心中十分歡喜，便問他們是甚麼人，住在哪裏。

"陛下，"大王子回答道，"我們是王上的已故的園林總管的兒子，我們現在的住宅是他生前建造的，這宅子造好不久他就去世了。"

蘇丹說道："我看你們兩個都喜歡打獵吧？"

"陛下，"那哥哥回答道，"打獵是我們兩人的一種鍛煉，凡是有志於將來在王上的軍隊中建立戰功的，都不應該疏忽鍛煉自己。"

蘇丹聽到這小伙子的回答十分得體，心裏很是高興，就邀請這弟兄兩人隨他一起去打獵。那弟兄兩人身手不凡，投射出去的標槍，沒有不中的，蘇丹滿心喜歡，就約他們到他的宮裏去做客。

沒有想到這兩兄弟面有難色，竟謝絕了蘇丹的邀請。蘇丹一定要知道這是為的甚麼緣故，大王子這才解釋道：他家還有一個妹妹，兄妹三人相處十分和睦，他們兄弟兩人有甚麼事，一向總是先要和妹妹商量之後，才決定這事該做不該做。

"你們兄妹之間的感情這麼好，很是不錯，"蘇丹說道。"儘管去和你們的妹妹商量吧，明天還是到這裏來見我，給我一個答覆。"

兩個王子回家後卻忘了把白天在林子裏遇見了蘇丹，承蒙蘇丹邀請他們進宮去做客等情況告訴公主；不過第二天他們倒是如約去見蘇丹。他們不得不承認昨天回家把事情忘了，竟沒有對妹妹說起，同時請求蘇丹的寬恕。

蘇丹真是寬宏大量，並不計較，只是要他們答應明天一定給他一個答覆。

誰知道這兩位王子一錯再錯，第二次又把事情忘了個乾淨。

雖說蘇丹秉性溫和，第二次又寬恕了他們；不過他從錢包中取出三個小金球，放進了大王子的衣襟中，微笑着囑咐道：

"給你這三個金球，免得你第三次又把事情忘了；你解開衣服的時候，這三個金球掉在地上發出響聲，那就是在提醒你。"

果然不出蘇丹所料，大王子直到晚上解開腰帶，準備上牀，聽到金球落地的聲音，這才想起白天的事來。他急忙奔到公主的閨房裏，把他們兄弟兩人三次和蘇丹見面的情況全都跟她說了。

公主聽了大哥所說的一切，十分驚奇，說道：

"我知道，都是為了我的緣故你才沒有接受蘇丹的邀請，你這樣看重兄妹之情，我十分感激；不過要違抗君王的意志，那是太危險了。如果我勸你別去王宮做客，你就此不去了，也許會使蘇丹生氣，那你我不免會遭到災禍。該去不該去，讓我們還是先去向能言鳥請教一下，再作決定吧；這鳥兒懂的事可多呢，牠答應過我們遇到甚麼困難，可以向牠請教。"

公主叫人把鳥籠取來，她把兩個哥哥遇到的情況都告訴了鳥兒，於是問牠該怎麼辦。那鳥兒回答道：

"你的兩位哥哥務必接受蘇丹的邀請，到他的宮中去做客，然後他們就好回請蘇丹到你們家來做客。"

第二天早晨兩位王子又見到了蘇丹，這樣回話道：

「陛下，我們聽候您的驅使；我家妹妹聽說陛下有請，竭力贊成我們應邀做客，不僅這樣，她還責怪我們像這樣有關向君主表白忠誠的事，還要回家去先和她商量，真是太不應該了。如果我們已經冒犯了陛下，那麼請陛下多多寬恕吧。」

「你們兩人不必為了這點小事而於心不安，」蘇丹回答道。「我非常讚賞你們的行為，只是我希望，如果你們也願意和我交個朋友，那麼你們怎樣看重你們的妹妹，請同樣地看重我吧。」

蘇丹說完就吩咐回王宮去。他讓兩位王子騎着馬一人在他一邊。他們進入京城的時候，老百姓都擁到街上來觀看，他們的目光都盯在那兩個陌生的年輕人的身上，都很想知道他們究竟是誰。羣眾中有很多人但願蘇丹有這樣一對英俊少年做王子，那就好了。

回到宮中之後，蘇丹引領兄弟兩人參觀宮中的各個大廳、正房；那兩兄弟看到宮廷建造得那樣宏偉，佈置陳設又那樣典雅富麗，讚不絕口，顯示出他們有很好的鑒賞力。

蘇丹設盛宴招待；他十分喜歡這兄弟兩個；飯後，要兩兄弟坐在他身邊，心中想道：「看他們是那樣聰明，那樣有見地，就算他們是我的一對兒子，才藝見識也不過是這樣罷了。」

夜幕降臨了，兄弟兩人起身告辭，他們俯伏在蘇丹腳下，感謝蘇丹對他們的說不盡的恩寵。在離開王宮之前，那做哥哥的說道：

「陛下，不知我們是否可以提出這樣一個心願：下次您到我家附近打獵時，想恭請您給我們兄妹三人賞臉，光臨舍間？寒舍很不像樣，不配君王駕臨；不過我們想，有時候君王也會降尊紆貴，暫且在茅屋裏棲身的。」

"我的孩子，"蘇丹回答道，"你家宅子一定是很漂亮的，不會叫宅主感到慚愧的。我願意來看你們，也看看你們的住宅，這是很高興的事啊。這事也不必耽擱，我明天就來看你們吧。第二天一清早我就來到第一次碰見你們的地方，你們到那裏去迎接我，做我的嚮導。"公主聽到兩位哥哥說，蘇丹明天將要光臨她家，於是說道：

"我們必須立即準備可以款待君王的宴席，讓我們趕緊去向能言鳥請教，也許鳥兒能指點我們，蘇丹最喜歡吃的是甚麼菜餚。"

兩個王子覺得這個主意不錯，他們回房去休息，公主獨自去和鳥兒說話。

"好小姐，"能言鳥說道，"你家廚子燒菜的手藝很高明，讓他們多燒幾道好菜；不過要緊的是關照他準備一道用南瓜做的菜，南瓜裏面塞滿了珍珠，就拿這作為第一道菜端到蘇丹的面前。"

"南瓜裏面塞滿了珍珠？"公主嚷道，"這可是從來沒聽說過的一道菜啊！再說，把我的珍珠全都拿出來，也塞不滿一隻南瓜啊。"

"你說珍珠不夠嗎？"鳥兒說道，"明天一早到林園去，在你看到的右邊第一株樹的腳下，挖開泥土，底下的珍珠比你所需要的還多呢。"

第二天早晨，公主按照鳥兒的指示，帶着一個園丁，來到右邊第一株樹邊，那園丁在樹腳下挖起土來；挖了一會，就發現泥土裏埋藏着一隻約有一尺見方的金匣子，他拿起金匣子，交在公主手裏。公主打開一看，匣子裏裝的全是珍珠。

公主回到宅子後，把廚師長叫了來，把有關宴席安排的事吩咐了一番，接着又這樣說道：

"除了這些之外，我還要你為蘇丹準備一道特殊的菜餚，端上席來放在他面前。這道菜用南瓜燒成，把這些珍珠塞在裏面。"說罷，公主打開金匣，露出裏面的珍珠。

那廚師長從沒聽說過有這麼一道菜，真是目瞪口呆。他不知道說甚麼好，從公主手裏接過那金匣退下去了。

這時候，兩個王子在約定的地點見到了蘇丹，大王子陪着蘇丹做嚮導，二王子搶先趕回去，通知家裏的人蘇丹就要光臨了。

等蘇丹進入庭園，來到門廊前跳下馬來時，公主早守候在門前迎接，她一看到蘇丹駕臨，就跪倒在他腳下。蘇丹把她攙扶起來，看到她長得這麼美，說道：

"有這樣兩個哥哥，真不愧有這樣一位妹妹；有這樣一位妹妹，真不愧有這樣兩個哥哥！現在我不再感到奇怪了，做哥哥的為甚麼有事先要和妹妹商量。"

公主引導着蘇丹去看了她家的那許多佈置陳設各有特色的房間(只有大廳沒有去)，得到了蘇丹的稱賞；於是蘇丹要求去看看她家的園林。

公主隨即打開了通向園林的門，伴着蘇丹來到了唱歌樹那裏。蘇丹耳邊只聽得一陣陣他從沒聽到過的那麼好聽的音樂，他回頭問公主道：

"我的孩子，音樂師在哪裏呀 —— 怎麼我只聽到音樂不看見人呀？難道他們在地底下，或是隱藏在空氣中嗎？這樣的演奏高手是應該出來和人見見面的呀。"

"陛下，"公主笑着回答道，"這不是音樂師在演奏，這是就在陛下面前的那株樹上的樹葉在發出音樂聲。如果您不相信，只消走近幾步就可以知道了。"

蘇丹於是向唱歌樹走近幾步，那一陣陣美妙的音樂聲真把他迷住了，他要公主告訴他這奇妙的樹叫甚麼名字，是從甚麼地方弄來的。

"陛下，"公主回答道，"這樹並沒有別的名字，就叫做'唱歌樹'。我們國家是不長這種樹的。要說到它的來歷，那就要連帶說到'金黃水'和'能言鳥'。等陛下休息過後，再去看看那鳥兒和那水，這以後，如果陛下願意聽的話，我就把這三件寶貝的來歷講一下。"

"我的孩子，"蘇丹回答道，"你給我看的東西太奇妙了，叫我把疲勞全忘掉了。我一心只想馬上去看那'金黃水'，去欣賞那'能言鳥'。"

公主陪着蘇丹來到了那盛着"金黃水"的大理石盆邊，那噴射得高高的水柱簡直使蘇丹看個沒有夠。公主向他講述了這"金黃水"的妙處之後，他終於戀戀不捨地轉過身來，說道：

"好吧，今天也就算看過了，不過我打算以後還要經常來看看呢。現在讓我們去看看'能言鳥'吧。"

他們向大廳走去，只見周圍的樹木上棲息着許許多多的鳥兒，只聽得一片囀鳴聲。蘇丹感到奇怪極了，便轉身問公主這是怎麼一回事。

公主向蘇丹解釋道，這許多鳥兒是從四面八方飛來和能言鳥作伴的，這能言鳥蘇丹馬上可以在大廳的一個窗口的籠子裏看到了。

公主陪着蘇丹走進大廳之後，她提高了嗓音説道：

"我的小奴隸，蘇丹光臨了，快來向他請安吧。"

這鳥兒正在唱歌，聽到公主的吩咐，果然立即停下歌聲，這樣説道：

"真主保佑蘇丹！祝蘇丹萬壽無疆！"

宴席特地設在靠近窗口，蘇丹就座時回答道：

"鳥兒，謝謝你的忠心，你是鳥類中的蘇丹，我今天能看到你，心裏真高興！"

端上席面的第一道菜餚是一大盆南瓜，特地放在蘇丹面前。蘇丹伸手取了一個來，放在盆裏用刀切開，裏面竟是塞滿了許多珍珠，蘇丹奇怪極了，問道：

"怎麼把珍珠塞在南瓜裏呀？珍珠怎麼能吃呢？"

他向兩位王子看看，又向公主看看，想弄明白這究竟是怎麼一回事兒。這時候那籠中的鳥兒搶着替他們回答道：

"陛下何必這麼大吃一驚呢？南瓜塞珍珠這道菜明明放在您眼前，您還信不過來，那麼從前您一聽説王后 —— 您的妻子 —— 生下了一隻狗、一隻貓、一根木條，怎麼就這樣輕易地信以為真呢？"

"我相信有這等事，"蘇丹回答道，"因為那保姆跟我説這是千真萬確的。"

"陛下，"鳥兒回答道，"那兩個保姆就是王后的兩個姐姐，妹妹比她們幸福，她們心懷妒忌，就利用陛下的輕信，把您騙了，好給自己出口怨氣。您只消把這兩個女人抓來審問一下，她們就會供出自己的罪行。你眼前看到的那兄妹三人就是您的親骨肉呀

——是您從前的園林總管把他們從河裏救上來，當作自己的子女，扶養他們長大成人。"

"鳥兒，"蘇丹嚷道，"我相信你對我説的這一番話，是要叫我睜開眼睛，看到事情的真相。我第一眼看到他們兄妹三人就從心底感到喜歡，這清楚地表明了他們是我的親骨肉。來吧，我的兒子；來吧，我的女兒！讓我擁抱着你們，我要讓你們第一次得到父親的慈愛。"

宴席結束後，蘇丹要回宮去了，他起身説道："孩子們，現在你們看到了自己的爸爸，明天我要把王后帶來，讓你看到自己的媽媽。你們準備好接待她吧。"

蘇丹一回到宮中，第一件事就是命令宰相把王后的兩個姐姐抓來。這兩個壞女人被從家裏抓走後，不到一小時就被定了罪，判了死刑，立即被押出去執行了。

就在這時候，蘇丹率領着朝廷中的大臣們徒步去迎接那被幽禁在小屋裏的王后。可憐的王后在那簡陋的小屋裏度過了十多個寒暑，好不淒涼；現在總算重見天日了。蘇丹眼中含着淚水，向她説道：

"從前我冤枉了你，現在特地來請求你的寬恕。你那兩個壞心眼兒的姐姐編造出一套鬼話欺騙我，現在已經得到了報應。不消多少時候我就可以讓你看到你那兩個才藝出衆的王子和可愛的公主。跟我一起回到宮裏，重新恢復你王后的高貴身份，享受你應當享受的榮譽吧。"

這令人歡樂的消息很快就傳遍了整個京城。

第二天一清早，蘇丹和王后，由全體朝廷大臣陪同，前往園林總管營造的宅院。到了那裏，蘇丹親自領着兄妹三人去見他們的母親。所有在場的人看到他們骨肉團聚的歡樂情景都感動得直流淚水。這時候，那王后看到有這樣兩位王子做她的兒子，有這樣一個公主做她的女兒，她心中的高興再沒有人能比得上了。

當蘇丹騎着馬回京城的時候，右邊是兩位王子作伴，王后和公主在他的左邊；朝廷的大臣和侍衛前呼後擁，組成一支浩浩蕩蕩的隊伍。滿城的老百姓都擁到街上來觀看，發出一陣陣熱烈的歡呼聲。大家的眼光都集中在王后和她的王子、公主身上。公主手裏捧着的一隻鳥籠更是引人注目；許許多多鳥兒都被能言鳥的美妙的歌聲吸引着，一路跟了來，從這個樹梢掠到那個樹梢，從這個屋脊跳到那個屋脊。

兩位王子和公主隨着父王母后，進入了宮裏，那場面好不氣派。整個晚上，燈火輝煌，有歌有舞；不僅在王宮裏舉行着盛大的慶祝活動，而且整個京城，整個波斯王國都在為宮中的天大喜事而熱烈地慶祝着。

5

神馬

在元旦節的聚會上，設拉子[4]的蘇丹剛剛結束對大家的講話，一個印度人帶着一匹人造的馬出現在他的面前。這匹馬栩栩如生，乍一看活像是一匹真馬。

這印度人拜倒在蘇丹腳下，指着馬説："這是一匹神奇的馬。只要騎上它，我就可以到地球上最遙遠的地方去。如果你下命令，我願意讓陛下親眼看到這個奇跡。"

蘇丹對任何新奇事情都很感興趣，他從來沒有看見或聽見過神馬這種怪事，就要印度人操作給他看。

這印度人立刻把一隻腳伸進馬鐙，翻身上馬，隨後問蘇丹希望他去哪裏。

"你看見遠處那座山嗎？"蘇丹用手指着説。"騎上你的馬到那裏去，從山腳下的棕櫚樹上摘一根樹枝帶回來給我。"

蘇丹話音剛落，印度人就扳動安裝在馬鞍的前橋旁邊、馬頸子凹陷處的一隻木釘。這匹馬立刻離開地面，駄着它背上的人以閃電般的速度飛向空中。蘇丹和全體在場的人都大吃一驚。在十五分鐘不到的時間裏，他們就看見印度人手裏拿着棕櫚樹枝回來了。在人們的歡呼聲中神馬降落到地面，印度人下了馬，走向蘇丹的寶座，把棕櫚樹枝放在他的腳旁。

蘇丹目擊這從未聽説過的怪事，覺得十分驚奇，非常想把這匹馬佔為己有，便對印度人説：「我想把它買下來，如果你願意賣的話。」

「陛下，」印度人回答説，「只要答應我一個條件我就願意賣掉這匹馬，那就是：把公主——你的女兒——嫁給我。」

蘇丹身邊的臣子聽見印度人提出如此荒唐的要求，忍不住都大笑起來。蘇丹的長子費魯茲·沙赫王子更是火冒三丈。「陛下，」他説，「請你乾脆拒絕這種厚顏無恥的要求，不要讓這可憐的小丑自鳴得意，以為能夠高攀上世界上最強大的家族，不要讓他抱有片刻的幻想。請你想一想吧，對於你自己和這個高貴的家族，你負有多麼大的責任！」

「我的兒子，」蘇丹答道，「我不會同意他的要求。不過，撇開我的女兒不談，我可以換一個方法和他做交易。但是，在這之前，我要你把這匹馬檢驗一下，你親自去試着騎一騎，然後告訴我你覺得它怎麼樣。」

聽了蘇丹的話，印度人趕緊走上前去想幫助王子騎上馬背，並打算告訴他如何駕馭和操縱這匹神馬。但是，他還沒來得及這麼做，王子已經騎上馬背，扳動木釘——如同他先前看見印度人所做的那樣。神馬立刻如離弦之箭竄到半空，一會就不見了蹤影。印度人看了大驚失色，趴倒在蘇丹的寶座前，請求蘇丹不要發怒。

「陛下，」他説，「你和我看得一樣清楚，這匹馬飛得多麼快。我一時驚呆了，忘記説話。不過，即使我説了，即使我把方法教給他，他也已經離我們太遠，不可能聽得見。不過，希望還是有的，王子將會發現另一隻木釘，只要他扳動那支木釘，神馬就不會繼續上升，就會緩緩地降落到地面。」

儘管印度人這麼說了，蘇丹仍然十分為兒子擔心，他分明碰到了危險。他對印度人說："你必須以腦袋為我兒子的生命作擔保，三個月之內他一定得安全地回來，或者我能聽到他還活着的消息。"說完這些，他命令武士們把印度人關進監獄嚴加看管。然後，他回到皇宮去；想到元旦節結束得如此不吉利，他覺得很難過。

這時候，王子正被神馬載着以驚人的速度在空中飛行。一小時不到，他已經升得非常高，往下看去，地面上的山脈和平原聚攏在一起成了一堆。他這才想到該回去了，於是他再次扳動木釘，先往左再往右，又牽動韁繩；但是這匹馬繼續上升，王子開始緊張起來，並深深地後悔在騎上馬背之前沒有完全弄明白應該怎樣操縱它，這真是太愚蠢了。他開始仔細檢查馬的頭部和頸子，發現在它右耳朵後面另有一隻木釘，比馬鞍的前橋旁邊那一隻小一些。他扳動這只小木釘，很快就感覺到神馬開始降落，同上升時一樣神奇，不過速度稍慢。

王子發現小木釘，把它扳動的時候，天色已經暗了下來。在神馬降落的過程中，太陽最後的光芒漸漸從他的眼前消失，不一會，天就完全黑了。他只得放鬆手中的韁繩，耐心地等待這匹馬自己選擇着陸地點，不管是沙漠、河流還是海洋。

最後，大約在半夜時分，神馬降落在一片堅實的土地上，王子下了馬。他已經餓得渾身沒有一點勁，因為從早上到現在整整一天甚麼都沒吃。他發現自己正站在一座富麗堂皇的宮殿的一個露台上。他慢慢地摸索，不一會來到一個台階旁，這台階向下通到一個房間，房間的門此刻半開着。

王子在門口停住腳步側耳細聽，隨後小心翼翼地走進屋去。燈光下，他看見幾個黑奴在睡覺，出鞘的劍放在身旁。很明顯，這是某個蘇丹或公主的衛兵的屋子。他踮着腳再往前走，把一道簾子拉向一旁，看見一間豪華的內室，裏面有好幾張牀，其中一張比其餘的高一些，因為放在一個略高於地面的平台上，顯然這是公主和她的侍女的屋子。他悄悄地走近平台向牀上張望，看見一位異常美麗的少女，一下子使他驚呆了。他跪倒在地，輕輕地牽動公主的袖子。公主睜開眼睛看見一位英俊的小伙子跪在自己面前，臉上卻毫無懼色，她大吃一驚。王子站起身來，深深地鞠了一躬説：

　　"美麗的公主，現在你看見，跪倒在你腳下的是波斯王國蘇丹的兒子，由於一場極為離奇的歷險他來到了這裏，希望能得到你的幫助和保護。"

　　對於費魯茲・沙赫王子這一請求，美麗的公主答道："王子，你並不是在一個野蠻的國家，而是在孟加拉王公的王國，我是他的大女兒。我答應保護你，我的話是可靠的。"

　　波斯王子想表示感謝，但公主制止了他，她説："儘管我非常迫切想知道你用甚麼神奇的方法從波斯首都來到了這裏，又是靠甚麼法術躲避了衛兵的監視，可是，我要抑制住自己的好奇，讓你先去休息，恢復疲勞。"

　　公主的侍女們十分驚訝地發現一位王子在公主的房間裏，但是她們立刻遵照公主的吩咐，把王子帶進一個漂亮的房間。到了這裏，她們有的安排牀鋪，有的端來豐富可口的飯菜。

　　第二天，公主打算會見王子，比平時更加精心地打扮自己。

她把所有的珠寶都戴在脖子上、頭上和手臂上，並穿上只有國王、王子和公主才有資格穿的、用最昂貴、質地最好、色彩最豔麗的印度綢緞織成的衣服。最後一次照過鏡子以後，公主讓人請王子來見她。

王子接到邀請的時候剛剛穿好衣服。他懷着十分榮幸的心情立刻來到公主的閨房。他向公主敍述神馬是如何了不起，他從高空飛到這裏的經歷是多麼奇妙，以及昨天他是怎樣進入這個房間的。接着，他感謝公主的熱情接待，並表示想回家去，以免父王擔憂。

公主回答説：“王子，我不同意你這麼快就回去。請答應我再多待一段時間，那樣，你回到波斯以後，就可以把你在孟加拉王國的所見所聞詳詳細細向那裏的人敍述了。”

公主誠懇的挽留使王子覺得盛情難卻。這以後，公主忙個不停，熱心地安排各種活動，如打獵、聽音樂、參加盛大的宴會等，使王子日子過得很愉快。

整整兩個月，波斯王子完全服從公主的意願和安排，彷彿除了一輩子和公主生活在一起之外，再沒有別的事情要做了。但是，他終於還是向公主表示不能繼續待下去了，請求公主同意他回到父親身邊去。

“此外，公主，”他還說，“我還想不揣冒昧地請求你跟我一起回去。”

對於波斯王子的這一請求，公主沒有回答，但是她的沉默不語和下垂的目光，向王子明白表示了她願意伴隨王子到波斯去。她說，她只擔心一點，那就是王子恐怕還沒有完全弄懂怎樣操縱神馬。但是王子很快就消除了公主的擔心，他向她保證說已經有了經驗，現在甚至敢說比印度人本人都操縱得更好。於是他們進行了周密的思考，想好了如何祕密離開王宮的計劃，不讓任何人懷疑他們的意圖。

第二天拂曉前，僕人們都還在睡覺的時候，他們兩人來到王宮的平台上。王子把馬頭轉向波斯，公主騎上馬，在他身後坐穩，並用雙手抱住他的腰。王子扳動木釘，神馬立刻飛上天去，跟以前一樣，速度非常之快，兩小時以後，波斯王國的首都進入了他們的視野。

王子沒有把馬降落在王宮，而是讓它飛到城外不遠處的一座涼亭。他把公主帶進一個漂亮的內室，命令侍從們供給她一切需要的東西，還對她說，他要去告訴父王他們兩人來了，隨後馬上就回來。他命令下人備馬，便出發到王宮去。

蘇丹見了兒子，高興得流了眼淚。他懷着熱切的心情聽王子敍述他的歷險——他在空中的飛翔、孟加拉公主的熱情款待，以及由於他們兩人互相愛慕而造成他在那個王國這麼長時間的逗留。他還說，他答應要娶公主為妻，並且已經說服她來到了波斯。"我讓她和我一起騎着神馬來到這裏，"他最後說，"現在把她安置在您的夏宮，等您表示同意我們的婚事之後我再回去告訴她。"

聽了這些話，蘇丹再一次擁抱王子，說："我的兒子，我不但同意你們結婚，而且還要親自去把她接到王宮來，你們的婚禮就在今天舉行。"

這時候蘇丹下令將那印度人從監獄裏放出來帶到他的面前。蘇丹說："我把你關進監獄，是為了萬一王子生命有危險的時候可以拿你的性命來抵償。感謝上帝，我的兒子現在安全回家了。走吧，帶上你的馬離開此地，不要讓我再看見你。"

從把他提出監獄的那些人的口中，印度人瞭解了全部情況，知道費魯茲·沙赫王子把公主帶到了波斯，安置在涼亭裏，便立刻想出一個復仇的辦法。他騎上神馬直接飛到涼亭，對守衛隊長說，他是奉命來把孟加拉公主用神馬從空中帶到蘇丹那裏去。蘇丹正在王宮前的大廣場等候公主。

守衛隊長看見印度人從監獄裏被放了出來，就信以為真。公主以為是王子叫他來的，也就聽從了他的安排。

印度人看見他的陰謀如此容易得手，心裏高興極了。他騎上馬，讓公主坐在自己後面，扳動木釘，神馬一下子就升到空中。

與此同時，波斯王國的蘇丹由眾臣陪同，正在去涼亭的路上，王子則急急忙忙地想要在他們之前先趕到那裏，好讓公主作好迎接蘇丹的準備。出乎他們意料之外，印度人帶着他的俘虜突然出現在他們的頭頂上方。先前他受到了粗暴的對待，現在他為自己報了仇。

蘇丹看見印度人的時候，感到特別的驚訝和惱怒，因為此刻他束手無策，沒有辦法懲罰印度人的惡劣行徑。他只能站在那裏，用各種各樣的話來罵他；親眼目睹這一奇恥大辱的眾臣也跟着一起罵。但是，最痛苦的還是費魯茲·沙赫王子，當他看見印度人帶走了他心愛的公主時，他的悲傷筆墨無法形容。他的心碎了；他憂鬱地來到先前與公主分手的涼亭，守衛隊長已經瞭解印度人的詭計，這時候跪倒在王子的腳下，詛咒自己，還説要自殺，因為自己輕信了印度人的謊話，造成了致命的後果。

“起來吧，”王子説，“失去公主這件事我不責備你，而要責備我自己缺乏警惕。不過現在我們不要浪費時間，快給我拿一件托缽僧的袍子來，但不要讓別人覺察是拿來給我穿的。”

守衛隊長把袍子拿來之後，王子立刻把它穿上，偽裝成一個托缽僧，帶上一盒珠寶離開王宮，下決心要把公主找回來，否則就死在外面。

這時候，印度人騎在神馬上，帶着公主來到克什米爾王國的首都。他並不進城，卻停在一片小樹林裏。他把公主留在靠近一條清澈小溪的一塊草坪上，自己去尋找食物。他回來之後，兩人一起進食，隨後印度人就開始迫害公主，因為公主拒絕嫁給他。

恰好在這時候克什米爾王國的蘇丹和他的臣子出外打獵，經過這片樹林，聽見一個女人求救的呼喊，便趕來幫助她。印度人竟無恥地説，誰也不能干涉他們之間的事，因為這女人是他的妻子。

公主一聽急得大叫：“老爺，上帝派你來救我了，不管你是誰，可憐可憐我吧！我是一個公主。這印度人是個邪惡的巫士，他把我從就要娶我為妻的波斯王子身邊搶走，用一匹神馬把我帶到了這裏，你們可以看見此刻神馬還在那邊。”

公主的美貌和高雅的氣質，以及她的眼淚，表明她説的是事實。印度人的無恥行徑激起克什米爾王國蘇丹的義憤，蘇丹下令把他抓起來，砍下他的腦袋。這個命令立刻被執行了。

公主得救了，擺脱了邪惡的印度人，她感到無比欣慰。她以為克什米爾王國的蘇丹會馬上把她送到波斯王子那裏去，但是她的希望完全落空了。救她的人自己想要娶她為妻，並決定把婚禮安排在第二天，還向王國內全體居民宣佈，要舉行一次盛大的慶祝活動。

第二天黎明，孟加拉王國的公主被響徹王宮的鼓聲、喇叭聲和歡呼聲所吵醒，卻一點想不到這是怎麼一回事。後來克什米爾王國的蘇丹來了，向她解釋說這些喧鬧和歡呼聲是慶祝他們的婚禮，並請求她同意他們兩人的結合。聽了這些話，公主昏厥過去。

在場的侍女們趕緊跑過去攙扶她，費了很長時間才使她蘇醒過來。恢復知覺以後，公主下了決心，既然克什米爾王國的蘇丹強迫她結婚，她就偽裝發瘋。於是，她開始胡言亂語，還做出精神失常者的各種舉動，甚至從坐椅上跳起來，做出要向蘇丹撲過去的樣子，使蘇丹大為震驚。他把全體御醫都請來，問他們能不能治癒公主的病。

蘇丹眼看御醫們無法治好公主的病，就把王國裏所有著名的醫生都請來，但他們也無能為力。於是他又向鄰近的王國的蘇丹們求救，答應要是有人治癒公主的病，一定給予優厚的報答。各個地方的醫生都來施展他們的本領，但沒有一個獲得成功。

這時候，化裝成托缽僧的費魯茲‧沙赫王子在各地周遊，每到一處都打聽孟加拉王國的公主的下落。最後，在印度斯坦的一個城市，他聽說有一位孟加拉王國的公主在即將和克什米爾王國的蘇丹舉行婚禮時發瘋了。他相信，這一定就是他的那位公主，就急忙趕到克什米爾王國的首都。在那裏，他聽人說了關於公主的事，還瞭解了印度巫士的結局。這使王子確信，經過這麼長時間的尋找，他終於找到了心愛的人。

王子穿上醫生的服裝，勇敢地來到克什米爾王國的王宮，表示願意為公主治病。已經有一段時間不見醫生來了，蘇丹對於公主能否治癒，已經開始喪失信心，儘管他仍然想和她結婚，所以一聽說又來了一個醫生，便立刻下令把他帶進宮裏。見了面，蘇丹對王子説，公主一看見醫生，她的病就會發作得更厲害。因此，蘇丹把王子帶到一個小房間，在那裏，王子可以通過一個小窗口窺探公主而不被公主看見。王子看見他心愛的公主無比悲傷地坐着，嘴裏哼着悲歎自己不幸命運的哀怨的曲子，淚水從一雙美麗的眼睛裏流淌下來。王子離開小房間，對蘇丹説，他可以肯定公主的病是能治好的，不過，為了幫助公主，他必須單獨和她談話。

蘇丹下令打開公主的房門，王子走了進去。公主立刻像前一陣看見醫生時一樣，做出種種威脅着要撲上前去打人的樣子。王子進一步靠近她的身旁，用低得只有他們兩人可以聽見的聲音對她説："公主，我不是醫生，我是費魯茲・沙赫。我是來救你，讓你恢復自由的。"

孟加拉王國的公主熟悉王子的聲音，儘管他的鬍子留得很長，認出了他，立刻平靜下來；能夠這樣意外地見到自己的情人，她心裏暗暗感到高興。在簡短地交換了自從分手以來彼此的情況之後，王子問公主是不是知道印度巫士被殺死以後那匹神馬的下落。公主回答説不知道，但猜想它一定被當作一件奇特的東西而被小心地看管着。王子接着對公主説，他在思忖有甚麼辦法把那匹馬弄到手，兩人一起回波斯去。他們商量定當後，為了達到這個目的，王子要公主在明天先見一見克什米爾王國的蘇丹。

第二天，蘇丹非常高興地發現公主的病大有好轉，認為王子是世界上最了不起的醫生。陪同蘇丹一起去看望公主的王子就問，公主是怎麼從她遙遠的國家來到克什米爾王國的。

蘇丹於是把印度巫士的事情敍述了一遍，還告訴王子那匹神馬現在被當作神奇的珍品存放在他的寶庫裏，雖然他自己並不知道如何駕馭它。

"陛下，"這位假冒的醫生說，"這個消息使我想到一個治癒公主的辦法。當初她被神馬帶到這裏來的時候，遭到了巫士的魔法的侵害，我知道有一種香可以解除這種毒害。明天，讓人把神馬帶到王宮前的大廣場上來，其餘的事就交給我吧。我保證讓你和所有在場的人都看到，只消幾分鐘的時間，孟加拉王國的公主就能在精神上和肉體上完全得到康復。不過，為了確保我的計劃得到成功，必須讓公主穿得儘可能地華麗，還要用你的寶庫中最貴重的珠寶給她打扮起來。"

蘇丹急切地表示一定照辦。為了達到和公主結婚的目的，比這困難得多的事情他都願意承擔。

第二天，神馬被人從蘇丹的寶庫取出來帶到王宮前的大廣場上。有一件不尋常的事情將要發生的消息傳遍了整個城市，人們從四面八方趕來觀看。克什米爾王國的蘇丹在貴族和大臣們的簇擁之下，在一個特地搭建起來的平台上各就各位。孟加拉王國的公主由侍女陪伴走到神馬跟前，在她們的幫助下跨上馬背。隨後，這假冒的醫生在神馬周圍放上許多有木炭燃燒着的罐子，又將一小把一小把的香投入其中。做完這些儀式之後，他繞着神馬走了三圈，口中唸唸有詞，裝作好像是在唸咒語。不一會，罐子裏冒出濃濃黑煙，把公主和神馬籠罩起來，把人們的視線都擋住了。趁此機會，王子敏捷地跳上神馬，坐在公主後面，扳動木釘，神馬飛上了天空。這時候，蘇丹清楚地聽到這些話傳到他的耳邊：

"克什米爾王國的蘇丹，當你想要和那些請求你保護的公主們結婚時，先要學會得到她們的同意才行！"

就這樣，王子救出了孟加拉王國的公主，當天回到波斯王國的首都。他的父親，也就是波斯王國的蘇丹，立刻着手準備，為他們舉行了一場隆重而熱烈的婚禮，為王子和公主的成親而舉行的慶祝活動，持續了好幾天；過後，蘇丹指派一名使節去孟加拉王國，通報了這一消息並表示希望兩國結成聯盟。孟加拉的王公覺得十分滿意和榮幸，非常愉快地同意了。

6

漁夫的故事

很久以前，有一個年邁體弱的漁夫，他家裏有妻子和三個孩子。他很窮，因此難以弄到足夠的食物養家活口。他每天很早就出海打魚，還限定自己每天只撒四網。

一天早上，當天空還能看見昨夜的月亮時，他就出門了。到了海濱，他脫去外衣撒下魚網。收網時，他感到很重，心想這一回捕到大魚了。但是，等到把網拉上岸來一瞧，裏面不是魚，卻是一頭死驢子，這使他十分懊喪。他補好被死驢的重量扯破好幾處的魚網，把它第二次撒下海去。

這一回還是很重，他又以為大概捕到了滿滿一網魚。但是，結果使他非常失望，魚網裏只有一隻大籃子，裝的全是泥沙。

"啊，命運之神！"非常悲哀的漁夫語調憂鬱地呼喊道，"停止對我發怒吧。我從家裏到這裏來打魚謀生，你卻以死亡來威脅我。我沒有別的養家活口的辦法；就是靠這樣辛辛苦苦地打魚，也只能讓一家人非常勉強地吃上一口飯。我這樣抱怨雖然不應該，但是你為甚麼要以欺騙正直的人為快樂呢？為甚麼要讓好人默默無聞，卻又偏愛邪惡的人，還要頌揚那些沒有道德因此是不值得你頌揚的人？"

這樣發過牢騷之後，漁夫憤怒地把籃子扔到一旁，洗掉魚網上的泥沙，第三次把它撒到海裏。

這一次他得到的只有石塊、貝殼和爛泥。他的絕望無法形容。這時候天快要亮了，他是一個老實的穆斯林，從不輕視早禱，所以又這樣哀求起來："我的主啊，您知道我每天只撒四網，現在我已經撒下三次，一點收穫都沒有，只剩最後一次了，我求求您讓大海行行好吧，就像您從前對摩西所做的那樣。"[5]

早禱完畢，漁夫把網第四次撒到海裏。這一次和前面三次一樣，他拉網時感到很沉重，他又以為捕到許多魚了。但是拉上來一看，網裏一條魚也沒有，只有一隻黃銅製的瓶，根據它的重量來看，裏面一定裝滿着甚麼東西。漁夫注意到這瓶是用鉛蓋封口的，蓋上還打着印。"我要把它拿去賣給鑄造工，"他高興地自言自語，"再用得來的錢買穀子。"

他仔細觀看瓶子，把它搖動，想根據聲音來判斷裏面裝的是甚麼。但是一點聲音也沒有。這個情況，加上那鉛蓋上的封印，使他覺得瓶裏一定裝着貴重的東西。為了弄個明白，他用小刀不很費力地把瓶蓋撬開，然後把瓶子顛倒過來，這時他驚訝地發現沒有任何東西從瓶口掉出來。他把瓶子放在自己面前的地上，全神貫注地觀察，只見從瓶口慢慢地冒出一股煙來，這煙非常非常濃，使他不得不後退幾步。漸漸地，這股煙向天上升去，幾乎和雲一樣高了，籠罩了大海和地面，就像濃霧一樣。可以很容易想像，漁夫看見這個情況非常驚異。等到瓶子裏的煙統統到了外面，它又重新聚集攏來，形成一個具體的形狀，一個妖怪，一個比任何巨人都要大得多的妖怪。看見這麼一個魔鬼出現在自己面前，漁夫想撒腿逃跑，但是他恐慌萬狀，呆呆地一動也不能動了。

"所羅門[6]，所羅門啊，"妖怪叫道，"真主的使徒，原諒我吧，請求你。我再也不違背你的意願了，我服從你的命令。"

　　漁夫剛聽完妖怪的這些話便鼓足勇氣説："高傲的精靈，你在説些甚麼？所羅門是上帝的使徒，他已經死了一千八百多年了。現在你把你的過去告訴我，告訴我你是怎麼會被關在這個瓶子裏的？"

　　妖怪輕蔑地望着漁夫回答説："説話要有禮貌一些。你稱我為'高傲的精靈'，膽子真是夠大的。"

　　"那麼，"漁夫又説，"稱你為一隻報告吉兆的鳥，也許就比較禮貌吧。"

　　"我告訴你，"妖怪説，"在我殺死你之前，對我説話要有禮貌一些。"

　　"請問，為了甚麼你要殺死我呀？"漁夫問。"你已經忘記是我把你放出來的嗎？"

　　"這一點我記得很清楚，"妖怪答道，"但那不會阻止我殺死你。我只答應你一件事。"

　　"甚麼事？"漁夫問。

　　"那就是，"妖怪説，"答應讓你選擇怎樣去死。"

　　"可是，"漁夫又問，"我怎麼得罪你了？你難道就這樣報答我給予你的恩惠嗎？"

　　"我只能這樣對待你，"妖怪説，"為了使你相信這一點，現在聽我把我的過去告訴你吧。我是那些反抗真主權威的精靈當中的一個。他們那些傢伙後來都承認和服從上帝的使徒所羅門，只有薩卡爾和我兩人認為屈服是可恥的。為了懲罰我的抗拒，這位強有力的君主派他的宰相巴拉基阿的兒子阿薩夫來抓我。阿薩夫抓住了我，用武力把我帶到他的主人所羅門王的寶座跟前。

「大衛的兒子命令我放棄我的生活方式，承認他的權威，服從他的法律。我倔強地拒絕了他，拒絕按照他的要求發誓忠於他和順從他，任憑他大發雷霆。為了懲罰我，他就把我關在這個銅瓶裏，還在鉛蓋上加上他的封印以防止我衝出來，那上面還刻着真主的名字。這樣做妥之後，他把瓶子交給一個服從他的精靈，命令它把我扔進大海。真叫我非常傷心，這件事它立刻照辦了。

「在我被囚禁的最初階段，我發誓，如果有人在頭一百年以內救了我，我一定使他成為一個富翁，即使他死了也還是個富翁。但是一百年過去了，沒有人來救我。在第二個一百年，我發誓如果有人放我出去，我一定把地球上所有的寶藏都找出來給他，可還是沒有人來。在第三個一百年，我許下諾言，要讓我的救命恩人成為一個最強大的君王，永遠執行他的命令，並且每天滿足他三個要求，不管這些要求是甚麼。但是，和前面兩個一百年一樣，第三個一百年又過去了，我仍然被關禁在瓶子裏。這麼長時間的監禁終於使我憤怒了，我發誓要毫不留情地殺死任何放我出來的人，只答應他一個條件，那就是由他自己選擇死的方法。今天，你既然來到這裏把我放了出來，那麼你現在就決定怎樣去死吧。」

漁夫聽了妖怪的話十分悲傷。「我是多麼不幸啊，」他叫道，「我到這裏來，難道只是為這麼一個忘恩負義的傢伙幫大忙嗎！我請求你，想一想你這樣做是多麼不公正，收回你那沒有道理的誓言吧。你如果放過我，那麼真主同樣也會饒恕你的。如果你慷慨地讓我活下去，那麼真主也就會保護你，使你的生命不受傷害。」

「不，」妖怪回答，「你非死不可，只是決定讓我怎樣殺死你。」

看見妖怪這樣堅決地要自己死，漁夫傷心極了。這一方面是為他自己，更主要的是為了他的三個孩子；當他想到自己死後三個孩子的悲慘處境，心裏十分痛苦。他繼續哀求妖怪。

"不要浪費時間了，"妖怪吼道，"你的話不會動搖我的決心。快一些，告訴我你怎麼死。"

常言道：急中生智。漁夫這時候想到一個計策。"既然我免不了一死，"他說，"我服從上帝的意志。但是在我決定怎樣死去之前，我以偉大真主的名義懇求你 —— 真主的名字就刻在這銅瓶鉛蓋上大衛的兒子所羅門王的封印上 —— 真實地回答我一個問題。"

當妖怪感到他將被迫正面回答問題時，渾身顫抖，對漁夫說："你要問甚麼？趕快問吧。"

一聽妖怪答應說實話，漁夫立刻對他說："我想知道你剛才是不是真的在那個瓶子裏。你敢不敢以偉大真主的名義起誓？"

"敢，"妖怪回答說，"我以偉大真主的名義起誓，我剛才確確實實是在那個瓶子裏。"

"說實話，"漁夫說，"我無法相信你。這瓶子連你的一隻腳都藏不下，怎麼可以容納你整個身子呢？"

"儘管如此，"妖怪回答，"我向你起誓，正如你剛才所看見的，我的確在那瓶子裏。我這樣正式起誓你還不相信我嗎？"

"不，確實不信，"漁夫說，"除非我再親眼看見，否則我不相信。"

妖怪聽漁夫這麼說，便立刻把自己重又變成濃煙，籠罩了大海和地面。隨後，這煙聚集起來，開始進入瓶子，慢慢地、連續不斷地，直到瓶外一絲都不剩。一個聲音隨即從瓶子裏傳出來：

"現在，你這不相信人的漁夫總該信服了吧，我不是在瓶子裏嗎？"

漁夫根本不理睬他，卻迅速抓起鉛蓋扣在瓶口上。

"妖怪，"他大聲說，"現在輪到你請求饒恕了，選擇一個最適宜於你的方式去死吧。哦，不，我最好還是仍然把你丟進海裏，然後在岸邊、在你被丟下海去的這個地點造一間屋子住在裏面，警告那些到這裏來撒網捕魚的漁夫，不要救起你這麼一個邪惡的妖怪，因為你發誓要殺死讓你獲得自由的人。"

受到漁夫的嘲罵，妖怪大怒，使出全身力氣想衝出瓶子，但是辦不到，因為瓶蓋上有大衛的兒子所羅門王的封印。他意識到現在漁夫佔了上風，便開始把自己的怒氣隱藏起來。"你要注意，"他的語調溫和下來了，"哦，漁夫，你要注意現在你在做些甚麼。剛才我說的只是開玩笑，你不該當真。"

"哦，妖怪，"漁夫答道，"幾秒鐘之前你是妖怪中最了不起的，現在卻是最沒有用的了。不要指望說些好話會對你有甚麼幫助。你非回到海底去不可。先前我以上帝的名義懇求你不要殺死我，你拒絕了，現在我同樣拒絕你的請求。"

妖怪說了各式各樣好聽的話來打動漁夫，想得到他的憐憫，但是都不起作用。"如果你再一次讓我得到自由，"他對漁夫說，"你就有權利要求我表示感謝，你會得到滿足的。"

漁夫說："你這傢伙太奸詐了，我不相信你。要是我愚蠢到這個地步，第二次讓你獲得自由，那麼我就活該丟掉性命了，因為你准會像祖曼國王對待醫生杜班那樣對待我的，讓我把這個故事說給你聽。"

國王和醫生的故事

從前，波斯有個祖曼國，百姓的原籍是希臘。他們的國王患麻風病，吃足了苦頭，醫生們採取了他們所知道的每一種方法來給他治療，都失敗了。這時候，一個名叫杜班的非常有學問的醫生來到了這個國家。

他聽說國王生病，而醫生們又都束手無策，便穿得乾淨整齊來到王宮，設法使國王接見了他。

"陛下，"他說，"聽說所有那些醫生都沒能治好你的病；如果你願意給我這樣的榮譽，願意接受我的治療，那麼我既不用藥片、藥水，也不用油膏，就能給你治好那麻風病。"

國王聽了醫生的自我推薦非常高興，回答說："假如你果真如你剛才所說的那樣醫術高明，那麼，我答應你，在我恢復健康之後，不但要賜予你和你的後代無數錢財，而且還要把你當作最親近的臣子。不過，你說這話是不是認真的？我用不着吞藥片喝藥水，也不需要敷油膏？"

"是的，陛下，"醫生回答，"我覺得，在上帝的幫助下，我能夠成功。明天我就開始給你治療。"

杜班回到家裏，製作了一隻球拍，拍子的柄是空心的，裏面塞進了治病所需要的藥物。球拍製成以後，他又準備了一隻圓球。第二天他再次去見國王，拜倒在國王的腳下。

這樣恭順地施禮之後，杜班站起身來對國王說，他不妨到他常去的地方騎在馬背上拍球。國王接受了這個建議。到了打球的綠草坪上，杜班把事先準備好的球拍交到國王手中，說：

"哦，陛下，使勁用這拍子連續地打球，直到你渾身出汗。當你手上的熱量傳到我裝在這拍柄裏的藥物時，藥力就會滲透你的全身。然後你就停止打球，回到王宮裏去，洗個熱水澡，用毛巾使勁地擦過身子以後上牀睡覺，到了明天你的病就好了。"

國王催馬上前追擊那圓球，被擊出的球由陪同國王的侍從扔回來，國王便再打；就這樣，他打了好長一段時間，直到他的手和整個身體都發熱，拍柄裏的藥物像杜班所預言的那樣開始發揮效力。這時候國王停止打球，回到王宮洗澡、擦身、睡覺，完全按照杜班的指示做了。

很快國王便感覺到這個治療方法效果很好，因為第二天早上他又驚又喜地發現他的麻風病已完全治癒，他的整個身體清潔得彷彿從來沒有生過這個病。他穿上衣服，立刻進入議事殿，登上寶座，接受文武百官的祝賀。他們這一天聚集在這裏一方面是表示他們很高興看見國王恢復了健康，另一方面是為了滿足自己的好奇心。

杜班進殿來，匍伏在寶座前國王的腳下。國王見了，叫他起來，讓他坐在自己旁邊，把他介紹給全體在場的人，當眾給了他各種他所應該得到的表揚。這還不算，在當天王宮裏舉行的盛大慶祝宴會上，國王還讓杜班和自己單獨地在一張桌子上進餐。

祖曼國王這樣做了還覺得不夠。到了晚上，當眾臣將要告辭的時候，他又要杜班穿上通常大臣們觀見國王時所穿的那種華麗而昂貴的服裝，賞賜他兩千金幣。可是國王覺得這還不足以報答這位醫術高明的醫生，因此一連好幾天，繼續用各種不同的方式表達他的感激心情。

國王的宰相生性貪婪、妒忌，隨時準備幹出各種各樣的罪惡勾當。這個傢伙眼看着國王給予醫生這麼許多賞賜，心裏怒火中燒，腦子裏頓時生出邪念，他決心在國王面前詆毀杜班的良好品格，貶低杜班的功勞。為了達到這個目的，他私下去見國王，説他有非常非常重要的情況需要報告。國王問他是甚麼情況。

　　"陛下，"他説，"對於一個國王來説，信任一個尚未證明是完全忠心的人是很危險的。現在你十分寵信醫生杜班，待他如上賓，卻不知道他是個奸細，混入宮裏來目的是要暗害你。"

　　"你怎麼敢對我説這些？"國王大聲説，"你別忘了是在跟誰説話；你説得這麼肯定，可我不會輕易相信你的。"

　　"哦，陛下，此刻我有幸報告你的是千真萬確的事實，所以請你不要再信任杜班了，這麼做是危險的。我要再説一遍，醫生杜班來自他自己的國家希臘的最偏遠地區，唯一目的就是要實行剛才我説的那個可怕的計劃。"

　　"不，不，宰相，"國王打斷他的話説，"我確信這個你認為是偽君子和奸細的人，是一個最有道德、最善良的人。你知道他用甚麼藥物——哦，還不如説是神奇的辦法——治好了我的麻風病。假如他想要害死我，那為甚麼還要這樣救我呢？所以，不要再往我的腦子裏灌輸對於他的不公正的懷疑。我不但不相信，而且現在還要告訴你，從今天起，我要每月給他一千個金幣的俸祿，直到他去世。他給我治好了病，即使我與他共享我的全部財富，甚至我的王國，也不足以報答他。我已經看到了這其中的原因。他的品德和成功使你產生了妒忌。但是你不要指望我會產生不利於他的偏見。"

宰相一心要害死醫生，所以不肯就此罷休。"哦，陛下，"他又説，"並不是妒忌使我憎恨杜班，我恨他是因為我關心陛下的健康。杜班是個奸細。你説他治好了你的病，但是誰説得准呢？也許，他只是表面上治好了你，實際上並沒有。誰能擔保，這樣的治療到最後不會產生最最惡毒的結果呢？"

國王的性格懦弱，他既沒有眼力能看穿宰相的邪惡用心，也沒有意志堅持自己原來的看法。"你説得好，宰相，"他説，"他可能是為了殺死我這個特殊目的而到這裏來的，這個目的他很容易能夠達到。我們必須考慮在這種困難情況下應該怎麼辦！"

當宰相看到自己的話已經起了作用，國王已經陷入自己的圈套，便對他説："能夠確保你的休息和安全的最好最有效的方法，偉大的國王，就是馬上派人去把杜班找來，等他在王宮一露面就立刻砍了他的腦袋。"

"的確，"國王應道，"我想我必須防止杜班實現他的計劃。"説完國王就命令一個侍從去把醫生叫來。

杜班絲毫沒有想到國王已變了心，急急忙忙地趕到王宮。

"你知不知道，"國王一見杜班就問，"我為甚麼派人把你叫來？"

"不，陛下，"杜班回答。"我把你叫來，"國王説，"是要砍你的腦袋，免得我自己掉進你設下的陷阱。"

筆墨無法形容杜班聽見國王這些話的時候是多麼驚愕。"哦，陛下，"他問道，"為了甚麼你要把我處死？我犯了甚麼罪呀？"

"我已經得到報告，"國王説，"你是一個奸細，你到我的宮裏來是要謀害我，為了預防這一點，現在我要殺死你。動手吧！"

他又對身邊一個侍從說了一句："把我從這個奸詐的壞蛋手中救出來，他到這裏來只是為了暗害我。"

聽了這些話，杜班明白了，國王賜予他的許多榮譽和大量錢財給他製造了敵人，輕信的國王已經讓自己被讒言牽着鼻子走了。他開始後悔不該給國王治病，但是已經太晚了。"難道，"他叫道，"我治好了你的病，你就這樣報答我嗎？"

誰知國王根本不理睬他的責問，第二次要侍從執行他的命令。杜班於是懇求國王。"啊，陛下，"他大聲說，"如果你延長我的生命，那麼上帝也將延長你的。不要殺死我，否則上帝將用同樣的方式對待你的！"

（"你瞧，"故事講到這裏漁夫對妖怪說，"國王和醫生杜班之間的情形和我們兩人之間的情形完全一樣吧。"接着他把故事繼續下去：──）

國王不理睬醫生的懇求，高聲喊道："不，不，你必須死，否則的話，你會用比治癒我的方法更神祕的手段奪走我的性命。"

於是侍從用一條布帶子蒙住杜班的眼睛，還把他的雙手也捆起來，眼看就要把短彎刀抽出鞘來。

在場的眾臣非常同情杜班，他們請求國王饒恕他，並且對國王說，他們願意擔保醫生是無辜的。可是國王已打定主意，不可動搖，他再次下命令時語氣專橫，眾人不敢再多說了。

杜班被蒙住眼睛跪在地上準備接受結束他生命的那一刀時，再一次對國王說：

"既然陛下拒絕收回把我處死的命令，我請求你至少准許我回家去一趟，安排我的葬禮，向親人最後告別，把一些錢送給窮人，並且把我的書交給那些知道怎樣使用的人。其中有一本我想把它送給陛下。那是一本世間少有的奇異的書，值得好好地保存在陛下的寶庫中。"

"那是一本甚麼書，"國王問道，"這樣珍貴，值得受到如此特殊的榮譽？"

"陛下，"杜班回答，"那本書具有一種最奇異的力量。它的主要功能之一是，在我的頭被砍下之後，要是陛下你不嫌麻煩，願意把書翻到第六頁，然後讀一下左手邊第三行的文字，那麼我的頭將回答你的任何問題。"

國王非常想看一看這麼一本奇怪的書，就把醫生的死刑推遲到第二天執行，並派了相當多的武士把他押送回家。

這不幸的囚犯把後事作好了安排。當消息傳開，說醫生的頭被砍下之後將發生奇跡，文武百官在第二天都聚集在議事廳，想要親眼目睹這不尋常的事情。

醫生杜班很快就被押了上來，他手裏捧着一本很大的書走到國王的寶座跟前。然後打開包書的封皮，把它遞給國王，説：

"希望陛下你樂意接受這本書。過一會我的頭將被砍下，請你命令一個侍從把它放在這個花瓶上，再把花瓶放在這包書的封皮上。這樣放妥之後，我的頭將立刻停止出血，隨後你打開書本，我的頭就會回答你的全部問題。不過，陛下，"杜班接着説，"請允許我再一次懇求你可憐可憐我吧，我是清白無辜的呀。"

"你是白白請求了，"國王回答，"單單為了聽你的腦袋在你死了之後説話，我也非把你處死不可。"他一邊說一邊從杜班手中接過那本書，命令劊子手把醫生處決掉。

劊子手的動作幹淨利落，杜班的頭恰好掉在花瓶上，而花瓶剛被放到包書的封皮上，血就立刻止住了。接着，國王和所有的旁觀者驚訝地發現，這顆頭睜開了眼睛，説："請陛下現在把書打開吧。"

　　國王照辦了。他發現第一頁和第二頁粘在一起，便把手指放進嘴裏舔一舔，利用唾沫來幫助翻書。就這樣，他把書一頁一頁地翻過去，一直翻到第六頁。他發現第六頁上甚麼字都沒有，就對杜班的頭説："醫生，這上面是空白的。"

　　"再翻幾頁，"杜班的頭回答。

　　國王於是繼續翻書，並一再地把手指放進嘴裏，卻不知道這本書的每一頁都在毒藥裏浸過；最後，書頁上的毒藥開始發生作用了。國王這時候只覺得心裏異常煩躁，這是過去從沒有過的；他眼前的東西也模糊了，接着便翻倒在地，一直滾到寶座底下，渾身激烈地顫抖。

　　當醫生杜班——或者還不如説是他的頭——看見毒藥已經發生效力，國王很快就要死去，便高聲叫喊：

　　"暴君，現在你看見了吧，那些濫用手中權力殘害無辜百姓的統治者將得到怎樣的下場！他們這樣不公正，這樣殘酷，真主遲早會懲罰他們的！"

　　杜班的頭剛説完這些話，國王就斷了氣；殘存在這顆頭裏的微弱生命緊接着也就死亡了。

　　漁夫講完國王和醫生的故事之後，對仍然被關在銅瓶裏的妖怪説："假如國王讓杜班活下去，真主也同樣會讓國王活下去，但是他拒絕了醫生的懇求，真主就懲罰了他。妖怪啊，這種情況同樣適用於你。先前要是我能夠使你的心腸軟下來，使你答應了我的請求，那麼我就會憐憫你現在的處境；可是，既然你剛才根本不考慮是我讓你獲得了自由，是我為你做了大好事，卻堅持一定要殺死我，那麼，現在我也不可憐你。我要讓你一直留在這瓶子裏，把你丟進海底，使你永遠成為一個廢物。"

"我的好朋友，"妖怪回答，"我再一次求求你不要幹這麼一件殘酷無情的事。你不要忘記，復仇並不是美德，相反，以德報怨才是值得稱讚的。"

"不，不，"漁夫說，"我不會放你出來，還是把你丟入海底來得好。"

"再聽我說一句，漁夫，"妖怪叫道，"我將教你如何變成一個富翁，這個方法是你怎麼也想不到的。"

漁夫聽說有希望可以改變自己貧窮的生活，可以擺脫缺衣少食的困境，立刻換了一個態度。"這個我倒想聽聽，"他大聲叫道，"如果我還有一絲理由相信你說的話。以真主的名義對我發誓，你保證信守諾言，我就打開瓶蓋。我想你總不敢違背這樣的誓言吧。"

妖怪發了誓，漁夫跟着就揭開瓶蓋，濃煙立刻從瓶裏往外直冒。妖怪恢復他的形體之後所做的第一件事就是把銅瓶一腳踢進海裏。他這個行動使漁夫大吃一驚。

看見漁夫驚慌的樣子妖怪大笑。"不要緊張，漁夫，"妖怪對他說，"拿着你的魚網跟我走吧，我要向你證明我是遵守諾言的。"

於是他們一起離開，經過城市，翻過一座大山，下山以後到達一個廣闊的平原，再往前走，便來到四座小山包圍之中的一個湖泊。

到了湖邊，妖怪對漁夫說：“撒網捕魚吧。”

漁夫看見湖中有大量的魚，毫不懷疑自己將有很大收穫，不過他十分驚訝地注意到，這些魚有四種顏色——白、紅、藍、黃。他撒下網去，捕到四條魚，每種顏色各一條。

“把這幾條魚拿進皇宮去，”妖怪說，“把牠們獻給蘇丹，他就會給你許多許多錢，比你一生中所見過的還要多。你每天到這裏來吧，在這個湖裏捕魚，不過要注意，每天只能撒一次網。如果你不重視我的警告，災禍就要降臨到你的頭上，所以你要小心。”

說完這些，妖怪以腳跺地，地面裂開，他的整個身子陷下去從漁夫眼前消失，地面重又合上。

漁夫決定嚴格遵照妖怪的忠告和指導，決不撒第二網。他心滿意足地回到城裏，帶着捕獲的魚來到蘇丹的皇宮。

可以想像蘇丹看見這四條魚的時候多麼吃驚。他把魚一條一條地拿起來仔細察看，欣賞了好一陣子以後，對宰相說：“把這些魚拿給希臘國王送給我的那個傑出的廚師。我相信牠們看上去這麼美麗，吃起來也一定味道鮮美。”

宰相親自把魚送到廚師手中。“這裏有四條魚，”他對廚師說，“是一個漁夫獻給蘇丹的，他命令你把牠們煎一煎。”然後宰相回稟了他的主人。蘇丹吩咐他賜給漁夫四百個金幣。從來沒有看見過這麼一大堆錢的漁夫喜形於色，幾乎覺得這一次奇遇就好像是一場夢。當然，他很快就肯定了這不是夢，是真有這回事。他用這些錢買了許多生活必需品。

現在我們得敍述一下蘇丹皇宮的廚房裏發生了些甚麼事。

女廚師把宰相送來的魚洗乾淨之後，就把牠們放進一個平底鍋，加入一些油，放在火上煎起來。當她認為魚的一面已經煎透，便把魚兒翻過身來。不料她剛給魚兒翻了個身，就看見廚房的牆壁上出現了一道裂縫，接着又向兩邊分開，從裏面走出一個漂亮的年輕女子。這美女身穿繡花緞子長袍，那刺繡手藝是埃及風格的，還戴着耳環、由大顆珍珠串成的項鏈，以及鑲有紅寶石的手鐲，手裏拿着一支桃金娘。女廚師非常吃驚地看着她走到鍋子旁邊，用手中的桃金娘枝敲了敲四條魚當中的一條，嘴裏說："魚兒，魚兒，你們在盡你們的義務嗎？"那條魚回答了一個字。這女子重複了她的問題，四條魚就一起豎起身子，非常清晰地回答："是的，是的 —— 如果你計數，我們也計數；如果你還債，我們也還我們的債；如果你飛起來，我們就勝利了，滿足了。"

四條魚剛說完這些話，這美女就把平底鍋打翻，回到牆壁裏面去，牆壁隨即合上，彷彿甚麼事情都沒有發生過。

所有這一切使女廚師萬分驚駭。待到稍微從恐懼中喘過氣來，她走上前去把掉在灰燼上的魚撿起來，發現牠們甚至比煤炭更焦更黑，根本不能再放到蘇丹的餐桌上去了。她十分苦惱，傷心地哭起來。"天哪！"她叫道，"這下我可怎麼辦呀？要是我把剛才看見的對蘇丹說，他是一定不會相信我的。"

正在這時候宰相進入廚房，詢問魚是否已經煎好。女廚師於是把剛才發生的一切向宰相敍述，他聽了深以為異。但是他並沒有把這件事稟告蘇丹，卻編了謊話將他的主人矇騙過去。然後他派人把漁夫叫來，對他說："再給我弄四條魚來，跟你送來過的那四條一樣，因為出了事故，那些魚不能給蘇丹送去了。"漁夫說路途太遠，當天不能把魚捕來了，答應第二天早上把事情辦妥。

為了不誤時，第二天漁夫在天還沒亮的時候就出發到湖邊去。他撒下魚網，收網時發現又捕到四條，和昨天那四條一樣，每一種顏色各一條。他立刻回去，把魚交給宰相。

　　宰相把牠們拿進廚房，鎖上門；他要親眼看着廚師煎魚。女廚師按照前一天所做的那樣，把四條魚放進平底鍋，倒入油之後放到火上去煎。一面煎好以後，她把這些魚翻過身來，這時候廚房的牆壁立刻出現一道裂縫並向兩邊分開，那年輕美女又出現了，手裏仍拿着一支桃金娘。她走到平底鍋跟前，敲了敲其中的一條魚，又重複了昨天說過的話，四條魚便豎起身子作了同樣的回答。然後這美女跟昨天一樣把鍋子打翻，接着回到牆壁裏去。宰相親眼目睹了這全部過程。

　　"這件事非常令人吃驚，"他大聲說，"真是太稀奇了，這事再不能隱瞞起來，不讓蘇丹知道。我要親自去把這個奇跡稟告他。"於是他徑直去皇宮，把前後經過一五一十報告了蘇丹。

　　蘇丹聽了非常吃驚，並急於想親眼看一看這奇異的場面，為此他派人把漁夫找來。"朋友，"他對漁夫說，"你還能給我再送四條魚來嗎？"

　　"如果陛下給我時間，"漁夫答道，"我保證再給你送來。"蘇丹給了他一個期限，於是他第三次到湖邊去。和前兩回一樣，他只撒網一次就成功地捕了四條顏色各異的魚。他趕緊把魚送給蘇丹，蘇丹下令賞他四百金幣。

　　蘇丹派人把這四條魚以及各種煎魚所必需的器具一起送到他自己的房間。他和宰相兩人留在屋裏，把門鎖上，開始煎起魚來。一面煎好了，他們把魚翻過身來，這時候牆壁立刻出現一道裂縫，並向兩邊分開，不過，從裏面出來的不是年輕的美女，而是一個穿着奴隸衣服的黑人。這黑人身材高大，手中拿着一根粗大的綠色的棍子。他走到平底鍋跟前，用棍子觸動其中一條魚，以一種可怕的調子大聲說："魚兒，魚兒，你們在盡你們的義務嗎？"聽見這話，四條魚豎起身子答道："是的，是的，我們在盡我們的義務。如果你計數，我們也計數，如果你還債，我們也還我們的債；如果你飛起來，我們就勝利了，滿足了。"四條魚的話音剛落，黑人就把鍋子打翻，使牠掉在燃燒着的煤炭中間，魚兒成了灰燼。隨後黑人進入牆壁，牆壁立刻重新合攏，跟原先一模一樣。

"我都親眼看見了，"蘇丹對他的宰相說，"這件事我不能就這樣讓它過去。這些魚說明，一定發生過某些很不尋常的事情，我必須弄清楚發生了甚麼。"

他派人去把漁夫找來，對他說："你送來的魚造成了很大的麻煩。你是在哪裏捉到的？"

"哦，陛下，"漁夫回答，"從這裏你可以看見那座大山，在它的那一邊，還有四座小山，四座小山中間有一個湖，那些魚我就是從那湖裏捕來的。"

"你知道那個湖嗎？"蘇丹問宰相。

"不，陛下，"宰相回答，"我甚至聽都沒聽說過，雖然我在那座大山附近，以及大山的那一邊打獵已經差不多有六十年了。"

蘇丹問漁夫那湖距離皇宮有多遠。漁夫回答說要不了三小時就可以到了。蘇丹估計，如果立刻出發，天黑以前還可以趕到，便讓漁夫做嚮導，命令全體文武都跟隨他一起去。

他們登上那座大山，然後從另一邊下山，這時候他們十分吃驚地發現眼前是一個大平原，是以前他們誰也沒有見過的。最後他們到了湖邊。這湖的位置和漁夫所説的完全一致，湖水清澈見底。他們看見湖裏的魚跟漁夫送進宮裏來的那些一樣，共有四種顏色。

蘇丹在湖邊凝視着這些魚兒，臉上帶着非常讚美的表情，隨後他對眾臣説，這個湖距離他們的城市這麼近，而他們卻從來沒有看見過，這難道是可能的嗎？眾臣答道，他們甚至連聽都沒有聽説過。

"既然你們都這麼説，"蘇丹宣佈，"而且我也跟你們一樣對這件新鮮事感到十分吃驚，那麼，我決心把它弄個明白，否則就不回去。我要弄清楚這個湖是怎麼會到這裏來的，湖裏的魚為甚麼只有這四種顏色。"説完蘇丹下令安營紮寨。

天黑了，蘇丹在營帳裏休息，開始和他的宰相進行一場重要的談話。"現在我的腦子被弄得很糊塗，"他説，"這個湖突然在這裏出現；那個黑人從我房間的牆壁裏出來；還有這些魚，我們聽見牠們説話了——所有這些使我十分好奇，我一定要弄個水落石出。因此我決心實行一個計劃。我將孤身一人離開營地，你必須嚴守祕密。你留在我的營帳內，明天早上如果眾臣來到營帳門口，你就要讓他們離開，就説我有點兒不舒服，想一個人待着。以後你必須每天這麼對付他們，一直到我回來為止。"

宰相費了許多口舌，講了許多理由，企圖説服蘇丹放棄他的計劃，但純屬徒勞。蘇丹不聽勸告，準備出發。他穿上一件適宜於行走的衣服，佩帶一柄長劍，待到營寨裏鴉雀無聲的時候，他就獨自走了出去。

蘇丹朝四座小山中的一座走去，不很費力地爬到山頂，從另一邊下山，就更容易了。接着他越過一個平原，繼續向前，直到太陽升起。這時候他看見前方一段距離之外有一個大建築物。這使他非常高興，因為此刻他想找人打聽一些情況。

他走近一看，這建築物原來是一個富麗堂皇的宮殿，由光滑的黑色大理石建成，屋頂是貴重的金屬，整個建築明亮閃光，好比一面鏡子。這麼快就遇見了至少值得探索的東西，蘇丹很興奮，他站在這宮殿的正對面仔細觀察，然後他走到其中有一扇是開着的那些折門跟前。儘管他可以走進去，但他覺得最好還是敲一下門。起先他敲得很輕，等了一會，不見有人回答，又敲第二次，這一回比剛才響得多，但還是沒有人答應他。這使他非常意外，因為他無法想像如此豪華的宮殿竟會被主人丟棄。

"如果裏面沒有人，"蘇丹自言自語，"我就沒甚麼可怕。要是有人來，我有武器可以自衛。"

他終於走進門去，站在門廊下叫起來："這裏沒人嗎？沒人來接待我這個旅途勞累需要休息的陌生人嗎？"他放開喉嚨這樣叫了兩三遍，還是沒有人回答。

這種寂靜無聲使他更加覺得驚異。他繼續向前，來到一個寬敞的庭院，環顧四周，卻看不見任何活的生命。隨後他穿過幾個大房間；這些房間的地上鋪着絲綢地毯，牆壁的凹處置有沙發，沙發上的飾物和墊子都是朝聖地麥加的產物。房間的門簾是最昂貴的印度產品，上面有金銀絲的繡花。蘇丹繼續向前，來到一個非常華麗的大廳。這大廳的中央有一個大水池，四個角上各有一個很大的金獅子。水池中央有一個噴泉，水柱幾乎高達大廳那繪有阿拉伯風格美麗圖案的圓屋頂，從獅子嘴裏噴出的水匯入中央的水柱，令人賞心悅目。

這個宮殿被一個花園從三面包圍。花園裏有色彩絢麗的各種花朵，有泉水、樹叢和其他許多美麗的景致，使這個地方非常迷人，不過，在這方面比所有這些美麗風景更迷人的是許多繚繞在空中的美妙的歌聲。這裏是鳥兒們常駐之地，因為有網覆蓋着整個樹叢，不讓這些漂亮的歌唱家逃跑。

蘇丹依次穿過一個又一個屋子，繼續漫步了很長時間，身邊所看見的一切都是那麼富麗堂皇。他覺得有點兒累了，便在一個開着門的房間裏坐下，從這裏眺望花園。正當他這樣對着眼前的景色沉思的時候，突然聽見一個悲傷的聲音，發出撕心裂肺的叫喊。他側耳細聽，傳來的是這樣一些好不叫人感傷的話：

"哦，命運之神，你沒有讓我長久地過幸福的日子，卻使我成了最最不幸的人。求求你，不要再這樣折磨我吧，快點結束我的生命，讓我擺脱痛苦吧！"

蘇丹被這悲傷的哀求所震動，立即起身向發出這聲音的地方走去。他來到一個房間的入口，掀開門簾，看見一個年輕人坐在一張略高於地面的類似國王寶座的椅子上。他外表英俊漂亮，衣着華貴，但是滿臉愁容。

蘇丹走上前去和這陌生人打招呼。年輕人深深地低下頭去表示回答，卻並不起身。"當然，"他對蘇丹説，"我理應站起身來接待你，對你表示敬意，但是有一股強大的力量阻止了我。相信你不會因此而誤解吧。"

"不管是甚麼原因使你站不起來，"蘇丹説，"我都願意接受你的道歉。你的抱怨引起了我的注意，我是來幫助你的，希望能幫你擺脱痛苦。但是，首先請你告訴我，那個湖——裏面有四種

顏色的魚 —— 是怎麼回事？這個宮殿是怎麼會出現在這裏的？你是怎麼會孤身一個留在此地的？"

年輕人沒有回答這些問題，卻好不悲傷地慟哭起來。"命運之神是多麼喜怒無常啊！"他哭喊道。"她把人高高舉起，卻為了捉弄又把他們狠狠摔下來。誰能誇口說命運之神讓他享受了平靜的生活，讓他享受了純粹的幸福？"

蘇丹很同情年輕人的處境，再一次問他為甚麼這樣悲傷。

"啊，大爺，"年輕人回答，"我怎麼能不悲傷呢？"說完他撩起身上的袍子，這時候蘇丹才發現，他整個身體只有腰部以上還保持着原樣，下半身已經變成了黑色大理石。

我們很容易想像當蘇丹看到年輕人可悲的狀況時那大吃一驚的神態。"你這種情況，"蘇丹對他說，"讓我看了十分害怕，同時也使我好奇。我很想立即瞭解你的遭遇，我還相信，那個湖以及湖裏的魚都和你的過去有關係吧。因此，我誠懇地請你把你的故事說給我聽。"

"我將滿足你的要求，"年輕人回答，"不過我必須首先提醒您，要仔細地聽，仔細地想 —— 甚至於要仔細地看 —— 因為我要說的有些事情是令人難以置信的。"

黑島國年輕國王的故事

"首先我要告訴你，"年輕人開始說，"我的父親馬哈默德從前是這個國家的國王。這個國家叫'黑島王國'，得名於附近的四座小山 —— 它們從前是四個小島。我的父親居住在王國的首都，現在卻成了一片湖泊了。你聽我往下說就會瞭解這些變化是怎麼發生的。"——

我的父親是在七十歲去世的。我接替王位之後就馬上結了婚，王后是我的表妹。我從她那裏得到的愛使我心滿意足，我也以同樣的柔情報答她。我們的結合使我享受了五年純真的幸福，但是當五個年頭即將過去的時候，我開始覺察到王后不再愛我了。

一天，晚餐以後，她去洗澡了，我覺得困乏，就倒在沙發上睡覺。王后的兩個侍女正在屋內，便一個坐在我的頭旁，一個坐在我的腳邊，為我扇扇子。她們兩個以為我睡着了，就悄悄地說起話來。其實我醒着，只是閉上了眼睛，所以她們的對話全讓我聽見了。

"真可惜，你說是不是？"其中一個說，"我們的國王是這樣地溫柔可親，王后卻不愛他了。"

"誰說不是呢，"另一個回答，"我真弄不明白為甚麼她每天晚上離開丈夫到外面去。國王沒有覺察到嗎？"

"他怎麼會覺察到呢？"第一個又說。"每天晚上王后在他的茶裏滴進某種藥草的汁，使他整夜酣睡，王后就可以想去哪裏就去哪裏了。黎明時分王后回到國王身邊，讓他吸入一種特殊的香味，把他弄醒。"

你可以想像我聽了這些話是多麼吃驚，多麼氣憤！不過我還是儘量控制住了自己的感情。我假裝從睡夢中醒過來，彷彿甚麼都沒有聽見。

不多一會，王后洗完澡回到房內。在上牀睡覺之前，她同往常一樣把茶遞給我。然而，我這一回沒有喝，卻乘她不注意的時候把茶從一個窗口倒了下去。隨後我把空杯子交回她手中，好讓她相信我喝了茶。接着我們就上牀了。不一會，她以為我已經熟睡，就放心大膽地坐起身來，甚至還大聲說道："睡吧，我希望你再也不要醒過來。"說完她很快地穿上衣服出去了。

王后一走，我立刻起身，儘快穿衣，帶上短彎刀，緊緊跟隨在她後面，連她的腳步聲也能聽得見。她唸動咒語，一連穿過幾道門，最後進入了花園。我躲在花園門旁以免暴露，目光盯着她，看她穿過一個草坪，進入被稠密的矮樹籬所包圍的一個小樹林。我從另一個方向走近樹林，隱蔽起來，這時候看見她正和一個男人走在一起。

我仔細地傾聽着他們的談話。"如果我給予你的愛還不足以使你相信我的誠意，"王后對她的同伴說道，"那麼你儘管下命令吧——你知道我有多大的力量。只要你願意，我將在太陽升起之前把整個城市和這個富麗堂皇的宮殿統統變成可怕的廢墟，只有野狼和貓頭鷹在這裏出沒。你要不要我把這些石塊和這些堅固的城牆都移到高加索山的那一邊去？或者更遠一些，把它們弄到荒無人跡的地方去？只要你一句話，這地方就會徹底變樣。"

王后這些話說完之後，她和她的情人已經到了小路的盡頭，折上了另一條道，從我面前經過。這時我已經把短彎刀拔出了鞘，讓那男人走過去之後，我從背後一刀砍在他頸子上，把他砍翻在地。我只想殺死他一個，而且相信已經把他殺了，就迅速逃跑，沒有被王后看見。

雖然她的情人受了致命傷，但是王后施展魔法，沒有讓他死去，而使他處於一種半死不活的狀態。我回到屋裏就立刻上牀。

既然已經懲罰了那個冒犯我的壞蛋，我帶着滿意的心情進入夢鄉。第二天早晨我醒來時發現王后睡在我的身旁。我說不準她是真的睡着了還是假裝的，不過我起牀時沒有打擾她。待到我上朝之後回來，王後身穿喪服，蓬頭垢面地走到我跟前，說：

"國王，我請求陛下不要因為看見我這個模樣而生氣。剛才我聽說發生了三件事情，使我心中感到強烈的悲傷，簡直難以用言語表達。"

"發生了甚麼事情呀，王后？"我問道。

"我親愛的母后死了，"她回答，"我的父皇陛下在前線陣亡了；還有我的兄弟，從懸崖上掉下去，摔死了。"

她編造這些藉口來掩蓋使她悲傷的真正原因，可見她並沒有懷疑是我殺死了她的情人。

"王后，"我說，"你很悲傷，我怎麼會責怪你？相反，請你相信，我同情你。不過我希望，時間和哲理的思考能使你恢復往常那種快樂情緒。"

從那以後她一直留在自己的那幾個房間裏，度過了整整一年，有時啜泣，有時痛哭，盡情地抒發心中的悲傷，哀歎情人不幸的命運。一年過去之後，她要求我允許她在王國的中央為她自己建造一座陵墓，並說要在這陵墓裏度過她的餘生。我沒有拒絕她。於是她造起一座圓屋頂的豪華陵墓，把它稱為"淚宮"。

陵墓竣工之後，她把她的情人從那天晚上被我殺死以後臨時安置的一個地點搬過來。在這之前，她一直親自給他吃一種藥，維持他那不死不活的狀態，住進"淚宮"之後，她繼續每天給他吃那種藥。

然而，她的一切魔術都沒有起到多大的作用，因為她的情人不僅不能走路、站立，而且連說話的能力也喪失了，只是看上去好像還活着。王后每天都要去看他兩次，就這麼看着他，只顧跟他說許多充滿着柔情蜜意的話，這就是她僅有的安慰了。

受好奇心的驅使，有一天我到"淚宮"去，想看一看王后在那裏究竟做些甚麼。我隱蔽着不讓她看見，聽到她對她的情人這麼說：

"啊，眼看你這個樣子，我的心裏多麼難受！你的痛苦也是我的痛苦。可是，我最親愛的人！我的生命！我一直在對你說話，你卻始終一個字都不回答我。回答我一次吧。啊！離開了你我就活不下去。經常能見到你，隨時能見到你，這對於我來說，比得到整個世界更珍貴。"

這一番屢屢被哭聲所中斷的哀告使我完全失去了耐心，再也無法繼續躲在暗中。我從藏身之處衝到她的面前，吼道：

"王后，你已經哭夠了，現在是結束這種哀悼的時候了，對於我們兩人這都是很不光彩的。"

"王上，"她回答說，"如果你對我還是關心的話，我求你不要打攪我，讓我痛痛快快地哭吧；時間並不能減輕或消除我心中的悲傷。"

我竭力規勸她不要忘記自己的義務，但是徒勞無益。我發現儘管我擺出了全部道理，她卻變得更加頑固；最後我放棄了要她回心轉意的念頭，離開了她。在以後的兩年裏，她的情緒始終悲傷憂鬱，仍然每天去看望她的情人。

後來我第二次到"淚宮"去。我看見了她，便和上次一樣隱蔽起來，只聽見她說："你已經有三年沒有跟我說話了，對於我的一片癡情也沒有任何反應。陵墓，是你把他對我的柔情統統毀掉了嗎？是你讓那雙眼睛——那雙曾經閃耀着愛情光芒、曾經是我全部快樂的眼睛——永遠閉上的嗎？"

不瞞你說，大爺，我聽了這些話火冒三丈。你決不會想到，她所鍾愛的情人，她所崇拜的這個人，是甚麼樣子的。他是個印度黑人，是一個土著居民。剛才我說了，我火冒三丈，驀地從躲藏的地點跳出來，像我妻子剛才那樣對陵墓叫喊："啊，陵墓，你為甚麼不把這個如此醜惡、人性不容的魔鬼吞掉？或者，還不如把姦夫淫婦一起埋葬掉？"

我的話音剛落，坐在黑人旁邊的王后憤怒地跳起身來。"啊，畜生！"她罵道，"是你造成了我的不幸。你那野蠻的手把我的愛人弄到現在這種悲慘的境地。你這麼殘忍，居然還到這裏來幸災樂禍地侮辱我？"

"不錯，"我怒吼道，"我懲罰了那個魔鬼，那是他活該；我後悔當時沒有把你也一起殺了。我不能容忍你一直對我這麼忘恩負義了。"說完這些，我抽出短彎刀舉起手來就要朝她砍去。

"火氣不要這麼大，"她臉上帶着輕蔑的微笑對我說。緊接着也不知她嘰哩咕嚕了甚麼，於是她又說道："憑我的法術，我命令，從現在起你一半是人一半是石頭。"

她的話音剛落，大爺，我便立刻變成了你現在看見的樣子，說是死人，還有一口氣，說是活人，卻已經死了。

這殘忍的女巫婆把我變成這麼個模樣，又運用妖術把我移到這個房間之後，立刻摧毀了我的首都——它原先是那麼繁榮，那麼人丁興旺；她毀掉所有的宮殿、公共場所和市場，把整個地區變成了一個湖或者說一個池塘。她把我的國家——正如你所看見的——變成荒無人煙的地方。湖裏的四種魚是原先住在首都的居民，他們信仰四種不同的宗教。白色的是穆斯林；紅色的是波斯人，火的崇拜者；藍色的是基督徒；黃色的是猶太人。那四座小山是四個島嶼，王國最初就是根據它們來命名的。

所有這些情況都是那女巫後來告訴我的，是她親自向我描述了她的憤怒所造成的這些災難。毀掉了我的王國，使我成了殘廢人之後，她的怨憤卻還沒有得到徹底的發泄。每天，她都要到這裏來，用牛皮鞭子在我的雙肩抽一百下，每一下都抽出血來。這樣鞭打我以後，她把一塊用山羊皮製成的粗糙東西蓋在我身上，再加上一件華貴的織錦緞袍子，這當然不是給我榮譽，而是嘲笑我的絕望處境。

說完這些，黑島王國的年輕國王不禁潸然淚下。

這個離奇的故事深深地打動了蘇丹，他迫切要為不幸的國王復仇。

"告訴我，"他大聲說，"這背信棄義的女巫住在哪裏？她那無恥的情夫，那還沒有死就被她送進了墳墓的傢伙在哪裏？"

"大爺，"年輕的國王回答，"正如我剛才對你說的，那姦夫在'淚宮'，在一個圓頂的墳墓裏；那個建築與皇宮之間有一個通道，是在入口的那個方向。我不知道那女巫的確切住處，但是我知道每天太陽升起，她來殘酷地折磨我，你很容易想像，我只得聽憑她擺佈。她把我折磨個夠之後，就去看望她的情人。她總是隨身帶着一種藥水，只有這種藥水可以讓她的情人維持那種不死不活的狀態。"

"年輕的國王，"蘇丹答道，"沒有人比你更值得同情了。誰的命運都沒有像你這樣坎坷。以後要是有人為你寫傳記的話，會寫出最令人驚奇的故事來。只有一件事還等待去做，那就是你的復仇，而我將千方百計達到這個目的。"

接着，蘇丹先把自己的姓名和地位告訴年輕的國王，又對他説了自己是怎麼會進入這個王國的，然後，為確保成功，兩人商定了必須採取的步驟，並決定在第二天開始執行計劃。夜已經深了，蘇丹準備就寢。年輕的國王自從被施行妖術之後就一直無法睡覺，只能睜着眼睛打發時間。

天一亮，蘇丹就起身，把外衣和袍子脫下留在房間裏，以免它們妨礙行動，隨後到"淚宮"去。他發現"淚宮"被許多白色的蠟燭照得通明，還聞到令人愉快的香味，這是從那些排列得整整齊齊的各式各樣美麗的鍍金花瓶裏散發出來的。他看見一張牀，上面躺着那受了致命傷的人，便毫不猶豫地抽出長劍，一下子結束了那傢伙殘餘的生命。接着他把屍體拖到室外，扔進一口井裏。然後他返回屋裏，冒充那印度黑人躺在牀上，一隻手握着隱蔽在被單下面的長劍，等待時機來到，好完成預想的計劃。

不一會，那女巫來了。她的第一件事就是進入監禁着她丈夫的屋子，把她丈夫的衣服扒掉，野蠻地抽打他。年輕國王的慘叫聲整個皇宮都能聽見，他苦苦地哀求他的妻子發發善心，可是這狠心的女巫繼續揮舞皮鞭，直到抽滿一百下才住手。"你對我的情人沒有絲毫憐憫，"她説，"那麼你也就別指望我會憐憫你。"幹完這件殘酷的事情之後，她把那件山羊皮衣服扔到丈夫身上，再罩上那織錦緞袍子。然後她到"淚宮"去，一進門就開始哭哭啼啼；待她走到那牀邊，以為牀上躺着的還是她的情人，便放聲叫道：“天哪！像我這樣一個溫柔多情的女人，生活中還有甚麼樂趣和安寧呢？這是多麼殘酷啊！無情的國王，當我用憤怒的火焰來燒你時，你責罵我沒有人性，可那是復仇，難道你的野蠻行為不是更加沒有人性嗎？你這奸徒，你毀掉了這可愛的人，難道不是把我也一起毀掉了嗎？天哪！”接着她把蘇丹誤以為是她情人，對他說道：“我的生命之光，難道你就永遠這樣保持沉默嗎？難道你決心不給我安慰 —— 不讓我再聽一聽你大聲宣佈你愛我 —— 就讓我死去嗎？說話吧，我求求你。”

這時候蘇丹裝作從沉睡中醒來，模仿印度黑人的語言，語調嚴肅地答道：“除了萬能的真主，誰也沒有力量。”

女巫萬萬沒有想到還會聽見情人說話，興奮得尖叫起來。“我親愛的郎君，”她喊道，“你是跟我開玩笑嗎？剛才我聽見的是真的嗎？說話的真是你嗎？”

“該死的女人，”蘇丹應道，“誰願意來答理你呀！你每天這麼野蠻地折磨你的丈夫，他的哭喊、眼淚和呻吟不停地影響我的休息。如果你停止折磨他，那麼我早就可以恢復健康了，早就可以重新開口說話了。”

“那麼，”這女巫說，“為了使你滿意，我準備聽從你的命令。你是不是要我把他恢復原來的樣子？”

“是的，”蘇丹說，“趕快使他恢復自由，那樣就不會有哭喊聲不斷地打攪我了。”

王后立刻跑出“淚宮”，取了一杯水，對着它說了一些話，這水就沸騰了，彷彿放在火爐上燒過似的。她拿着這杯開水到年輕的國王也就是她的丈夫的房間去。

"如果造物主造你出來就是這樣的，"她把水潑在她丈夫身上說，"或者造物主正對你生氣，那麼你就保持現在的樣子吧；如果是我的法術使你變成這樣，那麼你就恢復你原來的模樣吧。"

她的話音剛落，年輕的國王便恢復了原形，滿懷喜悅地站起身來，向上帝表示感謝。

"走，"女巫對他說，"立刻離開這個城堡，永遠不要再回來，否則你就沒命了！"

年輕的國王被迫離開了王后，一句話也沒說。他躲在一個隱蔽的地方，焦急地等待着蘇丹完成他的整個復仇計劃。現在他們的第一步已經成功了。

女巫回到"淚宮"，對她誤以為是黑人的蘇丹說，"我的愛人，你的命令我已經執行了。所以，現在你盡可以站起來跟我說話了。滿足我的要求吧，別再叫我失望了。"

蘇丹仍然模仿黑人的語言，帶着嚴厲的語氣說："你所已經完成的事情還不足以使我恢復健康。你只消滅了部分邪惡。"

"你這話是甚麼意思，我的情人？"王后問。

"還能有甚麼意思？"蘇丹大聲說，"還不是指你用妖術摧毀了的那個城市和它的居民，以及那四個島嶼？每天到了半夜那些魚兒就從湖裏仰起頭來高聲喊叫，要向我們兩人復仇。這就是為甚麼我這麼長的時間不能康復的真正原因。趕緊去把一切都恢復原來的樣子，等你再回到這個房間，我就會把手伸給你，你就可以幫助我起牀了。"

王后聽他這麼說，覺得有了希望，興奮地叫道："啊，我的生命，你很快就能恢復健康了，我要立刻去執行你的命令。"

她來到湖邊，在手心裏盛了一點水，然後灑向空中，同時面對着湖裏的魚口中唸唸有詞，城市立刻恢復了原來的模樣，魚兒又變成了男人、女人和兒童，變成了伊斯蘭教徒、基督徒、波斯人和猶太人，每個人都是他原來的面目。房屋和商店裏的人發現所有的東西都在原來的位置上，都放得整整齊齊，跟女巫施展妖術之前完全一樣。駐紮在平原上的蘇丹的文武百官和侍從們驚訝地發現自己突然來到了一個很大的、有美麗的建築並且人口眾多的城市的中心。

女巫把城市恢復原樣之後，懷着無限希望，急急忙忙趕回"淚宮"。她一進門就叫道："親愛的郎君，你就要康復了，我回來和你共享快樂，因為你要求我做的事情我已經全部完成了。起來，把你的手給我。"

"那麼你走近些，"蘇丹依然模仿黑人的語言說。王后照辦了。"再近一些！"蘇丹大聲說。王后又走近了些。這時候，蘇丹坐起身來，一把抓住王后的手臂。他的動作非常迅速，這女巫還沒有明白過來，蘇丹已揮動長劍，一下子就把她攔腰砍成兩段。

蘇丹處決了女巫，立刻出去尋找黑島王國的年輕國王，這年輕人正十分焦急地在外面等他。"快活起來吧，年輕人，"蘇丹擁抱着國王說，"你再也不必害怕了，因為你的殘暴的敵人已經死了。"

年輕的國王向蘇丹表示感謝，祝願他的救命恩人健康長壽，祝願他的國家繁榮昌盛。

"祝你在你的王國也生活得幸福安定！"蘇丹應道。"我們兩個國家相距這麼近，今後如果你想來訪問，我將真誠地歡迎你，那時候你會受到尊敬，就像在你自己的王國裏一樣。"

"強大的蘇丹，我的恩人，"年輕的國王説，"你認為這裏離你的國家很近嗎？"

"當然囉，"蘇丹答道，"我想，從這裏到我的國家，最多不過四五個小時的路程。"

"要走整整一年，"年輕的國王説，"雖然我相信先前你來的時候只花了四五個小時，因為那時我的國家遭到了妖術的詛咒。可是現在情況就不同了。不過，路途遙遠並不能阻止我在需要的時候跟隨你到天涯海角。是你解救了我，只要我活着，我將永遠感謝你。為了表示這一點，我情願放棄我的王國永遠陪伴你，決不後悔。"

蘇丹驚訝地發現，原來這個地方距離自己的國家這麼遠，説道："路遠算不了甚麼。我幫助了你，我們兩人建立了感情，我覺得你好像就是我的兒子，我沒有孩子，就把你當作兒子吧，從現在起你就是我的繼位者。"蘇丹説完這些，和年輕的國王極其親熱地擁抱，隨後這年輕人立刻去打點行裝，準備上路。三小時之後，他們準備就緒，就要離開黑島王國了，文武百官和百姓們對他們的國王戀戀不捨。年輕人指定他的一個近親接替了王位。

蘇丹和年輕的國王終於出發了，隨行的一百匹駱駝馱着從黑島王國的國庫裏挑選出來的不計其數的財寶。五十個全副武裝、威風凜凜的大臣騎着戰馬陪着兩位國王一同前進。一路上他們十分高興。蘇丹預先派了信使回國去通報説他就要回來了。當他們接近首都的時候，宰相和大臣們出來迎接，百姓們也都擁上前來向他歡呼。

回國的當天，蘇丹就把文武百官召集在一起，向他們詳細敘述了他的經歷。然後，他宣佈，黑島王國的年輕國王放棄了一個很大的國家隨他來到這裏，並且將永遠和他住在一起，現在他決定把這年輕人收為義子。最後，他傳諭，按照官銜和地位，把財物賞賜給每個人，獎勵他們的忠誠。

至於那位漁夫，年輕國王的得救多虧了他，因此蘇丹重賞了他，使他的一家從此以後永遠能過上幸福、富足的生活。

完

註解

1 當時風俗，在某人家吃鹽，就是做某人的客人。強盜頭目去阿里巴巴家是為了報仇雪恨，絕非去交朋友，所以拒絕吃他家的鹽。

2 大教長，蘇丹或哈里發的稱號。

3 打蘭，衡量單位，等於十六分之一盎司。

4 設拉子，在當今的伊朗。

5 據《聖經》，摩西率領希伯來人逃離埃及擺脫奴役，他們到達紙莎草海濱，前有海水，後有埃及追兵，突然海水向兩邊分開，出現一條乾燥的通道，希伯來人沿着這條道通過，隨後海水重新合攏，將埃及追兵淹沒。

6 所羅門，《聖經》上記載的以色列的賢明國王，他的父王是大衛。